Seven Red Sundays

RAMÓN J. SENDER

SEVEN RED SUNDAYS

Translated from the Spanish
by Sir Peter Chalmers Mitchell

ELEPHANT PAPERBACKS
Ivan R. Dee, Publisher, Chicago

First ELEPHANT PAPERBACK edition published 1990 by Ivan R. Dee, Inc., 1332 North Halsted Street, Chicago 60622. Manufactured in the United States of America.

Library of Congress Cataloging-in-Publication Data
Sender, Ramón José 1901–
[Siete domingos rojos. English]
Seven red Sundays / Ramon J. Sender ; translated from the Spanish by Sir Peter Chalmers Mitchell. — 1st elephant pbk. ed.
p. cm.
ISBN 0-929587-29-4 : $9.95
1. Spain—History—Revolution—1931—Fiction. I. Title.
PQ6635.E65S513 1990
836'.62—dc20 89-25926
CIP

Contents

Fifth Sunday: Collapse

Sixth Sunday: Aftermath of Dejection

Seventh Sunday: Only in the Future

Samar in Gaol

Translator's Introductory Note

AN OVERFLOW crowd gathered in front of a theatre in Madrid in which a revolutionary workmen's meeting was being held. Against regulations, loud-speakers were installed to carry the voices of the speakers to those outside, and the military intervened. Some of the megaphones by a mysterious accident continued to sound. The military fired, and three of the workmen's leaders were killed. But there was also killed a member of the Parliamentary socialist party, and the Government decided to permit a public funeral of the four victims. That ceremony also got out of hand, and there followed street fighting, sabotage and an attempt to institute a general strike throughout Spain.

On this theme Señor Ramón J. Sender has written a book of terror and beauty. Of terror because he describes the course and the failure of the insurrection with stark realism. Of beauty, because he is an artist, and because in his own words he is seeking a human truth and not a political truth. There is no cause so foolish, it has been said, that men will not die for it; and Señor Sender has found behind the confused and conflicting theories of his revolutionaries a sublime faith in what the Revolution could accomplish, and a generous willingness to give their own lives, not in a spirit of romantic heroism with flags flying and even the enemy applauding, but naturally and without fuss, in the street corner by day or in the furtive night.

Although Señor Sender in his Preface disclaims making a political assessment, it is not to be supposed that he chose the subject of *Seven Red Sundays* merely because it suited his powers of vivid description and psychological analysis. He was born in Aragón in 1901, the son of small farmers, educated in a monastery school and afterwards at Saragossa. At the age of eighteen he went to Madrid to read law at the University, supporting himself by assisting in a chemist's shop, and spending more than his leisure reading in the Ateneo library. But he abandoned law, became entangled in revolutionary movements, and escaped punishment only because his parents claimed him as a minor. For three years he lived with them, editing a small country paper, and then passed his military service in Morocco. His experiences there, described in his first novel *Imán,* a translation of which has been published in the United States, showed his reactions to war, especially as waged by an incompetent government. In 1924 he joined the staff of *El Sol,* then almost a Republican organ, but was imprisoned for activities against the dictatorship of Primo de Rivera. He made his experiences in prison the basis of his second novel *El Viento en la Moncloa* (*The Wind in Moncloa Gaol*). In the winter of 1933-4 he went to Russia, not as a tourist but on a proletarian ticket, and his book *Madrid-Moscú,* published in 1934, is an acute and sympathetic description of the achievements and efforts of the Union of Soviet Republics. His *Viaje a la Aldea del Crimen,* a study of the governmental outrage at Casas Viejas, also shows his sympathies. *El Problema Religiosa in Méjico* and *El Verbo se Hizo Sexo,* in which the life of Saint Teresa de Jesus is interpreted with a mixture of naturalism and mysticism, show another side of his powers. He is regarded as the young hope of Spanish literature, and has been awarded unanimously by a jury containing Pio Baroja, Machado, Répide and other writers who cannot be supposed to have a great sympathy with the Revolution, the National Prize for Literature of 1935.

Seven Red Sundays, in my judgment, is the greatest book he has yet written. Naturally it is extremely Spanish, but is even more difficult for English readers, accustomed to neat plots, because the confusion in the minds of the revolutionaries is emphasized by a deliberately loose construction in the book. Although his "Reds" agree in their revolt against the existing order of Society, against *bourgeois* politics from monarchism and republicanism to the kind of socialism which accepts office, against capitalism, against religion, against art, against history, against philosophy, they are as pedantic, as opinionated and as ready to wreck concerted action by debate on first principles as are respectable ratepayers. There are three types of doctrine distributed amongst the individuals in unequal proportions, much in the fashion, say, that the abstract conceptions or doctrines of conservatism, liberalism and socialism are distributed in unequal proportions amongst the politicians of Great Britain. There are the communists who would use the Revolutions as an opportunity for imposing by force a Marxism, modified in the direction in which it is being modified in Soviet Russia. There are the syndicalists who wish to replace wage-slave labour (knowing not what, nor for whom, it is producing, but knowing only that it must produce or starve) by a self-conscious, self-controlling labour rejoicing in beneficent creation. There are the anarchists, pure idealists of human nature, who believe that the Golden Age will come when all authority is abolished. These men and women, revolvers in their hands, love in their hearts and shibboleths on their lips, are killing or being killed, are fighting against the laws of God and of man. And it is amongst them that Señor Sender asks you to see a human truth, a human beauty.

Is then *Seven Red Sundays* a defence of murder and of sabotage? I think not. Perhaps not even an explanation. And if you read Señor Sender's Preface and submit yourself to his book, you may agree. But I hazard one general observation. In almost every country the principles of civilization and the fabric of civilization are under discussion. Gone, possibly for ever, are the days when those in authority could believe with a clean conscience that in defending the State they were not merely defending their own privileges and interests, that in repelling disorder, they were also punishing the wicked. May it be worth while considering if what are certainly the legal crimes of the "Reds" are an inevitable reaction to the tremendous forces of repression with which science has armed authority, and that authority, no longer absolutely convinced of its own integrity, is more ready to use violence? And above all, is there not a flicker of hope for humanity, if it be the case that a selfless love and a generous purpose glow through the cloudy dreams of the "criminals"?

P. CHALMERS MITCHELL.

Author's Preface

My own voice is heard seldom in this book, but nearly always the voice of my characters, and so I say something here, not much, but necessary. From the political and social points of view this book will satisfy no one. That I know. But it is not an attempt to make political capital or to describe the social struggle, and still less to praise or to blame. I am in quest of no utilitarian truth—social, moral, or political—and not even of that seemingly harmless aesthetic truth—always false and artificial, in the quest of which many young writers lose themselves.

The only truth, the reality, at which I aim in these pages, is the truth of living humanity displayed in the convulsions of a Spanish revolutionary episode. I seek it in the words and the emotions of my characters and in the circumambient light and air with which they blend, to form a moral atmosphere, cloudy or limpid, logical or incoherent. Nor am I seeking the consistent sequences of a novel. My reality is human, sublime it may be, stupid it may be. There is stupidity, because my description is not coloured by that intellectual bias of a man for men which, as you find it amongst novelists, is no more than a pedantic and repulsive bias in their own favour. The persons in my book do not recognize the social conventions, cannot make elegant phrases and have never been respectable ratepayers.

You will see that my book is not directed to your intelligence, but to your sensibility, for the deepest human truths must be felt rather than understood or analysed. They are the truths which men have neither spoken nor tried to put into words, because their message is delivered in the shining confusion of the emotions. When he has read the book, the reader who has submitted himself loyally to me will have understood, or will have failed to understand, the social and political phenomena which are my subject, but in either event he will have passed through a new emotional experience. By addressing the emotions, the sensibility, and not the understanding, at least I gain the advantage that no one will have the right to call me an intellectual.

My book sometimes appears confused and loosely wrought. If the reader is of those who can see and grasp, he will admit that my method is logical, because chaos has its own logic.

Nevertheless, I permit myself a word about my own position. It may help those who cannot deduce concrete formulas from the evidence in this book. In my view the anarchosyndicalist phenomena are due to an excess of vitality in individuals and in masses, to a generosity and exuberance characteristic of over-vitalized men and societies. Let my readers ponder the enormous disproportion between what the Spanish revolutionary masses have given, and continue to give, and what they have gained. And between the forces that are in them and the efficiency with which they employ them. There are many consequences, but what interests me most is the emergence of a generosity at times truly sublime.

If anyone should ask me what anarchosyndicalism really is, apart from its superficial political significance, I refer him to this book. If there are still persons foolish enough to ask me whether anarchosyndicalism is good or evil, I shrug my shoulders and offer them this book. If anyone should ask me: "Do you think that anarchosyndicalism is an ultimate factor in Spanish politics?" my answer is "Yes", and that neither today nor ever can it be neglected. Lastly, if anyone should beg me to be explicit as to my own view of anarchosyndicalism as a political fact, I return to what I have said already. Here is my formula; it is a non-political formula. People too full of humanity dream of freedom, of the good, of justice, giving these an emotional and individualistic significance. Carrying such a load, an individual can hope for the respect and loyalty of his relations and friends, but if he should hope to influence the general social structure, he nullifies himself in heroic and sterile rebellion. No man can approach mankind giving his all and expecting all in return. Societies are not based on the virtues of individuals, but on a system which controls defects by limiting the freedom of everyone. Naturally the system takes a different form under feudalism, capitalism and communism. Let anarchosyndicalists invent their own system, and until they have attained it, go on dreaming of a strange state of society in which all men are as disinterested as St. Francis of Assisi, bold as Spartacus, and able as Newton and Hegel. But behind the dream there is a human truth of the most generous kind—sometimes, let me insist, absolutely sublime. Is not that enough?

Chapter 1

Comrade Villacampa Explains

THERE IS a calendar on the wall of my room. I like tearing off the sheets before the days have come to read the proverbs and the instructive stories printed on the back. "Dog does not eat dog." "Idleness is the root of all evil." Great truths. Then I learn that a dog called Napoleon was sold to an Englishman for twelve hundred pounds, and that the moon is a lump of the Earth torn out of the bed of the Pacific. Also a short history of Viriathus and of the assassination of Sertorius. Of course the calendar is arranged regularly. After Monday comes Tuesday.

Pulling the sheets off before their dates isn't a sign of my impatience for the future. Such an elegant pastime is not for me. My creator, the author of this book, has made me nothing better than a grocer's shopman. I tear off the sheets and read them, partly because I sometimes get bored in my room, but also because I am a friend of Samar, a young man who writes for the newspapers, and so I have to know who Sertorius and Viriathus were, and be able to talk about them. I don't like always to have to agree with him simply because he knows more than me.

On the wall, alongside the calendar, the damp has made a stain like some monster. It reminds me of the witches on Goya's monument. Tramcars 11, 6, and 49 stop just outside, and I often travel on the platform, to have a chance of talking to someone, because people don't talk inside, and also because I am often carrying parcels—a gallon of oil and a few pounds of sugar, for example—and the conductor lets me put them down beside the motor. I was on a 49 one day when I saw Samar with a very pretty young lady and her companion, what we call a wardress. Their presence turned the car into a first-class coach. The girl was like an actress I once saw at the cinema, who seemed to talk and to move her arms as if to music. He was stiff and serious. I didn't know if I ought to recognize him. It might worry him to have been seen in such *bourgeois* company. But he smiled to me, made way for me to pass with my parcels, and nudged me with his knee against my leg to make me bow. That was just like Samar. I had to bow to his sweetheart just like bowing in a church. What did Samar mean by it? It was all done quite simply, but there seemed to be something behind it. He goes about and lives and talks as if he were a philosopher, but that doesn't mean anything because suddenly he'll smile as if to say "what good friends we are". I can't understand these *bourgeois,* least of all those who belong to our side. All right. I am a grocer's porter, and he writes in the newspapers. You could call him an ink-sucker and he wouldn't turn a hair, just as it doesn't worry me to be called errand-boy. Damn it all. With these *bourgeois* in power everything is false and silly, but if we are to take things seriously as I took Samar and his young lady, then my bowing was quite in order.

I am twenty-five years old, he is twenty-eight and wears a coat with wide lapels and has a sweetheart. I haven't a coat like his, but all the same there is a girl who is sweet on me, the daughter of Germinal García, who is one of the oldest of the active members of our organization. She is fifteen or sixteen and wears a red jersey. I don't like her, but the time is coming when I'll have a sweetheart too, perhaps not so pretty and scented as Samar's, but a bit better than Germinal's daughter. I've told you already that she isn't my sort. When on a Sunday I brilliantine my hair and wear my red tie it isn't for her—although we go together to the Centre—but because it is necessary to be smart and well-oiled so that the boss may see me and raise my wages. Clothes and tidy hair count for everything with the *bourgeoisie.*

Germinal's girl is called Estrella, but her father calls her Star—it means the same—because he was in England, and because he likes a brand of revolver with that name. She is dark and has big eyes, quiet like those of horses, but blue. Her face is round and dusky. When she laughs there are two dimples in her cheeks and she stares and stares and says nothing. She is shorter than me and I am five feet eight in my stocking soles. Although she says that she has passed her eighteenth birthday, she is not more than seventeen. She says it to make her father buy her stockings. But it is no good. She goes about in bare legs and shoes without heels. She wears rough socks of her father's and rolls them over her ankles. All the same she isn't ugly. But she is too ignorant to be my sweetheart. I have just missed being chosen my syndicate's delegate to the local federation, and although I have a lower position, I'm a member of the committee. She is scheming to be made delegate of the syndicate in the lamp factory where she works, but who is going to propose her, as she is too ignorant to do anything better than sell leaflets at the meetings? She is Germinal's daughter, but that hasn't the pull it would have amongst the *bourgeoisie*. With us you must be the son of your own deeds, like me who——

Never mind. What does it matter? One day, when he came back from church, my father had a row with my mother and beat her to death. Why? Bah. That was their own business. I was twelve years old; I left the house. I was often hungry and slept out of doors in all weathers, but, as I've said already, these sort of things don't matter. Today I am comrade Leoncio Villacampa. If you don't know what that means, go to the syndicate and ask. I know enough about syndicalism never to make a slip in questions of organization. All the rest counts for little. I don't read any newspapers, except those of the organization, which are the good ones. The *bourgeois* papers, except for their pictures, are rotten. They don't know how to report. You should see what they say about our meetings and the movement. Everything to keep people ignorant. They know nothing of our affairs and about as much of their own. They tie themselves up in knots with words. Columns and columns to say nothing. Sometimes they get hold of a new word, and then the whole lot of them take it up. The other day I saw one I didn't know; "juridicity". Samar told me it became fashionable when the dictatorship fell. Words and fashions; just like women! I laugh myself sick when I read the boss's paper.

When the Republic came, I knew that everything would go on just as before, but all the same I was a little surprised. When the King bolted, I saw at once that there was something new in the streets, the people and the houses. There seemed to be weddings and fairs all the time. And then it was said that there was going to be a Parliament. I wished to know what that was, as I had only heard about it. I was only a kid when there was one before. It seems that what had upset the *bourgeoisie* enough to make them have a Republic was the abolition of Parliament by the King and the military. Parliament must be something important. I had to go to see it with my own eyes, as the newspapers couldn't be trusted. On the opening day, I put on my new jacket and my tie. I smoothed my hair with brilliantine and off I went. Didn't you see me on the first page of the daily papers where I was in the photographs? Alongside me was the President of the Government, a man of about fifty who didn't look a fool.

I walked right in and found myself in the great hall. All was red and yellow. I looked to see who was in charge and went to a man who was said to be President of the Chamber. I asked him what it was all about; he became stern and looked at me as a woman does when she won't have anything to do with you, and at last said that it was the opening of Parliament. I'd have asked him a lot more, but he was dolled up in black and white, like the dummies in a tailor's shop, and it seemed that another question would have made him stain his shirt-front. Up above in the galleries there were bishops and women; down below, rows of benches and clusters of electric lights. Photographers everywhere. When I saw the pole with the flashlight being pushed up, I insinuated myself forward and got in front. I came out in all photographs. I talked again with the President and then with one or two others, who, it appeared, were ministers. Decent people, Sir, although no one of them seemed to be quite sure of what he was doing. They stared at me and weren't a bit ready to reply. Then one of them spoke up, in quite a homely way, and all the rest applauded. Then another made a speech and they all cheered, although he had hesitated over his words and had to repeat himself. It reminded me of the "Mickey Mouse" films, where the poor animals are in a theatre, get excited and applaud. One of them was like a young goat, another like a rat. Most of them were good enough chaps, but there was a yellow-faced fish so small that he could hardly be seen. When the others cheered, he whistled, and when they protested, he cheered. They stared at him as if they'd like to eat his head off. I burst out laughing at the sulky little bloke. Then I went up to the man they called the President of the Government and spoke to him again. They all fixed their eyes on me, and one of them up and said, "There are strangers in the House." It was said in such a nasty way that I looked him in the face and sang out, "Meaning me?" I couldn't be a stranger in the Republic. I was one of four who nearly upset the Royal train in 1927. I was a year in gaol. The King's police had beaten me nearly to death and my revolver had given a good "blighty" to a socialist blackleg who had refused to come out when we organized the general strike against the monarchy. I had a right to be there, and anyone who didn't like it could lump it. I said all that to a young man with a portfolio full of papers and repeated it to eight or nine deputies who were looking at me in a way that didn't suit me. The young man with the portfolio, who afterwards mounted the pulpit and began to read a long manuscript, didn't pay any attention to what was being said round about him, but replied "Yes" to everything. And so that was Parliament! I didn't see much sense in it. When it was all over I went up to the President in the lobbies and asked him if he thought it was any use. He turned his head to one side, stretched out his arms and said, "Well, well!" He didn't seem very sure about it.

But it hadn't lasted long enough to bore me too much. And they hadn't upset me, for when I came out I was still a republican. I hadn't quite followed all that they had been saying, for the atmosphere, the lights and the whole show had dazed me a bit. And so I said to the grey-haired gentleman, in the proper republican fashion, that we would have to do in the bishops. I had seen them up above in a gallery and I felt like hunting one of them alive. The President made off without replying. But when he got to the entrance steps I caught him by the arm. They were taking more photographs. You must have seen me on the first page of the daily paper. Then I had to leave the President as he got into his car.

In front of the Parliament House, infantry soldiers were posted along the street as on gala days. Amongst them was Joaquin, packed up like an oyster in his new uniform. He was in the 1930 levy and served in the 6th Saboya. I thought that I would roll him a cigarette secretly, and he asked me if I had changed my views and was a friend of the President. I said "No". I had gone to see things for myself.

"What about it?" he asked me indifferently.

"Don't you think," I said, "that it is so bad! They are clever people, just like those in a theatre."

I finished rolling the cigarette, lighted it and gave it to him to suck while I kept watch. For a good while we didn't speak, and then I said to him that after all the best would be to set fire to the whole shoot. Joaquin shifted his weight to the other leg and then nodded "Yes". Some aeroplanes droned across the sky. The crowd began to press. A priest got mixed up with some young whores and Joaquin and I were amused to see him puffing and struggling. Joaquin was sulky because he had been unable to go out with his sweetheart, a pretty girl from Lower Carabanchel. All the same, Star García, Germinal's daughter, with better clothes, would have no need to be jealous of her. But you mustn't think that Star is so very pretty or that she is fit to be my sweetheart. The poor girl has a lot to learn yet, although I am not the sort to be uppish. Besides, I remember something disagreeable. In my calendar, behind the packet of dates, there is a coloured picture of a girl in a white wig very like her. Her skirts are flounced and her breasts show above her bodice. She is sitting on a bench and another girl has come through the trees behind her, with fair braided hair and lace round her neck, who is going to kiss her. She is dressed like a man and the pig is going to kiss her. I don't like women with these *bourgeois* vices. But certainly Star reminds me of the calendar and the calendar of Star, although the manners of the picture are quite different from Star's.

Today is Saturday and we have a full list of committees. I am going to tear off a sheet. Sunday. Hello! printed in red. But let us see what's written on the back of Saturday. "Guzman the Good threw a dagger on the rampart to tell the enemy that they might kill his son, but that he would not deliver up the city keys." And above in capital letters, "Patriotic Anniversary". How idiotic the world was until now. They might just as well commemorate what led to my leaving my father's house. "A father kills his wife with a stick to prevent the slightest deviation from family morality." What people! Sticks handy behind the door! "The more I beat my wife, the better the soup!" The Fatherland! Murder of a boy to keep the key of a door! Religion!—Lies and dirtiness to thwart the instincts of the people to the gain of money-lenders and whores! How stupid it all is! It makes me want to laugh or to set fire to things, or to do both. Let us tear off another sheet from the calendar. What? Behind Sunday the seventeenth, there is another Sunday, also printed in red! Another Sunday. Damn it all! One Sunday is enough for me. Once a week I oil my hair and go to see Star. She gazes at me also once a week, nodding her head without saying anything. When I go on looking at her she smiles in a silly sort of way, and the two dimples show on her cheeks. Away with this wrong Sunday! But let's see what is behind it. Another Sunday! Sunday the nineteenth, and then another, Sunday the twentieth, and so on. Seven Sundays following each other! The calendar has gone mad! Time has stopped ruling! Seven Sundays in succession and the seven with numbers red as blood! If it is a silly joke of Time, it suits the picture with the white wigs. These swinish vices of the *bourgeoisie* can't lead to anything good!

Chapter 2

Loud-Speakers Sabotage a Meeting

THE WARD theatre in which our meeting is to be held is in a wide street with tramways. Beer-vendors on the pavement pour out their foaming glasses. At the corner where the street widens into a square, there are three hawkers. An old woman offers cakes of soap from a tray strapped to her neck. The theatre stands higher up, with its first floor level with the trees. No one who wasn't a member of our party worked on its construction. "That first floor," said a member of the Syndicate of Construction, "has a beam more than a foot thick and could carry eight thousand men without noticing. A good beam! A daughter of the forges of Biscay, tempered under swift hammers, shaped by the skill of workers in metal; its fibrous strength won't flinch under the weight of thousands of workmen. The echo of our speeches and of our applause will reach its entrails and make them throb with pleasure. Even while it was still in the workshop, it heard the workmen speaking the same language—its own language. The beam knows nothing of the 'common good', of democracy or of parliaments. Its whole universe consists of work committees, of the delegates of sections, of subscriptions, of the ups and downs of the Movement, of 'tools down', of sabotage and of boycotts. In the middle of the hall it is helped by two alert round pillars, and these also speak the same language. The tall beams of the vault, the lights hidden under the moulding on each ledge, the doors, the fireproof curtain, the wooden chairs, the orchestra pit, the straight rafters of the second story, and the oval windows, more like those of a ship than of a cathedral. All speak the same language, bolts, nuts, artificial lights, and glass;—machine, workshop, daily wages, disputes, strikes, revolts. What does it matter although on a Sunday night a magistrate goes there to gloat on the legs of the chorus girls? For such a *bourgeois* it is only a theatre. Revues, knees, and thighs. Drama—domestic tragedies within the limits of the Common Law. Comedy—pleasant adulteries in a setting of fine sheets and honeyed words. For the beams and planks, the pillars and panels, it is a co-ordinated piece of work wrought like the poop of a ship. Let the pretty girls show their thighs! If the theatre is to be kept going, the pretty girls must sometimes doff their petticoats to dance! But today, wood, iron and crystal find their soul in the sunlit morning—the Meeting. 'Against oppression! For the release of our comrades in gaol!'" The theatre laughs from its balcony with its arc of blue windows.

Among the groups on the pavement Progreso González says that today he is going to see the theatre at his leisure—which hasn't been possible before. He speaks, leaning against the door-hinges, scraping with his thumbnail a spot of dry mortar on his trousers. Then he puts two fingers into his mouth and whistles a greeting to a friend on the platform of a tramcar. The sellers of labour papers display bills like banners, with the words "Solidarity", "Land and Liberty".

When Progreso was working on the construction of this theatre the police one day came in search of him up to the vaulted roof where he was fixing rivets. He was three months in gaol.

"Yes," one of them interrupts, "that was the time when Dot-and-go-one escaped."

"No. Later. It was the last time."

When he was released he said to himself: "I must go to see how the job is getting on and collect my tools." Many were the bricks he had laid. He knew the cold on the top of a scaffolding. "Let me get up to the level of the great beam and the splendid vault of the second story." He was a good foreman and no small part of the work had passed through his own hands. Straight from gaol he went there.

"What-ho! My good walls, noble lines, curving steel and glass! How the light sings in the round eye of a gable! With what grace arrows of light shoot out from the hanging lanterns of the ceiling!" He gazed and smiled. Alongside him two old idlers in front of the posters discussed the legs and thighs with lustful eyes. They chewed the sensual cud of their old monastic days. Progreso asked them for a match, kept half the box and blew a puff of smoke into their faces—one doesn't come out of gaol every day! He raised his eyes and moved towards the door. "Paranymph Royal!" What elegance! He couldn't have believed that the impresario was such a scholar. There was no performance that afternoon. So much the better; he would go in, take a look round and see if by any chance he could find his tools.

The impresario was having a snack in the bar. He had to speak to him. Progreso didn't take off his cap, and the impresario didn't take his eyes off him. The position was a little strained. How do you speak to a *bourgeois* in the cabin of a ship anchored in a Castilian street? He told him what he wanted. Between sip and sip the impresario shook his head:

"There are no tools here belonging to anyone, and you have no business here."

"But I worked on this job for more than six months."

"If you did work, they paid you for it—clear out."

The impresario pointed to the door. Progreso pointed to the inside staircase. "I am going up. When I've seen everything, I'll look in to say good-bye. Or I'll stay here if I like. All this —" and he pointed to the walls and the roof and the hangings—"is more mine than yours."

He began to go up. The impresario wanted to speak, but a gulp of beer went the wrong way and he began to cough and to choke. Then he ran to the telephone. "Why the hell isn't the police number among the urgent calls? 92741, I mean 92417!" Meantime Progreso disappeared round the corner of the second-floor landing. He inspected everything at his leasure. He examined the level of the beams, the quality of the timber; the hangings pleased him, and although he could not trace the distribution of the electric wires, so far as he could see it wasn't too bad. He stroked the great cross-beam and another smaller one, and patted the pillars. He climbed up farther to the highest row of seats on the top gallery where there was a curved range of glazing more than six yards round. The light from the lantern, rosy and mellowed, tinged the glass. He stared and smiled down from his high perch. He sat down on a step and finished his cigarette. The glow of the stump on the carpet seemed the red seal of approval on his work. But "Paranymph Royal"—what could the words mean?

When he was about to go down, two policemen appeared at the foot of the stairs. When they saw him, their hands went to the pockets of their uniforms. Progreso also stood still. He knew that action of the police and what it meant.

"Come down!" they ordered.

Progreso played the fool.

"What for? Are you going to take a film?"

"Come down at once!"

Progreso raised his hand to his pocket where he hadn't a weapon, and continued:

"If you want to take a film, all right; I don't mind."

In the end they took him. The sergeant charged him. He had just come out of gaol and instead of going to see his wife and children, like any decent man, he risked his liberty again.

Progreso argued. "Everyone has a wife and children. You look after them yourself or a neighbour does it for you. Work counts for more. The products of our labour are our true children, and there is an instinct making us think more of honest work than of a woman and children and a few shillings. Your way is the narrow way of the *bourgeoise*. Besides, it is false." Progreso didn't say all that, but he felt it boiling in his blood.

He laughed with the comrades as he recalled it all. The sun gave the morning its benediction of peace. The groups grew bigger. More than half the theatre was full already. Samar hurried in with long strides. He was of average height, strong, thick-set. Voices from a group hailed him. He nodded to them and looked up to the galleries on which the white sun of May was throwing a lacework pattern. It was still half an hour until the opening of the meeting. The meeting was of little importance, a mere affair of procedure, an incident in the constant war of the syndicates against human and divine law. Against socialists, republicans, priests and generals. Against the tenors and the baritones of the *bourgeoisie,* who played for time in Parliament, against the intellectual highbrows. Against everything, sometimes even against themselves. Samar reflected, a little puzzled. What were these men seeking? What did they wish? He asked himself that every day, and yet he was with them, and with them full of faith. But whither?

Star García arrived, bringing new wares. She was selling rosettes of red flannel for the benefit of the comrades in gaol. Absorbed in her duty, she was an image in marble. She came to Samar and put a real carnation in his buttonhole. Seriously, gravely. But she had trouble in keeping solemn, and once she began to laugh all the solemnity vanished. Samar gave her a shilling, after asking, rather slyly, about Villacampa. Star shrugged her soft shoulders, raised her eyebrows and warned him:

"Just listen! I don't want to hear about Villacampa."

Then she passed inside. Her bare legs above the shabby socks of her father were like the legs of a shepherdess on a lacquered cigarette-case. She went into the theatre and her passing seemed to take the light away from the corridor.

Meantime the crowd were entering the theatre in a babble of talk. Two comrades were climbing up to place loud-speakers. When the hall was full, workmen were still trying to crowd in. An old man, almost blind, with a white beard like a seal's whiskers, moved in, humming "The International" in a low voice. Belief in the revolution straightened his old back. Others wandered about offering leaflets and journals.

The lower third of the front of the theatre was covered with bills and cartoons; C.N.T., F.A.I.[1] The letters "C.N.T." emblazoned the good ship "Paranymph", and gave a new meaning to replace the "Royal" which the theatre had lost on the declaration of the Republic. A little farther off the peals of a church fell on the heedless working district. Small craftsmen and shopkeepers leaned out over the closed doors of their shops in unbuttoned Sunday coats. Into the peaceful calm, the sun suddenly threw disturbing flashes of blue and violet light, reflected from the windscreen of a car, the sign of a dentist, a midwife's gilded placard. Scarlet words were on all lips and the clenched grin of revolt. The air quivered with the initials C.N.T., and C.N.—which are not the same—and F.A.I. The Social Revolution was based on denials. Down with Politics. No Collaboration. No Voting. No Pacts. Direct Action! After twenty minutes of wrangling, of displaying formulas, badges, slogans and chaff, of the flaunting of initials, the C.F.A.N.I.T.[2] replaced the C.N.T. At five minutes to ten the hall was choked with men and thousands of others were in the street unable to enter. They looked up with hope to the loud-speakers whilst they idly turned over the coppers in their pockets, mapping out their Sunday outings. The trumpets of the loud-speakers protruded from the balcony and seemed to be clearing their throats for the speeches. The street seemed wider as the sun rose. And Justice? God's Justice? The Justice of the Constitution? Or the Justice of Progreso who built the theatre? But Justice is not an absolute. It is a slogan!

The sun is reflected from the façade to the asphalt of the pavement. A young girl leaning out from a balcony to two youths going towards the church called out:

"It is my first dance tonight; I am going to have a real good bath in the afternoon and you can come for me about nine o'clock."

It turned the street into a nuptial chamber. You could feel in the voice of the girl the subconscious tremor of anticipated defloration. She throws the reference to her nudity amongst the workers, and the morning is crowned by her erect breasts and her upraised naked arms. Star, who has come out again, offers her wares from the door, and her scarlet jersey and ripe throat were so vivid in the shade of the porch, that she seemed to feel the effect of her presence, and almost running, went back inside.

[1] C.N.T., National Federation of Labour; F.A.I., International Federation of Anarchists.
[2] National and International Federation of Labour.

"Leaflets for the benefit of the Prisoners! Treason of the Fascist-Socialists! Price twopence. Confederate Badges!"

She carried her wares over her unripe left breast, rocking from one foot to the other as if she were dangling a doll. Suddenly she noticed Villacampa in a chair. With her hand she replaced a lock that had slipped from her coiled hair, bit her lip and looked away. The hall was now full and showed a sea of faces and voices at rest after six days of labour. Neither impatience nor boredom. Star saw friendly glances and familiar faces. Suddenly an altercation arose near the door. A young man, revolver pointed, was signalling to a man to go out. Progreso hurried to them and made the comrade lower his revolver. "But he is a police agent." Progreso begged the agent to go. He protested:

"They have threatened to kill me."

"What nonsense! Damn it all! It isn't possible," said Progreso.

"All of them can bear witness."

Progreso questioned those round about, and they all denied it. Not one of them had seen a revolver.

"Now you see! You are excited and imagine weapons and threats everywhere. Go off, and tell your chiefs that we won't tolerate spies at our meetings."

The incident closed. People laughed and began to talk about other things. Star looked at Villacampa again. He was near her father. He had the air of a *bourgeois* as he drew out a nickel and beckoned her with an authoritative gesture. She went up to him and for a moment her eyes rested on his new suit with admiration. Villacampa's eyes replied, "Don't think that I am dressed up to make silly little chits fall in love with me." She sold him a leaflet, and then put a carnation in his buttonhole. "I had two," she said, "and I gave the other to Samar." Villacampa knew that, as he had seen it already. Then he praised her and was sympathetic for a little, and then got up to look for Samar. The crowd with its rows and rows of caps, hats and white shirts hid him completely. He sat down again and followed Star with his eyes as she passed up and down the central gangway. Her badges and leaflets were selling well, and seemed to Villacampa to make the revolution so childish that he was almost ashamed to be a revolutionary. Shouts came from the upper galleries to comrades below and bits of discussions of revolutionary doctrines. A dirty-looking, self-confident type with a bundle of papers under his arm, came and went. He was an agent of three Amsterdam Jews who were bears of Spanish currency and kept smelling out the future in political and proletarian circles. He was a financial spy, greedier and less brave than spies in war, but with the same slinking indefiniteness in appearance and actions. There was another curiosity in the third row of stalls, a mysterious South American who claimed to be an author and dressed almost like an Indian chief covered with trinkets and rings. He had come to us with the scheme of destroying the whole Civil Guard in a single night by a new scientific dry powder. We called him "Al Capone", and the name suited him. He hoped to get a special committee to carry out his idea. Now he bought from Star a set of her leaflets, a red rosette, and the confederate badge. Bundles of leaflets, the manifesto of the local federation, were being thrown down from the galleries. Star caught one of them and began to distribute them in an absent-minded way. Hands and arms were raised and waved about. The atmosphere grew warmer, and the words of the manifesto saturated it with a fertilizing pollen.

The unlighted stage began to fill up. The President took his seat. The *bourgeois* journalists—why do they come here?—at the reporters' table affected the air of curious visitors at a Zoo. Then someone came forward and asked that the comrades in the street should be told to come in and fill up the lobbies and passages where the amplifiers were placed, as the police had prohibited any assembly in the street. Growls of protest. Passages and door become blocked. A comrade disconnects some wires and the meeting opens with a few words from the President, before he makes way for the first speaker. The loud-speakers in the street raise their hoarse voices, pouring out the usual phrases, "The Government, slave of capitalism, is murdering our comrades in the street." "The Cabinet Minister is abusing the authority we put in his hands." Someone protested. "We mustn't say that; it gives a weapon to our enemies. The organization must not admit any relationship with the *bourgeois* revolution." A storm of protests tried to drown the voice of the interrupter. But he insisted. "It would be opportunism." Someone replied, "Very good, and why not?" The loud-speakers continue, "The meanness of the *bourgeoisie,* always covetous of its own privileges, is heaping oppression on the proletariat. It is filling the prisons, turning ships into dungeons, shooting down our brothers." The loud-speakers hurl out the phrases like stones from a sling. Three thousand workers who could not get into the theatre are packed in the street. The officer in command of the troops pulls his moustache and throws angry glances at the loud-speakers. He sends messengers. "I have ordered the loud-speakers to stop." Confusion. The electrician swears that he had disconnected them. But the loud-speakers continue. "We shall destroy all the corruption which you represent and impose. The thick head of the *bourgeoisie* shall fall by its own weight as fell the head of aristocratic feudalism." "Quick now! Disconnect these wires!" Someone disconnects them. But the loud-speaker above the veranda and those of the second floor continue. It is the voice of the second orator who is denouncing the "Law of Flight". He was the first who had suffered under it, in 1919. They hadn't actually killed him, and upright and bloody, he had been unable to denounce them. His words came out in boiling jets, hissing and burning and wounding the sky like comets. "Treachery, Cowardice, Misery, Crime, Gun-powder, Guns, the Revolution, F.A.I., C.N.T., F.A.I., C.N.T." The loud-speakers growl. The crowd in the street becomes more dense and circulation is stopped. The tramways impatiently ring their bells, in serried columns. A "Viva el Revolución" comes from a thousand throats and from thousands indoors, drunk with words. Cornets sound the alarm. The human crowd keeps silent, faced by the armed troops. The loud-speakers continue: "Hurrah for the C.N.T. Death to the Bourgeois Republic." A sergeant arrives with orders. A telephone message had been sent to the central police station and the order had been issued to stop what was going on, because of the violation of the order forbidding the use of loud-speakers in the streets. The soldiers stand motionless. The cornet shrills again, and the assault begins, to the sound of cries, the sudden lowering of shutters and the closing of doors. The tramcars empty, their occupants flying in terror. A lady trips and, as she falls, screams out, "Rascals! rascals!" A workman lifts her up and asks:

"Who are the rascals?"

"You, the working men."

The worker laughs and replies:

"Don't upset yourself, lady, raping doesn't begin until noon."

The loud-speakers repeat the declamation of the orator:

"They are murdering our brothers in the street."

The loud-speakers are sabotaging the meeting. There is neither installation nor electric contact. The wires have been dragged out of a channel ten feet deep. They ought not to have spoken. They were children of fertile labour. They came from the hands of the workers, like the windows and the beams of the façade, but they came with delicate and gentle curves, feminine and *bourgeois*. The loud-speakers sabotage the meeting, speaking of their own free will. They recapture the words of the speeches, the noise of the crowd, roaring out of the three doors. The first advance of the troops pressed back the crowd, but now, as the theatre empties, the crowd re-forms and presses forwards. Although the hall is empty, the loud-speakers go on talking: "Death to the Bourgeois Republic." They are completing their mission of incitement. Is there not a bullet for the traitors? Pim! Pam! Down comes the loud-speaker over the porch. But the others continue, and the sound of firing aggravates everything. "The International", weak and flickering, pants through the cries. A tramcar is made into a barricade and a car is turned over with the noise of crashing glass. Half the crowd has taken refuge behind the theatre. From one of the windows shots are fired. The Madrid morning has turned livid. A single loud-speaker, high up, bellows:

"Barbarians! What are you about? Remember the soul!"

Telephonic communication has been established with headquarters. More troops. Now the Civil Guard. From amongst them more shots against the loud-speakers. The street is a clamour of shouts, disorderly noises, explosions. The revolution? Ha! Ha! Ha! What more can you want? The loud-speakers are not going to provoke the revolution of their own will and pleasure. Civil Guards on horseback invade the street. They dismount and fire. Half an hour of battle. The entrances to the Underground in the square are held by workers who lean out and fire. The loud-speaker stutters a moment and then calls out:

"The true interests of the country are based on order and peace."

But what about the spirit? Do not forget the spirit!

Shots at the windows, shots from the windows. The loud-speakers, now in fragments, are silent. Horses paw the street; one slips and falls, striking sparks from the ground. More shots. Another motor-van with troops. Another half-hour of fighting, and silence falls on the deserted street. Three comrades lie plastered against the pavement. More than fifty, hand-cuffed, are led off, surrounded by mounted troops. The beer-seller begins to open the metallic tap of his barrel, shaking his head. "It is chaos! Much use my having voted socialist!"

Chapter 3

Post-Mortem on Three Comrades

THE WORKMEN who lay dead in the street were Espartaco Alvarez, Germinal García and Progreso González. A list of three names isn't much. Three young and strong workmen, dead on the city pavement on a Sunday morning, mean more. These very men, half an hour before the meeting, were no less than signs of a new order of things. Espartaco belonged to the syndicate of agricultural labourers. Germinal to that of gas and electricity. Progreso to that of building construction. When they were picked up, they were in different positions. Espartaco had fallen face downwards and his teeth had been knocked out against the paving-stones. There he lay, kissing his own bloom. Germinal, with his mouth upwards, near a tree-trunk, had his head in the gutter. Progreso hadn't died instantaneously. He had been creeping with his chest on the ground, his heart beating against the asphalt. He died on the way to the ambulance. Then he was taken to the mortuary, to join his two comrades. And the Police surgeon dictated: "Espartaco Alvarez, forty-two years old; two gunshot wounds in the right temporal region, with the brain protruding; wounds necessarily fatal." "Germinal García, fifty years of age, bullet wound in the chest with no aperture of exit, another mortal wound in the groin with rupture of the femoral artery and contusions on several parts of the body." "Progreso González, aged thirty-two, three wounds from firearms, respectively on the fourth right intercostal space, the liver, and the frontal bone. All three with apertures of exit. The injury to the head certainly fatal."

The Police surgeon had to certify them as dead and that they were there. But the post-mortem scrutiny did not go so far as to indicate the size of the bullets or if they had been fired from short or long weapons. These facts remained unascertained so that the newspapers might be doubtful whether the victims might not have fallen to the revolvers of their comrades in the confusion of the struggle. When there is doubt, the papers select and impose their own view. But when there is evidence all they can do is to darken the air and create doubt.

But a post-mortem is a trivial affair. It tells nothing about comrades Espartaco, Progreso and Germinal and of the men they were. Who were they? Perhaps the personality of three corpses doesn't interest you, readers, but it may be told in a few words. There is seldom much to be said about men who die for an idea. If they were idealists of the other kind, those who at the club suddenly say, "It would be a good idea to go to the cinema, or to a cocktail party," and in pursuit of such an idea die of a cold they have caught, then we could possibly write a good deal about martyrs of that kind. But what can we say about Progreso, Espartaco and Germinal? How make you understand what can be said about three illiterate workmen who, in the time left them from their daily toil, dreamed of a juster society based on living realities and not on high-souled and highbrowed falsities?

Espartaco was a countryman who lived in Tetuán de las Victorias, near the demolitions of Fuencarral. Countryman? "Better call me," he used to say, "a poacher." He lived by hunting on the estates of the ex-King which remained closed land when the Republic came. His house seemed almost a palace to the vagabonds and thieves of the neighbourhood, and to them it was a dream of comfort. At one o'clock of the morning he rose from bed, kissed his mate and his son, took the ferret and some cord and went off to the Pardo. He caught some rabbits, sold them to a dealer before six o'clock, and by eight was home again with a few shillings. His expeditions covered the household budget and there was something left over for his expenses as a militant. Coupons of the Prisoners Relief Committee, subscriptions to the syndicate, assistance to those who were being prosecuted, dues to the Federation of Groups.

His mate admired him. Never in his house were quarrels or angry voices. Espartaco's receipt for keeping the peace at home was what he called—he had read the phrase in a leaflet—moral suasion. He himself behaved well, and any difference from his own conduct stood out as criminal and monstrous. They were happy without sentimentality. She sometimes asked him if he loved her, and Espartaco froze her with a look as he replied:

"Don't you see that I live with you?"

In the early months of their living together, Espartaco wasn't a countryman but a gambler. Every night he went out to play. He wasn't a pedant. When he saw that another member of the party was cheating, he did a bit of handling himself. As he was clever, all the money found its way to his pocket. But it was a risky profession; his mate suffered and used to lie awake in her bed. "One night," explained Espartaco to his friends, "I was playing as usual, and I pictured her to myself as sitting up in bed and crying. I left it all and went off home! Since then I haven't played again." "I gave up that easy job to be a countryman." It wasn't so easy to square his work as a poacher with that of a labourer so as to be accepted in the syndicate. But he was a first-rate militant, and to see him at work digging out rabbits showed that he was a good labourer!

He had taught himself to read when he was thirty years old. He didn't really understand the problems of capitalistic production, rationalization, excess production and artifical restriction, but he was unwilling to dim the clarity of his opinions about the social revolution by doctrines tainted with *bourgeois* intellectualism. In his life he had one hatred: the communists of the party. He could not endure their theoretical doctrine, and he was accustomed to say that in half an hour's argument he could knock them over. No doubt he was right, but what enraged him most was to see his own arguments exploited by his opponent with the unscrupulous personal vanity of a "leader", and he thought that the way of the communists. When an argument began to reach his limits, Espartaco used to stop speaking, shut his left eye and say slowly:

"Anyhow, comrade Espartaco can say that he has a tidy little shooter dancing in his pocket."

The shooter was a 6.35. But comrade Espartaco was neither unbalanced nor hot-headed. Never had he killed anyone from rage or without reason. He had hated the communists of the party for long, but his hatred became stronger after, one day, he had seen a fine young gentleman with the sickle and hammer, the emblem of the party, embroidered in silk on his shirt. He could not bear a *bourgeois* in the party's clothing. When there was trouble, as during the revolutionary strikes, or when there was a wages struggle, he carried out sabotage wtih precision and boldness. Wherever a daring hand was needed, his was ready. He carried out whatsoever he was asked to undertake, without comment, without vain boasting, and without asking useless questions. At home he was the same. He never missed a chance of working for the cause. He spent his free time in reading and in completing the education of his son who used to come back from school with follies stuffed into his head. But already the boy was a good critic.

"They told me," he said, "that the army was to defend the country."

"And what did you say?"

"That the army and the idea of the nation are only to defend the *bourgeoisie* and to enslave us more."

Espartaco burst into laughter. That was the kind of joke which made him laugh until the crockery rattled, times when the "cause" gave him a moment of real pleasure. But now he didn't laugh so heartily. In fact, he hardly smiled on the mortuary slab; he was nothing but a little lime, phosphorus, moisture and other chemicals.

Progreso González was a very different kind of man. We have already seen him in the "Paranymph" affair. Talkative, merry, an optimist. He was so sure of himself so confident in his own logic that his hatred of the *bourgeoisie* sometimes turned into a proud disdain, even pity. But that did not hinder him from fighting with zeal and with faith. He looked on the world and smiled, went about or slept, in all moods a free-thinking communist. He was so fervent an idealist that his views not only controlled his personal behaviour, but were carried over into physics and chemistry. It followed that he never had quarrels in the syndicate. He never bothered about their arguments. He thought of nothing but the immediate triumph of the revolution from the beginning of his own mental evolution, which, starting with the hatreds of his adolescence, was nurtured in the syndicates. Apart from his belief in social reconstruction, a belief confirmed and clarified by theory and by practice, there was the emotion of a man of tomorrow, of a tomorrow without injustice and without *bourgeoisie*. And so in fact he did not hate the *bourgeoisie* with the concentrated and aggressive hate of his comrades. When in a labour dispute the unfairness of the present constitution of society became evident, he was much surprised. "Very likely they don't understand! Oh! if I could have a chance of talking with the ministers!"

On the few occasions when he was on a deputation to the Police Headquarters to ask leave for the reopening of the syndicates, or for the ban to be removed from a newspaper, he tried to convince the Chief. For that reason they no longer put him on these deputations. "But," he used to say, "our ideas are so beautiful and so easy to understand!" But the Government as a body, which ordered slaughter in the streets, did not know the protective spirit in which Progreso González spoke of it at such times. "It would be better for the Government itself. The ministers would live in tranquillity and we should not have to kill them." That was how it seemed to him. Isolated acts of terrorism accomplished nothing, but when there was a great revolutionary scheme being carried out, he would reserve for himself, and in the past always had done so, the most dangerous and bloody tasks. He always had that idea in his mind. But it was no pleasure to him, and one day, talking to Leoncio, he found a solution. "I shall be a man of blood until the *bour-*

geoisie has been smashed. Then my fury will be turned to propaganda and constructive work." There was no anger in him, which was the more extraordinary because he had passed two years in a cell, chained by the leg so that he could not move more than two paces, and had seen comrades sentenced for life without proof, shut up in dark dungeons, chained by the ankle like himself, but with the chain riveted breast high to the wall, so that the prisoner had to stand night and day with the chained leg doubled up and to sleep on one leg. In him there was no urge for vengeance, because he felt that on the day after the revolution cruelty to the conquered would be unnecessary, and because for him it was now the day after, the moment the revolution had been made in his own conscience. Progreso, in the material sense, had come in conflict with the *bourgeois* monster without the chance of trying to persuade it. The monster, although he did not hate it because he felt it only as something aloof and outside him, killed him.

As for Germinal, he was a good plumber. He installed pipes and glass. He earned a regular wage and lived with his mother and daughter. His mate had died years ago and he hadn't chosen another, because in matters of sex there was always a *bourgeois* skirt available, and in matters of feelings, he loved his mother and his daughter Star. His house was on the outskirts of a northern workers' district where the police were always busy. His door was on the latch, day and night. Germinal didn't believe in thieves or in ghosts. When a comrade arrived at three in the morning, seeking a shakedown, he got it, and before he left next day, shared Germinal's hearty breakfast. The same treatment was given to those he knew and those he had never seen before. Germinal asked no questions. The mother served them distrustfully until she saw in Germinal's eye his sympathy with them. When that happened she came and went at her ease and called the stranger "son". Afterwards, if the police came nosing, the old lady received them suitably and had some unsavoury language for them about their dirty job. Some of the police feared her more than their own chiefs, because out of that gentle grey head there poured bitter insults and searching words. Even when she had routed them, she would follow them to the door hurling at them a final insult and sometimes a stone. In the district a police agent was always spoken of as a dog. They knew it well, and when it happened that the neighbours heard the old lady speaking, they aided her with a chorus. Other women appeared at the windows and the balconies adding to the trouble. Some barked, others smacked their lips and called out "mongrel".

The old lady, Auntie Isabela, became more insolent, and, with her arms akimbo, would cry out:

"To hell out of this, you bloody bastards."

Germinal, Auntie Isabela and Star lived in their red-brick house. There were more. A cat and a cock. "Makno", the cat, belonged to Auntie Isabela. The cock had no name and belonged to Star. The cock and the cat often quarrelled because the cock got bored and wished to play. The cat, voluptuous and pampered, took things seriously and drew its claws. Then the family had to interfere. Auntie Isabela picked up the cat, and Star took the cock, which she defended against the reproaches of the old woman:

"He only wanted to play."

She punished the cock with a few slaps and it crowed at each blow, pecking at her hand. It was an aggressive bird, feared by the children and the dogs of the street from its habit of lowering its wing and making a dash for the bare legs of children or the muzzles of the dogs—unless they were wolf-dogs, the only kind it respected. The cock slept in a little shed alongside the house. There were no hens, but in fact all the hens of the neighbourhood were at his disposal without his having to fight for them, as they had learned to come discreetly to him.

Star, Germinal and Isabela, the red cottage, the cat and the cock. Germinal was wrested from that group, his chest opened by bullets. Where could he be? Neighbours would invade the house and Auntie Isabela would pour out bad words, because as it was a matter of a corpse and the corpse that of her only son, she would be driven to desperation. Leoncio might go up to the house, but what would be the use? After each battle there was no point in going to condole with the families of the victims. It was not Germinal's death, but his appearance and last words that were troubling Leoncio. They had come rushing out of the theatre. The police had fired. They almost fell over Germinal's bleeding body. Star wished to go to him, but the crowd prevented her, carrying her off her feet. Germinal cried out to those who were trying to raise him: "Leave me alone; it's all up with me! Find my girl!" When he saw that Lucas Samar was kneeling beside him and calling to others to come and lift him, he stretched out, pushed them off and cried out again, "My little girl! My little girl!" Lucas supposed that she had been wounded and looked round for her. The firing continued. Finally Star appeared and Lucas picked her up in his arms and carried her off. Germinal smiled to see them, let his head fall on his arm, and in a few minutes he was dead.

Leoncio Villacampa thought more over these facts about

Star than about Germinal's death. He knew that deaths happened when fighting happened. But most of all he wished to go and see Germinal, to guess what he had meant to say with his last look about the future of Star, if any of the look remained on the mortuary slab. Also he wished to know if there were other victims, because there were rumours that two comrades of the "Gas and Electricity" were missing. The coming and going of the workmen in the secretariats of the syndicates in an alarmed and rustling swarm, as well as words he actually heard, convinced him that a general strike would be declared. Leoncio got up and walked towards the street. He saluted his comrades, read some of the notices on the walls of the lobby, and went down. The light faded to the dull grey of a sunless city. He took a tramcar. Progreso, Espartaco, Germinal. A white-bearded old man shook his stick on the platform and tried to lure the conductor into an argument. The conductor maintained his own opinion and the old man was annoyed. The tramcar, on the upgrade, struggled round the corners, halted at a wide avenue, rang its bell and halted. High above the houses a golden ray of sun streamed out. Leoncio went to the mortuary. When he reached the walls of the Civil hospital, the first lamps had begun to shine against the crystal opaqueness of nightfall. The suburb, deserted and dreary, livened up round about the huge building. There were the Main Gate tavern, Mickey's Bar, two sweet-shops, and a taxi rank alongside the corner café. The city seemed to be erupting in the taverns and bars. In an hour the public would be leaving the theatres and cinemas and ebbing towards the suburbs. Leoncio looked at it all and smiled. "Fools, tomorrow there will be a different kind of amusement for you." The indifference of the city life revolted him whilst Espartaco, Progreso and Germinal were lying awaiting the nameless void. "Fools! What will you say tomorrow?" Tomorrow the general strike would crash on them! "Why are there no newspapers, no tramways, no bread, no amusements?" they would bleat. "What has happened?" Every citizen would react in his own way. "Is it a sin to go to the pictures? Why shouldn't we get drunk on whisky? Because we take our best girl for a day in the country, is that a reason to rob us of the necessities of life? We haven't done any harm. It isn't our fault!" Leoncio smiled as he climbed the staircase to a ward. "Fools!" He took a deep breath and looked back. In the melancholy little square a dwarf tree struggled up from between the flagstones. The wall reached up to his feet. Behind it rosy haloes marked the lighted parts of the city. "Fools!" Leoncio Villacampa, the grocer's porter, with his scarlet Sunday tie, heaved a deep sigh and muttered, "Don't you all know that this morning you murdered three of our comrades? You the merchant, you the priest, and you, my lord judge, and you, my lady whore! But you have to pay for it! Tomorrow you are going to pay." He had to cross a lobby, traverse a passage with several doors and staircases. After an argument with some watchmen and persuading the police that he was a relative of the deceased, he came out on the other side of the block and began to descend another stairway like the first. Another little courtyard. The mortuary was in the block facing him, down in the basement. The courtyard was paved with dull slabs. Above the black outline of the walls and the slated roof the sky was luminous and blue, and two stars shone over the chimneys. Close to the wall, leaning against it, were Samar and Star García. For a moment Leoncio felt uncomfortable. Star, the daughter of the victim, would be in distress and he would have to find some *bourgeois* phrases telling her how sorry he was, difficult things that meant nothing. But he said nothing, for he found Star just as usual, as if nothing had happened. When he came up, Samar put his arms round her shoulders and drew her to him paternally. Leoncio found a significance in that action and kept silence a minute. Lucas Samar asked a question with a glance and Villacampa had to reply, but turned to Star: "A general strike is being arranged for tomorrow."

The girl brightened. As her father was dead, something must be done against the assassins. Lucas withdrew his arm, raised his eyebrows, frowning.

"A general strike?"

Leonico looked through the window into the mortuary. Star said in a strangely indifferent way:

"They have made the post-mortem."

The journalist repeated:

"A general strike?"

In the present conjuncture a general strike might mean everything. It would precipitate other events, stir up the rebellion latent in the whole country. It was a mutiny. It might mean everything. But it might also be a bitter failure. He crossed to the window, looking in. Star also. In silence the three stared into the mortuary. Three slabs alongside each other with the bodies of Progreso, Espartaco and Germinal covered with sheets. Two employees passed in and out carrying buckets. Leoncio thought, "Is it possible that everything ends like this, in nothing?" But he didn't speak, because he thought that Lucas would think of something deeper to say. And in fact Lucas said almost at once:

"There is no death; Germinal, Espartaco and Progreso still follow the rebellion, in our ideas, in our memories."

"But is not death real?" objected Leoncio.

The journalist rolled a cigarette to dispel the strong smell of disinfectant. He added:

"There is no death. If our comrades there could speak, you would hear them discussing the advantages of the general strike, without remembering the incident of their own deaths, facts of no importance among real things. Death which comes to us from outside—a shot, two cries, blood and loss of consciousness—all these are small things outside our own will. The real evil is the death that comes from within us—failure."

Star's eyes shone.

"It's true. My father could never fail. He could not die. My father hasn't died."

Her face broke into smiles. Then suddenly she added, disdainfully:

"Let us go. There is a bad smell."

They went off through the courtyard.

The doctors had finished the post-mortem. They had opened the skulls of Progreso and Espartaco who had received head-wounds. They found red blood and blue veins. In the brains there were none of the toxins familiar in the lovesick, in suicides, in unbalanced persons. The brains were healthy. The only abnormality was an intoxication about the future. A doctor with the gift of observation might have made an interesting note, as it is rare to examine brains free from metaphysical fears or hopes. All the organs steeped in material faith, daring and generosity. Ambition? Personal anxiety for the future? Impatience? No trace of these. Material faith, self-sufficing faith. Daring and generosity come only from faith in oneself, from one's own faith! And when there is confident faith in one's own faith, of what value are material ambition and hope, memory and illusion, phantasms which make death dark and oppressive, a haunting menace to feebler minds? Faith! but not metaphysical or intellectual faith, but organic faith! The faith of the rock and the tree.

As they walked on in silence, Star García suddenly turned to Leoncio:

"But, after all, my father is dead."

"Yes, he has died for the cause," replied Villacampa.

She reproached the journalist:

"You were deceiving me; my father is dead."

Lucas repeated:

"Death does not exist. I have not deceived you."

Villacampa interposed obstinately:

"Tell him that he has, Star."

"What do you know? What do you know about death?" asked Samar.

The grocer's porter replied hotly. Star looked from one to the other. Samar added:

"Death does not exist, dear; death is *bourgeois.*"

"And what about that, what about these?" said Villacampa angrily, pointing to the mortuary.

Star hesitated. She raised her closed hand to her face, rubbed her chin, sometimes biting a finger. Then she said dubiously:

"But, Samar, my father is dead. It is no use telling me anything else."

Samar gave up explaining. He saw that Star was struggling to keep back her tears, and he said roughly:

"All right. Let us go on."

The girl took Villacampa's arm.

"No! I am going to stay here."

She quivered and began to cry. Lucas rather crossly took her other arm. "Home. You can do nothing here. Your father is dead. You are right. The *bourgeoisie* has murdered him. Never again will you hear him speak; he'll never go to his bed again or buy you sweets on Sundays, or kiss you again." Star broke into a flood of tears. "His chest has been broken by bullets and his skull has been opened. You are the most unhappy of women. Cry! Cry!" Star appeared to be going to abandon herself to weeping and Lucas went on: "But your tears are only killing him a second time, because if you let your feelings get the better of you, you'll kill what you have of him within you, what you have of your father. Cry! Cry! Like a *bourgeoise*!"

Star pulled herself together with difficulty. She wished to say something. Her eyes shone with a faraway look. From being a cold and lifeless statue, she turned to a furious savage with eyes full of hate.

"Let us go in."

She entered the mortuary, went up to one of the slabs and uncovered a victim. The two others followed her in amazement. She stared at the gaping hole in the chest, and with a mystical air, murmured, "Father! Father! You are not dead! No!" The journalist added, "You are not dead! Sleep in the justice of tomorrow!"

Star repeated: "Sleep in the justice of tomorrow." She was going to kiss him, but the journalist gently held her back. She had to get close to the living warmth of someone and submerge her own despair in it. She hugged the journalist and also wetted Leoncio's breast with her tears. Clinging together they went out. She turned round at the door and repeated, sobbing, "Sleep in the justice of tomorrow." She wanted words, more words. Her eyes renewed what they had seen, her ears repeated the cries, the voices and shots of the morning, her heart beat wildly; she breathed in gasps and clenched her hands. All her being was a wild protest. Words she needed, and Lucas found them for her.

"We shall avenge you and the *bourgeoisie* shall know your justice."

She repeated them, interpolating the sonorous incantation of wrath: "We shall sweep away the God of the *bourgeoisie*."

The brutal and criminal God of the Civil Guard!

And the Christ, the pander of evil!

God, death, Christ, evil, broke from her lips as flowers of a burning infection. Lucas felt his entrails wracked with hate. He had lost his serenity, but he controlled himself and led them out. Once in the street, he called a taxi and they moved away in silence. Star had subdued her sobbing, but from time to time sighed deeply. When they were near her house she started and made the driver stop. They didn't know why. She told them:

"We must stop a minute over there"—pointing to an alley—"I must buy corn for the cock. As there is going to be a general strike I must have a store for him."

Chapter 4

Comrade Star Left Alone in the World

I AM at home. My grandmother has gone to the hospital to watch by my father. They won't let her go in, but that doesn't matter, as it will be enough for her to see the walls of the hospital. If she doesn't see them, she'll believe that her prayers will go to the benefit of a money-lender or even of one of the Civil Guard. The neighbours have been here to ask me to sleep in one of their houses, as if I hadn't my own bed here I have stayed because I wish to begin being alone today now that my father has gone, and I know that I am alone in the world. The neighbours tell me I'll be frightened, and so I would be, but for the cock which is walking about the room wide-awake.

It is on the alert; it knows that something has happened, although I've told it nothing yet. "Come here and listen. Don't you know that they have killed my father? You think little of that because I am still bringing you corn. But anyhow I am left without a father or a mother I am eighteen years old and the neighbours are sorry for me. I am alone. My grandmother doesn't count because she is on her way out of the world, and I am on my way in, and as she is wrinkled and old, and I am young and pretty, she does nothing but scold me. I've been crying. Perhaps I'll cry more now, and you are gay. But no! It is the last time in my life that I'll cry. I am alone, and a girl alone in the world mustn't cry. Still less an anarchist girl. I am an anarchist like you and like my father. I work in a lamp factory and earn eight shillings a week, almost the wage of a forewoman, and they have to feed Makno, you, grandmother and me. You on corn, the cat on liver, and grandmother and me on potatoes. Sometimes cat's-meat and corn are as dear as potatoes, but your stomachs are small and you'll be filled first. You may be glad of that, now that troubles are coming, for you'll still be able to crow and mew and swank round the district." The cock drooped his wing and came at me sideways, but I gave him a little kick to quieten him. Then he crowed, came up to me and jumped upon my knees. I caught him and we began to talk again. Now that we are alone, I have a lot to say. "Listen, dear; I am going to tell you something very important. Wait till I see that we are really alone. Let me see that the bolts are all shut. My father is dead because it was his mission to die, and the mission of the Civil Guard to kill him. I am not the kind to tear my hair in despair. And that which was my father I loved as I loved you. He is dead because in all his life he did what he had to do, and he died in the way a revolutionary dies. That brings nothing new to me, my cock. Until today I was Germinal's daughter. Now I am Star García, of the syndicate of Various Duties. Do you understand? People say that I was born in 1916, but I don't remember that. I think I was born today. With Saturday's money I'll buy my first pair of stockings and embroider my sash with 'Land and Liberty' and my name. You don't think much of that? Of course. But although I've some respect for you, as my father admired you and said that you were more of an anarchist than he was himself, I won't let you go to sleep. I am alone. I am myself. I was born today and I have to live a life which is beautiful in a society which my father thought criminal, but I think merely foolish and simple. The neighbors say that they will give me my mourning. But how silly to wear black with my first pair of stockings! Also the neighbors tell me that at my age it is very dangerous to be left alone, and that I may go wrong. But it is old Cleta who says that, and she is the widow of a soldier and thinks that what happens amongst them may happen amongst us. I asked her what she meant by 'going wrong' and if she thought that I had the stuff in me to go wrong. Then she smiled in a mysterious way and kissed me. What can have happened to these people in their lives that in the end they should want to kiss one in that sort of mysterious way? Because there is certainly something wrong about it. As for the thing itself, I've never had time to think about it. I know well enough that I like men. Some of them, of course. But they must be comrades, because the others don't seem to me any better than priests. I don't want children until we have made the revolution, and as for the rest—sometimes when I see a handsome fellow I wonder if I'd like to kiss his mouth, but the idea always disgusts me."

The cock jumped from my lap, crowed, and drooping its wing, raised itself on its legs. It made a short rush, kept crowing, retreated, then attacked me, pecking at my legs. Never was it in such a temper. I got up and ran at it, but it got in front of me and drove me into a corner. Then I picked up a stick from the wall and threatened it. It gave in sulkily and I sat down again with the stick handy. The cock began to crow and wished to go out. I put some corn in my lap and it came to sit on my knees, pecked at the corn and was contented. I clasped it over the wings, put a grain of corn in my ear which it took with its beak. That always tickles me. Good, where were we? "There are only two men I can think of kissing without disgust, and even then I'd clean my mouth afterwards." The cock crows and threatens me, and I give him a couple of slaps. "I shan't tell you their names, silly goose of a cock. To no one, and not to you. If I were to tell you it would make it important, and really it doesn't matter at all." And the cat? There is a noise on the roof and it must be him. Not even on a night like this will he stay at home. Our cats have always been shameless. Father never said that the cat was an anarchist, and if I ever called him one, it was when he was a kitten and didn't know his tricks. I think that cat is a dogmatic communist, but I don't object to them as my father did, because it seems to me all of us who are alive should join in the fight against capitalism, the cat, the cock and me. As for ideas, I think that the character of the individual is more important than the views he holds, and among men I like the communist character better than the anarchist. Samar isn't an anarchist, but he is with us because he relies more on organization and the revolutionary force of individuals. I don't care what he thinks. He is a communist. Villacampa is not. He is an anarchist. His face is tranquil and his eyes are steady and besides he speaks very little. The anarchists are like that, but the communists always seem to be in a hurry, look superior and often don't know what to do with their hands. Samar has given me a note telling what to do tonight with the papers and the rest of my father's things. He gave it to me in an envelope and I've been keeping it under my jersey. Let me see what he bids me to do before the police come to investigate. What a long letter! But what is this? "Dearest little girl, forgive me. Until now, seven o'clock, I couldn't write to you." A letter to his sweetheart! He has made a mistake, and now I am going to read it right through, to see what a love letter is like. The paper is elegant and the writing is small. "I am not going to write much, but you know I love you, little darling, desperately. I am hungry for your arms and your lips. I would like to give you a life you don't know, and to fill it with light and peace. But I don't believe it can be. In the whirlwind of my life, love has no place. I want for you all the peace and quietness that is in my soul when I forget everything but our love. But can I give it to you—the peace and quietness which are so far from me? The peace and quietness which fly from me! I am laughing at myself in spite of everything, as I think how all these marks of exclamation, or interrogation, and these dashes, will annoy you because they take up space in my letter. As I laugh, some of the happiness which you keep for me and give me is with me. If you only knew with what impatience I watch the passing of the days without you! What a wild longing to get to you! But sometimes life, everything, seems to push me away. What wild rage, little darling of my heart! Life is stupid, but our love will save us, because a kiss from you will be the secret begetter of worlds and lives and new joys which I know already a little, darling, from your gentle eyes, but the day when you are mine will make me a god. The longing for a God which is in all the religions, I shall assuage in my own religion —your love, your hands, and your lips! How can I tell you how much I love you? I know only that I have passed through great joy and great sorrow. I have known life in its most secret corners, in sweetness and in bitterness. I believed that my soul held all the secrets, knew everything, had reached everything. I knew why people were happy one day and killed themselves the next: how one flower grows out of a dung-heap and the same day another more beautiful, and the sun which begot them, kills them. I know how water is born from the clouds and forms rocks, how rocks make mountains and mountains volcanoes, and how from the colour and the light and the love of the rocks and the seas there arise little beings as independent as the plants, but like them, subject to love. Amongst these there are persons in whose hearts something of the sun remains. They call themselves men, and the sun within them turns into the poison we call knowledge, and sometimes, poisoned, they die or kill themselves. I knew all that, and knew the roots of my own knowledge and the paths by which it would lead me, and I closed my eyes and sang sad songs, and sometimes I wished to kill, sometimes to kill myself, as many have done, or perhaps I had already killed myself, and was laughing with the grin of the dead. Suddenly, my lovely darling, I came to know you. Think of it! I came to know you! I went on as before, but my sorrowful wisdom turned into faith, into passion. I was drunk every day with the light in my own heart, with the sun which had been hiding there and suddenly shone, filling all my being and rising to my brain and turning it. I sang songs of joy and gave way to fits of laughter. Shall I tell you why I laughed? I laughed at the poisoned wisdom of men, at the sad consciousness of the rocks, at the hurrying destiny of the rivers. The mountains became the tiny figures of a map and the outpourings of the volcanoes, frivolous and ridiculous, the flowers despicable in their vain levity. Everything passing on to ruin in foolish levity. Everything except you and me! The secret of the universe, immense and everlasting, I found in the depths of your gentle eyes, and my heart quickened its beats in joy. Outside ourselves all is sadness. Except our love, all is ugly, all but me sigh and weep. All but me have been poisoned by the sun. My poisoned wisdom melted in the light and evaporated under the sun in my heart. And now I know nothing and wish to know nothing. I live like a new-born planet, wheeling in happiness and careless of the laws which it obeys. You and me, darling! You and me! Others don't exist. They are quenched in desolation, for I have robbed the world of its joy to offer it to you, I have stolen all its pleasures to carry them to you, I have plunged its soul in darkness, to cast every ray on you! You and me, darling!"

I never could have thought that love-letters were written like that. Nor that Samar—— Now I understand that man. I didn't see clearly. There was always a dark zone round him, but I set it down to communism. He is a communist, I thought, and so we don't understand him completely. But all the same he knows a lot of things and is not confused like me, a poor girl in a lamp factory. But all the same it is a bad job for Samar to have forgotten his letter. If he knew where it was, to get it back! Or even if he had put the address on the envelope so that I could have delivered it for him, and when I saw him tomorrow morning I could have told him. What will he think of me when he knows that I have read the letter? Could I pretend and hide it up? But, dear me! She is a neighbour of mine. Daughter of the Colonel of Artillery, 75, Light, who lives in the house at the side of the barracks, and the barracks are quite close, at the end of the street. In love with a *bourgeoise* girl and—what love! —— I couldn't help laughing at a man if he were to write that sort of stuff to me. Amparo García del Río. It is a pretty name. I'll try not to forget it. As for the note with the warning to me, it is a pity I haven't got it. My poor father must have been in some trouble with the police and I ought to know what it is. Here in this loneliness and with the light so bad, throwing shadows everywhere, I am likely to lose my wits and not remember. Be quiet, dear! What is the matter with you? Oh! a knock at the door. It must be the police, as I might have suspected. If grandmother were here, she would give them what for! A pity! I must let them in. Hallo! Whom do you think it is? Samar? I hurriedly offer him the letter. He looks at it without taking it, pushes my hand aside in a careless way and comes in. Looking all round he says:

"The syndicates have been closed and the central committee is going to meet in the country tonight. A general strike must come, and now that we are moving we must push forward and do all we can."

I am going to speak to him about the letter, but he interrupts me whilst he moves the night-table and takes two revolvers which are under it.

"There is fear in the air. The *bourgeois* are afraid. Tomorrow trouble comes."

I say to him innocently and in good faith that the best thing to do in this quarter would be to attack the barracks.

He starts with his eyes staring. The revolvers tremble in his hands. Then he asks for a knife and goes to the yard where he makes a hole in the ground in a particular spot. Soon he comes on two boxes of cartridges, another revolver and a small drawing. In a satisfied way he puts them all in the pocket of an overcoat which he is carrying over his arm. He pointed to the roof and said:

"In a hole, there should be two dozen hand-grenades. Tomorrow you must stay indoors all day."

I objected. When there is a strike I must be in the thick of things. "Although you don't think it, I am useful in all sorts of ways."

He replies, "All right, but you must give me the key of the house."

I give it to him. Then when I offer him the letter, he tells me to keep it and deliver it tomorrow.

"Have you read it?" he asks.

I make such a face that he can't help laughing. Then he goes off, slamming the door. I laughed so much that all the neighbours must have heard. Then suddenly I became quiet. What can the neighbours think, hearing me laugh when my father is dead? I read the letter again, and remembering the words and gestures of Samar, I am sure that what the *bourgeois* call love must be a disease like typhoid or influenza. What do you think, my cock?

Chapter 5

Lady Moon Looks Down

I ROSE in the East, wide and scarlet. Then I lingered over La Mancha, small and pale. I have two large mirrors, the lake of Casa de Campo and the marsh of Lozaya. First I have to pass over some domes from which telescopes protrude, observing me. I thought at first that they might belong to an institute of beauty culture, from the attention they paid to my spots, but then I saw that they were only a few poor scientists who were gazing at me. It is true that I haven't yet convinced poets that I am old—what follies they think—and that I am dead—what a joke it all is! Fortunately there are terraces quite near the observatory where young people dance to jolly music and love each other, and say all sorts of things as they look at me. Thanks to them the Earth has still some interest.

But to be interested and to love are different. I don't love the Earth for what I've been telling you, but for other reasons which are my feminine secret as the fatal planet. I am not a star but I have the gift of fatality. As I pass over the Earth against its solar course, it pleases me to see the shadows fly and take refuge in their terror. Under the bridges, behind the houses, hurriedly, tumultuously. I exert an evil influence, because at my pleasure I change the grouping of atoms and cause odd magnetic changes in things and in human beings, the effects of which vary but are always exciting. The news columns and society gossip of the papers are really an intimate diary of me. There are peculiar beings who love me without knowing it—the best kind of love—and although most of them don't write me poems they respect me more deeply than the poets. They don't sleep if I wish them not to sleep. They change their appearance at my pleasure. They quarrel with their wives and families, ruin themselves or even die or commit suicide for my sake. Men call them lunatics. When they devote themselves to politics, I amuse myself playing them merry tricks. Monarchists establish a Republic, and don't know what to do with it. Other republicans get up to speak and lose themselves in communistic declarations. One man really believes that he is saving the country and all he does is to give it new clothes. I like them because they are my true lovers, but I laugh a good deal, although a laugh is not becoming to my broad face. But as for politicians, the most changeable and feeble people on the Earth, it is easy to turn their heads, although indeed the change isn't much noticed. A politician's head is light enough without my interference. I have more trouble with scientific men. One of them wrote tedious essays about me; I made him loony and kept him for two years with his right hand clenched and raised, begging people to tell him what to do with an atom of hydrogen he held in it! As for poets—those that hymn me are better called soothsayers—I have my group in every town, a chorus which issues a bulletin—although they don't yet call it the Lunatic Bulletin. These are the green poets who love me with a love sweeter than men's love, with a feminine love. I influence them in a very different way from my effect on tomcats, in which I arouse masculinity. The sweet sensuality of the young and tender verses of my lovers quite thrills me. To plunge into their images is like bathing in the sea of milk and roses of the Pleiades. My magnetic influence turns the heads of young gentlemen to follies. But enough; night advances; the stars are shining with midnight brilliance. My gentle poets are sleeping in their soft sheets, and towards the East where the dots and dashes of Morse have been spluttering out at me, shots are heard. That must mean that on the other side of the town groups of men who hate me or despise me are collecting to discuss something. Police cars are rattling towards the seat of disturbance. That is what those syndicalists wish. A ribbon of shadow under the cars rolls through the streets and alleys. Tonight you can distinguish between the police and the syndicalists by this; the first seek the light and the others cower in the shadows. But I am more cunning than the police, and instead of shining where the shots are being fired, I pass to the other side of the city. There hotels and villas have little gardens between them, where the country has inserted its fingers. A balcony is open on a hotel and I pass through the transparent curtain. I shine on the mirror of the dressing-table and slide through to the bedroom wall. A woman, wrapped in lace, one breast uncovered, weeps into her pillow. Alongside her a man talks without stopping:

"You think that simply because the police are after them, respectable houses should give them shelter!"

"He is not a criminal," she sobbed.

"I've heard that before! He is your cousin and he is a communist. He wears a dark flannel shirt with a Zip fastener, and he is sullen. Right, he is a communist. But why should he seek refuge with peaceable citizens? Let him look after himself!"

The woman started.

"You are going to throw him out? You are going to hand him over to the police?"

"Of course not. The sense of pity is *bourgeois*!"

"When it suits you! You'd forget it now very willingly."

The husband laughs.

"I suppose you are a communist, too."

She says nothing, but has stopped sobbing. She listens anxiously and is comforted by the silence.

"A nice kind of communist, with an income of one thousand five hundred pounds a year!"

"And what about it? Does it bring me happiness? Isn't an ideal better?"

"Be quiet! Or perhaps you hope the communist is listening?"

"Beast!"

"Have I offended you?"

"Yes."

She rises and makes to leave the bed. She displays a plump and rounded leg.

"Where are you going?"

"To my own room."

The husband raised himself, opened the drawer of the night-table. He took out a strange object and hissed: "I love you too much. If you put a foot in the passage I'll shoot you."

I fled from the scene. Once before I was shot at in a mirror, and although it didn't injure me, it gave me a bad shock. Besides I've seen scenes of that kind too often. I must confess that it was I myself who suggested to the husband the fear and the risk of his wife going to the communist's bedroom. My rearrangement of atoms had put that into his head. It would have been easy to make him shoot, but I tell you I am afraid of shooting.

The men can't be far off who have misled the police by sending some of their friends to the other side of the city. Behind the blocks of flats there are two clover fields. Then a rounded hill. Then the highroad. Then a short belt of trees along a canal, then a slope where boulders cast short shadows, then another little hill with a ruined hermitage. I could not cast my beams across it to the other side. There is a line of shadow. From time to time a waterproof cap appears above the wall and with a little trouble I drew glints from the barrel of a revolver there. In short, there are two men on the watch, and the others must be quite near. Let us sharpen our ears and listen! My hearing is very acute, and as there are no frogs or crickets about, there are no distracting noises. I hear two words distinctly: "sabotage", "capitalism". This means that they are at the beginning, because the first word reveals the impulsive attitude of an anarchist from the federation of groups, and the second is the keynote of a syndicalist delegate. And in these reunions they discuss tactics more than revolutionary action. But at first the two camps are not clearly defined. The President is a fat man over whose face I pass my rays without revealing anything but curves. There are about twenty delegates. Now the secretary speaks: "A communist delegation has come to tell us that they will follow our decision. They have brought their credentials. I've told them that all they have to do is to follow us." The others applaud. "I have announced to them that the general strike is for tomorrow. But they wish details of our plans. As nothing else has been definitely arranged, I confined myself to insisting on the general strike and asking them to help to make it complete. There is only a minority in the organization for that, because the constitutional reformers have the upper hand, but thirty thousand of our people must drag the others into the strike. The communists, although not numerous, are very active and can help us."

The speaker is a dry and melancholy workman who has other troubles on his mind. His mate is in hospital, and they have not let him visit her for three days as the nuns were at her bedside day and night persuading her to confess and take the sacrament, and urging that the conduct of her companion was criminal and suicidal. With her, he had struggled and suffered. They hoped to convince her even at the point of death. Perhaps they had already persuaded her, in the clean comfort of the sheets and by the apparent generosity and humanity of their sentiments. Perhaps she had already made her confession and received unction, and perhaps she was thinking that the nuns were right. When she asked why her mate had not been to see her, they would have told her that she deceived herself about men, that trust was to be put only in God, the supreme Consoler. She and her mate had not been married, and the sister would not let him come in, nor tell her that he had been twice every day trying to visit her. The poor were in their power and they took advantage of it with firmness and persistence. They wished faith in life to be lost. They kill matter. They do well. I like religion because it is romantic. And these nuns are worthy people. What a work they perform to support order and social peace! How it touches me to see them, without any thought of gratitude from others, arrange the sheets, give the bed-pan, take the temperature—and not from humanity, which they modestly disclaim, but for the love of God and their hope of eternal bliss. I am never happier than when I see my own whiteness reflected on their clean hoods. But this barbarian hates them. He has left his revolver on the ground, between his feet, and looks at me thinking of happy days. Then he sighs, passes his hand over his unshaven chin, rubs his jaw under its yellow skin and begins to listen. Another speaker gets little attention because he has too many familiar generalities, such as, "the cruelty of the *bourgeoisie*, the need to avenge their dead comrades, the hope of moving towards a rebellion of infinite duration and wide results". All that has been said to satiety. Now two manifestoes have been approved—that is something concrete. One is to be set up and printed this very night and distributed at dawn. Another is a reply to the advice of the social-democrats, who as usual are exhorting their members not to stop work. Another delegate, who is of more weight and something of a poet, but no friend of mine, but in fact in his own way a leader of the opposition to me—to the moon—asks leave to speak to say that steps must be taken about another manifesto, the one that "the socialists" will issue in the afternoon, declaring a general strike as an expression of grief over the death of the comrades, and asking, as a token of reconciliation, the dismissal of the Director-General of Public Safety.

An old anarchist protests: "that it is a political point of view," and launches into a tirade against politics. They remind him that Samar himself had not written the manifesto but had warned them that the socialists would issue it. But the old man kept mumbling the same two phrases through the hollows of his teeth. He ends with a compliment to me: "We are as clear as the moon that is presiding over us." Samar shrugs his shoulders: "No politics!" and then adds, "Everything is political, even your long white hair, old friend!" People laugh and then Samar goes on, "And as for the moon, I denounce her presidency as she is *bourgeoise* and a bawd." Then they all laugh again and so forget the socialist manifesto. Samar insists that the socialists "are bound by the adhesion of their syndicates to our protest, and therefore to avoid being ridiculous must declare the general strike. We must make the most of this triumph and make it known to all the comrades." Then the old white-hair begins to repeat Samar's phrases about the ridicule the socialists would incur if they did not join, and on the same line of argument suggests the unfortunate position in which the constitutional reformers would be if they were forced into the strike by the unanimity of the movement. Samar smiled and began to arrange pebbles with the butt of his revolver. At last he said: "I am glad that the comrade has come to my opinion." But then the old man recovered himself, and in order to say something that Samar had not said, begins to praise free love. Next he proposes a vote of thanks to the moon. I am much obliged to him. But I don't understand these men. I can't influence their brains because that would require a power of assimilation they haven't got. Some of the young delegates don't know what to do about the vote of thanks, whether to vote for it or against it. They can't see how I could help them against capitalism, and so the old man recites some verses to convince them. The President gets impatient and recalls them to the agenda of the meeting. The vote is passed idly, and the secret meetings for the next day are then settled. Next came instructions to the committees and the agreement with the delegates from the district to act with the federation of anarchist groups. In reference to the latter, the old man became eloquent again about universal brotherhood and spoke about the harmony of atoms in molecules. The young men didn't listen to him but counted their cartridges. The old man droned classical doctrines and quoted from some members of Parliament. The young ones smiled sadly, but Samar noticed that none the less the old man was having some influence on them, in the fashion of the sentimental and rhetorical *bourgeoisie*. A vote of thanks to me. I had to be grateful, but only in a formal way, because I despise them, but gratitude is always pleasing. Now they are wrangling over the significance of a word, and the three most opinionated delegates argue and discuss irrelevant matters with the logic of somnambulists. The three are sure that the comrades from the syndicates do not grasp the force of their arguments. A young man, also an anarchist, with self-possession and sense of responsibility, very different from the three, comes forward in the name of common sense and the interests of the revolution. He succeeds in imposing his will. But the three old men attack him about the exact meaning of what he has been saying and analyse his orthodoxy with the meticulousness of Church Fathers. The other delegates keep silent. One of them suddenly asks for silence with a gesture. A loud whistle is heard near the hermitage and here I take a hand.

Police motors and the horses of the Civil Guard appear between the blocks of flats, and are pouring into the fields. I seize hold of a cloud and place it so that it throws them into shade. With another cloud, I hide the revolutionaries, who keep silent, feeling safe and waiting for the second whistle, the warning to fly. When the scouts in the hermitage wish to give the warning signal, they are already surrounded by the police. Nothing could have been better. Now the police move on to the others. I withdraw the cloud as if raising a curtain. On the motion of the old anarchist they had passed a vote of thanks to me, and now I have done them in! There they are, in full light. Now they have seen you! No use hurrying to escape, old friends! But the young ones get out their revolvers and take cover in the slope. And now there is a problem. Can they keep together and escape in a body? The ground is too open for them to escape singly. They are bound to try to get away, but they have to move forwards, firing all the time. That is a bad business, but, after all, I am a *bourgeoise* and the least I can do is to help my side at the cost of a headache.

Two lads shrug their shoulders and call out to the police: "Halt! We are going to have some fun!" The agents throw themselves on the ground. A dozen shots come from the revolutionaries in a volley. The police retire and the horses of the Civil Guard waver and separate into two groups. A pair dash off at a gallop. They are sending for reinforcements. The delegates exchange rapid glances and search the ground over their shoulders. Three creep back cautiously and take up positions in the rear. The comrade who was secretary picks up the wrapper in which he had put his notes. A grey-faced little fellow calls out as he fires: "This for Germinal! And now one for Espartaco!" There have been no losses. The group separates and they retreat more rapidly than the others advance. When they reach the trees along the canal, an agent is seen three yards off. He and the syndicalists fire at the same moment. The agent falls, and the others fly. One is holding his arm which has been wounded. Samar is alongside him and with his belt and handkerchief improvises a sling which he adjusts without ceasing to run. The helmets of the Civil Guard are visible across the canal. They have misjudged the ground, and now the canal helps the fugitives. Samar already feels in safety as he runs between the wounded man and the old man with white hair. For a moment he thinks of something very far away; of Amparo García del Río. He feels ashamed about her. But then he thinks: "If she were to see me now she would think me a criminal, a footpad. Perhaps she, too, would be ashamed of me." Shots are heard farther off and a ball whistles over their heads. There rings in his ears the voice of the old man proposing a vote of thanks to the moon. To the moon which has betrayed them. Samar looks up angrily at me and curses me. But he doesn't know that at this very moment I am flooding with my beams the workmen's quarter in the East, the barracks of the 75th Light Artillery, the Colonel's garden, and that I am entering Amparo's room by the open balcony window and am caressing Amparo's soft and rounded arms as she lies asleep dreaming rather sadly. What an inspiration for a tender poet; the tears of a pretty, sleeping girl! But Samar has killed sentiment and buried it in the depths of his soul. He can no longer say anything tender aloud.

Samar, now that he feels out of danger, and because I am influencing him, remembers that he hasn't seen his betrothed this Sunday, and that he hasn't yet been able to get his letter to her, and that she has probably tried in vain to telephone to him at his house, several times, and still worse, that probably a police agent must have replied to one of these calls with irony and insults. And so when by roundabout ways they reach the first streets of the city, he leaves the two others abruptly.

"Where are you going?"

"Home."

"The police will be there and you mustn't let yourself be caught that way! You must lie low just now."

Firing is heard in the distance.

"What for?" laughed Samar; "to pass votes of confidence in the moon?"

Now the voice of the third is grave and low:

"We aren't old and our hair isn't grey."

"Anyhow, we must separate after what has happened."

The groups break up, and as they skip into the shadows under the eaves, I cannot follow them. I suppose nothing more will happen tonight. But what has happened in the La Mancha quarter to make the enemies of my gentle poets so restless? Doubtless I'll find the answer in the Civil hospital, in the mortuary. Let us go there. I can't enter by the window, as the roof of the ward in front is in the way. In the courtyard there is a tall slender tree with a heavy black crown. The flagstones are slimy, large and porous. You can hear some coffins being dragged along. They must be going to put corpses into them. Now you can hear a hammer, and by the sound the coffins can't be empty. Express delivery to the nothing. My gentle poets would make tender verses, were the coffins white and heaped over with white lilies. They have delicate minds! In the street an old woman in black is moaning as she leans against the hospital wall. I don't like old people. Old age is terrible as it bends people's backs and prevents them from looking at me. Now a young man goes up to her and says:

"I am Leoncio Villacampa. Where is your granddaughter?"

"At home."

Then the old woman tells how they have kept her from seeing her son, larding her words with curses, prayers to God, blasphemies and insults. She holds her rosary in her left hand and she has told half of it. With her other hand she gropes under her skirts and pulls out something rounded.

"I am going to throw this at the head of one of these sons of bitches!"

It is a small bomb. Leoncio begs her to give it to him, calling her "Auntie Isabela", and she hands it over. It is clear that she wasn't much interested in it and that she showed it only to let Leoncio ask for it. Leoncio looks sadly up at me and interrupts the prayers of the old woman:

"Poor Star! What a misfortune for her. She is left alone in the world!"

"What about me?" cries Auntie Isabela. "She is on her way up in life, and at sixteen all you want is a comb and a looking-glass. But me? Who is going to look at me now?"

Hillo! There are three comets, new and scarlet. From the rate at which they are moving they are likely to stay seven days in our System. Three new comets! Hillo! you there. What are your names?

—Espartaco.

—Progreso.

And you? What do you call yourself?

—I am Germinal.

Chapter 6

Comrade Samar Blunders in "Action"

I'VE SLEPT for five hours in the house of a comrade. The bugs woke me up, and I rose to go to find Star at her house which is quite near. Before I reached it, I heard her voice, singing. A neighbour stood in the door of the next house, listening and murmuring:

"And her father a corpse, at this moment!"

As I entered, Star noticed and was silent, with her hand on her mouth. I didn't wish to tell her that the neighbours were shocked at her behaviour. Auntie Isabela had not come back. Star looked after her as a mother looks after her child. I told her that, and reminded her that she was her granddaughter, and she said, laughing, that sometimes the old woman was more of a child than she herself. Then she added, pointing with her hand to the height of her knees:

"So high. Sometimes she's like that. And so I am not angry when she scolds me."

"Why does she scold you?"

"Because I am young and my skin is smooth and firm."

I asked her to come with me. She looked hard at me.

"Is it to be 'action'?"

She meant "were we to be on a definite job". I said that it was so, but that there would be no danger.

"A pity," she lamented, putting her head on one side. "I have to go to get the socialists up to the scratch."

To get them out of the workshops and factories, she meant. That was to say that they were not going to support the strike. I sat down on her bed. She pulled out a grey beret and put it on. Then she took it off, took from under the mattress a small plated revolver, hid it in the beret, folded it up, kept it in her hand, and stood in front of me.

"As soon as you like."

"But do you know how to use that little toy?"

She didn't condescend to answer. Then I picked up from the floor a kind of skeleton of a doll shedding sawdust through tears, lifted it up by a leg and asked:

"And this?"

She told men that she made dolls with sawdust and rags,

but never could manage to finish one, because when it was nearly finished and she showed it to Auntie Isabela, the old woman used to laugh and say: "That isn't a doll, it's a big toad."

Then she used to examine her work closely and had to admit that the old woman was right. She at once loathed her production as a kind of bastard frog. Soon after, she would begin to make another, but with no better fortune. As she was at the door she added:

"And so since I was eight years old, I've gone on without succeeding over a single real doll."

We went into the street. Certainly Star was very sensitive. As soon as anyone said that her work was like a frog, she thought it was foolish and useless. When Auntie Isabela forgot to give her opinion, Star would love her doll and think that she had made a success of it. But it would have pleased me more if toads had not disgusted her, if their stiff and gracious beauty had attracted her.

Presently Star went back to the house, saying that she had forgotten something. She came out with a large letter of a pale violet colour. The night before she had taken my letter to the Colonel's quarters where the sergeant on duty had met her and given her that one from Miss Amparo. As the letter was ready, Amparo must have been expecting what happened and could not have been very frightened, as she did not go out to see Star. I kept the letter without reading it. At once the air took on a different colour. Perhaps it was only that the dawn was breaking. We walked in the direction of Moncloa.[1]

We go a little out of our way, because I wish to see her balcony. The red-brick wall is covered with creepers up to her windows. The most daring of them climb up on one side. Some blue campanulas tremble, moistened with dew. The morning is female; pink like her; tall and of a slender grace. Blue-eyed, luminous—like her, tender and sweet, with gentle arms. The morning is feminine and sings in the springtime.

In the air with the scent of pines,
In the wind with the scent of May,
Through the air it came laughing,
Through the air it departed singing,
What shall we call sweet love?

[1] In the nort-west of Madrid.

I put her letter hurriedly in my pocket. It seemed to me that everyone had arisen and was watching from the windows. We left the Colonel's quarters behind us. She must be sleeping like a three-year-old child, her consciouness not yet awakened, a dream of carved wood and marble. Star looked askance at me and asserted:

"Your betrothed is a *bourgeoise,* isn't she?"

But beauty, limpid morality, purity, aren't *bourgeois.* She was born in a *bourgeois* house, educated in a convent school for daughters of the rich; she left it and came to me with the open arms of youth. She knew nothing of capitalism of social injustice, of the *bourgeoisie.* She was the fine flower of factors of which she knew nothing. We came to know each other. She accepted my love, became drunken with it, and wished to know nothing in the world I didn't know. As for me, the less said the better. The reveille sounded in the barracks. A resounding harmony. Force and purity. They opened the windows of the imagination wide to infinite things, and I cursed those notes which so comforted the ear. I hated any assault on her ears save that of my passion, any harmony except that of my words. What is all that beauty compared with what I keep for her? But the sounds of the reveille are not only purity and harmony. They are the trappings and trimmings of *bourgeois* denseness, of blind, and arbitrary power, of the vanity of capitalism, mingled with *bourgeois* artistry and patriotic falsehoods, all the things that pursue me and sometimes threaten to crush me. The reveille which is sounding wishes to remove me from her, or even to capture me and intoxicate me.

"Isn't she the Colonel's daughter?"

I turn violently to Star:

"Yes, and what about it? You don't know anything about these things."

Star smiles in a wise way. Perhaps she does understand.

"I know her. She is lovely. But she is not for you, comrade Samar."

"What do you know about her?"

"Sometimes I go into the barracks to get the leavings of the mess for comrades on strike. The men themselves go, but when I go, they give me two or three times more than they would give the men, and I share them amongst those who have nothing. Also I go to the Colonel's quarters by the service staircase."

"Have you seen her?"

"She has given me old clothes which I give to the neediest

comrades. Haven't you noticed Floreal? The coat he wears belonged to Colonel García del Río."

All this annoys me. My friends are beggars from her father. The thought wounds me, and I am vexed that it has come into my head. But then I can't help asking her why she says Amparo is not for me. Star looks steadily at me.

"You are an anarchist. Or a communist. You won't wish to be married by the Church, and she won't be able to give up everything to go and suffer discomforts with you. You know that quite well."

The simplicity of her words upsets me. Here all my uncertainties and all my dreams are reduced to a simple common-sense phrase. The little girl, although she doesn't often offer an opinion, shows good sense when she does give one. Good sense which terrifies me.

We walk on in silence. The morning has remained under the influence of the reveille and the grey tone of the sky does not lighten. When we are near Moncloa I ask her:

"My dear, what do you think of life?"

"What a question. I can say only that I've never thought about it."

I stop and look her in the eyes:

"Have you never thought that it might be better or worse?"

She shrugs her shoulders. In the blue of her eyes, as in the blue of the sky, there is a star. They are quiet eyes, restful and not penetrating. Then she replies:

"You must think me a fool."

I go on walking.

"I don't think anything, my dear."

She knows that I am going to "act", and has said that she will go with me. She would follow me to the end of the world. We kept descending when we left the suburb. As we were not going to the centre but to one of the suburbs and there were neither railway nor tramline, it was better to go across country. The landscape was enlivened with the buildings of the University City across the river. It took us about an hour to reach an isolated place where there were two metal standards and an electric transforming station. I looked all round. The highway was at a distance. There were no buildings near. The silence and loneliness were complete. The air is soft, sweet and heavy. In a bend of the river the bottom is clear and pebbly. A slight reflection makes the surface more glassy.

"Have you had breakfast yet, Star?"

"No."

"Would you like to bathe?"

"Yes, but I can't swim well. Won't you laugh at me?"

We began to undress. As she took off her jersey I thought my suggestion unwise. But she was showing so great delight that she infected me too. The water, the air, the light were intoxicating. Before we finished undressing, we wet our heads. Then I took off my shirt and drawers and dived into the water. It came up to my waist. It was chilly, but not so cold as in January. I hugged the water, splashed in it, and felt light and active, against its cold resistance. I hadn't turned my head when I heard behind me splashing and laughing. There was little Star who had overtaken me, her arms and legs scattering shining beads. Panting, we spoke.

"You, who didn't know how to swim!"

She laughed her satisfaction. At least as well as me, and with better style.

"If you can't 'act' better on land than you do in water, I'll have to denounce you to the committees. Isn't that so?" she added, leaving me behind.

I overtook her with an effort. When I was alongside her, I tried to swim in my best form.

"Over there is Madrid. In an hour they'll be finding out that no one is at work, and the *bourgeois* will have to take their breakfast without fresh toast. The strike will go well. Even the socialists are joining."

Star laughed and imitated the whining voice of a beggar:

"A crust of wholemeal bread for this poor *bourgeois.*" I added:

"For he is a diabetic, the poor fellow."

"Do diabetics take it?"

"Yes."

I try to float, but the current is pulling me. I begin to run, lose my balance, and take to swimming again. She goes to the bank and begins to tremble. I ask her if she is cold, and, panting, she says "No". She is a graceful statue of marble, with her toes, the points of her breasts, and the tip of her little nose rosy pink. Under her slenderness there is an unbelievable strength. I look all round again. There is no one. Who would come here at such an hour? The fields here are not tilled. She understands.

"If the *bourgeois* were to see us, they would think us mad."

"Or they would go mad over the little anarchist."

She laughs from the bank:

"Or perhaps over you. You can't tell what the *bourgeois* will do."

I think she is making a fool of me. I look at her to see. She is busy cleaning the mud from the sole of one of her feet, and seems to have forgotten what she said. All the same I laugh loudly. Then, still busy with the mud on her feet, she adds:

"The *bourgeois* are such pigs."

I tell her to run about or to go back into the water. She chooses to swim. The sun has risen, and will soon reach us, because it is already shining on the metal standard and the transformer. I swim to the other bank. It must be about twenty-four yards. Then I come back. I think how Star knows everything, knows without curiosity or mystery. Different from my little *bourgeoise* girl. Amparo thinks that a baby comes from a kiss. One day she read the word "homosexual" in a newspaper and asked me—she asks me everything—what it meant, forcing me to tell her a fib. I ought to have told her the truth, but it seemed to me that I would have been corrupting her, and, besides, she wouldn't have understood my explanations. I lied to her. Sometimes that doesn't trouble me—my relations with her are a string of pretty lies—but sometimes it does bother me. Were I a millionaire—could I be one?—I'd take her to the country with me in a land the language of which she didn't understand, and, like Pygmalion, mould her character, securing that her life would be passed in ignorance of all but beauty, in an eternal drowsy dream of delight. Keep her for ever in moral childhood! Keep all sounds from her except my voice, all the facts of life which I did not put before her. What an artist I should be!

I sit down on the bank. As I come out, my feet get soiled and I have to wash them. Star has gone in again, and under the water her skin is soft, and she glides like a fish in the blue shadows. But I reflect that the existence of an Amparo jars my convictions. For me the simplicity and purity of the *bourgeoisie* are ignorance, which today is a defect and tomorrow will be a crime. In the society of my hopes there will be only two crimes: sickness and ignorance. Lack of cleanliness and of prophylaxis in body and mind. Injurious to others and therefore to be punished. What a little criminal, my darling! And what a good judge, me! And Star? Now she is floating without swimming, much better than I could. Although she is still only a girl, her legs and arms are shaped, her hips softly rounded, and although she is light, she displaces plenty of water. Star is the comrade. I see her as a figure of crystal, not stirring to the senses. She is not yet a woman, and her flesh is still asleep to love. How will love come to her in the future? The water is dark under the bank, then comes a light band, and then over the bottom it is colourless and transparent.

The whistle of a train, repeated three times, is heard. The horizon bends and makes way. Star repeats the whistle, not with her lips, but with her throat, and calls out in her shrill little voice:

"The express from the north!"

Then she tells me that on the south railway those out of work have kept going by robbing the goods' trains. The delight which such revelations bring to her is strong with a health lost for ever by the weary, worn-out, and hide-bound *bourgeoisie*. Now it is Star who calls to me from the water that I must take exercise. I am cold. I wish that the sun would reach me. That will be a few minutes later.

"You are a pretty fish!" I said to her.

"Are you admiring me?"

"Yes."

She comes out of the water, straight to me, with her hands on her hips:

"Then I won't swim any more."

She tells me that ever since she was a little girl she had been fond of the water. She used to pass the summers with some relations in a village. Old women in the villages are always catholic and *bourgeois*, however poor they may be. She was eight years old and had gone with some young ragamuffins to bathe in the pools of the river. One day they came on her quite naked, with her clothes under her arm, after she had been bathing. She was singing at the top of her voice a song she had heard from her friends:

On Christmas morn the Christ was born,
Let Christmas come and I'll cover my bum!

The old women spanked her, prophesied that she would come to a bad end, and kept her shut up for a week. When Germinal heard about it, he went to fetch her, had a quarrel with his relations, and would have no more to do with them. She rather surprised me, as Star didn't seem in any way a wild girl. But of course these were not signs of badness, but only natural results of health and gaiety. The sun now reaches us. Let's see. A last plunge before drying under its golden rays. Star's hair is all wet, and her head looks like a smooth unripe fruit or like a hairless little baby. But she tells me that she has a little comb with which she can tidy her own hair, and mine too. We come out of the water and put on our socks, drying our feet with my shirt. Then we wait until the sun dries our skins. We laugh and chatter on out-of-the-way things; "Let

Christmas come and I'll cover my bum." Star wishes to sit down. I lend her my jacket and shirt, making a rug for her. She falls down, rather than sits. From time to time she raises her head and shakes it, sprinkling me. She laughs. I make her lift one of her legs so that I can take the letter of my betrothed out of my jacket pocket. She has to turn over so that I may get it and a pencil falls out of the pocket on the other side. Star grumbles:

"To read the letter from a *bourgeoise,* you make a comrade uncomfortable."

"I am not going to read it, my dear."

I stay by her side. I look all round, and with the pencil draw some curved lines on the back of the envelope. Then a straight line. More lines, mapping the landscape. I make a little sketch. The standards, the transformer where the high tension current drones. Here and there I write figures. The river is about thirty-one yards wide, and about four feet deep. Although there is a current, it is quite easy to wade across. A scout on the left curve could see for nearly three miles round. Star raises herself.

"Are you sketching me?"

She looks over my arm, putting her hand on my shoulder.

"It is a map. You can see the river. And the standards."

She strokes my shoulder, and tells me that I am dry now, and that if I wish to dress, she'll give me my clothes. But in the position I had taken to make the drawing, water had collected in the pit of my stomach. I shake myself, turning to the sun, and Star calls out laughingly:

"The whistle, the whistle!"

She passes a finger down my stomach and presses on the navel. At the same moment, an engine whistles. My navel is the alarm button of the country. The locomotive stopped whistling when my little friend took off her finger. She is quite confused, and looks round the horizon to solve the mystery. She pushes again, and again the engine's whistle sounds from East to West across the landscape. We both laugh, unable to stop. I tell her that it isn't surprising. A naked man is the defender of the country. The locomotive and the country are parts of the same whole, and besides, when I was young, I was in love with a steam-engine.

"Not me," she said. "The tramway is mine. You don't know how sorry it makes me to think that the tramway staff belongs to the Reformist Party."

We finish dressing, in the sun. Star looks at my watch and starts.

It is half-past seven.

At eight o'clock she has to be at the gate of the lamp factory, as a picket against blacklegs.

"Do you attack the blacklegs?"

"I don't. But I tell the comrades in the other factories which they are, and they go for them."

I also have business in hand. We return by the Segovia Gate. We stop at a bar to have breakfast. After taking a cup of coffee and milk and some biscuits, we are still hungry, and take a second. After paying I find that I've only sixpence left. It will be a bad job if an article of mine doesn't appear tomorrow in the paper for which I write. If it does appear, it will mean that the strike is not complete, and that the compositors are still working. That would be worse. All right. I mustn't think about it. Star is in a hurry, and is off to the factory still nibbling half a biscuit. When I am alone, I sit beside a window and take out my sweetheart's letter. I hear workmen coming in and going out. I listen to their views. One of them has our manifesto in his hands, and discusses it, brandishing it and reading it aloud. The strike is attracting attention. A chauffeur comes in saying that he is going to lock up his car, and that in the centre the syndicalists are active. A band passes singing "The International" and carrying a piece of scarlet muslin on a pole. Now cries are heard in the street, and people, turning round, begin to run away. I hear a noise. They have stoned the windows of a shop which has dared to open, and a group of strikers are pushing and kicking, and hurling insults at a blackleg baker. The keeper of the bar calls out to close the shutters and leave only one door half-open. I can hardly read the letter, but I make an effort and comfort myself with the angular writing, the tender words and the laments. As we didn't see each other yesterday, the letter is spotted with tears. There are two sheets. She tells me that she shares my "ideas", and that in the last part of her trousseau on which she has been engaged and which will cost three hundred pounds, there will be materials and work which will benefit a great many humble people. Embroiderers, dressmakers, etc., etc. "I think that will please you." "Tonight, ring me up. If you like we'll go to the Royalty Cinema. Papa doesn't wish me to go as he is afraid of disturbances, but with the car we can get there in no time, and when you telephone, you can say that it is all quiet. If there should be any trouble, probably they will shut off the light as they enter the cinema, and during the dark, you can slip down in your seat, and be pretending to read so that the rascals won't recognize you." Two pages of tenderness and anxiety. "I am afraid that now, with the revolution they say you are making, you will love me less. I've always known that the revolution comes first, and then me; it's no use telling you that I think like you, and that they know it at home, for papa said it to me the other day in joke, but I know he meant it seriously, and you, my Lucas, don't believe it." I see her restless eyes, her heaving breast, her hand laying down the pen to wipe away a tear from her eyelashes. And her complete longing to be with me. I keep on reading, completely absorbed. The coffee-machine whistles and startles me. Instinctively I raise my belt, as if it depended on my navel, and the whistling stops.

I read to the end of the letter. The restlessness in the street increases. I hear a shot. The blood pulses in my brain. The silence and the animation outside are the intermittent silence and animation of a Sunday. But the shot belongs to a red Sunday. And this letter! This dose of morphine with which I am injecting myself through my eyes! This *bourgeois* love! I roll up the envelope into a ball and throw it away. I keep the letter and get up to go. An individual stooped over the spittoon, picked up the ball I made of the envelope, and has put it in his pocket. Then I who had lost consciousness of what I was doing, drunk with the sentimental intoxication of the letter, recovered my senses, and in real terror remembered that. . . .

SECOND SUNDAY/THE INSURRECTION PROCEEDS

Chapter 7

A Vote of Censure, but Forward!

I CARRY my revolver in the leg of my boot. The handle outside, with a string tied to it and to my belt. Through a hole made in my right-trouser pocket I can pull the revolver up the string. In case of trouble I leave it with the muzzle in the boot, and although they search me, the police won't find it. It is an old dodge. There are others, but I prefer this one which has never failed me.

It was a good thing that the comrades were advised not to go into the streets unarmed, and neither to be without them nor to fire them in a moment of panic. We cannot go into the streets today without arms, because disorderly throngs of tramps have come among us, and I remember very well that when I was out of work and wandering the streets aimlessly, I didn't quite care or know what I was doing. I went about as if I were another person with all the world against me. Bad times these! But Sundays were the worst. Everyone had been sitting down to a meal, and getting up from a meal to stroll through the park, whilst I was prowling through the city without table or chair. The houses came up against me and the sun smote me in the face. A hell of a time! Once when I was completely done in I made myself walk as if I had an object, but people noticed that I was going nowhere. When I saw one of them by himself I hated him like hell. What hurt me most was that when they saw me in rags and hungry, the *bourgeois* enjoyed their own happiness all the more. Then I sat down on a bench and planned an assault or robbery. What can a man do who has come to the world with nothing but a rag in front and a rag behind, except work, rob or beg? I had no work, and I didn't know how to beg. No one can be surprised that I planned a new robbery every few hours. As it happened, I didn't carry out any of them. A tramp has no definite ideas, and an unarmed striker in the town feels just as helpless as a tramp. But we were saved from that. We of the Federation of Groups have come out ready to tear the guts out of heaven, to see if angels are there, or bombs of incense, and if the flag of the future is to be a soiled swaddling cloth from the infant Christ!

In the meeting of the groups we passed a vote of censure on Samar. I proposed it, and it was the first grave error made by the comrade. If he doesn't pull himself together, he won't be in favour with us. I don't know if I am still angry with him, but it is plain that if I hadn't done it, someone else would have accused him. By his fault, part of the sabotage arranged by us for tomorrow must fail. By an inconceivable imprudence. He had made the sketch for which he was asked, and then had thrown it on the floor of the bar, where it was picked up, it seems, by one of the police. And now there is nothing to be done. How easily the best-planned matters go wrong! The transformer will be protected. But there is worse; the police will have guessed that we were going to deal not only with a single transformer, but with all the stations which light the city, and probably they'll have put guards round them all. There couldn't have been a graver reason for the vote of censure. Now the sabotage may cost one of the companions his life, and, what is worse, the whole plan will go wrong. Samar was very stupid. But we may contrive to trace the agent, and somehow prevent him from taking the sketch to the police. Recover it at any cost! Samar has given particulars of the agent, and three comrades have gone to seek him, but I fear they won't find him. Samar thought it useless, and went off after making an appointment with me and the out-of-work committee to meet at ten o'clock in a public-house in the Plaza Mayor. The out-of-work comrades are to be in this quarter half an hour later, and we'll see what will happen.

So far the strike is going well. The socialists are backing it. A mere glance at the city shows how things are going. The strike will be general tonight. Last night a deputation of our syndicates went to the leaders of the constitutional reformers who refused to receive them. Today those people have issued two manifestoes which are being distributed by the police, telling the workers not to listen to irresponsible counsellors who will only lead them to chaos. But they are such fools that they let the police do the distribution. A manifesto of that kind in the hands of the police carries every mark of treachery. Even the members of their own syndicates look on it with disgust, and its results are almost nothing. All the taxis have now been withdrawn. In the centre of the city the shops dare not open. The department of public works has completely stopped, including all municipal services. The waiters are out. Draughtsmen, transport workers, house-fitters, metallurgists and timbermen have come out as usual. Even the masters are treating blacklegs as worthless slaves. There is peace in the streets. Very little movement. The tramways are running on some lines, but only to serve the Civil Guard, as the public do not dare to use them. But we'll have to give them a lesson. We must force the whole city to go into mourning for the murder of our three comrades. I come to the Puerta del Sol. In the corner to the left, those out of work belonging to the building trade are airing themselves in the sun as usual. Very few of the *bourgeoisie* are to be seen in the streets. Workmen are much more numerous, and they proclaim themselves strikers by the mixture of amusement and suspicion with which they walk the streets. The streets belong to no one yet. We shall see who are going to conquer. The Civil Guard, the Public Safety Agents, the Shock Police lurk in the entrance halls of public buildings and in the usual stations, the doors of which are half closed. In the Home Office there are black visors, chin-straps fastened, and eagle eyes looking in every direction. Telephone calls, telegraphic "tickers", although there is still no reason for expecting anything outside Madrid. All the same the Regional organization has acted spontaneously. Although there are no newspapers, we have received word that the local Federations in the two Castiles are meeting to discuss the matter. That means a lot. A pity that there is little to excite them. But the out-of-work people will soon put that right.

Voices, disturbances. This Puerta del Sol is like a bay of the sea, always in agitation. I have sometimes seen all the street openings occupied by troops which had cleared the open space completely, and suddenly men, coming as it were from the asphalt itself, began to gesticulate and shout. Suddenly, firing. The rebels appear on the great electric light standards and in the entrances of the metro. What happens in the Puerta del Sol happens all over Spain. The strength of our tactics is that the Government never knows where the enemy is. And these tactics are not our own, but come from the Spanish temperament. They say that the monarchy fell in that way. A moment comes when passion has infected the air, and no one can breathe, and the most extraordinary events happen independently of any of the preparations which have been made. We ourselves have determined on a general strike. No doubt we should be content with making the strike as complete as possible. But when we go into the street and see one of the Civil Guards, we feel that we have to kill him. The organization is always behind us ready to go forward to anything. Someone calls, "So far," and a thousand voices call, "Further." Amongst these voices workers and women, well-dressed people and beggars. We move on, and soon we see that the syndicalist plans are overruled. We halt a little, and resolve again, "Thus far." The air and the flag-stones, the light and the buildings call to us, "Further on." We consult the Local Federation, and they say "Further on," signed and sealed. We go to the Regional and they say "Further." Next the National Committee and the Peninsular Central are consulted. All reply, almost without words, a single sign, the sign of today and tomorrow. The eternal sign. "Always further." Today the starting-point is in Madrid. Sometimes it is in Barcelona or Seville. The whole organization, without conference or even telephonic communication, is behind us as we are undermining, without discipline and without any real organization, the defence system of the State. Whither we don't know. Comrades Progreso, Espartaco and Germinal! On the Sunday night they closed our syndicates, deployed all their forces against us, but the general strike was agreed on, and as Samar told me, arrangements were made in the secret meeting at night for instructions to be sent in all directions. We would not have gone further than a strike of forty-eight hours, but they have driven us into secrecy, into the dark, really pushing on our side, and we shall see what will happen! The National Committee has issued its dictate, without the need of orders or telegrams. The dictate is in the air, "Forward." Now we know it. "Forward." "Always further on." Sleep in peace, murdered comrades! We'll go wherever you would like us to go. The sky is blue; the old beggars wait at the doors of the churches; and the smell of powder fills the air with fear.

To reach the appointed meeting-place I ought to pass through the Puerta del Sol, but seeing the precautions that have been taken, I retrace my steps and thread a labyrinth of little side streets. I am on duty, and have to deprive these gentry of the pleasure of putting me in gaol. Two newspaper sellers are shouting an issue of today, the *Leaflet*. It is Monday, and there is no other newspaper except this *bourgeois* and half-official sheet. Even in the little streets the strike is evident, for the small shopkeepers have shut up, or have their doors half-closed. The solitude and quietness are gloomy. A red Sunday, a true Sunday. Not like those that were Sundays only for me, when I was out of work, and slack in body and mind, nor like the *bourgeois* Sundays in which the rich were not resting because they had never worked, and when we rested from labour only because the fire of battle kept us burning. Not those Sundays of individuals, black and filled with a shabby hunger, nor the white Sundays of bells and best clothes, but the real red Sundays, our own Sundays. Sundays without taxis, without tramways, without idle *bourgeois* wandering through the streets. Sundays in which the empty streets and the air are a delight, and we are going to conquer the Civil Guard with shots, to shoot the varnished hats from off the weary and sleepless police. I am in the Plaza Mayor; columned portals, houses of the seventeenth and eighteenth centuries, Philip the Fourth. Stinking with History. The City Archives. Files of papers and peals of bells. Dwarf trees and gigantic trees. Again Philip the Fourth. Neither history nor art are of any use to us. Neither the history of kings nor the decorative art of their courts! Away with it all! There they are, on the panelled walls with their feet in the air. We must pull down a few of them, and replace them by our own brilliance, our own grandeur. Away with history! This square is said to be very beautiful. It represents the epoch of the Austrian royal family. That doesn't interest us. We live in our own efforts, for ourselves, and we fight not for the past but for our own ideas and for the future!

In a corner, under a portico, a narrow passage opens with stone steps leading down to a small cobbled space. At the foot of the steps there is a glass door with a red curtain concealed under a kind of balcony. The Out-of-Work Committee, the Federation of Groups and Samar are to meet there. It is exactly ten o'clock. I represent the Federation, and am the first to arrive. Before sitting down, I look round for a way to escape if it should be necessary. They bring me wine, and I take the darkest corner. Next comes Murillo, the communist, who has his head honeycombed with a thousand cells, and in each of them, as he says, an emergency and its solution. He dresses rather like a *bourgeois,* but never gives up his grey jersey however hot it may be. He is pale and lean, and always talks as if he were half asleep. He is like a piece of pumice-stone. He comes up to me and stands on the other side of the table.

"The strike is going well," he says, "although the socialists are trying to restrict it."

"And your lot?" I ask.

"Our position is determined by the need of helping to radicalize the masses without getting out of step."

"But what have you done?"

He hesitates and pulls out a printed circular.

"Here is the letter of the Third International, determining our position."

"What is it?"

"To help to radicalize the masses."

I look at the clock. Murillo sits down insisting obstinately:

"We must go step by step."

Voices are heard in the street, and the sound of horses' hoofs on the flag-stones. Murillo listens a moment:

"There is no doubt about it. The letter of the International supports the position of the Regional Committee. The masses are being radicalized. Are we to get out of step in order to join you? That is what the Executive will have to decide. Are we to get out of step for that? This letter supports my view."

"I hope they'll turn you down, Murillo."

Murillo keeps talking and eyeing his paper. Every now and again I interrupt him, "I hope they'll turn you down, Murillo." But as he never listens when one is speaking, he goes on talking. At last, when I thought he had forgotten my interruptions, he asks me:

"Why should they turn me down?"

"For dividing labour."

We are waiting impatiently. The members of the committee are too late. And Samar? Has anything happened to them? I suggest to Murillo:

"How are you going to make the masses in Spain reject the communist solution, State capitalism, as a piece of *bourgeois* intellectualism? In your case I should feel a terrible responsibility."

Murillo was silent. At last he said:

"What is your position?"

"Well; for the present to stir up an agitation among the out-of-work. If you want a more general answer, I was brought up as a Marxist. But Marx has made me more Marxist than himself. I mean that I seem to have gone beyond him, driven by his own force, and I don't believe either in the spontaneous activity of spirit or intelligence—that is a *bourgeois* conception, but in actual deeds. The mission of intelligence in our campaign is simply to interpret deeds and co-ordinate them for the future. Never to explain them in terms of party principles, and still less in terms of past experience. Let us make the revolution! We shall make it! That will tell us today what we must do tomorrow. All together we shall accomplish victory. And the victory will be for all. That is enough. I know that all this is a little vague and more difficult to grasp than your plan. But if the masses accept your programme, I shall be glad and accept it, in the sure belief that you have gained a step towards our revolutionary programme. But the masses will reject it, and will prefer a smoother road. This very preference of theirs is a force and a reason, which I understand very well. Because I too feel myself one of the masses, my friend Murillo. My intelligence never takes me to minorities. I am for the logic of the spontaneous deed, and I accept its consequences, rather than my own prejudices. Do you understand?"

The others had already arrived when Murillo, after thinking a few minutes, said to me:

"You are only a *bourgeois*, anarchist and opportunist!"

I burst out laughing. It was an insult, but Murillo is rather unreflecting in his judgments and unreflecting judgment is a brother of the direct and spontaneous deed, and equally pleasing to me. Samar arrived with the news:

"They have taken out the machine-guns in Cuatro Caminos."[1]

"Which? Ours?" I asked.

Murillo opened his eyes wide.

"You have machine-guns?"

The members of the Strikers' Committee smiled in a mysterious way, but kept silent. One of them asked Murillo:

"How many are there of your party, here in Madrid?"

"About three hundred. But we are going to separate off at the next congress because we understand that the executive is moving to the left."

Samar commented:

"But aren't you in too small a minority to assume power?"

Murillo took out his document again and began to hold forth about the radicalization of the masses. Cipriano Gomez, a mason, made a sweeping gesture with his hand and said:

"Enough, comrades! Let us quit these follies now that we have to take action."

We began to discuss what was to be done at once. The quarter was thick with police reserves. The points of action, our objectives, were a provision shop where the assistants were blacklegs and which Villacampa had told us about, and a well-stocked gunshop in the little square in front of the provision shop. Most of the strikers required weapons.

"How many are they?"

Comrade Cipriano replied:

"Those who are on the look-out in the quarter are about one thousand five hundred. Among them there are a few communists and socialist strikers."

Murillo insisted that there could be no objection to recognition of the communistic collaboration. Cipriano got impatient and looked at him as if he were an odd kind of creature. Cipriano was an anarchist. Samar explained to him:

[1] A district in the north-west of Madrid.

"Don't you know that Murillo is a communist?"

But Cipriano was already explaining his plan without troubling about Murillo, but seeking the approval of the others. In his opinion it would be best to attack the gunshop and the provision store simultaneously. I made some observations about difficulties that might arise. We ought to avoid, if we could, risking the death of some of the comrades. Murillo intervened:

"Why? It is natural that they should fall; the strikers are the vanguard."

Cipriano threw an angry look at him and went on to say that he and another had twenty hand-grenades between them, but that these were not weapons to put in the hands of starving men, but should be entrusted to serene and safe people. He would divide them amongst us. If we made the best use of them, they would be effective. Besides, they had revolvers. Murillo excused himself. He had something to do. He left us some leaflets and was about to go off, saying that he wished us success. Cipriano nodded his head.

"This man is neither a communist nor anything else. An intellectual gent! Out there are real communists. Communists, heart and soul with us, whilst you——"

Murillo sat down again. He said that he would not throw bombs, but that he would be alongside us as a representative of the Spanish section of the Communist Party. Samar reserved himself, with Cipriano, for the duty of watching for the arrival of police reinforcements. Ten comrades would go with them, and they would break up into groups of three. Villacampa undertook the direction of the attack on the provision store. He accepted his mission with some pride. It was more dangerous and more enterprising than Samar's job. Villacampa and Samar treated each other with some distrust, because Villacampa had joined with me in my charge against the journalist two hours ago, so that Samar really had had two accusers. Everyone accepted the appointed duty calmly and firmly. They realized the feebleness of the *bourgeois* party, and the growing force of the comrades; possibilities and contingencies of the brightest were in their minds.

"If the strike is general tonight," they thought, "we shall only have to ask the other regional bodies to join with us."

They expected that the socialist leaders would have to accept the strike, if only to prevent the appearance of impotence. Samar did not quite agree with them.

We went out, divided into three groups according to the arranged details. Murillo commented on the phenomenon of the adhesion of the socialists and the advantage of united action.

We descended by the seventeenth-century monument where Quevedo's knaves were scratching themselves, blaspheming with pleasure. The little square was deserted. Two streets lower down, near a public market, groups began to give a Sunday air to the streets. As there were many women who had come out to make their morning purchases from the street vendors, the groups attracted no attention. I noticed, from many known faces, that in this section there were at least two thousand comrades awaiting the signal for the beginning of the attack. Our committee scattered. Here and there our comrades stopped and were at once surrounded by three of four who listened to them attentively. These are the preliminaries. These three or four move off and pass on the directions. In an instant a network of words has spread, reaching all the vegetable market of the street, and the cordon of strikers who are pretending to take the air at the entrance of the square. They are men of all sorts but made alike by hunger. As I pass by a group someone says:

"If I were to join the socialists I'd get some help. Is half a crown enough to buy a man and his ideas?"

Of course they deny it. The sun gets paler and little clouds pass over the sky of the aluminium tint of cinema screens. At the other end, a number of workmen crowd together and are seen suddenly to rush down a little street. My post is with Cipriano and Samar; I look for them and go to them. The comrades are running headlong. I separated myself a little from the committee, because I saw Eugenio Casanova seated in the shade of a doorway, nodding with sleep. He has stayed there since noon yesterday, without moving, hoping for the return of a comrade whom he heard saying a few days ago that he had two revolvers. He himself has none. I told him to come with me, and we joined the others. We followed the streets leading towards the gunshop. No one could say anything, because three men, without uniform, passing with an idle air round a corner don't cause suspicion. But each of us has four hand-grenades and a revolver. The same is happening in the other streets. If troops come the collision will take place far away from our point of attack, and the comrades will be able to get weapons and food. Murillo comes up, agitated, with the news:

"The communists are in the front. They have torn down a scaffold-post and are using it as a battering ram against the closed shutters. The out-of-work are not the vanguard. Those who are using the ram are strikers, not out-of-works. It isn't going as was arranged. I am off to find out why."

He goes off, and Cipriano nods his head:

"He has got water on the brain. The comrades themselves will play the fool with him, if he doesn't look out."

The blows of the ram against the metallic blinds resound. The workmen swing their blows rhythmically—

"Ah, a, a, u! Ah, a, a, u!"

The noise is heard through the confusion of cries, yells, hurrahs. The comrades are madly excited. Let the forces of the Civil Guard, the Shock Police, the Public Safety men come. Keep up with your fury, comrades, for we shall defend you! Hand-grenades number 9. Clear eye and resolute hand. But the tumult keeps us from hearing whether the enemy is coming or not. Cipriano moves forward alone. Then he comes back running, with the flap of his cap pulled down and his coat collar raised:

"Look out, comrades! Let us go under these arches in the corner. If trouble should come, we can get round the corner and escape to shelter." We take shelter under the sheds of a big old house. The noise of the ram tells us that the doors have been destroyed. Samar is very pale. He also has raised his coat collar and pulled down the brim of his hat so that only his nose is seen. The two of them grasp their revolvers. I have a grenade in each hand and a lighted cigar in my mouth. The grenades have a fuse about an inch long. Now we'll see! The noise has begun to increase in the side street, where they are attacking the provision store. Cipriano looks flustered again. The enemy are not visible. We hear our own breathing.

They must have taken the other corner. We'll know soon!

In fact, the comrades who have the same duty as ours in the other street fire three times. The horses slip and rear. They retreat at a trot, and they are heard more close to us each second. Samar leaps back and presses against the wall:

"Look out! Here they come!"

We can hear the muffled report of muskets and mausers. Some of the guards keep firing whilst the others go back to come by our corner.

"Here they are, comrades!"

Cipriano puts out his hand, supporting his weapon against the corner of the archway, and fires. Samar does the same. A horse must have fallen down. I have lighted my fuse, and although it is not now absolutely necessary to throw it, as they are on the point of retreating, I can't keep the bomb in my hand, and so I throw it. The explosion was violent. They are in disorder. Almost all the horses have turned round. Three remain close up against the doors, and make a fine target. We fire. A guard retires wounded, and Cipriano mutters some words through his clenched teeth. In the side street there is a similar scene. The explosion of the bombs is followed by cries of pain.

And now there comes an avalanche of strikers, rich in weapons and in enthusiasm. One of them carries a machine-gun, but not knowing how to work it, throws it on the ground. Then, in spite of the firing, he sees a sheet with printed instructions, and begins to finger the gun as directed. Two workmen have fallen, and the rest move on. The guards retire and the horses flee in terror. Murillo comes on the scene. I ask him, and he replies with diabolic joy:

"The provision store is now empty. The gunshop also. There are a few with cuts on their hands because they broke the window panes with their fists, to get the revolvers."

"You must retire now."

"Retire? Why?"

"Now the Civil Guards will come and they won't leave a puppet with its head on."

"And what about it?" replied Murillo with a face the colour of ashes.

"The strikers will do their duty, waiting for them."

"Letting themselves be killed?"

"Yes."

Four communist workers arrive. Murillo gesticulated and asked some questions I didn't hear. Then he put his hand against their breasts to stop them. They weren't strikers!

"It is your duty not to intervene."

They push him away and move on. Bullets continue to come from far away. Murillo kept dancing about among the spent bullets and muttering:

"The stages are being reached. You cannot wound me. I can't fall because I am not a striker. Nor you, companions." He meant us three. Cipriano withdrew his revolver and we come out of our hiding-place. He seizes hold of Murillo by one of his sleeves and drags him along to the other side of the corner. Once there he said:

"We are going to accuse you in the committee."

"Why?" asked Murillo fearlessly.

"Because you are a blasted fool."

Then Villacampa came up, very pleased. We have to fly. We can't stay there another moment. Samar looks at him very queerly because Villacampa had been the accuser at the Federation of Groups that morning. Villacampa meets his look. I fear that they are going to fight, but all at once I see that Samar has put his hand on the other's shoulder and is smiling.

Villacampa also smiles. Then the two speak at once, exchanging their experiences in surprised relief.

The rout has been general. We have hardly fired a dozen shots. All has been too easy. A few of the comrades stay behind, because nothing in the world would make them retreat.

They exchange shots with a few heads so far away as to be hardly visible. Three comrades who arrive laden with food, when they hear the firing, throw down their load, move forward, taking out their revolvers. Samar smooths his coat collar, puts his hand in his pocket where he keeps his revolver. His finger comes out through a hole. He pulls out some papers. They are pierced by a bullet which has grazed his hip. Among the papers is Amparo's letter. He tears it into fragments, throw them into the air where they fall in a fine rain. Alongside they call out:

"Six have been arrested. They are hustling them through the streets with blows."

Chapter 8

Wreck of the Coffins

TWO STRIKERS and I have eaten in an inn close to the hospital and it cost us very little as we had nothing to pay but the wine and the cooking. We brought the food with us. We had first-quality rice, bacon, tins of peas, and also elegant dainties such as *foie gras* and caviare which the others just tasted because they didn't like them. I really didn't like them either, but because I am in the trade, and we know what is good, or at least what costs a lot, I couldn't think them bad but rather that my palate was out of order, and so I ate them. The strikers were pleased because they had weapons. They believe that all will go well now, and that the *bourgeoisie* are done for. The monarchy fell for less. In a corner Auntie Isabela is sleeping over a bottle of wine. She has spent the night praying at one of the gates of the hospital. At dawn they made her come in here. Her hair is white and straight, and her face is like a peeled nut. The glass is the one they put before her at six in the morning and she hasn't touched it. Every now and again she asks for water, repeats a paternoster, or curses, in the same tone of voice. Who knows what is going on inside that old woman? It is more than the case of a mother whose son they have killed, or of a greedy old woman whose treasure they have stolen. Rage against us, against the innkeeper. We offered her food and she swore at us like a bargee. One of the two strikers burst out laughing and said: "The old woman is dotty."

Then an Argentine came in who sometimes comes to the syndicates and who is elegantly dressed. He speaks with a rising drawl like the singers of a tango when the music stops and they recite. I understand that he is very rich and that he is a newcomer to the organization. When he speaks, he moves like athletes in a slow-moving cinema picture. Samar tells me that if I pay attention I'll see that he is always using headlines from the *bourgeois* press. It is true. As soon as he came in he said to me:

"The funeral is arranged for three o'clock"—and added, shaking his head: "More Serious Outlook."

He had wished to order a wreath of scarlet carnations, but the flowershops are not open. One of the strikers said:

"Leave these follies alone and give the money to the relief committee."

The Argentine looked bewildered:

"What follies?"

I soothed him:

"He means compliments; that it is no time for gracefulness."

He went on commenting:

"It has been terrible. The police have exceeded their functions. Public order should not be maintained by bullets. The conscience of the proletariat will be outraged."

He put the whole force of each phrase in a single word and then slurred half of that word. He raised his arms rhythmically and swung on one foot.

"It was an inevitable decision."

"Which?"

"The general strike. They were terrible."

"What were terrible?"

"The grave events of yesterday."

We all agreed and he went on:

"Three proletarian families in misery."

Again we agreed. I didn't know what to say to him. Never out of our minds for four and twenty hours and now a *bourgeois* comes to tell us about it. I pointed to Auntie Isabela:

"There you have Germinal's mother."

He looked at her pitifully. The old woman stared at him:

"And who are you?"

"One more for the revolution."

"One more? Aren't you a spy?"

"O, madam!" he cried out, "I am on your side. Like your son."

"There aren't many like my son."

The Argentine sat down and told her to order what she pleased. She refused without thanking him. She kept looking at him, and yet didn't seem annoyed with his company and his civilities. She must have been thinking: "He treats me like a real lady." Meanwhile I told the comrades that recently the agents had made a search in his house—the house of the Argentine. He was quite pleased because his chief wish was to be thought a revolutionary. The agents cross-examined him about his political theories, and he told them that he was an anarchist. They talked to him for a time and one went to the gramophone whilst the other took notes. From time to time they stopped their investigation and put on a new disc. They discussed which was the best, and when they agreed, they turned on the music whilst they searched casually. The Argentine was indignant:

"Aren't they going to take me to prison?"

Then he explained why he had not been arrested by saying that the agents were afraid of diplomatic complications. But the fact is that they did not stop their search until the discs had all been played, and that they took off a box of expensive cigarettes.

The strikers laughed, and the Argentine moved uneasily on his chair. Then old Isabela began to speak very excitedly:

"All the women in the world, although they aren't decent and honourable like me, can go to the judge or to the police or the courts if their son has been murdered. They are protected and defended. But just tell me to whom am I to go? Who are going to punish the murderers of my son?"

She was quiet for a minute and then added:

"If only I were young!"

She clenched her fist and thumped on the table. The Argentine said something I didn't quite hear; "justice of the people", "tribunal of the revolution". Auntie Isabela began to curse with tears in her eyes.

"For nearly thirty years, Germinal believed that the revolution would come in a month or so, and used those same words. I think you're just like him."

The Argentine agreed, and then she nodded and gave him something under the table. The Argentine's face changed at once. By feeling it he knew that it was a hand-bomb. He got up with it in his hand. She made wild signals to him to hide it, but the Argentine behaved like a somnambulist. He smiled to the old woman with a sour face and nodded "yes", to the nods of the old woman. In the inn there were two other old men and a youth from the quarter. I can't tell you the fright I got. One of the old men went to talk to the publican. He was the doctors' assistant, a kind of mortuary porter. He came and went with pails and bottles of disinfectant. He helped at the post-mortems and had become quite hardened to his work. He had an unconcerned and contented appearance, and was rather like the cashier in the shop where I work. He had acquired rather good manners from the nuns and doctors.

He spoke about the post-mortem on Germinal as if he had made it himself.

"The wall of the skull was very thick. We had to put the chisel in the forehead three times. At the third hammer stroke, we got through."

Auntie Isabela listened with her eyes round like a bird's. She wasn't surprised at anything. The old man went on:

"That man was as strong as a lump of concrete and young. Now I am weak, old and tottering, and I've to go about on my two legs setting down and carrying away buckets."

Auntie Isabela said tenderly:

"His was a head more friendly to hammer and chisel than to his old mother's kisses."

And she felt proud of having given birth to that body, to have formed a skull that three strokes of a hammer were required to open. The Argentine trembled. A comrade took the bomb from him and kept it. Then the Argentine went to the door and began to look through the panes to hide his nervousness. I went across to Auntie Isabela and sat down in front of her. I asked her rather savagely:

"Why did you do that? How many bombs have you with you?"

"Four others."

"What for?"

The old woman hesitated before answering. Then she said unwillingly:

"I wished to finish up everything, but then I didn't dare. It isn't easy."

"Give them to me."

She gave me them under the table, taking them from her bodice. I asked her where she had found them, and she answered weariedly:

"Although he didn't think it, he never took a single step

without my knowing. In the hollow of the fireplace he had about two dozen."

I ordered her not to touch anything again. She told me that there was a written paper with the bombs, with an order of some committee or other. I wrote another: "Four have been used in the matter of Germinal, Espartaco and Progreso," and signed it with a number.

"Be sure you put this paper with the other. How do you get at the hiding-place?"

"By a hole inside the fireplace."

"Do the comrades know it?"

"Yes; all the comrades know it."

The innkeeper, plump and rosy, without eyelashes and almost without eyebrows, went on gossiping with the mortuary porter.

"As you say; what kills a pig kills a man. Cutting the throat, of course."

The other insisted on something that I didn't hear, and the innkeeper replied:

"Oh, with a rifle it is another matter."

He showed in his little eyes the fright of a pig for whom Christmas-time has come. I don't jeer at him because I am a revolutionary and the poor man sympathized with us.

When I went back to the table where my friends were, the Argentine called out from the glass door: "Three lorries of the Shock Troops have come, and they are clearing the people from the street. The forces of the State have resumed action. Disorders are to be feared at the Funeral." Then he added suddenly, "A dangerous position has arisen. The police are searching for arms, and they seem to be coming here." We take our revolvers and hide them in the folds of the tablecloth. The bombs remain on the ground ranged against the wall. The police come in. Searching. Orders to the innkeeper. The barman goes out to shut the door. We look quite unconcernedly at the police and the result is all right. When we have been searched without anything being found, they go to the back of the room. They search the others. Auntie Isabela notices that they are police and begins to click her tongue against her palate, mocking them. The agents don't at first understand that it is against them, and the old woman sticks out her foot and kicks as if she were chasing away a dog. The agents stop in front of her a minute, and are in doubt.

"You dirty hound, get out!" she says.

"A dotty old woman," says one. "She's silly. There isn't a dog here."

Now they've stirred her up. Auntie Isabela rises to her feet, letting the rosary fall on the floor, and stands akimbo. Small and fragile, she displays a high-pressure force. She pours out a torrent of words, civil enough at first, then a little harsher, and finally foul and furious. From time to time she comes up close and almost overwhelms them. The innkeeper tells them that she is Germinal's mother, and the agents hesitate a minute, thinking that those persons, killed in the name of public safety, after all may have mothers just like decent people. Auntie Isabela beats the pit of her stomach with her closed fist over her petticoats and cries out:

"I bore him. Yes, me! So that you might kill him, you think? What do you know about the bearing of a son? What do you know?"

They chose to treat it as a jest. They say that they don't know it and don't want to know it, and they clear out. Auntie Isabela follows them to the door and hurls after them her favorite phrase:

"To hell out of this, you bloody bastards!"

Then she returned to crouch in her corner like a heap of rags. But her corner behind the table became a solemn place. She picked up her rosary from the floor and kissed it. At that moment Star came in with her cock in her arms. She told us that the public forces were going to prevent the workers from reaching the hospital. She had brought the cock with her because the police were in the house and would have been likely to eat it.

The old woman tore at her hair.

"Scoundrels! They wouldn't have gone in if I had been there."

Through the door I see the guards beginning to surround the building. We'll have to clear out as soon as possible. Star has no business to be here in this place, and with us. Wherever we go, she'll be in the way. Women are a difficulty nowadays. The innkeeper seems to be watching us. Perhaps he has been aware of everything, and I don't know why these fatheads haven't yet seen what was on foot. The two old men have gone off to the hospital again. Now they can be seen in the doorway with their uniform hats and their grey coats. The innkeeper keeps nosing about, and then rolls over to the telephone and picks it us. He telephones to his wife and tells her not to worry. I keep thinking of his home, and of the home Auntie Isabela used to have, that old woman full of bitter experiences which have done nothing for her except to swell the muscles of her arm when she clenches her fist in rage. He knows about nothing except glasses and mugs. And the two have made their home and had love. What can love be? They all have made love, and yet they have come to this. But if Star and I? With her cock, that little girl is more distinguished than duchesses in paintings with greyhounds and peacocks. And yet a cock is a stupid sort of thing. So I think, but she thinks differently.

"If you want to go off, don't bother about us."

She looks at me, and as I don't say anything, she tells me that she had come here because she knew that Samar was coming. Then she scolded me for having asked for the vote of censure on him, and told me that what he didn't like was having been proved to make the sketch as they had been together and she would be implicated. That didn't make things seem better than before and I was ashamed to have thought well of him.

I shrugged my shoulders and said that Samar would certainly come because there was something we had to do at once.

"Can one know what kind of thing?"

"One may know, but one mustn't say."

Samar came in almost at once. When we saw him, we were about to go at once, but he asked us to wait and went across to the telephone. He used his voice as if he was speaking from a great distance. He said curious things, in monosyllables, laughed unwillingly, and then spoke quite vaguely again. It was clear that they were asking him from where he was speaking, and that he was lying when he said, "From the Ateneo." Then the name of a cinema, and his voice lowered to say something sweet. I thought of his pretty fiancée I had seen on the Goya tramway. Was he speaking with her as if miles and miles away? Her world is very different, where there are silks and coloured lights and people say, "How kind of you", "How interesting", and never give a direct "Yes" or "No" to anything. From Samar's face when he came back, it could be seen that he was thinking the same sort of things. "Oh, this telephone which in an instant brings together two worlds as different as the Earth and Mars!" What he actually tells us is that we must read a short manifesto which he has in his pocket, and in which the socialists proclaim a general strike. "What are we to reply to them? We must answer." I don't think that it is very important.

"The chief thing," I tell him, "is that they were forced to support the strike. This manifesto of theirs doesn't matter, because it is only the political side of the matter."

And it is true. Samar always sees only the surface of that kind of thing. Auntie Isabela comes frowning with a set purpose. We are all standing up, and without any intention were in a row. She wished to read what was really in our minds, by looking into our eyes. The Argentine said:

"Since I was a boy they have always said that I was mentally deficient. If I become a revolutionary, my stupidity will take on a mysterious and unusual air, and they will stop calling me a fool. They will rather say: he is an anarchist; and perhaps they will say it with a suspicion of dread of me."

The oldest of my friends:

"I have come out to let them kill me as they killed Germinal."

The other:

"I want to stop the breath of Madrid. I wish to make the people here fly in fear, to work in the mines and the fields. With old clothes and week-old beards, like me."

Samar:

"To force men to use what intelligence they have got and make of it a social system in which there will not be grades of society. I mean to socialize all the wealth, but even more the mind and the will."

Star:

"To save the cock from the teeth of the police."

Me:

"To carry out the resolutions of the Federation of Local Syndicates."

Auntie Isabela wrinkles her brows and twitches her left ear, strokes her nose as if to measure its size, and goes back to her corner. Then she stares at the innkeeper. He says, whilst we are silent:

"I am in sympathy with you."

As she sat down the old woman reflected resentfully that no one had said the words for which she was longing. The moral force which the death of her son had created in her sank and now she was giving way to her old age.

"Don't give way like that, Auntie Isabela."

When she saw that the others had realized her state of mind, she raised her head and spat out:

"Bastards; a lot of impotent bastards."

We left the inn, and Star and the old woman stayed behind. The men thought that there wouldn't be a funeral, that the authorities wished to avoid it, and that the three bodies would be rushed off in a swift lorry, at full speed through side streets. The men wanted to have a real public funeral with three open hearses. The homage of the city to the martyrs, just as the *bourgeoisie* made us take a public holiday on the anniversary of their patriotic martyrs. Until the last minute everyone thought that there would be no funeral. But at last sensational news came. The socialist leaders were in the hospital. There were not three corpses, but four. Besides Progreso, Espartaco and Germinal, they had wounded an out-of-work socialist, a man called José Pérez Rodríguez, and he had died last night, and the socialists were pleased, because it gave them an excuse to justify the adhesion of their followers to our plans, and to demand from the Cabinet a funeral and public mourning. Poor José Pérez Rodríguez had caused by his death a very pretty political opportunity! When they had reflected on their collapse of this morning, the socialist leaders began to think that they were not the *bourgeoisie,* that it was bad business to seem to be so, that the social-democrats had failed in other countries, in Germany and in England, and that to call themselves proletarians was sometimes quite as good as to be in the Ministry. They demanded a public funeral, and the rest of the Government agreed on the condition that the socialists should go at the head of the procession. And there they were. Comrades Progreso, Espartaco and Germinal. Now you have them. Fifteen years ago they were your comrades in the socialist syndicates. Now they wish to join you again, through the thin, cheap wood of the coffins, because the masses are in the streets, and shots go through the windows to the most secret bedrooms. They haven't yet accustomed themselves to *bourgeois* authority. As Samar says, it is because the political centre of gravity has moved away from social-democracy. But he isn't very cheerful, the journalist. He is depressed and melancholy. Tonight there will be many committees. But first we have to meet the delegates of the groups. But there is nothing to be done except to explain to those who don't know about it the impossibility of carrying out our plans for sabotage. Samar must come with us because he will have to explain again what happened. He will have a bad time. It is very hard on a man in such cases to confess his own stupidity.

The guards withdrew, and remained on duty in the streets close by. The socialist leaders arrived, and the look of things changed. The workmen came in an avalanche. The guards intervened to clear a passage for the hearses and the leaders of the procession. Detectives insinuate themselves into the crowd, but, uselessly, because they would have to search all of us and take all of us to prison. The sun is overclouded for a few minutes, and when they bring out the coffins they look as black as the inside of a bat, and much larger than we could have believed. The hearses come, but the crowd prevents them from drawing up at the gate, and some men push forward ready to carry the coffins on their shoulders. There is confusion. In the end they permit it and choose six comrades of the same height for each coffin. The socialist coffin comes last, and behind it comes an empty coach with four wreaths of flowers. Ours have no flowers.

No one knows how it has happened, but the fact is that suddenly the three coffins were seen to be wrapped in the black and red banner. The socialist leaders come out, and take places at the head of the procession. Their presence was enough to make it seem that everything had been due to their initiative, a thing which to me at least was insufferable. All the same, we are tolerant enough, although it doesn't seem so. Samar denies it:

"What happens to us is that we have no aptitude for successes, to make the most of our triumphs. All that we know is how to turn our failures to the best advantage."

"That isn't a small thing."

"No, but it isn't enough."

He said no more, and we followed amongst the crowd. When the vote against Samar had been passed, not one of us was capable of reminding him of his mishap, and still less of using it as a weapon against him. But he knew that, was pleased about it, and didn't wish to join in any disputes about trivial matters. And so for a time we walked in silence, when there came elbowing through a dried up yellow-faced person, as lean as a rat. He greeted Samar and asked him what was the significance of the presence of the socialist leaders.

"They have definitely joined us to form a united revolutionary front."

The unknown man opened his eyes wide. He seemed thunderstruck and we passed him. Samar laughed and explained:

"He is a financial spy. He will be rushing off to wire to Amsterdam. Tomorrow morning the news will be in the papers all over the world."

"And what will be the result?"

Samar shrugged his shoulders:

"If only a couple of bankers are ruined, we shall be so much to the good."

Now I happen to recognize one of the socialists who are leading. I spoke to him in the Congress where very likely he is the most powerful man. I look backwards. The river of human beings is lost in the curve of the street. Seeing the crowd all rather disturbed, it is easy to guess at their feelings. They are all thinking the same, "What the hell are the socialists doing here? Why are we following them?" Some insist, respectfully, that one of the dead was a socialist. Looking in front we can see our three coffins being carried with slow and swaying movements. Looking sideways and half-closing the eyes, one can see the helmets of the Civil Guard, huge, hollow and hard. Now a little bill is being distributed. Another manifesto of the socialists promising to bring to book those who were responsible and giving the route of the funeral procession. "It will traverse the Paseo del Prado," it said, "to the Plaza de Castelar where the hearses will set out for the cemetery and the public manifestation will terminate." That is the order. They rely on being in the majority. It is now half-past three. There is still a long afternoon—the May sun does not set until half-past seven—and the procession must be diverted by the Plaza de Neptuno and go up to the Puerta del Sol. That is what we have secretly told those who are carrying the coffins. Samar went on:

"The *bourgeoisie* must be compelled to see our martyrs. When Pablo Iglesias died, the socialists kept the cold meat on public view for three days."

The manifesto was creating an uncomfortable atmosphere behind us. The forces which were watching in the streets looked at us suspiciously. The events of this morning have given us a formidable moral triumph. When the procession reached the Paseo del Prado, it had become three times as numerous. A red Sunday, the colour of glowing coals, with the city shivering and the three coffins tossing like ships above the crowds! Our red flags challenged the *bourgeois* purple. The socialist coffin went behind with no banners. Samar remembered that he hadn't had time to eat, and went on to say:

"If they give me a wound in my belly or stomach, I'll heal all the better."

I begin to wonder why Samar should be a revolutionary, although indeed good revolutionaries have no reason for it in their lives. They have become so almost without noticing it, from some moral need which they have felt since they were children, and which has grown with their education.

We begin to hear songs. In this forest in which one is only a single tree, there are groups singing as if it were Corpus

Christi day. At nightfall we used to carry lighted candles like torches and sometimes there rang out the song of the exterminating angels who went robed in white before the clouds:

Let us gather together
In the last struggle.

Now I feel the same religious emotion, exactly the same, as I felt when I was a small boy in church. Naturally there are neither saints nor priests. Samar is thoughtful. Without meaning it, we are marching to the rhythm of "The International". A group of the International Federation of Anarchists round the coffins sings "Son of the People, bound with chains", and it seems as if the heavens had lowered and the air was heavy, and it was difficult to breathe. The procession goes on and its head has almost reached Neptuno. Probably there are more than 70,000 workers in it. The *bourgeois* must be shivering in their lairs. I say so to Samar. "If they were real revolutionaries, we would overwhelm everything tonight. How easy it would be to grasp power, if our organization really wished power!"

It is a communistic remark, but I don't retort. We march on to "The International". From their horses, the guards look at us as shepherds watch their flocks. We are no longer hating. We are strong and we can do everything. Forward, following Germinal, Espartaco and Progreso on their slow way to infinity, just as we are going. We are going to the infinity of liberty and justice. Samar interrupts:

"Liberty is not an end. It is a banner."

"Bah; we are strong and nothing will turn us aside. The coffins of Progreso, Espartaco and Germinal follow the high old path. Death or Victory. Everything else is a concession to the *bourgeoisie,* is 'liberalism'." Samar and I decide to ascertain the average feeling of the men. As we are near the front, all we have to do is to walk slowly, let others pass us, and listen as they pass. I'll set down what I recall. "I've two revolvers, but I need them both. A man can't do with less?" The other made a reply I didn't catch. They pass us, crowding on, black coats, grey coats, glossy or patched. "Counting in our three comrades there are two hundred and fifteen who have fallen since the Republic came." More jackets. One out at the elbow and with its collar sodden with sweat. "Sixteen, because the socialist has to be counted." Someone protests, "Socialists are not proletarians."

Samar replies: "If they had not killed the socialist, we couldn't have had this procession." They say nothing, because there is no denying it, and we are always being thwarted in our wish to make a demonstration. Another supports the last man: "If they would only let us act in this way, there wouldn't be so much use for revolvers." Another: "Wait; it isn't all done yet." Lower down they are talking about the "dictatorship of the proletariat". They all reject it but would accept dictatorship at the hands of the F.A.I., with financial control by the National Labour Federation. Samar holds that it would be a sure thing if the F.A.I. had sufficient strength and ability for a national offensive. I tell him:

"You aren't an anarchist."

Samar shrugs his shoulders:

"Anarchism is all right as a negation of the State. Abstract anarchism is a religion and doesn't interest me, because, like all religions, it is based on superstition, and besides, aims at a utopia. Anarchism has nothing to do with revolution. Our revolution cannot be based on a spiritual factor. The Spirit today, including our form of it, is *bourgeois*. Our revolution will come about in spite of spirit."

I don't exactly understand him, but his accent of sincerity impresses me. To our right, workmen are saying that the syndicate of construction is the best. Another intervenes: "But the syndicate of waiters has organized support for the out-of-work." Further back, we hear the name of Germinal. The comrades recall him always by stories and episodes of the struggle. All his life was in the struggle, and from the barren plane of death, his continued effort proclaims itself even more. The name of Espartaco is heard less often, but he still wanders through the groups with his ferret, his dark lantern and the snares of his nocturnal exploits. Progreso gives the impression of not yet being dead, because everyone talks of him as if he would be met again within the next half-hour. Of Germinal they say that "he was a man"; nothing more. Of Espartaco that he was an "anarchist". Of Progreso that he was a first-rate foreman mason and that he organized the syndicate. The three compose a complete being. Espartaco the spirit, Germinal the body and Progreso the action. Samar wasn't pleased with that.

We continue to drift backwards. All are singing. There are many socialists, but they are almost all silent. Samar looks at the sky and keeps on walking.

"There is no chance of striking an average opinion today," he said. "Anything may happen tonight."

Here and there uneasy voices call out. "To the Puerta del Sol!" On grasping the order of the socialist leaders, the crowd has rebelled and has resolved on following the order of the F.A.I. By the Puerta del Sol! The cries keep increasing. The coffins have now reached the Plaza de Neptuno. Samar and I push forwards and quickly reach our old places. As we passed along, we made the plan known, and behind us voices rise in a swelling flood. The sky is grey and doubtful. The faces are whiter and the trees are an unnatural green. "Puerta del Sol!" I hear only the last word of the cry. "Sol!" repeated from thousands of throats. "Sol!" The coffins wish to turn to the left. The entrance of San Jeronimo is completely blocked by troops on horse and on foot. "Sol!" The cry, gathering to it new voices, rolls up to resound like a trumpet under the grey vault of the skies. "Sol!" The multitude has stood still. "Sol!" Samar laughs. The heavens, obedient but astonished, open a porthole through which yellow rays emerge. The sun sheds a pallid sparkle on the black of the coffins. But that isn't the cause. The crowd hangs on the three letters. "Sol!" Samar goes on laughing. It is a bitter and crafty laugh. He explains:

"What a lovely word for forty thousand throats!"

But he hasn't told everything. That isn't the cause of his laughter. His happiness is deep and bashful, secret, and, like morphine, not to be admitted. His fiancée is mixed up in this, in this gaiety of his. "Sol!" "SOL!" I am suddenly frightened by my own perspicacity. She, his fiancée, must call him "Sun", very likely, "My Sun", "Sun of my heart". She is a *bourgeoise*, but now he thinks her transfigured in the revolution, identified with the masses. "Sun", "SUN". It is she who is calling out. Now everything is possible for him. The revolution and his own personal happiness go together.

The demonstration has divided. Our lot are crowding round the coffins, and the others have gone on towards the Plaza de Castelar. The socialists are in tense alarm. Our men still cry "Sol!" And they are threatening. The plan is realizing itself in action, and the multitude has changed its cries for the communist and anarchist "International". We go in confidence and resolution against the troops. They block the street, but presently they will open it. On one side the Palace Hotel, on the other the Ritz. Now, you rich and international tourists, look on our three dead men! They have put the other body in a swift hearse and have taken it away. Don't be frightened! We know well that you call all this bad taste, but in Spain bad taste is not an argument. Here they are, Progreso, Espartaco and Germinal. The three coffins can make a fine commemorative obelisk. Sepulchral of course. But it would be our obelisk. We have as much right to display it to you as the *bourgeoisie* with their obelisk of May 2, over there among the trees. Progreso, Espartaco and Germinal. Hillo, Samar, look at the pale moon up there. THE MOON: "Three new planets: Progreso, Espartaco and Germinal."

Now the sun appears again. Forward, comrades! It is not the sun but the Puerta del Sol. Even the heavens are trying to cheat you. Be damned to the Heavens! Sing! Sing! Take no notice of the cornet sounding to warn us off. Sing! Our voices will penetrate anything. Our ideas, like gunshots, will pierce heads armour-plated with selfishness. Sing! Sing!

A shot. Then more shots. The crowd is silent and the coffins reel above their heads. The cornet sounds again. It is the Law. First comes the Law, and then the deed. Thus in the old civilizations. In those that are being born—like ours—first the deed and then nothing, and much later the Law. With the last note of the cornet a volley sounds. The guards have raised their rifles to their shoulders. Each volley is followed by a mortal silence. Who will fall? Why have I not fallen yet? The coffins move on, tottering above the heads. The crowd has shrunk back, but the comrades carrying them move on. They are alone now. Our shots ring out in a scattered fire whose echoes are lost in the borders of the Plaza. The guards have broken their line and have grouped themselves at the two sides. One of them has fallen. The horse of another is plunging, wounded. Now we fire, retreating, seeking the cover of a tree or of a pillar from which we may continue to fire. They reply with close volleys. Thousands of demonstrators escape to the Retiro Park and the Cibeles. The volleys go on. In the empty spaces of the roads, there are black spots writhing and groaning. Firing continues everywhere. The coffins still move forward. An officer goes up to one and with his revolver in his hand orders it to stop. In the invisible waving stream of bullets, two bearers of the first coffin have fallen. The coffin rocks, crashes and comes to rest on the paving-stones. The wounded bearers creep along and the others pull out their revolvers and retreat firing. I have taken cover behind a bench and continue firing. Samar, with his hands in his pockets, curses and looks up and down. The Plaza is marked with lines of flying men. We go on firing. Another coffin has fallen on the ground. The bullets are reaping the flowers in the gardens and splattering on the paving-stones, throwing out chips. Presently people come running from Cibeles. From there and from San Jeronimo, more troops come down. We must fly or die. We fly, because we mustn't die. Tonight there are the committees.

THE MOON: "Three new planets: Espartaco, Progreso and Germinal." The coffins are on the ground. The third has fallen from the shoulders of the wounded bearers and has cracked, like the dry shell of a nut. It has split open, and the fruit, white and yellow, has been spilled out. The Plaza now seems deserted, but shots still come from several places, and there are wounded men crawling towards safety but firing as they crawl. The troops don't dare to come out into the open. A wounded horse, with its backbone broken, plunges forward, with its muzzle in the air, and its rump sloping down like a giraffe. It crosses the Plaza in a mad dance, and the reins get hooked in a plank of the coffin which turns over on the pavement. The animal dances to the music of the bullets, dragging the coffin. I am flying like the others, but I stand still. For half an hour no one dares to move a step. The horse remains in the Plaza carpeting it with scarlet rosettes. On the pavement there are now only four men. Four dead men. Besides comrades Espartaco, Progreso and Germinal. The last, with his naked arms exposed to the light, outside the empty coffin. The wounded men have all fled. They will get cured where they can. Or in any case they can die where they please. Not, as the *bourgeoisie* would wish, in the "act and at the place of the rebellion". The coffins—all three—are riddled with bullets. Now they have taken to killing the dead!

Auntie Isabela and Star arrive in the Plaza, hurrying. One of the men on horseback throws them out, and makes them flee. In the confusion the red cock escapes from Star's arms and gets between the coffins. It jumps on one of them and shrills out its evening song. Samar and I have contrived to climb over the railings of the Retiro Park, where we meet Urbano Fernández of the committee of federation. Without stopping he says to us:

"At ten o'clock tonight, in Cuatro Caminos, for sabotage."

Samar protests:

"But don't you know that we have had to give it up? Now we can't do anything."

Urbano gets angry.

"Don't you know, damn you? Two comrades who were in the same bar and saw what happened, knew the spy. They followed him and did his business. Here is the sketch."

We stole through Lealdad Street, leaving our revolvers and notebooks buried in the Retiro. We'll go to recover them before they close the park. From the top of the street we see the Plaza de Neptuno. Seated on the edge of the pavement are Auntie Isabela and Star. Their eyes are fixed on poor Germinal, naked under the evening sky. The horse is still dancing with its broken spine. When I see that Star has the cock in her arms again, I breathe more freely.

Chapter 9

Samar Between Love and Revolution

WHEN I entered the cinema, the performance had already begun; a pretty troupe of fairies appeared to receive me; thighs and golden heads. American music, staccato in throats of brass, and African drums. A lively rhythm recalling motors rather than banjos. Clean and firm sensuality. Gymnastics and swimming, the exact opposite of Eastern drugged sleep and poisoned spinal cord. This is not Madrid but New York. Nothing here recalls our high-brow spiritual culture. Nothing of the internationalism of Geneva. Down below gymnastics, swimming, heavy jaws. Above, the way of the spirit, with as its climax—Roosevelt! Politics without psychology, spirit so identified with the body and with mechanical necessity that no one could say it exists. A most complex ideal which places the greasy pole leading to moral aspirations on the head of Theodore. That ideal is crystallized in a complex abstract formula: "Deeds are worth more than words." To that point has been developed the spirit of the golden land which dances to the sound of motors and jerks its body to the rhythm of infantile negroid tunes. One day it became aware that words were controlled by an obscure intellectual force, a dangerous threat of the spirit. It hastened to issue an order against words. Theodore sank into deep reflection before adopting it, and then sounded the sirens of alarm: "Yes, Sir. Deeds are worth more than words. Have no confidence in the spoken word." Having attained this masterpiece of theory, he went to sleep, tranquilly, in history. The American cinema is the only anti-spiritual religion which has taken root in Europe. And I come to it—alas—to give the spirit a treat, whilst down in Carabanchel, evening firing is winding up the day.

I find my place, in the dark, guided by a flashlamp. Someone on the stage says with a firm voice, "We must close the ranks." The music of motors supplies a fine melody. Action. Struggle. Co-ordinated effort and firmness in conduct. "We must close the ranks." I take a measured leap into space, resolved to find my feet not too far off. Action, successful struggle. And harmony without spirit. The music goes on. I have sat down. My betrothed is on my left. I can see nothing. A hand takes my arm, another rests on my shoulder. I hear my name and the voice which pronounces it thrills with the joy of seeing me: "Lucas! Lucas!" I can now see her features. Her ripe cheeks, her sweet smile, her sparkling eyes. Involuntarily I remember the sketch and the vote of censure. With her rounded arms, her perfume, her gay bodice, the gloves which she has taken off, I see her sprung from all I hate, from the house of my enemies. But she is beautiful. And she has no soul of her own. I have poured mine into her.

"If you only knew the trouble I had to persuade Papa. The maids brought in terrible news from the street. It was only when you rang me up, and I told him that all was quiet, that he decided to let me come out."

From the next seat her aunt leaned across to ask:

"What is happening, Lucas? Is it really the revolution?"

My fiancée hurriedly answered:

"No, aunt, there won't be a revolution until a more conservative government comes into power and forces all the working classes to unite."

I don't remember when I said that to her, but I must have done so because she takes in all that I say and forms her judgments from me without the slightest alteration. I confirm what she said and the aunt sinks down in her seat lamenting:

"What must come will come, but I hope there will be no blood."

Amparo pressed my arm.

"Don't talk to my aunt."

We looked at each other. She smiled. I remembered too many things. They didn't suit this sweet intimacy. Feeling. She is nothing but that—her body, her voice, her eyes. But I can't smile back and don't wish to smile. She is like still water, transparent, and changeless. Water to mirror the infinite skies. Or to nourish a white rose in an ugly vessel. A pool among myrtles, lilies and pleasant paths, when all is naked rock and angry sea and no one can find his way. She smiled and pressed my arm. I looked at her and thought: "Why have we not yet accomplished everything? Why have we not yet reached even a social equilibrium in which we could rest?" Then, looking into her eyes, I added: "Why in your gentle eyes and in the lovely harmony of your face and in your young mouth must there be death?" And with her hand in mine, "Why should I, who do not believe in the spirit, have this longing to submit myself and give way to the spirit?" She looks at me smiling. I know only two moods in her: smiles and tears. She passes from one to the other almost instantaneously unless I am careful. I keep looking at her in silence. I look into her eyes again. Light and nothing else. And then I ask myself: "Why does one have this longing to be done with this world which must always be, and to be reborn in the marvellous new world of a home?" I kiss her hand and her arm fresh as if it were bathed in dew. On the stage the graceful fairies dance. The music mocks my madness, and the voice of the honourable Theodore Roosevelt keeps repeating, "We must close the ranks!"

Yes. Yes. We must close the ranks. But your line passes through a *bourgeois* paradise and our line doesn't. For me there is death in her eyes, and a wonderful material life far away from them. I can't give up death, and that is not my fault, but the fault of the spirit within me, a vaccine against happiness. The spirit keeps me in love. She asks me:

"Is it the revolution?"

I don't know if it is. Perhaps it is. But I don't wish her to be deceived if we should fail, and I answer, "No."

"So I thought," she went on, "because there hasn't yet been a change of government."

Then she told me what she did yesterday. There is such conviction in her actions, such a *bourgeois* solidity, assurance of the force of her principles, that one is terrified. She had paid a visit. With whom had she spoken? What did they say to her? How did they look at her as they spoke? Did they recognize what she was and respect her childishness? Did they refrain from improprieties? She is talking to me about her trousseau. "I think all my pretty things will please you." Luxury trades, dreams of machines and of men have surpassed themselves to decorate our happiness for us, and have worked tirelessly for it. Then she tells me how her wedding-dress is to be made. I see her, amid all these American phantasms, like a simple flower, bright and pure like a child. I ask myself, "How can a decadent civilization and a rotten society produce fruits like this?" She fixes her eyes on mine and implores:

"Speak to me. Tell me about our happiness."

She wishes some inspiration. Shall I not pervert her if I give her some of mine? She puts her pink shell of an ear close to me and waits, with quickened breath. Nature is whispering to her, but she doesn't know what. I tell her in the simplest words I can find what my dreams are. They are becoming definite. They are more real than the phantasms on the screen. Her breathing quickens. She smiles and looks at the illumined pictures, arranging them to her taste.

"One day your lovely body will melt in mine."

She agrees, smiling.

"Then my darling will be a woman. And we shall have a son."

Immediately she closes her eyes and her lips and looks down. And she stays like that a while with her chin on her breast. I can't make her raise her head. I smile and wait a minute. "Doesn't my darling wish to have a son?" She keeps silent and seems to shrink into herself. At last when I ask her again, I seem to see her say "no" with her head. I get closer to her ear.

"No?"

She replies with a whisper almost inaudible. I get close to her lips, ask again, and this time I hear:

"No, a little daughter."

"All right, dear wife; whichever you please."

I can't help smiling, and she notices it, and becomes more serious than ever. To make her raise her head I have to tell her to look to the other side. At last she raises it, but by then I am far away.

"Don't look at the screen, Lucas."

A pause. I am with Roosevelt, but I am carrying an anarcho-syndicalist revolver, and the sullen scowl of the "International". This is morphia. This is an artificial *bourgeois* paradise. The spirit at my side, intoxicated with emotion, cries:

"Lucas, my sun. Don't look at the screen!"

And tonight, sabotage. That music, those pictures so well arranged—without soul—the men as perfect as machines, the women as wise as puppets, are a tonic. We don't know whither the sabotage will lead us. Nor do the new victims of tonight know. Perhaps tomorrow the other cities will join us and Andalusía . . .

"My sun, don't look at the screen!"

From the tone of her voice I know that she is weeping.

"Don't be foolish!"

She cries again and pulls away her hand from mine. I see the tears trembling on her lashes. They must be cold, and they could madden. I seize her hand.

"Come! Come!"

The usual questions. Do you love me? Then why are you looking at the screen? I do love her, yes, but on a condition.

What?

Presently she stops. It is one of the familiar devices of lovers. She must be made to smile, nod her head and show the tip of her tongue between her teeth. I implore her to smile and to stop crying. She obeys at once, but she is still frowning, and a suppressed sob keeps her from showing the tip of her tongue. I pretend to be satisfied and kiss her hand. At that moment a guffaw resounds through the hall. It is Theodore Roosevelt, persisting in his materialistic misunderstanding. Not that he has returned to matter, loathing the soul in an European fashion, but because he has never attained a soul. But his guffaw has contrived to alienate me from my fiancée again. I think of what she was telling me. Of her trousseau. Of her wedding-dress. Then I remember that the wedding-dress is worn at the religious ceremony. I ask her more questions, and, understanding what is in my mind, she explains to me her good reasons for what she has arranged. Her lace train will give work to dozens of people. But she doesn't know what I wish to be at. She understands only when I ask her if the wedding-dress is also worn at a civil ceremony. She is slow in replying. "Because of the revolution," she says, "you don't love me."

"Don't you know that we won't have anything but a civil marriage?" I insist.

She tries hard not to cry again and succeeds. But her self-possession is so insecure that if I say anything tender, if I take her hand she will burst into tears. I take good care to prevent that. When I knew her first she was conspicuous amongst her friends for her poise, her self-possession and control. Now she breaks down not merely with a look, but at a word. She asks me timidly:

"Will you tell me the truth?"

"I always tell you the truth."

"Give me a real answer, my sun. Will you tell me the truth?"

"Yes."

"Give me your word of honour?"

"Nonsense. Honour isn't a thing I recognize."

"I'm sorry. Will you give me your word?"

"Yes."

"Is it true that sometimes you don't want to love me?"

"Yes."

True that sometimes you hate me?"

"I hate myself."

"But it is my fault?"

"Yes."

She is silent and shrinks away. She rests her elbow on the arm of her chair and rests her chin on her hand. Her eyes become dreamy and she whispers:

"I knew it when you were looking at the screen. Isn't it true that you've been like that for some time?"

"Yes, ever since I knew that I was in love."

I am following, without seeing, the images on the screen. There are moving drawings. A cat is making love to a rat, and as he lifts his eyes to the moon with both hands on his chest, his drawers fall down. The rat blushes. I am far away again. Thinking of the struggle and its consequences, the recent events and what is going to happen tonight, entangled in the deeds of the revolution—deeds, my friends—I am far away. The drawers of the lovesick cat have made me smile. She must be watching me, for I have heard her weeping quietly. Also I seem to hear her chewing her handkerchief with her white teeth and whispering as if she were calling her mother like a little lost animal. And Mr. Roosevelt keeps bawling from the sketches: "We must close the ranks."

Like a little lost animal. But it is me who has lost my way. I left my moral plane when I came to know her, and lost myself in the pure labyrinth of her feelings. I knew the love of the senses, good and pure without spiritual perversions. The women with whom I was concerned gave me affection and I gave them passion. But it was always the love of the senses without the feelings. I was free. I never dreamed. I was not enslaved by my own dreams. They knew it and didn't object. Shots and manifestos awakened me, tore me from dreams. But, Mr. Roosevelt? A doubt. Are not dreams more real, more alive, more "deeds", than manifestos and firing? The doubt brings me a moment of pleasure. Mr. Roosevelt begins to laugh again on the stage. Impulsively I turn to my betrothed:

"If you go on like that I'll go off."

I get ready to go and she makes a great effort to recover her serenity. And so I stay. But in any case I should have gone only materially. My spirit would have remained in the chair enveloping her, surrounding her, controlling her looks and her thoughts, seeing what she saw, adapting everything to her, imposing my wishes on what was wrong and ridding the screen of its implications. I would be far off, but still wounded by suspicions. A word overheard in passing might be corrupting. A newspaper left on the table in her house might bring her the bitter dregs of experience, or the offence of mere stupidity. Nothing ought to touch her. No one must fret her with a word or a thought. There are too many men and women who feel ruined themselves and secrete a poison from which I wish to keep her. I wish to censor words, looks, photographs in the newspapers, and even combinations of light and colour. Neutral words, the vacant looks of statuary, photographs of things, of objects, never of persons, clear and direct light, the blue of heaven, a soft blue never changing. But thinking like that, how could I leave her if it were still possible to stay an hour with her? And yet my motive in rising was sincere. Perhaps deeper than all these reflections.

I go on looking at the cinema. It is a psychological film. Sketches of straightforward characters as simple as those of a dog or a horse. Mr. Roosevelt proceeds with his metaphysic linked to elementary facts, as colour is to precipitates in chemistry or the light of a fire. On the stage the curtains, the glass, the lamps and the white shirts laugh. My betrothed suffers, seeing me follow the movements of the film. But there is something more powerful than my will, which unites me with my comrades or with Mr. Roosevelt. It doesn't matter that I am not gazing at her, for the spirit unites us. She has none, but I have given her part of mine. The spirit is decadent in all but her who has absorbed it as damp clay takes a shape. We begin to talk, but about things that don't matter.

"Have you the articles I gave you?"

They are essays on Pierre Louys from a French review. She hastens to answer, already forgetting everything else. She has read them and asks me the meaning of some words, amongst them "hedonism". Such words on her lips grieve me. This dear child ought to be, and will be, as she is now, without self-consciousness. A flower with a complete idea of its origin and purpose becomes the grotesque wooden model which you see in botanical museums. These articles don't please her. I could convince her that an essay of Pierre Louys had importance, but at the cost of intellectual superstition. And besides, it is much better that she shouldn't like them, but keep them and file them. In truth none of this interests me, but I carry on with it, because I wish to help myself somehow; thus we interpose facts—one for you, Mr. Roosevelt—in our intoxication of illusion.

In the interval, the lights are turned up. I slip down a little in my seat and lean on one of the arms whilst we talk. It would be a pity if one of the agents were to recognize me. She looks carefully all around. . . . She is not afraid. I like seeing her repel with a look the equivocal people who come close to pass up the central gangway. Her lips are full, both provocative and pure, pressed in a gesture of indignation. I manage to avoid laughing. My guardian angel feels herself a panther, with her beautiful throat, her eyes of velvet, with her charming costume. She is prepared to say in all good faith that she is a communist, and if she were to do so, I couldn't help a burst of laughter. She takes my hand and says with quickened breath:

"There is a man who has been watching you for some time. He must be a policeman."

"Don't you look at him."

Staring at me, she asks:

"Are you carrying a revolver?"

"Yes."

"If he comes, take it out and go out by that door. If you hear me cry out, come back at once and kill him!"

I jump a little, partly because she talks of death, and partly in case they hear her. I press her hand.

"All right; but be quiet."

She is frowning. What does her expression remind me of? It is a resemblance so extremely unlikely that I am not sure. Suddenly I remember the expression of Auntie Isabela. I close my eyes and try to shut out the memory. But now the voice of the old woman forces itself on me. "To hell out of this, you bastards!" I recover my tranquility and, looking at her, think serenely that if she had to endure the bitter experience of Auntie Isabela I would be capable of killing her and killing myself too. It would be too dreadful that these lips . . . And then I assure myself: "I should kill her; we should kill ourselves." My imagination turned round and round that idea until I began to be giddy. I haven't had a meal today, and last night I didn't sleep. I am excited and it almost pleases me to feel light, weightless. I keep staring at her. She, even she, talks about killing, about escaping, about revolvers with a simple and natural ferocity. But, darling I know all the harmony of your soul. You gaze at me, anxious to follow me blindly. What do you know? Rough roads, darling, for your little feet. I love you too much to take you with me. But to leave you—how? With whom? Where? Whither? I cannot do it. The suspicious individual has gone off. There is now no one standing up near us, and she takes the opportunity of asking me in the full light:

"Why did you tell me a few minutes ago that you didn't wish to love me?"

"Because it is true, darling."

"Then I don't make you happy?"

"You fill me with illusion and dreams. Often it is nice to dream."

Now she tries to convince me that she is a revolutionary. Of course she makes an exception about religion. And she can't approve of killing people. I ask her that to see if she will contradict herself:

"Not even the police?"

"If they are going to take you away from me, yes."

She cannot be a communist. But the trouble is—I must be sincere—if she were to become a communist I would stop loving her. She could not remain what she was when I knew her. This is another side to the problem, perhaps the most vital, which makes me sometimes feel far away from her, the root of the hatred of which we were speaking. When I am by her side neither my soul nor my heart are demented—as the poets write about—that would not have the slightest importance—but what is worse, what is really tragic, my reason suffers. My reason, straight and resolute, becomes baroque, in rising curves, with ridiculous fore-shortening, with cheap ornamentation, covered with tinsel. My reason twists about, scatters in the effort to concentrate, hurts me like a neuralgia. I confront her with the idea of marriage without the intervention of the church. She can't believe that abstract principles can matter in an affection like ours. I turn the argument round and ask her what she cares about a church marriage. She says it isn't for herself, but for her people. Sentiment comes over her in waves and everything is smeared with its sticky syrup.

I try to lead her back—Mr. Roosevelt again—to the region of simple facts.

"You would leave your family to come with me, without marrying?"

Her silence says "No". I don't wait for her to speak, for with her words would come tears.

"Would you agree to a civil wedding?"

She keeps silence.

Then I see that we are wasting time.

Fortunately the lights have been lowered again. Her seat has become a place of torment. I look at the screen. Mr. Roosevelt: what would you do in my case? I consult him because it is a spiritual question. Our principles give only the alternative: violation, or leave her alone and forget. But I am in the web of the *bourgeois* spider. What would you do? At last she speaks.

"I am an obstruction in your life."

I insist:

"Will you agree to a civil wedding?"

"Stop looking at the cinema and I'll tell you."

I obey. But instead of answering she tries to wheedle me. She doesn't know that I am completely and hopelessly hers.

"My Lucas; my sun!"

"Answer me!"

She delays, but then nods consent. At the same time she is thinking "No". I know that it isn't settled, much less than that; but I give myself up to the illusion for a little and am happy.

A question, Mr. Roosevelt: won't shots kill an illusion?

We go out before the lights are raised. When we are in the street, I gently press her arm and bend down to her ear:

"You know what you have promised?"

"I don't know, but always, always, whatever you wish!"

The chauffeur has opened a door and waits with his hat in his hand. His servility extends to me, too. All his kind make me ashamed. She lowers the glass and puts out her hand. The car is already moving off when I let it go.

Without turning my head I set off on foot. The streets are almost empty. There are no tramcars. A few of the picture-houses are open as the order to strike had come late or because the socialists did not wish to annoy the good *bourgeoisie* too much. I walk up towards Cuatro Caminos. By a few words I catch from a passer-by I gather that the Metro is still running and go to the nearest station. Is man free? Ought he to be free? If so, has he the right to grasp his own happiness? I have only one life to lead, only one. We are the least significant result of a set of mechanical laws which dominate us. We have no power over them. We are born, we live, we die, not by our own will. And we obstinately create worlds, or direct those that exist, infecting them with ideas. Must I sacrifice everything for an idea that has been born in the heat of a thing so alien, so adventitious, so *bourgeois* as my spirit? There is a solution: that others must sacrifice themselves for me. It is a natural law. It doesn't matter if I go to the mountain or the mountain comes to me. Or that it is blown into a thousand pieces, is destroyed, and with it my longing to possess it. So I go on meditating, continually coming back to my true nature, when the train reaches the terminus. I come out into a suburb, luminous and gay. The working quarter of Cuatro Caminos. Beside the station a set of youths are dancing round a bonfire in which two bundles of newspapers are burning. I pick up a copy that has fallen on the ground and go off at the moment when some police come up. The newspaper is *The Watchman* which has had the insolence to appear tonight.

I avoid the centre and pass down some narrow streets of the marine quarter. There comes a salty and damp breeze—it is in the centre of Castile—and then I see the inn, "Casa de Nicanor". Inside some workmen are finishing a meal. Nearly all have with them proletarian women carrying traces of their housework in their soiled clothes and weariness. I don't know any of them. My comrades have not yet arrived as it is very early. I open the newspaper. A narrative by a cheap novelist who when he is travelling in a sleeping-coach is politely addressed by the attendants—"as the gentleman wishes", "did the gentleman ring?", "will the gentleman permit me to inform him", and thinks it necessary to give an account of it, and incidentally to speak about his silk pyjamas. As he writes for the middle classes, his readers are thrilled by such exquisite luxury. Then there are three columns of threats of war against the Soviet, on the leading page. The French whiskers of Stalin on one side and a Japanese puppet on the other. "The end of the Union of Soviet Republics is in sight." The poor, greasy and apoplectic editor can't sleep for thinking that the Soviet Republic still exists, and that he may be publishing too often the same Japanese portrait as the President, as the delegate to Geneva, and sometimes even as the Emperor. Without being on the side of the Soviet, he feels anti-Japanese for the quick way in which they are apt to declare war without giving *The Watchman* time to get new photographs. Then a column, or two of jokes about cookery, high rents, pretty girls, iced lemonade and such matters of universal interest. A caricature of a lady wishing to buy a new dress and her husband refusing and saying that he himself is going to go naked. And underneath great headlines: "On page 2, Sensational information on the Criminal Revolutionary Outbreak begun yesterday." But before that an invocation to "Our Lady of the Peseta", Exchanges, Foreign Credit. This is a pretty way of insulting the despairing hunger of working men. Invoking the health of our credit in the Stock Exchanges of Paris and London. The editor knows that the invocation will please the President of the Council, who is crazy about foreign trade, and on a famous occasion wrote a set of articles dealing with the subject. Then there came right across the page two headlines, "A Firm Hand against the Hirelings of Disorder"; "Stern Measures against yesterday's Outrages." Below these, "The Whole Country supports the Government." And on the front page an editorial in large type. Rage, fear, contempt, hatred. All the elements of Greek tragedy and all the rhetoric of last century have been spilt in these comments. The Republic must be saved—the Republic under which the editor became a member of Parliament, which gave him in the recesses a soft job on a committee, and increased his income by fifty pounds a month. The editor doesn't speak in Parliament, doesn't sign his articles, never gives his opinion about anything—a device which, after fifteen years of diligent service to the managing board, put him into the editorial chair and finally convinced him that all these pleasant things which surrounded him were "the nation", the "public interest", "social order" and "culture". His howl reached to heaven when he was defending them against the "anarchosydicalistic-communistic" rabble. It is the only party against which he ventures to pronounce, because it is the only party from which he can get nothing. The comrades, I think, are going to play a nasty trick on him. There is also an article by a "learned professor" deploring the bad feeling of other people in politics, in social affairs and in art, but at the same time showing between the lines his own resentment not so much against another modern professor of greater social celebrity, but against the fame of Napoleon, Viriathus and Hamilcar, which gives him no moment of repose.

Then comes the news. As was to be expected, the death of the comrades is assigned to shots fired by the workers themselves, and this view is helped by the vagueness of the post-mortem reports. Believes that there is a risk of a national disturbance. Appeals to the sense of responsibility of the socialists and reminds their leaders that they would be the first victims of an exasperated populace. Praises the good feeling shown in decreeing the strike, so that the workers might be present at the funeral, regrets the death of the four, and insists that the public authority had never been more secure. But the manner of these lines shows that their writer had an entirely different view.

Separately and with a heading across two columns I read: "One of the Bodies has disappeared." Further on they mention Germinal. This notice brings him to life again. The Cid won battles after he was dead; and Germinal, although he didn't win them, lost them, which is much the same. The police had been busy.

"Does anyone know whose body this is?"

As the body was naked they began to surmise that he was one of the Shock Police or an agent stripped by the revolutionaries to his underclothes, and as he bears traces of the post-mortem they imagine that the revolutionaries had ferociously mauled the body. Finally on the list of corpses taken into the mortuary, there appeared this, unidentified, "with bullet wounds and stabs". Poor Germinal has died twice. The others have been buried in the common grave-pit.

Two of my friends arrive. While I begin my meal, they talk to me about the matters which have to be discussed. A manifesto to prevent the socialists from going back to work. A proposal for negotiations with the provincial parts of the organization, the fusion of the Local, the Regional and the Committee of the Federate Groups into a revolutionary organization with full powers, and as immediate plan of action, an outbreak in the northern quarter as a preliminary to an attack on the barracks of the 75th Light Artillery. Amparo, my betrothed, lives in the Colonel's quarters of that regiment. For a moment I thought that they were trying to test me to see how I'd behave. When I became sure that they knew nothing, I became tranquil and went on eating. One of them said that they could get to work in those barracks.

"Why?"

"That's easy. I live near. And when I pass by, I sometimes talk with the sentinel. 'How about it when we finish off your officers?' I said to one of them the other day."

"And what did he say?"

"Nothing. He asked me for a cigarette and laughed."

Chapter 10

Successful Sabotage

I WAS in prison and I promised myself that that warder would pay for it, and he did pay for it when I came out. Mallows are growing out of his carcase in the Eastern cemetery. I got a life sentence. But they treated me differently. The warders didn't annoy me. I was as if in an hotel. Some of them wished to be friendly, and patted me on the shoulder. "Bah," said I, letting them pet me. "They know that I am a killer," and I wasn't grateful. Prison was a university to me, as it is to many. I learned to distinguish between the grades of society and the different notions of what it should be. And also the kind of things to learn from one's own judgment without talking to anyone. I learned then that to have any success with the *bourgeoisie* one has to carry a revolver and to brandish it now and again for the common benefit. And here I am. Don't they kill us with hunger and cold and bodily exhaustion? At least that is what I tell myself. There is no more to be said about it.

I come into the street of the Three Fishes. It is dark and there are damp corners everywhere sodden with urine. The doors are shut and in one of them two labourers are sleeping. Alongside them there is a tall and strong chap stirring them with his foot.

"Get up, blast you! I am going to stand treat."

He is drunk. I know by his voice that it is Fau.

"Hillo! Fau."

"It's you, Urbano? Look at them. They are sleeping like pigs."

"What do you want?"

"To stand treat to them. Tonight I'll stand treat to God and the Mother of God. In there I've five other friends."

There is a small group beside Nicanor's pub. Voices call from it.

"Leave them alone, Fau."

One of the two sleepers pulls himself together:

"What do you want?"

Fau puts his hands on his hips and nods his head up and down:

"You must be the son of a bitch. Don't you hear that I am standing treat? When you are invited you don't ask questions."

The two are hungry, because they get up and follow Fau. I clap him on the shoulder, and when he spins round putting his hand to his belt I say:

"How about me?—aren't you going to invite me?"

He tells me that he doesn't like jokes of that sort. I wink an eye: "You are like me. Never without a dollar in your pocket."

"Not when there is work."

I keep staring at him:

"When there is work, oh yes?"

He moves his finger away from the trigger and returns my wink. I push him off and go into the inn. He is drunk and I don't bother about him.

There are few people. So much the better. We don't want crowds except at burials and processions. Sallent and Escuder, who had arrived from Barcelona today, are at one table and Samar at another. They don't know each other. Nicanor, the innkeeper, some years ago used to be a good fighter, but he married the daughter of a foreman and chucked everything. But he hasn't forgotten us, and one way or another keeps helping us. He has an idea of his own about us. He says that we are now like the early Christians of the catacombs. We meet each other everywhere, but everywhere the authorities are against us. He thinks that it is a question of two or three centuries and that we shall begin very badly, but that in five centuries or so things will go well with us. The day after tomorrow, as they say. But he is really a good sort and helps us. A little dotty, as will have been seen.

I go to Samar's table with the two comrades from Barcelona:

"These two that you don't know are Sallent from near Lérida and Escuder of Barcelona."

They are on their way to Andalusía to try to arrange an agreement between the Catalan region and the Sevillian organization. Escuder is short and wears glasses. Sallent is a stouter fellow. We talk. The two of them wish to join us in our sabotage, but I make Escuder admit that his eyeglasses prevent it. Samar says that as they have a mission in Andalusía, they oughtn't to take any risks in Madrid. I agree about that.

Escuder is astonished that the Madrid organization has been able to work up all this plot, and says that they'll hardly believe it in Catalonia. Sallent is crusty because we won't let him come with us. He is right. It isn't often that a man can suddenly and unexpectedly fall into a chance of direct action. Three others come in. We are now seven, counting the Catalans. No one takes any alcoholic drink, except Samar, who had a glass of brandy in front of him. This glass is just another of the ways in which he tries to be different. The Catalans are amazed at what our Centre can do. The three comrades who have arrived, Juan Segovia, Felipe Ricart and Graco, bring news. They tell us that all the organizations of Old and New Castile have joined in the general strike, and when we say that we are out for everything and that Catalonia and Andalusía will be unable to keep out, the Catalans look thoughtful but can't hide their emotion. We begin to arrange the details of the sabotage. Our job concerns the south-east cable according to the sketch plan which Samar made. At midnight two other comrades will be with us; they belong to our gang, and have to find Cipriano within the next half-hour to see if he has secured the length of copper cable we shall require. I see that the Barcelona comrades don't know all our arrangements so say little.

Besides, it is the same with the other comrades of our group. Why? It is quite enough for them to know what they have to do at any moment. We wish to force the *bourgeoisie* to declare a "state of war". That will be the signal for letting loose the whole of our organization. Samar asks me some questions and I reply:

"If you had been at the meeting tonight you would have known. These things are not to be asked about; you know them or you don't." But he guesses, to judge from some remarks he made. All the same, from an unexpected question by the Catalans I suspect that they know a good deal about things and are keeping it dark, in case I myself don't know: but what does it matter? The main thing is for each of us to do his part of the job. Samar is lost in thought. He is slow in replying and looks as if he would wake up. Suddenly he asks:

"Who killed the agent? Where?"

"What does the person or the place matter? Anyone would know you were a journalist. You want to know everything. Here is your sketch, and that is all there is to it."

I go on to show them the wires entering the transformer and those which leave it. Samar is thinking, for the face is the mirror of the soul, that by his fault one of the police has been killed, and that the policeman was just a man like ourselves. We can't all think the same way. For me he wasn't a man, but only a mechanical instrument of injustice. It would be a fine thing to become sentimental hypocrites, when we are in the thick of things. We go on studying the sketch. The innkeeper moves about. Samar keeps his eye on the envelope, and when I turn it round and the side with the address becomes visible, he cuts that off and keeps it. He says that the name might give a clue to the police. But he becomes pale, and to hide it, begins to smoke.

At that moment Fau came in followed by a swarm of beggars, and among them a man out of work. They look like scum from a drain trailing behind him. Misery and death in their dirty rags and in their slinking appearance. Nicanor fixes his eye on them and Fau makes a gesture of collecting them and says:

"I pay, I invite them."

Then he stares at the counter and suddenly turns round: "God Almighty, what are you doing? Sit down, can't you?"

He orders pork sausages, bread and wine. And keeps on chattering. This Fau is a queer character.

"Do you work?" I ask.

"Mother of God, I do work. Haven't you chaps given me work?"

Nicanor waits on him with extreme politeness, as if he were a gentleman. Although Fau speaks freely to him, Nicanor answers only No, or Yes. The others fall asleep or anxiously wait for the food. Fau thumps the table:

"Christ, can't you blighters smile? Is this a bloody funeral? And you, take your hand out of that man's pocket. I am watching you. We are all straight here."

"What is his is mine, and what's mine is his," replied the other.

"None of that; I don't allow that and I'll hit anyone on the snout who breaks my rule."

Everything being agreed, I beg for two No. 9 cartridges to fill up my revolver, saying that I had made good use of the missing ones. The journalist remembers that the policeman had been killed by two shots, and puts his hand in his pocket and crumples up the paper.

Fau goes off, having paid with a ten-dollar note for what had been taken and for some food he had distributed amongst his guests, repeating that he was an honourable man. Before he opened the door he hesitated, picked up his three bottles of red wine and raised his hand:

"So-long, comrades."

We didn't reply. The beggars had gone and there remain a few out-of-works sleeping fast, with their heads on a table. Nicanor takes Fau's note, lights a match, and burns it on a plate, on the counter. Then he beckons me and whispers:

"Watch your step with Fau."

"Why?"

"He is a spy."

I stare at him. That isn't the kind of thing to say about a man. Nicanor stirs the ashes on the plate:

"This money came from the police. Have him followed and you'll be convinced."

Then quite quietly he throws away the ashes, sits down and begins to read *The Watchman.* I come back. The comrades from Barcelona, and Ricart are detailed to watch Fau tonight. The rest of us go off hurriedly. I take a roundabout way to Cipriano's house, and the others go off towards Moncloa. We are to join them again exactly at midnight close to the river at Laundry-station No. 6.

I take the key and open the street door. It is almost a country house with the apartments round a court. The moon is shining, but the passages are so dark that I can hardly see my fingers. I don't hear a sound except someone snoring, and a partridge calling in a cage somewhere near. What a time to think of calling! It must be crazy.

Sometimes even animals go mad, and I remember the horse dancing in the Plaza de Neptuno. But this trick of singing at night when one is in a cage, is a thing I've done myself, because at night one's voice carries farther as if one were free.

The apartment is No. 37. The door chain has been put handy, and I've only to pull it. When I come in, I see Cipriano in his shirt-sleeves oiling a revolver. He tells me to speak low because his mate and the children are asleep.

"Have you managed to get the cable?"

He showed it me coiled round his body between his shirt and his vest.

"It is almost a centimetre in calibre. With it we can probably smash up even the dynamos."

Samar once said to me that anarchism was a religion, and I thought of Cipriano as one of its priests. Of course that's only a way of speaking. Religion and priests are rubbish.

We were just opening the door when Cipriano's oldest boy appeared, dressed, washed, and with tidy hair. The father asked:

"Where do you come from?"

He is eleven years old and his nose is shiny.

"Let me go with you. I know already that you are going to 'act'." Cipriano kept hold of his revolver and the boy couldn't keep his eyes off it. The father couldn't help showing me his satisfaction, but he shook his head. The kid insisted.

"Come on, father; I can help you. I know all the detectives by sight." Cipriano hesitated. Eagerness shone in the boy's eyes. Cipriano took him by the neck and pushed him in front:

"Come on, then, boy, and your father will show you how to finish off these swine of *bourgeois*."

The boy went out, frisking like a little dog with sportsmen. He ran in and out of the moonlight, and sabotage now became a sport for children. Once in the street, we set off for the place of "action". The boy ran on ahead, exploring. Before we turned a corner, he had a look to see that the way was clear. Although he said nothing, Cipriano was very pleased about his son. There was no knowing how far he would go, now that he showed such willingness at that age.

On the road to the laundries, once below Moncloa, nothing particular happened, although we changed our direction twice to avoid suspicious groups of which the kid warned us. There was bright moonlight and that helped us in the country, as the shadows concealed us better than if there had been no moon, and the expanses of light let us see anything that might happen round about. When we arrived, all were there. Seven of us in all. Cipriano and Samar undertook the delicate part of the job; we five watched behind them. Graco, who seemed drunk, although not from wine which he never touched; Juan Segovia, strong and ruddy, nineteen years old but looking more like thirty-five; Santiago, an excellent organizer; and Buenaventura, a grey little fellow who sells irreligious papers in front of the churches and every two or three days can't avoid having a row with some young swell! Cipriano and Samar re-examine the material. The boy has climed on a hillock and is keeping a look out. We were lucky in having chosen this meeting-place, because there is linen exposed at the laundries and from a distance we may be confused with that. Cipriano asks for the two other pieces of cable and the insulating suits. There are two pairs of gloves but only one rubber suit. Samar says that with only one pair of gloves no one must dare to manipulate wires carrying a voltage of 120,000. The rest of us are distressed at not having brought more material, and it is agreed that Cipriano shall wear the suit and both pairs of gloves, and do the manipulation by himself, Samar going with him only as helper. Cipriano has slung round him the three lengths of cable and has put on the suit and the gloves. He has made a double hook at the end of each bit of cable. He gives Samar his revolver, and they move away from us after having once more verified the position of the transformer, the metal post and their surroundings. When they have gone on about two hundred yards, we follow them, our revolvers in our hands. Cipriano, with his liking for the solemn side of things, had said to us:

"Don't forget that here are two men whose lives you must defend at all costs."

Then, without waiting for a reply, off they went. They reach the foot of the transformer, and, without hestitating, Cipriano climbs up by the metal steps. Samar watches down below, a revolver in each hand; his eyes question all round. We are about one hundred yards away. Everything seems to be going like clockwork. But presently Samar says something to Cipriano, who hesitates and then goes on climbing. Three cables enter the transformer on one side and three leave it on the other. More than a hundred thousand volts have to undergo the transformation necessary to adapt them to the industrial requirements of the city, to lighting and domestic purposes. Once he reached the top, Cipriano verified the condition of his helmet and insulating suit. A hair-wide contact through a scratch in a glove would be enough to turn him into a cinder. But Cipriano is prudent in everything. Quickly he attaches to a low-tension cable the end of one of the cables he has with him, and leaves the other end free. We look over to the river, to the lights of La Bombilla, to Rosales. Santiago is getting annoyed because so far there is no one to fire at. At the foot of Rosales, the North Station displays its beehive-like ranges of lighted windows. Graco mutters in a transport:

"To electrocute *bourgeois* Madrid now thronging the cafés and hoping that we are going to be crushed! To smash the motors of the blacklegs! To burn the fuses, send invisible shocks through the electric heaters of their silken-sheeted beds, the curling-tongs of their scented bitches, the electric stoves where their fine suppers are cooking!"

I nudge his elbow:

"Shut up! Graco."

But he goes on:

"It is the revolution, my boy."

Cipriano connected one of the low-tension cables with one of high tension. Half Rosales and Bombilla were darkened. I thought I heard something hissing, on the other side of the river, like the frying of brains or of eels. I thought also that smoke was appearing. All that I was certain about was the presence of a black pall over half Madrid. Graco trembled and said:

"Urbano, this is a historical night. Within five years we'll be celebrating this date, and instead of putting lights out, we'll be illuminating Madrid until it glows like gold. How about it, Urbano?"

"Shut up, damn you."

The second and third wires have now been connected and the rest of Madrid, all that we can see from here, is quenched in darkness. A single man's will has accomplished that. The windows of the Northern Railway Company, the lines, Rosales, Moncloa, all plunged into silence. At my side Santiago says:

"Civilization and mechanical progress have another side to them, my good *bourgeois*!"

Cipriano climbed down hurriedly. He let himself fall from the last ten feet and came running to us with Samar. He was in great spirits.

"The blacklegs who go into houses or workshops to repair the light will be electrocuted. The dynamos at Soler's factory must be pouring out flames. One hundred and twenty thousand volts over a part of Madrid must be like a rain of fire."

The small boy sees that all has been done, and joins us. Where are we to go? It will be best to separate and join again at dawn. Graco looks all round; the whole of the industrial districts of Carabanchel and of Cuatro Caminos have disappeared in a black pool. Graco says he wants to sing, and in a joke I threaten him with my revolver. Suddenly Graco looks as the sky and pours out a choice selection of insults, of *bourgeois* blasphemies and of evil-smelling and bitter words.

"What's the matter with you?"

"That great bitch," he said, pointing to the moon; "what's the use of our sabotage if she goes on giving light?"

Cipriano points out to us that the lower part of Argüelles is not served by the same line and that all the same its lights have gone. From that we know that our comrades of the other lot have done their job too. Samar insists that we must separate, and must certainly not go to our own houses to sleep. He gives Cipriano his revolver again. We all carry ours in our hands. Graco has stayed behind. He goes on cursing and pointing at the moon, and suddenly raises his arm, aims and fires a shot; then another "Paf! Paf!" We take to our heels. Graco goes on "Paf! Paf!" until he has emptied the magazine. Then he loads again.

LA LUNA, dimming herself, "Woe is me!"

Graco has stayed behind. Has he gone mad? He fires and at the same time jumps on the mound.

THE MOON: "Are there no Shock Police, not a Saviour of his country? Woe is me! It was better under the monarchy."

Graco goes on "Pif! Paf!" and insulting her until the moon completely disappears. We separate in the black darkness. Half an hour later I meet Graco and Samar at the Toledo bridge. And the others? Each of them has escaped as best he could. The effect has been magnificent, the alarm formidable. We have to pick our way here as if on a battlefield full of trenches and barbed wire. They must have put all their troops into the streets. When we were just leaving the bridge we hear a friendly voice:

"Samar! Samar!"

It comes from a girl of the Syndicate of Various Duties who was with a sabotage group charged with the job of cutting the communications of the official centres. Twenty years old. Her wages go entirely to her house to support her father, a Catholic and a slacker, and two sisters who keep on reproaching her for her opinions. Emilia is delighted at meeting us. She looks at us cautiously:

"Is is safe to speak?"

Graco protested:

"Damn it all, don't you know us?"

She is a resolute and brave girl. She wears a blue cloak. She tells us that although the telephone exchanges of the Home Office and the War Office were closely guarded she had managed to seize a moment when attention was distracted, to place a bomb.

"You?"

"Who else? Certainly me. The others were on the watch. We got away, and five minutes after we heard the explosion."

Emilia added:

"Eight thousand sets of lines out of action!"

It was dangerous to stand longer. Graco made a fuss of her, kissed her, and asked her how long she had been a member of the organization. Emilia said it was three months.

"Where are you going now?" I ask.

"Off home. To my horrid little house and my horrid family. I must get to sleep, for tomorrow I rise early."

"Is there a meeting?"

"No, but I am going to confession and to hear mass."

We stood in complete astonishment.

"To confess?"

"Yes. About the bomb. All the same, I won't tell the priest when it was or where. I'll tell him, too, that I am not asking for a penance. If he absolves me, good and well. If not, so much the worse for him. My conscience is quite clear."

Graco got angry just as quickly as he had become enthusiastic before:

"You are fanatical *bourgeoise,* and if you did do it, it was only a bit of hysteria."

This Graco is always like that. He never sees things straight. I defend her, but it is clear that she isn't annoyed with him. "And you?" she asked us.

To sleep, but we don't know where yet.

We kept quiet about our sabotage lest she should tell about that also to the priest. She is delighted with the action of tonight. She says that a state of war is about to be declared at any moment, and that the sabotage in the south-east has had splendid results. The *bourgeoisie* is done for. Of course there have been casualties and she is very sorry about them, but all the same at the funeral we also had had a smack at the *bourgeois*. She asked if we knew where to go to sleep, and when we told her we didn't know, she suggested No. 9, General San Martin Street, where people could go who had nothing but their membership cards. It was an anarchist who was well off, and had some warehouses of his own and a small house. He had never been marked down, and he helped needy comrades with money or by giving them shelter. I let her speak on, although I know that comrade myself; he really deserves all that she says about him.

"Have you given the address to any others?" I ask.

"No."

"Then we'll go there."

We hurry. Graco is enraged about this girl comrade who will place a bomb at night and next morning confess to a priest and take communion. He repents of having kissed her. "A woman like that," he says, "is quite capable of putting a bomb tomorrow in our syndicates." Samar bursts into laughter:

"What a face the priest will make!"

I also am in a state of joy from having spoken with the virtuous Emilia. It puts me in good humour to know that even those enslaved by *bourgeois* superstition can't help joining with us. Samar laughs, but for other reasons; he sees only the humour of the case. General San Martin Street wasn't near. But not very far off. Emilia had warned us to be careful because there were two telephone stations in the street which were important and were sure to be watched. But Graco has recovered his good humour. The darkness is blacker the farther we go, and the moon has disappeared completely. He makes some savage jokes, but although they aren't very good, he changes his voice so funnily that we almost tumble over with laughter. Near the viaduct shots are heard. Samar, listening closely, warns us:

"They are rifle shots. Up above there, they must be in strength."

Graco outdoes himself:

"These *bourgeois* always are getting into a panic. What can they be frightened about? There is really no reason!"

He says it with the voice of an imbecile and we burst into laughter. I make them stop. We are at the opening to General

San Martin Street. Graco swears that he didn't know that San Martin was a general. We can hear the feet of horses behind us. In the street at the side a halt is called. Clear enough. All the forces have been sent into the streets with urgent orders. In two breaths we get into our street and suddenly stop. As we can't see the numbers on the houses, there is nothing for it but that Samar should go back, and, flattening himself against the wall, count the houses. But there are two doors close together and we don't know if they belong to one house or to two. I think that No. 9 is one of the two and Samar thinks it is the next house. Graco suggests a plan. I stand against the door and he climbs on my shoulders and strikes a match. If he can't see the number lighted by the match, Samar may see it from below. There is no other way. If it isn't No. 9, at least we'll see which is the house. We agree, and with stifled laughs and polite words I hoist up Graco. His knees are bony and hurt my back. However, he gets up on my shoulders, flattens against the wall, pulls out his matches and takes hold of one, but he has hardly struck it, when a Mauser volley clatters out, and lime and bits of the wall fall down on us. The match has gone out and Graco has a very bad shock and we think that he is wounded, but it was only his suppressed laughter. Samar calls out in a whisper:

"It is number nine, the nine."

"Are you sure?" asks Graco.

"Yes. But why not climb up again and convince youself?"

Graco thinks he can do without that, and we are still laughing when the door is opened and a voice asks what is happening. The moment we are identified we enter. We wish to explain, but there is no need and we are taken straight to a room with three mattresses. They bring us a candle, and when we are alone Samar scolds us for doing our sabotage in such a way that we haven't wardrobes for our drawers. We go on laughing. All this is natural, for we are a bit excited. When we have put out the light we exchange a few serious words about what we have to do in the morning. Silently we are all putting to ourselves the same simple question:

"For what is the struggle? What is our goal?"

Graco says:

"The goal is destruction of capitalistic domination."

Samar says:

"The extinction of the *bourgeois* spirit and of the capitalistic theory."

And me:

"Free communism."

Clear enough, mine is the most concrete. Graco doesn't trouble about the government of the future if only capitalism be destroyed. Samar is interested much more in morals and logic than in systems. But we are all for revolution.

Chapter 11

An Informer in Trouble

FAU SPENT the night in Cuatro Caminos and in the morning went to the northern part of the city after having slunk through it like a hunted man. Looked as if he were wounded. Winged. Sallent, Ricart, and Escuder had passed the night following him, and had been very successful. First of all he wasn't nearly so drunk as he pretended. He went to No. 72 Gran Via, watched as if he were being followed, went in and shortly came out again. Thinking that he was alone, he counted out some notes and put them in his trousers pocket, keeping what seemed a larger bundle in the pocket of his jacket. Ricart noted the number of the house. They continued to follow Fau as he went down Gran Via, turned into Infantes, and stood still for a minute, spying all round the Central Police Station. He turned to look round several times, and it was really a miracle that he didn't notice his followers. Then he went boldly into the office.

He went straight to the information bureau, where he was received coldly by an elderly man with a grim appearance and frowning forehead.

"Anything new?" he asked.

Fau sat down firmly and confidently. Not because he was at home among the files tied with red tape, or that he was in sympathy with the police whom instinctively he despised and feared. But during his life he had very seldom worked, and always at casual jobs in which he could never be certain of the next week's bread. Life for him was a dismal gamble and since he was a boy he could not remember ever being sure of a half-crown in his pocket. He saw that on Saturdays the cashier was never quite certain that he had enough money to pay the wages. That sort of thing demoralized him, also because he could never assume initiative. Someone had to tell him, "Carry these stones to the mason's yard, or those planks to the scaffolding." He relied blindly on his jobs and not on himself. He saw that there was plenty of money in the police station, always ready to hand. It didn't depend on capricious persons, but on the solid and impersonal revenue of the State. Fau felt confident there. He was afraid of the guards and of the detectives, but he felt at home with the official and with the two typists, none of whom looked in any way like the police. The outdoor men were in another part of the building, the side facing Marques de Valdeiglesias Street, where there was a store of helmets and firearms and some dark lock-ups. Before replying to the old man, he scratched the back of his ear:

"Nothing; only a prohibited meeting."

The official, without raising his eyes from a sheet of ruled paper, asked:

"How many?"

"Seven or eight."

"Then it wasn't a prohibited meeting. How often have I to tell you? There must be at least nineteen. What people?"

"Syndicalists."

The official laid down his pen and folded his hands on his portfolio:

"Was there any sabotage?"

"I expected it," said Fau confidently, "but I convinced myself that tonight at least they weren't doing anything up there." He pointed towards Cuatro Caminos. The old man rang a bell. An orderly replied.

"Take this gentleman to the Assistant Director"—then turning to Fau—"go and tell him everything you know."

They took him along passages which were wide and well-lighted and left him in an office where there was nobody. When the Assistant Director came in, he felt uncomfortable. That man had the air of a policeman. He sat down on the arm of his chair and looked at him doubtfully. Fau repeated what he had said, and added comments so detailed that the police officer began to wonder:

"How did you find out that?"

Then Fau began to tell the tale. The Assistant Director seemed convinced and Fau added:

"You believe me and you'll see that nothing will happen."

At that moment all the lights went out. The beehive hum inside the building grew louder. Orderlies came in with candles and pocket electric torches. No one took much notice. Whilst someone went to the fuse-box to repair the damage, the Assistant Director took out his revolver and put it on the table.

"And about the men who killed our detective yesterday? Do you know anything?"

"I have a clue. Write it down."

The police officer took up a pencil and Fau gave him five

names. The Assistant Director knew some of them, and the two exchanged further comments on the men.

"The fact is that it seems there were only two men. And one of these fired the shot."

Fau interrupted him:

"I am not going to say that all five were in it, but I'll bet my shirt that among the five were the two."

The names were Liberto García Ruiz, Elenio Margraf, José Crousell, Helios Pérez and Miguel Palacios. Of these, the first two and the last were well known as organizers and propagandists. Fau knew that the Assistant Director had a personal grudge against them, and he himself had no taste for them, as their skill in questions of organization, the balance of their judgments, and the clarity of what they said had humbled him when he pretended to be "active", and although he could endure such qualities in a *bourgeois,* in a person who was his social superior, he couldn't endure them in a comrade who could put a hand on his shoulder. And so these names were written down on a sheet of paper. The Assistant Director rang and gave the slip to an orderly and told him to bring the records if there were any.

Fau added:

"Of course you must have them."

At that moment the Director, the Head of the Police, and two inspectors came in. They spoke excitedly. The Director demanded explanations from the chiefs, the inspectors and everyone else. Fau got up and stepped aside. He was unable to imagine anything like what had really happened. Although the Director mentioned high tension, darkness, and various other details—short circuits, fires and even electrocutions—Fau didn't understand in the least. The Director-General went out to see the Minister, gesticulating, shouting and threatening his subordinates. When he had gone, the Assistant Director at once confronted Fau with the inspectors. Then Fau understood what had happened. Sabotage. They had done their sabotage, and he had known nothing about it. The Assistant Director and the inspectors kept looking at each other in silence. One of them turned to Fau.

"And so there was no sabotage?"

He smiled like a hyena, showing his teeth. Fau thought that he was even more of a policeman than the Assistant Director. He tried to laugh himself, and he shrugged his shoulders, but the Inspector ordered him to walk ahead. When they make a man walk in front, it is because they regard him as a culprit.

Before then, the Inspector had told him to follow. In the corridor, without stopping, he was asked:

"And so the syndicates don't trust you?"

"Not much, but I do what I can."

Their footsteps echoed on the pavement of the corridor. The Inspector suddenly ordered him to stop in front of a door through which he passed. While Fau was waiting for him to come out, a fat man with a wide-brimmed hat appeared, stood looking at him with his finger on his coat collar whilst he chewed a cigar.

"This way."

He pointed to another passage. They met one of the employees who was being carried, as he had burns on his arm caused by a shock when he was trying to change the fuses. Fau, feeling the eye of the agent on the back of his neck, thought:

"This man, now, he is more of a policeman than any of the others!"

They came into a kind of lobby where there were fifteen or twenty arrested men. At his first glance, Fau recognized three or four of them and instinctively stopped and tried to retreat. They were syndicalist workmen. They had with them an important communist. There was also Miguel Palacios, one of those whom he had indicated to the Director as possibly the murderer of the detective. He saw his thin face and his hands tied behind his back. Fau stepped back and collided with the agent. The light was pale and raw as if a lemon had been fastened behind each of the six candles. The prisoners showed the uneasy exhaustion of animals trapped in a cage. The agent raised his head and stared at Fau. Then he gave him a slight push, and they crossed the lobby. At the other side Fau protested:

"Why have you brought me here? These prisoners know me and now I'll not be able to do anything. They won't trust me."

"Why not?"

"They've seen me with you."

The agent laughed and chewed his cigar.

"Fool! How do they know if you are an informer or a prisoner?" He continued laughing and chewing. He stopped his little chuckles. He summoned two policemen and at the same time told Fau, thinking it necessary to explain because of his sullen appearance, his puffed-out chest and his solemn face:

"Didn't you say that the syndicalists wouldn't trust you any more? We are going to restore your credit with them."

The guards brought some canes, and the agent searched Fau, took away his revolver and handcuffed him. At the first blow he remarked:

"You can't yell too much! It is for your good. We are giving you a great opportunity. You are paying for your carelessness of last night and your insolence to the Assistant Director. And at the same time you will win the confidence of the syndicalists again, because not one of them who hears you will doubt that you are suffering for the cause!"

The police gave him two or three strokes to show that they appreciated the joke. Fau stood them without crying out. As he did not cry out, a heavy-jowled fellow hit him on the nose with his belt-buckle. Fau writhed and yelled. The Sergeant consoled him:

"We are making a man of you, Fau: don't take it so hardly."

The air, set in motion by the vibrations of the rods and straps, made the candles flicker. Shadows danced on the walls covered with maps and statistics. The Sergeant with a grim smile inquired:

"Was there sabotage, Fau? What do you say now about it, you son of a she-goat?"

Fau writhed and shuddered. The police went on beating him with hearty goodwill. But they withdrew one of them who was putting all his might into it, sweating, and red with anger—this happens often and if they let it go on too long they kill a victim—and the others went on beating Fau more placidly. Fau screamed and begged for mercy. But he uttered no rash words against his torturers. They were doing their duty, and beating a man was only an occasional incident in their job. He yelled and snuffled. The blows sounded on his neck and shoulders like pistol-shots, and the rods whistled through the air. The beating lasted a quarter of an hour, until a blow on the eyes made him reel and fall down. He passed over his face a hand incredibly inflamed and purple. The police removed his handcuffs and had him taken to a cellar where they threw a couple of buckets of water over his head. The Sergeant then turned him out of doors, saying:

"Now let us have some better work from you."

"Yes, sir."

He was going off, but the agent called him back:

"I guess you won't again tell us the tale that they distrust you."

"No, sir."

As soon as he had turned the corner, he began to inspect

his sores. He had four or five weals on the back, one so bad that blood was oozing from it, and on one side of his forehead there was a lump as if he were growing a horn. He stopped to pull a trouser leg above the right knee. He searched his pockets. He had been given back his revolver. His money was there all right. He smiled as well as his face would let him, and setting off again in high content, grunted:

"Not so bad!"

When he reached Cibeles, he went to the fountain, and as it was now full dawn, he could look at himself in the water. He moved his head from side to side and examined the reflection of his distorted face. He got up and laughed so loudly that some early pigeons, startled, flew off. He went down towards the Prado, securing his trousers at the hips with his wrists, for his hands were so swollen that they seemed about to burst.

"That's nothing," he laughed, knowing himself to be free, with money in his pocket, under a clear sky in the soothing morning air. "With a good beef-steak inside me, I'll be all right.

He went to eat his beef-steak at Atocha. But as he was descending the street, the inflammation got worse, and his face broke out in spots. Fau felt his teeth, tried to chew and leaped with joy to find that they were all right.

He reached the Atocha garden, humming with joy. But the morning light, a clear metallic blue, came slowly and kept away from Fau as if to avoid him. Fau came into the crystal paths of the day, a sorry tramp. He came into May in the guise of a February carnival scarecrow, his face daubed with red and blue, his gait staggering, his tatters showing his nakedness. A woman's spirit in a hairy, bearded body. The dawn sang over a sheet of silver, the lovely flowers of the Retiro and the Botanic Garden, and Fau, looking at the blue sky, thought of the blue sea of the maps on schoolroom walls. He limped a bit, but had great faith in what the beef-steak would do for him.

But he was much disappointed to find the inn still closed, and he walked round the garden waiting. He was more than ever the deplorable carnival scarecrow in the alien light of May. The police had bestowed on him the ritual beating which they keep for those who won't play their part. "Skilfully questioned", is the phrase. Fau had nothing to say, but all the same he had been questioned with great skill.

He was very different from the strikers, from the revolutionaries, from the workers. But even different from veritable tramps. Enemy of the one and separated from the others! The shadows fled from him—he couldn't find out about the sabotage—and the light kept away from him not to stain itself. He wasn't a man although he talked loudly and blasphemed. Men don't sell themselves and aren't traitors. Still less was he a woman, although he lied to help himself. They didn't beat him as a revolutionary. They didn't trust him or respect him as an ally. They beat him as an informer, they would have beaten—other times they had already beaten him—as a revolutionary. He was neither man nor woman. A carnival scarecrow who speaks in a piping voice and has false nipples under his white jacket, a broom in his hand and a handkerchief on his head over his straw hat. He kept on wandering round the garden. When he saw that the tavern was being opened, he crossed to it. He hoped to ask the tavern-keeper, "Do you know me?" And that he would raise his hat-brim in astonishment. But he only thumped the table with his forearm and shouted for a steak. The waiter told him that there were no steaks as no animals had been killed the day before because of the strike. And they didn't expect any today.

He got up and went off towards Vallecas. On the way he fingered his revolver and cursed the strikers. What a farce that a few workmen grouped in syndicates could have more power than some good *bourgeois* bank-notes! Ought one not to have command of the world when his pockets were full? On his way he noticed that in the South Station there was more doing than usual. The trains came in slowly and the engines wandered about in the network of lines and sidings. Groups of workmen read manifestos and disputed. Fau squinted with the only eye that was open and nodded. All that meant a strike. Material things have their own language, and at that moment the high roofs of dark slate, the funnels of the engines, the dirty tenders and the grey connecting-rods all prophesied stoppage. But more than from all these things together, Fau got the impression of a strike from a stoker who was walking hesitatingly between the engines, with his badge of duty hanging in his hand.

He went on through Pacífico. He felt that his own vigour and natural force were weakening in the vigour and power of his surroundings: the houses, the trees, the church tower. Without knowing what had happened, he felt a mite, in the mass of the city, as if he had been disintegrated, a logical result considering that Fau weighed only eleven stone and had a height under six feet. His beating had left him no personality to distinguish him from the trees and the tramway-posts. He stopped. He took deep breaths. He was just going on again, when he heard behind the roll of drums. He stood still, and turning round, ascertained that it was a picket marching to proclaim the "state of war". Then he became wholly the carnival scarecrow as if with upraised broom, false breasts and bells hung from his belt, and set off running towards Vallecas in search of a "good beef-steak". He went on feeling resolute and safe. With each footstep he crossed a flagstone. Once more he felt assured in his surroundings. "To defend my beef-steak, there is the army, and then the police, and then the Civil Guard, then the Shock Police, then the cavalry, then soldiers of the line, and then the navy. The navy is something to think about." Not only did he now feel himself in harmony with the real world; he surpassed it; and now the tree and the light standard were what had been beaten at the police station. Far off he heard the drums rolling and the shrill call of a bugle.

He reached the bridge. There Pacífico opened into a large workers' suburb. He entered an inn and asked for a beef-steak. The innkeeper looked at him in surprise.

"They have made a Christ of me, don't you think? This is the work of the police." He had to go off again when he had drunk a glass. He was comforted by the charity of the innkeeper, who refused to let him pay for the drink, and that and the pain of the wounds made him feel for the moment an active revolutionary, almost a martyr. The suburb was quiet. The workmen were in their beds. They didn't wish to go to any work on which the *bourgeoisie* fattened. They wished only to go on sleeping in the illusion that they would wake up to a world without *bourgeoisie* and without slavery. Fau saw the closed houses and the women at their early morning tasks.

He entered yet another inn and asked for a beef-steak, but again there was none. It seemed to him incredible that the will of the labourers in the slaughter-houses and in transport could put one in the danger of not being able to get a beef-steak, not even as medicine. Another inn which he entered made jests about his request:

"A beef-steak? Would you like a chop cut from a banker?"

Fau was bold enough to reply:

"Shut up; I'd eat the blessed sacrament; you make my mouth water." He clicked his tongue against the roof of his mouth and went off. It was now six in the morning, and still no beef-steak. Leaving the last narrow street, he came out into the country. Beside the road there was a petrol station. Lower down, the reveille sounded in the barracks of the 75th Light Artillery. "State of war." All the army behind him. He went up to the petrol pumps and stopped to relieve himself alongside them. Listening to the reveille, he said to himself almost unconsciously: "The army; that is at my service. I make water and they salute me." But there was no beef-steak. He rubbed his eyes. He couldn't open the right one. Down below there was a small stream and he knelt beside it, but as he knelt there was a sharp pain in his knees. He pulled himself together and took out a dirty handkerchief. A wasp buzzed round him, circling in the first rays of the sun. He dried himself, put back the handkerchief and sat down. In front a cow was grazing. Steam was drawn from its loins by the sun. There was a long halter from its muzzle. Fau stared all round. There was no one in sight. "All the same," he thought, "the army and the Civil Guard protect me from behind." He crossed the stream and took hold of the halter. The cow followed him docilely. He tied it down tightly to a branch of a felled tree, remembering his time as a day-labourer on a farm and afterwards as a slaughterer's helper. He took out a knife, unsheathed it, and passed his fingers along the edge with gusto. The cow was brown, with white spots. He fondled the head and then suddenly with the knife made a semicircular cut above the shoulder. He completed the cut below and tugged. A bellow, loud and deep, seemed to come out of the bowels of the earth. The animal bent its leg double, and held its head in the air, the eyes wide open, not understanding what had happened. Fau ran off with his bleeding prize. He cleaned his knife in the ground and replaced it. Then he stopped to skin the piece, unsheathing his knife again, and then took himself to an eating-house some way off. They knew him there, as he had a room on the second floor.

"Have you any beef-steaks?" he asked mechanically.

They said they had them because there were three over from the day before. Fau was disconcerted for the moment. Then he recovered himself and said:

"They must be stale."

He threw his own bit of flesh on the counter.

"Roast this for me at once."

They questioned him whilst the old woman was cooking the meat, and he told them that he had fallen over the embankment and had just escaped being run over by the Valencia express. But nothing was said about his beef-steak. Presently a cloth was spread on the table and on it were wine and bread and a dish heaped with the roast meat. He ate gluttonously, putting his fork down only to seize bread and the jug of wine, and the olives, convincing himself that they all were his due. From time to time he scratched his head with the fork. From a distance came the bellowing of the cow which gave Fau a feeling of triumph. When he finished he went upstairs to go to bed. The staircase had windows open to the fields moist with Spring. Fau laughed and patted his belly. He tried to open his eye and did so without too much difficulty. The medicine was beginning to act. The bellowing filled the morning with pain, and Fau laughed in his safety.

"It is good to be full of meat," he thought.

When he reached his room, Eladio, the guard, came out on his way to duty. It was a modest lodging-house, but clean and well-managed by a widow who worked night and day to bring up her family. Fau asked if there was any news.

"What kind of news?" asked the guard in surprise.

"Have the police not been here?"

"No."

They separated and Fau went in, unable to understand why José Crousell and Helios Pérez were still free; these were two young workers who lived in the same house and whose names he had given as possibly the murderers of the detective. He stopped beside the room they occupied—a bedroom opening from the dining-room where shadows could be seen through the glass door. "They haven't taken them away yet," he thought. Seated at the table, a detective was breakfasting. He also lived there. Fau, preparing for eventualities, said to him:

"Probably these lads are for gaol. They have been too active in the syndicates."

Then he went off to his own room, thinking over the tiresome sense of their superiority these two used to give him when they talked about anything. Besides, one of them used to wear gentlemen's clothes and the other used to clean his teeth in front of him. Probably to humble him. It was well that their names had been put amongst the five. The detective went on drinking his coffee thinking that in private life he wasn't going to bother about anyone, and that he was an officer who carried out orders and nothing more. Fau coughed, and with the air there came in the bellowing of the cow. He began to laugh. He felt much better already. He undressed and went to bed.

In the dark bedroom José and Helios, two working printers, were kneeling at a trunk open in a corner. Inside the trunk there was a case of printing-type. They were delegates of the Ward and they were setting up in the dark and without proofs a manifesto which had to be distributed at seven o'clock. José held a handerchief to his mouth to ward off the metallic dust from the types, and was composing the lines in silence and giving them to Helios to put in the frame. There were still some to finish. In a quarter of an hour the two would go out looking as if they had slept well. Probably they would say "good morning" to the detective and take the frame to a printing press close by, where, without the proprietor knowing about it, in an hour and a half eight thousand copies would have been struck off. And afterwards? Ah, then eight thousand red pigeons—pigeons of war—would fly over the quays and railway lines, over the shunting-stations and cranes, and at the cry of the spirit of destruction, the trains would be abandoned and the asthmatic engines would cease to puff. Of course the Carnival Scarecrow knew that Helios had bought a fine new pair of boots, and that when he had put them on, they would take him to prison. But since it was certain that neither Helios nor José had had anything to do with the murder of the agent, Fau would be haled to the Central Station again, and would suffer under the rods, bellowing like a calf.

Chapter 12

Samar and Villacampa

AT DAWN the police came again and took possession of our house. It seems as if they have turned our house into a trap to catch any syndicalists who may come there. Or perhaps they suspect that weapons are concealed in it, and they wish to hinder people from getting them. My grandmother has taken refuge in the house opposite with Mrs. Cleta, and every now and then leans out over its balcony. She has changed her tactics and doesn't speak so much to the police. She replies to their questions with a dirty song, in which she talks of them as sexual perverts. The poor thing has the mad fancy that they have hidden her son's body, and she wishes to hunt all over Madrid to find it. We couldn't see what they did with it, because they pushed us out of the Plaza de Neptuno. My grandmother at this very moment is leaning out over the balcony and calling to the police. She has rolled up her sleeves and is smacking the railing saying:

"This for the Director-General of Public Security!"

She gives another smack and screams:

"And this for you!"

And again:

"And this for the one with the spectacles!"

She is compromising Mrs. Cleta, who is the widow of a soldier. I go into the street with the cock. The poor bird is badly upset. The cat came back at dawn, thin and with its fur all ruffled. That's what is going to happen to all of us. Grandmother and Mrs. Cleta are already like that. I am staying in the street, in case comrades should arrive, and I can warn them off with a sign. The cock walks step by step with me, or rather he takes three steps to each one of mine. I carry my cap in my hand and my revolver in my cap. The policeman with the spectacles has given me the glad eye, but I stood staring at him as if to say, "If I were a man I'd split open your face." I didn't invent that way of staring and making a man understand what I meant, myself, but I learnt it from a young gipsy girl when a swell tried to take her on.

On my way, I got close to the railing of the officers quarters at the barracks. The walls are of rose-coloured brick and are full of sunlight. Near Amparo's room they are covered with green creepers and blue flowers, all so clean and fresh, that I'd like to go naked and wrap them round my head and waist. But if you have anything to do with the *bourgeoisie,* you must be covered up with clothes. Looking at the blue flowers and remembering Samar's letter, the love affairs of Samar and Amparo seem to be like the coloured post cards they sell in shops. They are about to kiss. The pair of them good-looking, and all dressed up. And in the corner a white pigeon. I am disappointed with Samar. I thought that he had more sense, that he was an anarchist, and knew how to swim. Then I saw him letting the police get hold of that important document, and found that he is a communist, and not too much of that. But, and this is the truth, he is a good comrade. And although he writes for the newspapers and talks fine words like the *bourgeoisie,* it isn't a reason to denounce him before the organizations.

Now come Ricart and two I don't know. I make a signal to them to clear out, but they want to talk to me, and I put the cock under my arm and go to them. Ricart is completely worn out.

"Can't we get a sleep in your house?"

I tell them what has happened. The other two are also tired. Ricart tells me that they are comrades from Catalonia and we shake hands. Before going off they commission me to see the comrades of the committee of groups and to tell them that Nicanor was right, that they had proved it, and that they would give particulars in writing as soon as they could. They repeat it to me two or three times and then go off. Now I have a mission. I am very glad that the comrades have trusted me with something, for now my revolver won't be a toy; I am carrying it for a purpose. Now I am not going to be stopped; for I'll defend my freedom until I've repeated the words of the message to all the members of the committee. I'll know how to let anyone have it, in the chest. It is true that my revolver isn't loaded, but when one of us has to fire, the revolver really isn't much use. What the *bourgeoisie* want, is to corner us, and for us to fire, and then the steam-hammer of justice falls on us and crushes us. That is what I think.

It is nearly ten o'clock and I've had no breakfast. The sun is hot. I go to Auntie Cleta's house and they give me lump chocolate, bread and an orange. I go out to eat my breakfast in the street. I sit down on a stone, the cock comes to pick bread out of my hand, and so we share our food. It was almost eleven when Samar turned up. I go to meet him and we walk away together. I didn't expect him, and I don't know why I go, but I can't help walking with him. Samar stops and stares at me:

"Where are you going with that?"

He means the cock. I shrug my shoulders.

"I was afraid that the police would eat him. They eat everything they can find in the house. My grandmother had left some bits of sausage sprayed with rat-poison, but I don't believe that rat-poison will be any good for police." Samar doesn't listen. He pulls out some papers and scans them. I squint at them, but don't understand a word. They are ridiculous words: "Geyuwrewer, suhexmifoc, fimoxsamic, dihenthopay", etcetera, all written on a typewriter, in capitals, on oiled paper.

"I have to take this," he said, "to the Barcelona aeroplane."

He says nothing about the sabotage; nor about how the strike is going on, although anyone can see that it is complete, at least in my district. We never speak about the past, but about the future. For us there is no yesterday, only tomorrow. I ask him if he is a member of the committee of groups, and when he says "Yes", I give him Ricart's message. Samar stops and looks at me:

"Is that what he told you?"

"Yes."

"The scoundrel; we'll have to get rid of him."

We walk in silence. I don't understand what he meant about Ricart's message. Presently he asks me:

"You've made up your mind?"
"Yes, I am going to obey the order."
"Do you know where to go to see them?"
"Yes, most of them."
"I'll also tell any comrades whom I meet."

I asked him to tell me how he thought things were going. He waited and then did it rather reluctantly. Apparently the situation is very serious. Always when there is a critical situation, the comrades refuse to discuss it with me, or only discuss it with reserve. They think that it is not a woman's business, and still less the business of young girls. But suddenly Samar arouses himself and says:

"Do you know what you are carrying with these words of Ricart?"

"I don't care. That isn't my affair. I suppose that I am doing a useful service."

Samar stared in my eyes:

"You are carrying death!"

Then I felt his eyes on my yellow jersey and my bare arms, and he said: "Do you see how blue the sky is?"

I said of course, and he went on:

"A great storm is on the way. Behind it there are blackness and evil birds, my child. And also behind your lips and the words of Ricart there is death."

Perhaps he is right, but it won't be a black and evil death. And so I laugh and show my white teeth, and breathe on him so that he may see that if he is right about the sky, he is wrong about my lips.

"You women are good messengers of death."

It is clear that he was going to speak about his sweetheart, but he keeps silent. His head must be like the engines of an aeroplane when they start up. He keeps frowning and sometimes begins to say something and suddenly stops.

"Aren't you thinking about it?" he says.
I laugh: "About what?"
"About your being a messenger of death?"
"But to whom am I carrying death?"
"To a man, as if you were a passing-bell."
"Why?"
"He is a police informer."
"What is his name?"
"Fau."
"I know him. I knew already what he is."
"On your lips you carry his sentence."

I wipe them with my hand without answering. Then I laugh

and he replies only by twisting his mouth. Very good. It is right that they should kill him. Is there more to be said? We go towards the Ronda. There are foot soldiers between the houses, and the telegraph standards are guarded by soldiers. We go on in silence. Samar has given me his revolver to carry with my own, hidden in my cap.

Some Civil Guards come up and stop Samar. I go on and wait for him. The guards look me over, but as they see that I am small and look foolish—to look foolish is often an advantage, my comrade Villacampa—they don't say anything to me. Samar raises his hands. They find nothing. Then he shows them an identity card, and they let him go on his way. But first of all Samar asks them to certify that he has been searched, and they give him a stamped paper. The two of us go on in silence. When we are some way off, Samar says:

"Very well done, my child."

I tuck the cock under my arm, thinking that but for me he would have been arrested. But I don't tell him that, as I know that when you've done a person a good turn, you mustn't insist on the reasons why he should be grateful, in case he thinks he has to repay you. Although one is an anarchist, one has sense. I don't take the guards very seriously, for they seem nice fellows and they have grey coats and yellow straps. How I wish that instead of being servants of the State they were servants of the F.A.I., and that we were *bourgeois* and that they had arrested us and hit us on the head. I don't say this to him either, because it is stupid, and although our thoughts are free and sometimes foolish it isn't always necessary to say what we think. I look at Samar sideways, but he doesn't take any notice. He is thinking deep thoughts and is far away from me and all this. I want to sing, but even if I were to sing he wouldn't take any notice. The sun flashes brilliantly from the insulating cups of the telegraph standards, and the swallows, swooping on their wings, almost touch the broken tiles on a rubbish-dump.

But Samar bids me go tomorrow morning to the Artillery barracks to give some bundles of propaganda to a soldier who is already on our side. I tell him it is impossible now that there is a "state of war", for the troops are confined to their quarters, and not a single person is allowed to go in without a permit from the colonel.

"That is all right. You'll have the permit. Go in with the manifestos in a bucket and make for the kitchen. A soldier will meet you on your way. Give him the bucket and wait until he gives it you back. Then go out as if you had been to collect leavings."

The plan is good, if it works all right. Anyhow if they do take me, I am under age, and besides I can say that I didn't know what was inside. We walk on. The Ronda opens to a wide avenue. A motor-lorry comes up at full speed. It belongs to the hospital service and has a cross on it. It races past us, and turns towards the Eastern Cemetery. Samar stops and stares at it.

"Very likely," he said, "there goes your father." I heard him, as if suddenly I was being told in a gentle song that the universe was being pulled down on us. I saw Samar made sorrowful by his own suspicion, and to distract him, I told him that very likely tomorrow at the same time it would be he who was passing swiftly in the same lorry, in the same direction. Of course it was untrue, but it comforted him, and made him stop giving so much importance to the memory of my father. Samar smiled, and kept looking at me. I must be good to look at. He didn't make up his mind to tell me so, but I guessed what he was thinking. He made sure that I had guessed it, and as if he were shutting his eyes to take a plunge he said to me:

"I don't want to go a step farther until I've given you a kiss."

I stopped, stood on tiptoe and offered him my lips. Then he took my head in his hands and kissed me. I don't know how it happened, but I let the cock slip and it escaped. I pulled myself from him and ran after the cock. Between us we caught it. We went on walking. No one passed us in the Ronda. There were no buildings at one side. Samar said to me:

"And if they don't kill me today?"

He wasn't thinking about bullets but about some other kind of death which I don't understand. I am sharp enough to guess things which he doesn't say, but of course, as I am young and have little experience of life, I have sometimes only a glimpse of things which I can't explain.

"If they don't kill you today," I tell him, "so much the better, for you'll then see what is going to come of all this."

But he doesn't answer. Samar is ill, very ill.

I could cure him if he would let me, but he isn't the kind to submit. He could drag me with him I don't know where. I ask:

"Why did you kiss me?"

He shrugs his shoulders and walks on.

"Don't you know?" I insist.

He keeps silent and plucks a feather from the cock's tail and puts it in his button-hole, so that only a little piece shows. The cock cries out as if he were being murdered and I shift it to my other arm. I ask him again and he replies crossly. And so I keep silent. But I could cure him. The kiss he gave me told me the secret. I am sure I could cure him. How? I don't know. Keeping at his side. If he drags me along with him, I don't care. If they smash us up in the end, I don't care! Only thinking of it makes my head swim as it does on the last plunge of the Scenic Railway. Who knows? That letter I read was a kind of good-bye. But I can't go on in silence.

"Are you very fond of your sweetheart?"

"Yes."

"You are a *bourgeois.*"

"Perhaps you're right."

He said it with such depression that I didn't like to go on talking. But I looked at him from time to time. To see if I could find out what he is thinking. Since he was a boy he has read much and lived much, and has been happy, changing his women often, and without thinking about them more than a few minutes a week, because although he was with them, he didn't think about them, as he does now about me. He was happy, and had in his mind a set of things upon which his happiness depended. And he said—because it could be said with a gesture, without words: "Good. What more is there?" Everything is stupid and dirty and broken down, but I must seek out the best and make more use of it than anyone else, and keep a little happiness in the bottom of my heart for myself. And it may seem very good and fine to people, a kind of smiling with pity, or with the sympathy that a doctor gives to a sick child. Of course he was a little outside and not quite conscious of these things, and he didn't want them. But if the matter is there, the spirit will look after itself.

"And you?" he asked me, "haven't you a soul?"

"I? The soul is *bourgeois.*"

Now he is thinking something more complicated and I don't know what it is. The thought comes to him suddenly out of his own mind, but, none the less, he doesn't know how to express it, as happens to me when I think what the world could have been before there was a world. I wish to think and to know what I am thinking, but I can't. Then I get giddy. Perhaps he is thinking some of these thoughts which make one giddy. About love, before love exists.

"Where did you get to know her?"

He spoke as if he were speaking to himself.

"I went to the college to do something for some relations

who had a girl there. I was in the waiting-room at the same time as Colonel García del Río and his wife, acquaintances of my family. We exchanged greetings, and the nuns took us to a window from where we could see the girls at their morning gymnastic exercises in the garden. They were arranged in rows forming a large oblong with two diagonals, and were performing rhythmical movements. The amplifier of an electric gramophone directed their movements with one of Schubert's marches. The incongruity and monotony of their attitudes gave the girls the appearance of mechanical puppets. Schubert's march seemed to move all the flowers of the garden in manoeuvres of blue flags. Amparo was at the point where the diagonals crossed, the geometrical centre, you must understand, of the rectangle, the garden and the morning. If she had been at one of the sides, perhaps nothing would have happened. She made a vivid impression on me. She opened her arms, bent her head to one side, closing her eyes against the rays of the morning sun, and I was dissolved in that thin air of childhood and purity, and felt impulses and energy from an unknown source. We withdrew, and they went to summon the girl. A nun told us that gymnastics were the only part of the college course that Amparo disliked. She came running to the arms of her parents. She seemed to be fourteen years old. She sighed deeply and complained:

" 'I was terribly bored, Papa.'

" 'What about?' they exclaimed in surprise.

" 'With the gymnastics.'

"Another nun came in. It was plain that the girl was on difficult terms with the mistress, and the class tutor told them that she was rather inattentive at history.

" 'She tells us that it is no use our wishing her to learn the pedigree of some ancient queen, when she doesn't yet know that of her own family.'

"When we went out, Schubert's music sounded in my ears and the sun in my heart sent swarms of golden wasps into my brain. A choir of childish heads sang out my name in the broad avenues and at the same time threw at me branches of myrtle and white blossoms."

Samar became silent. He stopped and looked at the sky, then at the trees, and then at a window high up on a house, shaking in the wind and reflecting the sun in flashes like the explosions of a magnesium lamp.

"It was a morning like this."

I said nothing. We reached the end of the Ronda near Ventas. I couldn't go another step, with the cock under my arm and the two revolvers in the other hand. Samar noticed that.

"Come to the side here. The comrades of the committee are waiting."

Two Civil Guards on motor-cycles and a military motor-car passed. Once more I asked him how he thought things were going and he told me that the strike was not universal in Madrid, but that the proclamation of "a state of war" and the paralysis of the chief public services were making a serious impression. Things were going better outside Madrid, he added. But here the limited nature of the strike was partly compensated for by the successful sabotage, which, although not complete, had done much damage. I asked a question which I couldn't help:

"Are we out for everything?"

Samar responded. They were expecting definite news from Barcelona, Coruña and Seville. If the strike actually became general as a reply to the proclamation of a "state of war", things would go to the bitter end. There were many resources as yet intact. I saw that Samar was full of confidence. We came to a little café, a kind of suburban canteen. It was closed. It fronted on two streets and I saw a door half-opened. I saw a group assembled inside and recognized some of them. Once we were inside the owner closed the door. Some light came in under the eaves. The owner was old, and his moustache was stained with tobacco. He brought some cups of coffee and gave me one. I put down the cock, placed the revolvers on a table, and drank some of it. The old man didn't know me, but when he saw the revolvers he smiled and, looking at the cock, said to me:

"Are you very fond of it? Of course you are because you must have brought it up since it was a chick."

Villacampa was amongst the men. Now they talked about Fau with surprise and regret. Then there was an almost unanimous resolution, and Villacampa stated:

"We can't do anything until the other comrades of the committee know about it. And besides, we ought to send written information."

Urbano was in the chair.

Comrade Crousell. Statement about the M.Z.A. Railroads.

"That is quickly told. The Central sub-section is going on strike and can paralyse two-thirds of the traffic. We have printed a manifesto and have distributed eight thousand copies."

With that he hands out a few copies, and two comrades read it, whilst Crousell goes on speaking:

"As the leaders are in gaol and the centre shut up, it isn't easy to get exact information, but there is a majority in favour of the strike and much enthusiasm for it."

I look at Urbano and see that he has the solemn and serious manner of the Clerk of a Court. Crousell goes on:

"It is necessary to find out if the revolutionary committee approve of the last part of the manifesto."

This is a meeting of the delegates of the groups, not of the syndicates. But of course there are here three members of the local committee, and the national revolutionary committee is composed of representatives of the syndicates as well as of the groups. Urbano reads the end of the manifesto:

"We can assure you of the solidarity of the rest of the committee. By joining in the strike you will be leading to complete stoppage of all the railways in Spain. You will be securing the first step towards the triumph of the cause which at this moment is being menaced by all the forces of reaction——" And so on.

"The revolutionary committee therefore has sent orders to strike to all the sections."

"Is the position of the national committee with regard to this known yet?" asked Crousell.

Villacampa declared:

"The national committee has confirmed the revolutionary committee in principle and with respect to concrete points."

"Which points?" asked Crousell.

Urbano looked in a folio:

"Here you have them: 'Agitation against the repressions and the chains of the Government.—General strikes of protest whenever a comrade is shot down by the rifles of reaction. —Manifestos exposing the connivance of the socialists in the crimes of the *bourgeoisie*—sabotage—return to work only as circumstances determine.' But there is nothing about the national character of the committee. The points are no more than functions of a local federation."

"We can't accept these without referring them to a national referendum," said someone.

Cipriano declared, "What these comrades from Barcelona don't wish to accept is responsibility!"

Samar asked to speak and took out some documents:

"The fact is, comrade Crousell, that we are all ready to accept our part in the agitation on its negative side. But the national committee is quite right to wish not to be informed, when other organs such as the revolutionary committee try to lead the movement to triumph and to guide it constructively. They wish to know nothing, because there is no settled policy about the immediate future of the revolution, and they disclaim responsibility for what we ourselves do in that respect or can make others do. It is very natural. Very good, things being as they are, we must go all out and risk everything. If we are not to fail again, we must advance and make our road as we go. If not, we are going to our own ruin. The road we can map out here and force it afterwards on the national committee. If we submit it to their revision, they will repudiate it. They will think it a mere constitutional reform, and in any case will insist that it must go to a general referendum. And it is clear that everything would have to wait a fortnight. If we notify them and don't ask for their opinion and get ahead, they will say nothing and await results. My view is, either return to work at once, or tomorrow itself issue a mandate, definite, concrete and immediate, for taking over the power now from the *bourgeoisie*."

There was silence for a moment. All were in doubt. Villacampa said that he himself agreed, but the old man with the white hair said that he didn't believe we could destroy the power of the *bourgeoisie* this time.

"And so," he said, "as we don't believe we can do it, I vote for returning to work."

There were protests. The old man raised his hand and said:

"Comrade Samar has put a dilemma before us, and we can't avoid considering it. Either we replace the infamous rule of the *bourgeoisie,* or we accomplish nothing. I am not going to enter into long discussions, because I reject the first altogther, and so I can't possibly put forward in good law, that is to say in good logic" (he corrected himself quickly, as if the word "law" burnt his tongue) "that it is necessary before taking the second step to lay the foundations of the first. And we can't replace the power of the *bourgeoisie,* because to say such a thing is as good as saying that we should substitute for it another power, and I reject all forms of power as inconsistent with my lofty anarchist principles."

Samar laughed and commented:

"Lofty principles!"

The old man hoped to have a chance of explaining that there were two forms of nobility, another as well as the *bourgeois* idea. Samar was in a hurry and seemed upset and nervous. He said that he had prepared a communication to the national committee in which we would tell them what we were going to do without asking them to approve.

He began to read, but the old man interrupted:

"We can't trust that to the post."

Samar said that of course it was in cipher and that there mustn't be such silly interruptions. The clauses were simple. Things that we could really do, and which showed how easy the revolution would be. Then the old man shook his head sadly:

"I can't vote for that because comrade Samar has written it under the evil inspiration of Marx."

Urbano, although with all respect to Samar, was also unable to agree because it wasn't free communism. Cipriano thumped the table:

"I am an anarchist, but I am going to vote for it and sign it. We must not abandon our comrades who are fighting in the streets in the name of the purity of a doctrine which at present we can't impose."

Samar gazes at Cipriano, touched by his plain sincerity, and then at the others. The young ones were on his side. But they were few. Liberto García, the white-skinned giant with yellow hair, Elenio Margraf, the leaden-faced and sullen printer, and the other two also belonging to printing trades—José Crousell and Helios Pérez—supported him. None the less, when it came to voting, the old men won. Samar got up:

"I raised the matter here out of politeness. Although the federation of groups has turned it down, I shall take tonight to the revolutionary committee, because I know that it is the only way of getting things done."

But Cipriano was indignant:

"Let us be off."

"Off where?" asked Urbano.

"To let them kill us. It is the only thing to be done now."

Villacampa interposed:

"Well, that will give pleasure to the *bourgeois.*"

"But that is just what we are doing here—" urged Cipriano, "giving pleasure to the *bourgeois.*"

Urbano asked him to explain himself. The old man made excuses for Cipriano with the goodwill of a victor:

"Comrade Cipriano is an anarchist of the school of Nietzsche. I understand him, but——"

Samar interrupted him with a cross look and then said: "You understand us and know that we are right, which is worse. But you are nothing but a broken-down *bourgeois*. You fear revolution and wish to die an old man wagging your white head in a utopia." They understood each other. Samar spoke for Cipriano, who didn't wish to say any more. He said that they couldn't smash the resolution of a committee or of a meeting, although they had voted against it, and that as the agreement was to go into the street without plans and fight against everyone, that just meant letting themselves be killed.

He went off completely upset. With him went Liberto, Elenio, José, Helios and Cipriano, when the meeting wound up after a few minor resolutions had been passed. I went with them, taking my cock. When we were already in the street, Villacampa came running after us. He looked at the cock and wanted to come with me, but couldn't find an excuse for it. Perhaps he thought that it would be making too much of me. Cipriano said to José and Helios:

"Be on your guard with Fau. Don't go home, for the *bourgeois* hyena is thirsty."

But the two wished to go home to rescue the case of type as it was the only means in the district of printing clandestine manifestos.

"If we can set up the type," they said, "we can always find a place where it can be printed off."

It was settled that when they came back they should go with Samar to Villacampa's house to get something to eat. Villacampa was not a marked man, and with him they would not be in danger. They went off. Liberto, Elenio and Cipriano also wished to go to Vallecas to prepare what they had to do next day in the district. Liberto had his pockets full of papers. He was the walking Regional, Local and Revolutionary Committees. "This," he said, referring to Samar's draft, "has to be issued tonight." When we arrived in the Plaza de Manuel Bacerra, we saw some animation. It was time, because the streets gave the impression of a city deserted or infected with the plague. Cipriano said:

"How jolly Madrid is today!"

But I couldn't agree that it could be really nice without tramways. Cipriano and the two printers left us here. Villacampa stopped to look at a man sitting in a doorway and nodding to him. When he saw us, he got up and came across with uncertain steps.

"What are you doing here, Casanova?"

He rubbed his eyes and explained:

"Waiting for a comrade, who, I think, has two revolvers.

I've been here all night, if you please. Blast it all, you'd think it a bloody lie if I told you the trouble a man has to come by a revolver."

"But weren't you with us when we sacked the gunshop?"

"Yes, but all I managed to get was one of these that centuries ago lords used for duels. You load them by the muzzle and you have to carry a sack on your back with powder and shot."

Villacampa reflected:

"Do you know who has three revolvers? Serafin Urbez. He lives at the other end of Madrid." Casanova, without another word, turns round, looks about him for a second, and then goes off by a side-street. As he is very sleepy, he carries his head in front of his feet, and looks as if he were going to charge the lamp-posts. We keep descending. The street slopes gently downwards. There are a few shops half-open and a garage with its door on the hinge. Inside we can see some Civil Guards and a machine-gun ready for use.

As we descend, the street becomes more lively and people seem to be frightened. They are listening for any sound. There are a few working-men. The day is still and clear and seems safe after the terrors of the dark night, and they are out to see what is doing. An official edition of the *Vigia* has been issued, and they are calling out: "Grave events of last night; state of war proclaimed throughout the country." We buy a copy and Samar hardly opens it, only looking at the headlines: "The criminal outbreak of last night"—"Sabotage; victims"—"The Government's View"—"Public Proclamation"—"Discovery of all the Leaders of the Conspiracy." Samar smiled:

"What conspiracy? If there had been a conspiracy there would be no vestige of the Government by now."

He pointed to a paragraph with his finger, showing it to Villacampa:

"See, they have killed Murillo."

Villacampa reads: "It transpired that his name was Murillo and that he was a dangerous communist and the leading conspirator." Villacampa and Samar laughed:

"Poor Murillo!"

He had died in a riot, killed by a random bullet. Who would fall next? Would we be amongst them? Samar seemed to guess what we were thinking and said:

"The best of all this is that by sinking ourselves in the general mass, and losing individuality, they don't kill us, even when they get us through the heart."

Villacampa doesn't like that kind of talk, and so tells me

that on a day like this I ought not to come out in yellow, the colour of a blackleg, but in red. Samar retorts:

"It's because she is in love with the tramways."

"With them all?" asks Villacampa, thinking that I am quite mad.

"Now you're asking. To tell the truth, they are all alike. And so I am in love with one and with them all."

Villacampa looks at my legs and hums:

> *"A young parish priest*
> *Gave me stockings to wear*
> *But I called him a beast*
> *And preferred to go bare."*

"What a stupid song. What have I to do with priests? The fact is that he is angry because I am in love with tramcars."

"Have you been in love for long?"

"Ever since I was a child."

Samar laughs:

"She is still a child."

I could explain to them why I am in love with them, but this is not the moment to make them understand. I saw a tramcar being burnt when the Republic came. Poor tramcar; it had a plaintive voice like a lost child.

We hear shouts of terror. People flee in all directions. We do not see a guard and no one threatens us. Perhaps in the street, now almost empty, silent bullets are flying of the kind that come round corners and rise up to the roofs to hit a cook in some inside balcony. But we keep quiet. When everything near seems quite deserted, we suddenly see two children of four or five years old beside a heap of sweepings, turning the rubbish over and eating cabbage stalks or bits of stale bread. Villacampa insists:

"But is it true that you are in love with a tramcar?"

Samar replies for me and explains in a few words that the fragments of the *bourgeois* spirit which we still have, we keep far away from our feelings. Our feelings have nothing to do with the *bourgeois* spirit, but with the genital organs. When these are asleep or appeased, the spirit falls in love with anything. If the spirit and the feelings were working together, we should behave like the *bourgeois*. We should be sentimental. But we aren't like that. Our soul goes its own way and falls in love "spiritually", as the *bourgeois* say. With a tramcar, or like Casanova, with a revolver, or with a pruning hook.

I don't understand him. Neither does Villacampa, although

he says he does. But the fact is that now, after Samar's explanation, I am much more in love with a tramcar, and exactly at that moment one of them appears coming up the street. We stare at it stupefied.

"How can it happen, as the electricity is cut off?"

A workman tells us that the damage has been repaired on that line, and that the Government has given the order for the cars to be taken out. "But that one," he added, slipping away mysteriously, "won't get safely to its garage." He was right. Before it reached us, there was a loud explosion and paving-stones rose up in a fountain and fell on the car. The track was blown up, and the car thrown off its wheels and halted with one wheel spinning in the air. We run to take shelter in the nearest corner, and I get his revolver out so that Samar may use it if he wishes. The cock got such a fright that he has torn my skirt with his claws and I have to pin it up. We stop to watch. There are two Civil Guards in the car who have been wounded with pieces of glass and fragments of stone. They get out as best they can. The conductor has got out unhurt, but he rushes up the street without thinking where he is going. Threatening groups come from the side streets, and some approach, but others keep away down the street. I like the tramcar which isn't to blame. I smell petrol. They are going to burn it. But so far no one dares to go close to it. I give Samar the revolver, cross the pavement in a flash, jump the gutter and mount the car. When they see me so bold, they all come up behind, but I keep them back from the platform.

"Keep quiet. Don't burn it. The tramcar is a friend of ours."

We hear horses' hoofs lower down. And shots. People scatter, and I crouch down beside the engine. More shots. The tramcar is abandoned with me inside it. Some bullets hit the windows and scatter splinters of glass. The cock has escaped from my arm and jumps up and down on the seats and the window-sills in fear of the bullets. From where I lurk, I can see Samar and Villacampa, with their coat collars turned up and their hats pulled down to hide their faces, firing. Other working men are firing from all the corners. And I still hear the horses' hoofs coming nearer. The street is as empty as a tombstone. And the bullets sound against the tramcar as if it were the sun's heat stretching the panels and making them give cracks like a whip. I keep my eyes shut for a long time. Far off a machine-gun rattles. Four or five volleys, and then it stops. Then it rattles again and again stops. Then the hoofs sound all round about me, and someone calls me. "They are going to arrest me," I thought. I have my nickelled revolver in my cap. Another voice:

"That cock; catch it."

Before uncovering my face I wet my eyelashes with saliva. The guards console me, and ask if I hadn't been able to escape in time. They think that I was a passenger when the car was attacked. I asked for my cock and a guard brought it me, holding it upside down by the legs. The bird twisted up and pecked his hand. I put it under my arm and went off in great content to the street close by where I thought I saw Samar. When I was afraid that I wouldn't find them, they came out of a doorway. Villacampa was angry with me. He was jealous of the tramcar. He went into another doorway to hide his revolver in his boot, and Samar looked me in the face. He is placid and self-possessed as he always is when a bit of trouble like this one is over:

"Why did you kiss me before?"

I shrugged my shoulders:

"Because I like you."

He looked at me in a queer way. I added:

"All right. I like Villacampa too, but I didn't kiss him."

We are in a *bourgeois* street. It is a smart bit of the town. There isn't a soul about. Villacampa comes out of the door muttering. I don't know if he is angry with me for having saved the tramcar, or pleased because the comrades have escaped. But I do know that he won't look me in the face.

Chapter 13

Villacampa on the Merits of Violence

AFTER HAVING a meal with me in my house, the others have gone, leaving Samar and Star alone with me. I don't know where Star and the journalist are going to stop, but they are always of the same mind. I shall have to wear my red tie and pomade my hair to get Star to like me again. Ties and tidy hair have much effect with women, even although they aren't *bourgeoises,* and there are times when if Star and I could come to terms, I could take her away from Samar, which is difficult, as they are always against me. That is the only reason why it annoys me to see them always supporting each other.

Otherwise I don't care if they go about together. I've never thought that there could be anything between Star and myself except in affairs of the organization or in "action".

Star has made me search amongst my weapons for cartridges which will fit her revolver. A minute and neat bullet, because her revolver looks as if it were made to hold the kind of bullet that you might have in a powder-puff rather than one made to wound or kill. But at last I found one, a number five. It is like a toy and is painted. Brand new. She felt its weight and turned it round in her fingers. Then I offered to put it in the magazine, and she took away the revolver from me.

"Not yet; when the moment comes, I'll put it in myself."

We joked a little. "Whom did she wish to kill?" "Who is her enemy?" "Has she any enemies?" Who could take Star seriously enough?

Even Samar had laughed at her. But she scored over both of us in the matter of laughing. With the edge of a pocket-knife she tried to make a cross of two cuts on the point of the bullet. I told her that that could be done only with bullets with naked points. I showed her several. The result is that, as the bullet spins, it opens out like a cross, and does much more damage in the body. It has been known that a ball of this kind has gone into the belly of a man and has come out at his shoulder after having destroyed the whole of his inside and his lungs. They are good surgeons. Then with the point of the penknife I scratched on the bullet her initials: S. G. Then she gave the bullet and the knife to Samar:

"Take it," she said. "Put your initials too!"

Samar scratched down below, "L. S.", and asked me to add mine, when she stopped me, protesting:

"No, no. Only Samar and me."

Certainly that didn't please me. Why these distinctions? I looked at her an instant rather disagreeably, and she made a face at me and put out her tongue. This girl wishes to make the impression of being very clever, and her folly is only a disguise to put one off the track. I know her well. I know that it is all a pretence. I'm sick of her mysterious ways and her revolver. Such a fuss, and at the best she will fire her bullet at some cooking-pot, shutting her eyes. These girls aren't revolutionaries or anything else. They are like the vases people put on their pianos, delicate and dainty. And if they want to be taken seriously, they must stop falling for a tie or a sleek head.

I devote myself to cleaning and counting my little arsenal of deadly weapons, now that Star has put her hands in it. Meanwhile, as I take the revolver to pieces and wipe it with a rag dipped in oil, strange thoughts come into my head. For some time I've been sure that to be an intellectual—like Samar—one has got to have strange thoughts. I think them about the revolution. I am anxious that all should happen as we wish, that the *bourgeois* should come to offer us their bellies and that we shall only have to stick them. And that at the same time choruses should be sung, like those I heard once in Barcelona, joyful songs to greet the Spring in the gardens. And then when there are no more *bourgeois,* that we shall all sing and invent a new religion, some kind of religion of work and the statistics of production. Then all men will be able to look at each other without hate in their faces or jealously, and women won't blush with shame when we stare at them with the fever with which we sometimes look at them in the street. Everything will be made right, and children will grow up clean and happy, like plants with water and sun. We shall all be pleasant and charitable without that taint of sentimentalism which keeps girls from being full-breasted, makes little girls thin, and sends unshaven, fat priests after widows.

The rag comes out of the revolver stained with smoke. Which was the last shot? Was it this morning, in the Alcalá, over the tramcar affair? I didn't hit a single guard, not even the horse of a guard. When I was going to pull the trigger there came in the way an old man with a white beard, on crutches, with a black shawl round his shoulders and very clean varnished shoes. He limped and his face was miserable and tearful. He got in the way and stopped the bullet. His crutches went flying and his hat fell off, and he collapsed on the pavement like a sparrow. Of course it was shocking. It is worse in a war when a shell falls into a house and kills the women and children. But headquarters don't stop for that. And so with us. And besides, a lame man can't do much with life, especially if he has a white beard and *bourgeois* patent leather shoes. Now my revolver is clean. Looking at it in the light, it seems as if the inside of the barrel were made of glass. But I can't get out of my mind that shawl, black like a crow, which spun in such a foolish way when the man fell. A chauffeur comrade who was beside me told me afterwards that they had taken the old man away in an ambulance. He winked and added: "They are going to have some work with him."

I believe him. Those who go to the hospital don't come

back. It is a killing-house. I give my revolver another polishing, and when I look inside, it seems brighter than glass, almost as if it had an electric light inside. It's as bright as a medal. The *bourgeois* rear many birds with black shawls. Cloaks like those of a priest. I notice that when I put the revolver on the table I forget about the old man, but when I pick it up I remember him. It seems as if guns had consciousness. When we were attacking the provision-store I shot the hat off a guard. It was a great joke and the revolver seemed to say:

"Well, my friend. When you are talking with me, you've got to take your hat off."

When it was cleaned and oiled, with oil for typewriters—they sell neat little jars for a shilling—I fill the magazines. In one there was only a single cartridge left. I don't know why there is so much noise. They must be wasting a lot of lead.

In my chest-of-drawers I have an old pocket-book with three notes with the head of Philip the Second and a picture of the Escorial. I keep the case and nothing else. I feel like nothing myself. I put the revolver in my back pocket and feel plumped out and happy. If the mistress comes in I'll tell her that cows eat the heads of Philip the Second and the stones of the Escorial. For she has a face like a cow and I seem to have heard her bellowing like a cow when she is quarrelling with her husband, a leathery skinned old fellow who does nothing. I am happy with the revolver in my pocket, although these are days when pockets split, but mine won't split, because I've lined it with leather. General strike in the street; two full ammunition vans. Funds for our campaign; the federation committee now complete and at liberty. Now we are moving on, climbing. Violence—as is well said in the pamphlet I have on my night-table under the water jug—violence is the natural mainspring of all action and reaction, and without it there is no life or possibility of life. But things are so badly arranged in this dirty *bourgeois* world, that we can't be natural, what they call natural, because then there would be too much violence.

Here comes the mistress. Before she speaks I ask her:

"Do you want money?"

"No."

"Is the cow full of monarchial bank-notes?"

She shrugs her shoulders without replying. I remember old Auntie Isabela and point to the door:

"To hell out of this, you old bastard!"

She goes off screaming. Any natural action is violent. Then comes her husband and before he could speak I ask him:

"Are you coming to attack me?"
"No."
"To invite me to coffee?"
"Damn it all."
I pointed him to the door too.
"If you have come to speak to me, I tell you that I've nothing to do with a rotter. Get out!"
He also goes off. It works all right. But I can see that it is violence. It is our stupid civilization, more stupid than Star, and that is saying something. With a revolver in one's pocket, one's comrades in the street, and the revolution in the soul, we are as good as God, or better. Everything else is feeble, soft and smells like the sweat of a sick man. But now they are knocking on the door with their knuckles.
"Come in."
It is the servant girl. A poor girl, quite young and pretty. Today, after these days of close quarters with death, I feel as if I were drunk. When I think of the inside of the barrel of my revolver, all like glass, this drunkenness goes to my head and pulls me out of my Sunday suit and throws me on a heap of thorns. Here is the servant. It appears that the master and mistress aren't going to dare to come back. She is terrified and stares at me without being able to get a word out of her throat.
"What have you come for? If you were a conscientious worker you would belong to the comrades. As you are tricked by the priests, you have no use except to sweep out the rooms and have your behind pinched by the lodgers."
The girl opened her eyes wide and saliva dripped from her mouth. Once again natural action means violence. I get impatient.
"What is it now? Have you come to dust or do you wish me to pinch your behind?"
Still more frightened, she sobs out:
"He is dying."
"What?"
"Don Fidel."
I don't understand her.
"Come up here beside me."
She started, then came up instinctively protecting her behind with her hand. When she saw that I was laughing, she pretended only to be arranging her skirt.
"Speak now! What has happened to that silly old man?"
"He is dying!"

"That he is dying!" What a bit of news when I am just going off!

The servant goes out with quick and short steps. At the door she turned as if she were going to say something, but didn't speak. I don't behave that way with my own people, but I can't help it with the *bourgeoisie*. This Don Fidel is an old man employed in the tobacco trade. He wears stiff collars and cuffs, and always speaks about an uncle of his who was a Carlist general, and whom, he said, the liberals shot. When I cast doubt on it, he swears that in his country house there is a crystal vase in which is preserved the handkerchief with which they closed his eyes. He has the best room in the house, and hates the march of civilization. He would like to kill all the anarchists and communists, and falls into a passion every time he reads in the newspapers that a deputation of working men has been received by the President to complain about something.

"Why does he receive them?" says he, foaming at the mouth. "A thrashing, a good thrashing is what these scoundrels need."

He has remained a bachelor all his life because he thinks that a family would make a goose of him and that his wife would present him with a pair of horns. Now and again he spends a few shillings on a streetwalker. Through the wall of his room, which is next to mine, I heard him praying aloud one day. It seems that he isn't very satisfied with God.

"Thou leadest me into temptation, and then thou lettest me catch a disease. Oh, God, this isn't right."

And now he is dying. It would have been sport to see him die. When I go into the passage, I can hear them wailing in the kitchen. And so he is really dead! I enter his room. There is hardly any light. The windows are closed, and in a corner, from a heap of sheets, there come evil-smelling gasps as if a pot of cabbage were boiling over. I breathe through the nose and don't speak until my lungs are full of air and I can exhale. The mistress and her husband are at the two sides. They look at me suspiciously and she makes excuses, as if she had offended me when she opened my door a few minutes ago. I think that violence is uncivilized, but as it is natural, people pay respect to it. Look at these people. A few minutes ago I told them the truth about themselves, and all the same—— Of course respect for Don Fidel also counts with them. The mistress, when she moves away to leave me a seat at the side of the bed, accidentally shuts the window-shutter, and the master begs me open it again; explaining:

"Open air helps the death agony."

But I don't know what to say or what to do. It would have been better not to have come in. Once inside, the best thing to do is to hold the nose and to spit. They tell me what the illness is and try to convince me that he could be cured, whilst I think that the sooner he dies, the better. The master gives him water in a teaspoon. I say to him:

"Why are you nursing him? Leave him alone to die as he has got to die."

This seems so monstrous to the master that I justify myself, in a loud voice:

"But of course he is at the end."

He goes on:

"But don't speak so loudly, for he understands everything."

"He understands everything?"

And I think to myself: "What a fuss they make." The master calls to him:

"Don Fidel, dear Don Fidel."

I have a savage wish to laugh, especially when I see the master wiping away a tear. The master keeps calling:

"Don Fidel!"

And from time to time he looks at the gold watch of the dying man, which is on the table, and the tobacco pouch sticking out of the pocket of his black coat, and thinks that it must be of silver. The two call to him, and Don Fidel partly opens his blue eyes. They seize the opportunity to tell him that I am here, and then I see his dying gaze turning to my eyes. He shuts his eyes, without speaking. They have put a crucifix on his belly, and a scapulary near one ear. Presently voices are heard in the passage, and the mistress hurries out leaving in my hands a towel with which she had been keeping off the flies, and fanning. Then she appears in the doorway, and calls to her husband as if she were pleased. It must be a distinguished visitor, as it moves them so much. I stand alongside Don Fidel with the towel in my hand. From time to time I make passes with it over his head as the mistress did, but without meaning it, I couldn't help thinking of the bull-ring, and at each new pass I said out aloud:

"Olé."

And then from left to right:

"Turn again."

I was in a hurry to go, and he didn't seem in any hurry. Death has sharpened his face, but that is all. I go out into the passage and give the towel to the mistress.

"And Don Fidel?" they say to me, with the hope that he had died.

I replied as I went off:

"Just as lazy about it as ever."

I go into the street. A *bourgeois* isn't a person. Nor an animal. He is less than anything. He is nothing. Why am I to worry about the death of a *bourgeois,* when I am going out into the street to kill them?

Chapter 14

Samar, Amparo and the Informer's End

AMPARO AND I are in a summer-house in the garden. Near us, and visible through the green leaves, is her aunt at work. I am troubled by this *bourgeois* peace, the harmony of this bower, shaped like the half of an orange, with green and flowering creepers. I am ashamed at the way the orderlies show me as much respect as they show the colonel. I remember that when I was doing my service, my hatred extended even to the families of my officers. Coming in here raises in me an unpleasant sensation, as if I were a cynical *bourgeois* who had lost his senses and strutted elegantly about the streets on all fours. Besides, there are the strain and emotion of finding myself in Amparo's house, and in her presence, and my old perplexity: "Am I to go to the mountain or is the mountain to come to me? Or am I to destroy her and thus be done with the mountain?" But in any case I was in the snowy pass—a burning snow—and tried vainly to deceive myself. I had been on the mountain, and when I saw the sun reflected from the lovely ice crystals, I moved towards them, dazzled by thousands of little prisms. "The sun comes here bringing decomposition and death." Then I listened to the wind, and the wind only breathed the solitude of death with wailing of cosmic sorrow. I sat down and dreamed with the ice crystals in their gardens of colour. The cold burnt my skin. I felt the wind on my hair and my three-days-old beard, and took pleasure as it stung my purple-cold hands. I was alone on the heights; alone and far-off, high up in the wind and the ice. To enter the amber and azure heights, to come amongst the crystals of snow and the icy prisms and to warm them with my own pure heat, stronger than the cold of all the peaks, and to dream: "In the cold whiteness of these heights the impurities of down below must vanish, all the evil vapours must die, all the *bourgeois* corruption must disappear. She is pure and clear as ice, and the sun of my heart absorbs her and melts her, creating coloured gardens of pleasure. But the wind moans below. The wind screams above. The wind proclaims the solitude of the heights, and the cosmic sorrow of having to yield to unknown forces."

To give up—when everything invites us to raise our heads, to dispel mystery to deny *bourgeois* fatalism the mysticism of Palestine. To reject the icy peaks, the rainbow lights, and to rise against the wind of the wilderness and to raise a banner against the sun! If the wind wails, let us laugh and smother its groaning with our mirth. There is nothing for it but to surrender. The city down there below is outside our flowery arbour. The quaking streets. Black groups on the pale asphalt and mausers in the corners! White, deserted streets! Sand on the pavements and here and there droppings from the horses of the guards. The bow is strung and Espartaco's arrow is flaming. And so, in the presence of these things, are we going to give way?

I am at her side. But Star's words are dreaming in my ears: "Yours are the love affairs of picture post cards."

Amparo knows that the revolution is keeping me from her, and she startles me with her hope:

"If communism triumphs now," she says with childish pleasure, "then we'll always be at peace."

I agree, thinking of something else. Then I gaze at her. There is nothing behind her eyes. Everything seems to stop at the retina. Just like the heights and their stars of ice. As she sees that I am not talking, she persists with her revolutionary enthusiasm. I ask her:

"Are you a communist?"

"Yes."

"But that is impossible; you believe in God."

She begins to be disturbed, foreseeing danger.

"I thank God for giving me this happiness. But in everything else I wish to be a communist."

"If you had a chance of helping us, of proving it."

Her eyes shone with pleasure:

"Although I am a coward with animals, especially with hornets and bees, you mustn't think that I am not able to do everything that a communist woman can do."

My nerves are rasped by her childish words. There is silence between us, which she doesn't understand. Then she grasps my hand:

"Don't you love me?"

I think of Star and of the picture post card. I say craftily:

"I wish to beg something."

"What?"

"What I am going to ask might harm your father."

She hesitates.

"If you love me you won't ask me to do anything against him."

I explain to her. The sooner the better! It is that she should get for me three of the printed official forms with the stamp of the regiment at the foot. They are permits for entry to the barracks. The forms and the seal are on the colonel's desk. It is quite easy. Amparo, after being silent for a long time, says to me sadly: "You don't love me."

I insist as if I hadn't heard her:

"Choose, my dear! At a time like this our behaviour must be definite and clear. Compared with an ideal, the family counts for nothing. Think what was said to the poor man by that Jesus whom you say in your prayers you love so much: 'He that loveth his father or mother more than me, is not worthy of me.' 'For a man's foes shall be they of his own household.' Jesus offered an ideal. We offer you ours. Choose between God and me. Between your father and the revolution."

Her instincts struggle with her, and her soul flutters like a bird. Like the dove which Star put in the corner of the coloured post card. But now it can be seen on the glittering peak visible in her eyes. Burning cold. Flaming snow. And the loneliness sung by the wind of the peaks. No thought; light, wind, rocks, snow and the infinite harmonizing everything. No thought. She insists with a sob:

"You don't love me."

"We aren't thinking of that," I say sharply. "We are thinking of the revolution."

Almost weeping, she repeats:

"You don't love me."

With bitter directness—my pulse quickened by what lay behind my words—I say coldly:

"If I didn't love you I would marry you. It would be a good marriage. We'd have a brilliant ceremony, the church illuminated, and music. All that would be a fitting prelude to the possession of a woman so beautiful as you. You must see how easy it would be. But I love you in the only way I can love you, in a way that no one else could ever love you. I love you to despair."

I pierce her eyes with my longing.

"To despair, darling."

She trembled happily.

"Why do you say 'to despair'?"

"Because although you are my life, I have to give you up."

She ponders the meaning of my words. Soon she understands. Simple words laden with tragedy.

"No! Never! I'll go with you! I'll give up everything!"

"Will you give up God?"

She is silent and her gaze wanders in the light filtering through the creeper. I keep on:

"Will you give up your father?"

A tear trembles in her eyes, and yet light sings through the fringes of her lids.

"God," she says at last, "has given us this madness of our love. And as for Papa—he is so kind."

My expression changes. I recall my own parents, and this scene worries me. *Bourgeois* sentiment. Sugary. In the depths of my soul, a voice cries out to me despairingly, "Don't be an imbecile! What a tragedy! Don't be a *bourgeois* idiot. She'll love me all the same. An imbecile, an idiot and a revolutionary say the same elementary words to a woman like her. And these words are enough—like a fairy's wand—to discover this priceless treasure." She sees that I am away from her. She looks at my mouth because the decision to part which my words don't actually contain can be seen in the compression of my lips. She insists:

"I'll go with you! I don't care for anything in the world except our love. I'll——"

I stopped her in an imperative voice:

"Help us to make things easier for the comrades by getting these forms."

She asked doubtingly:

"Will it make the revolution come?"

"At least," I said, "the revolt will go further."

As yet she hadn't got quite enough to decide her. But she is on the way towards the heroic. What a charming creature, with her head leaning on her bosom, her eyes, bright like those of a bird, and her ripe lips apart.

"But you have just said, Lucas darling, that you have to give me up. If I get these forms for you, will you still be thinking that?"

"But there will still be God between us."

"Answer me Yes, or No."

"Yes."

She had become contented and serene, but now began to compress her lips. From a second she changed from radiant happiness to sheer desperation.

"Won't it be enough for you if I sacrifice Papa?"

"How sacrifice your father?"

"Yes. You know that you wish to suborn the regiment, and the first victim will be the colonel."

I said nothing. She began to weep, and I asked her:

"Do you think me a criminal?"

"I don't know what to think, Lucas darling. I would love you as much if you were one. I can't help myself."

Without knowing what I was doing, I lighted a cigarette. She took out her handkerchief, and when she heard me say that there was nothing we couldn't help, she began to bite it and tear at it. Her aunt, who saw that there was trouble between us, cast timid but watchful glances at us. Amparo sobbed:

"Oh, if only I could die."

Tears don't move me. I think of those that have been shed in the dark homes of hunger and in the prisons of injustice. Sentiment passes over me tonight without wounding me. Deeds, logic, possibilities. Argument doesn't suffice, as in the cinema the other day. I want deeds; I want the logic of facts. If I am in love, so much the worse for me. If I can't see a way out of this tangle, I'll shoot myself. I can't become a *bourgeois*. She can't come to my camp. I'll succeed if I can, or I'll die to a pistol-shot, smiling at the new theory which is more triumphant every day; which is stronger than her or me. How can she give up her silks, her toilet table, her garden, her gentle family, to come to the miserable hovel of those who are fighting, to adore a little wild flower growing from rubbish, she who lives with carnations and roses? What can I do with a revolver in my right hand and she with all her beauty and childishness despoiled, at my side? No! I have to give her up! Leave her to find happiness with someone else? I can't, I won't, I don't know how to do it, or how to learn to do it. I, who can think of myself with my brains blown out in the mud, like Germinal, without a shudder, cannot imagine her in the arms of another without feeling the earth shake below my feet. And she said:

"Oh, if I could die!"

I heard her without alarm. Thinking of it only troubled me a moment, for I remembered at once that she had said that she would love me even if I were a criminal. And I certainly hadn't thought of killing her, but only that she might die. But even if I were to kill her, she would go on loving me. I don't know why I bemuse myself thinking these things. She is ready to make me happy even after I had killed her. But I won't sacrifice to her white-bearded gods. I'd let them shoot me down in Germinal's mud, but I won't sit at that table with its vase of carved crystal, presided over by the *bourgeois* God. And yet her body calls to mine, and we are both quivering with passion and bubbling over with youth. Our bodies understand each other, far from the spirit, the detestable spirit which creates attractions and repulsions and which plays with death in the images of an old poet in love. Our bodies understand each other and call together her rosy cheeks and my three-days' beard. Our intuitions attract and repel us in flashes like lightning in a storm. She develops her suggestion:

"If I were to die you would be happy."

Her *bourgeois* morality should protest, but something arises within her and defeats it. I keep silent. She looks into my eyes, but I hide them in a puff of smoke. She waits until the smoke disappears, and then before she can look into my eyes I answer mechanically:

"What nonsense!"

Then I look straight at her with an expression that she might take for cynicism. She says nothing. Her eyes, her lips, the position of her hand and even the angle at which she bends her body all depend on what I may say to her, how I look at her, what she can guess to be in my mind. To be with her like this, to love her as I do love her, and still to hear her speak as she has spoken and to remain impassive! Our silence is deep, deep as eternity. She questions me again, turning the suggestion into a final query:

"If I were to die, you would be happy; isn't that the truth?"

When she said it before she was speaking to herself. Now she questions me, looking into my eyes. As my cigarette is finished I throw it away and return her glance in silence. Perhaps she thinks that I don't love her. Or that I am a scoundrel. It is terrible that I don't care what she thinks of me. And still I love her in spite of everything, with all my soul.

"If you don't answer," she says, "I'll understand."

I don't wish to go on talking. My mind wanders away, recalling that José Crousell and Helios Pérez didn't come to Villacampa's house to have food and that probably they have been arrested. Then I think about Fau and of my proposal which the revolutionary committee should have approved. Meantime I don't know what she is saying or thinking. I know that she is speaking, asking me strange questions, and that suddenly when I sit up, look at her and say "Listen to me," she starts and shudders from head to foot.

"Why are you frightened?"

What a question! She doesn't know.

"Listen to me. Now it is you who must give a definite answer. We must have—I must have (I added impressively) these forms with the seal of the regiment. Are you going to get them for me?"

She gets up and walks firmly away. She goes into the house. I am alone, far away, floating in a void between my passion and my reason. Then reason awakens as if it were neuralgia. I look on the ground, on the gravel. There are her footprints. But she is already something of the past. There are left only memories, deep-rooted in my heart. Always growing, always coming up. Her aunt thinks that for politeness she must speak to me.

"What is happening is terrible, Lucas. Do you know what took place last night?"

I hurriedly put away my lethargy.

"No, Madame. What?"

"The light. They shut off all the electric light in Madrid."

"Oh, yes."

"What do you think about it?"

"Well, well, what do you want me to say to you?"

"It was very wrong. In many houses there are sick people."

"Of course."

"And besides, there were fatalities."

I keep silence. I wish the good lady would leave me alone. Next, she asks:

"What do they want now?"

To make an answer, I say:

"Who knows?"

The extraordinary thing is that I am speaking the truth. We have force enough to try something definite, but we remain obstinately ignorant of what we want. All the same my conscience is clear. I know it. After all, what does it matter that I don't know where we are going, as no one can restrain or direct his will to rebel. The aunt continues to talk until Amparo appears again. She comes resolutely and free from care. On the soft gravel of the garden she steps in grace. I don't know why, but I recall cartoons of Greek goddesses. She sat down beside me and took from her bosom a little sheaf of papers.

"Here they are, Lucas. Do what you like with them."

I took her hand and raised it to my lips. She looked at me with a new and unknown serenity:

"Do you still think that it is impossible?" she said.

"What?"

"Our love."

"Not enough yet, darling. You must promise me not to let your father know."

"I promise; and now?"

I kiss her arm and then her lips. She strokes my hair silently.

"Is it really true?" she said after a minute. "True that we are going to be happy?"

"Not yet," I say, drawing away in a frenzy.

She opened her eyes.

"Not yet?"

"No. Do you believe in God?"

"Don't ask me anything more, Lucas darling."

"Do you believe in God?"

"Oh, this is dreadful."

"Do you believe in God?"

"I believe in you."

I look at her with curiosity. This girl has changed. She looks as if she had passed through ten years in a second. She questions me with a look which means, "Do you think now that our happiness is possible?" I reply, also silently, with a look that is another question: "And you, do you believe in it?" She understands my question and replies in a way that is a revelation to me. My little darling, so innocent, now has a placidity and a sweetness based on mystery. Sorrow brings wisdom. She gazes at me as she had never before looked at anyone and her gaze reveals a self-assurance far beyond the possibilities of human assurance. Her silent and gentle reply, sweet and deep, pierced the depths of my passion and made me tremble. "And you?" I ask again. "What do you believe?" "Is happiness possible for us?" Her eyes sparkle. I read in them a firm negative.

"No."

I seize her hands again. Notwithstanding the "No," I can't help asking her at once:

"Do you love me?"

She looks at me in silence. Her little hand passes up from my coat collar to my neck:

"What illusions! darling Lucas."

She speaks of them as if she saw flying away through the air a bevy of angels in which she believes. She goes on:

"What dreams!"

Yes, she loves me, but she isn't going to cry as I am so self-possessed. I move closer to her, feeling that I have to lose her, that I have to leave her. Her serenity doesn't last long. Now she raises her hands and buries her face. Her lips open as if she were forcing them, and her eyes look despairingly up at the ceiling. Almost sobbing, sobbing like a child, openly, but without tears, she laments: "My life's illusions!"

I put my arm round her waist and press her to me. She feels protected, and tries to smile. But she is still trembling as if with cold. And a last dream passes from her. I see it pass across her eyes, like a blue shadow, as she wails:

"Our baby girl. Now we shall never have our baby girl!"

She looks at me with her almost childish face discomposed as she seizes my hands.

"Now it can never happen, Lucas darling!"

She won't cry, I am sure of that, but she clings to my breast moaning, with her clenched right hand at her lips. I am afraid for a minute, as I feel her trembling and heaving, of what might happen. We separate.

"I have dreamed so much, my God!"

All the old knowledge of this bitter world has taught her its secret. She knows that there is nothing for us. I wish to tell her everything, but can say only:

"It is the revolution, darling Amparo."

No more to be said. Her low-voiced "No" has echoed to the world's farthest horizons. With her eyes round, as if she were in a trance, she replies:

"Let the revolution kill us, if it must. But our baby daughter? What has she done not to be born?"

High up the last rays of the evening sun catch the house. I

keep watching the "No" in her eyes, when she rises and with her hands on my shoulders gazes into my eyes. By thinking of my comrades, I have forced myself to absolute restraint. I see the "No" in her eyes. In mine she can read nothing but a chilled darkness. We part without words. There is one word between us which neither of us dares to repeat: impossible. "Impossible." There are now no more questions. She goes into the house, sobbing and calling on her mother. Once more she is a little lost animal! But this time lost for always. I grind my heels into the sand. "Never more," says the air of the garden. "Always something more," call my comrades as night rushes down. "Never more," says a fluttering curtain at a window. "Always more," cry the first shadows of the night. And I go off without saying good-bye to the aunt, who is frowning heavily, no doubt because she saw us kissing.

As soon as I am in the street I hear cries and an uproar. A monstrous figure comes on me, running and panting. I can hardly get out of his way. He reaches the garden wall, tries to jump on it, but fails. He runs along the foot of the wall. Little Buenaventura, Graco and Santiago arrive. Then I know who the monster is. Buenaventura gives the order:

"Quick. Watch for him as he comes back. He can't run far because his leg is hurt."

They run, they pass me. Buenaventura fires two shots and I hear Fau give a grunt as he crawls along. He manages to get up again, and makes for the part of the barracks beyond the garden. He flattens himself against the creepers, crushing the blue flowers. He is standing on the grass, gazing with staring eyes at his pursuers, with his arms stretched like a cross against the wall. A little lizard, caught under his boot, is thrusting out its snout gasping for breath. The three comrades go closer. They fire four, six, ten times, until the monster falls with his nose on the ground and his eyes staring without seeing. Then the comrades go off, hiding their weapons. Soldiers come out of the barracks and fire the prescribed shots in the air. Then they call the officer on duty. The lizard, its tail broken off, crawls slowly across Fau's trousers. There is still a glint of sun on the chimney of the house above my sweetheart's balcony, wreathed in creepers and blossoms; a real picture post card balcony!

Chapter 15

Auntie Discovers Our Lady of Wrath

MRS. CLETA doesn't wish to have me any longer in the house. But what a house! In the twelve hours I've been here, fleas have swarmed on me. And all the time she has done nothing but din into my ears how her husband gave her no peace with his jealousy. The husband must have been a fool. And as for her talk about her husband's jealousy, I don't think her a pretty woman, but a dirty bitch. To make me clear out, she has kept telling me how my staying here compromises her, the widow of a soldier! And so she thinks to make herself out better than me. She who had to wash four baskets of laundry when her husband was sick and didn't earn anything, what do you think of it? And bragging that her man was an officer in the Public Defence! I couldn't stand it any longer and I told her straight:

"My husband always earned enough for us to live on."

The old woman retorted:

"My husband commanded fifty guards."

She waited a little and then went on to be nastier:

"Of course when there was a revolt he was in charge of even more."

I told her:

"And my husband made the lot of them run away."

Then I knew that we were going to come to blows, and I stopped at that, as she was afraid of me, and she herself found me a lodging for tonight in the house of Lucrecia, the corporal's wife. The widow Cleta is very fond of Star. And I've said nothing to my granddaughter so that Lucrecia mayn't have too many living on her. She has stayed on with Cleta, she and her cock. She thinks more of her cock than of me or of anything. She has no heart. Now children come into the world leaving their hearts behind them in their mothers' bellies. When she heard of Fau's death, she never even thought that Fau had got her father sent to gaol more than once, but she only sighed with satisfaction and said to her cock:

"Now you may be satisfied, my little rascal."

"Little rascal" is her pet word for the cock. I have nicer

words for the cat. But why is the cock not to worry? With that mug that God gave her she goes on:

"Fau had cast his eye on you not only now, but even from before the Republic. Sometimes I used to see him sitting in a doorway and looking queerly at the cock. I rushed out, brought back the cock into the house, and then he spat on the ground, clicked his tongue and went off with a flea in his ear."

The old woman Cleta, who is just as foolish, loves to hear her chatter. But if the girl would listen to her old grandmother, I'd tell her things I know and keep under my jacket. There are many days, and God has given us a tongue to teach lessons to those who'll get up early.

It is nice to be in Lucrecia's house. There is more light there at midnight than in Cleta's at noon. And so there is cleanness. And as she has a husband, she keeps in her place. From the time she is young, a woman needs a man. Mrs. Cleta isn't too old for that yet, but as she hasn't got one, she is all out of sorts. Every time she goes to church and offers a candle she almost dies. I laugh myself sick seeing them so anxious, and without getting what they want!

Lucrecia's corporal built her house for her before he married. He bought the land by instalments on waste ground, and as he is a mason, the house was finished in a year. It has one floor, a partition and a cellar. Since then more houses have been built between it and the suburb and now it is close to the others. The corporal is not really a corporal, but people call him that because, when he was courting his sweetheart, he was in the army, in the cavalry, and used to come to the suburb with a big sword. He is a good fellow and was a great friend of my poor Germinal. I am on the best of terms with the pair of them, and as soon as I came into the house, I put on an apron and began to do my share of the work. There wasn't much to do, except to get the meals, but I fetched water, peeled the potatoes, and then went to my own house to get some little spring onions which were first-rate. The police were smoking in the courtyard.

"What have you got there, grandmother?"

I didn't look at them.

"Dung!"

The one with the spectacles laughed. And so, to keep them from talking to me, I pretended to be driving out dogs or calling them to me with a whistle, until I went out again. But you can't hurt their feelings, for they take everything as it comes.

The night is chilly, and the sky thick with stars. When I get back to Lucrecia's house I find in it Cipriano, Graco, Santiago, Buenaventura. Then came Elenio Margraf and Liberto. At the two corners nearest the house, two of our men are keeping watch. They have all been speaking quickly. Liberto opens and shuts his eyes when he is silent, and doesn't wink when he speaks. Elenio keeps very quiet and doesn't listen to what they say to him, because he thinks that from the beginning of his life he knew everything that they could tell him. These two and the corporal say that they'll have to change the meeting-place, and take the greatest care to keep it secret. The place has now been arranged. Then the corporal says:

"No doubt about it; this is a good party!"

They go off, leaving the meeting-place to be disclosed later on. Then I see that Graco and Santiago have their revolvers at their sides on a bench, and that they keep close to the side of a door. I lean forward in curiosity, but can't see anything. The room has nothing but a bed, a washhand-stand, two engravings of Liberty and the Revolution like the ones I have in my house. I look under the bed and see nothing except the chamber-pot and Lucrecia's old slippers. As they don't tell me anything, I don't ask questions, but I am very curious. I've always thought a lot of these comrades. A little stiff, but not babblers and with a good reputation. I think that the corporal is like my Germinal. Always keeping himself to himself. But I mustn't think about all that. It seems as if the corporal were the chief of the revolution. They take care of him—of him and of his wife—as kings used to be protected long ago, and it is more as if they were guarding a sanctuary than the bedroom of a married couple. The two sentinels outside won't let any suspicious person pass. Let the "dogs" come; let them come! I'd like to see the man with the spectacles coming here!

Two men whom I don't know have sat down where the others were, and these, after looking at the clock and taking their revolvers, have gone off. As they went out they said:

"Cheer up, old lady! We are going to make the lot of them pay for it!"

"May God hear you!"

"Or if He doesn't hear us! It isn't God who is going to stop us now!"

These aren't good words, but they come from the heart. Lucrecia puts on the table a bowl, bread and five plates. The two with the pistols come up with the corporal and sit down. They leave the best seat for me, and I object:

"We'll come afterwards. You eat now. Lucrecia and I will eat when you have finished."

The corporal says no. Lucrecia brings in the meal, and it seems that we are all going to eat together. We didn't do that in my house. The men come first, and a woman is born to serve them. They have given me the best place, but I know it is not for me myself, but because I am Germinal's mother. The meal is short, the meal of a poor house, but savoury, and as Lucrecia and the corporal get on well together, it is a pleasure to look at their contented faces. The two who were on the bench, guarding the bedroom door, have eaten their fill. Then they light their cigars and go back to their posts. The three begin to speak and the corporal says regretfully:

"It is a pity that we have to trust to shooting."

He thumps his knees with his fist:

"As for me, to get new ideas I've only to read and to hear what my friends say."

"Nonsense!" said one of the watchers, "we'll convince them only when we have a foot on their necks."

After eating I get sleepy. But I am afraid that if I fall asleep I'll be wakened by firing. It looks as if nothing were happening, but from their gestures and words, it is clear that something out of the way is going to happen tonight. The corporal says nervously:

"This is a party!"

As if to prove him right, two men come in. One is lame, and I think I've seen him before, begging. He has a grey beard and must be about fifty years old. The other isn't old, but his face looks starved enough to frighten one. They talk to the corporal and go into the bedroom. I lean out, but there is no one to be seen in the bedroom and there is no door to go out by.

Save us! there is witchery about!

But neither Lucrecia nor the corporal are taking any notice of it. People come in, disappear, and nothing happens here. I sit down again and fall asleep. The table is alongside me and tips up, and when it is going to fall I give a start. Lucrecia picks up the dishes and I tell her to wait a minute and we'll wash them up together. Then I nod two or three times, and wake up, and am quite ready to work. And this time I feel I am going to keep wide awake.

The corporal says to me:

"Auntie Isabela. None of us here has had a loss like yours."

It is true, but when I see them all eager to avenge my Germinal, I feel as if my son hadn't died. The worst will be when all this is over, and I have to go back to everyday life. The corporal says that that won't happen.

"Why not?"

"Because we are going to finish up everything."

I have seen too much in my life to be so sure. Many people will have to be killed, and for that uniforms are necessary. In a jacket and cap you can't kill more than a single guard.

I tell them about the bombs. I went out ready to blow up the town, and then I had to give them up to my son's comrades. The corporal burst out laughing. He laughed in my face, and as I didn't want to answer back, I went to the kitchen. Lucrecia doesn't want me to help her and would send me to bed as if I were a useless old wreck. But I insist on helping her. It would be the limit. Me to go to sleep when for forty years I've been the last in the house to go to bed and the first to get up! Bed is for old people; I am not old yet, and I must be the last to go to bed.

"Then you won't go to bed at all, Auntie Isabela."

"Why not?"

"There will be people here all night."

"All right; what about it? Surely sleep isn't the only thing in this life?"

When they see that I'll have my way, they let me help to clear up. There are voices in the room next door. I sit down and begin to nod. Every now and then I hear steps and wake up. More men come in. Some old ones who would be much better in bed. One in particular who drags his feet, has running eyes and a shaky hand. All go to the corporal's bedroom. I begin to pray so as to keep from falling asleep. I take out my rosary and get on with it. "For my son, that he may be in glory." When I remember that the agents are in my house, I can't go on praying. "Blessed Sacrament!" If only we could catch them in the woods! God says "Forgive your enemies," but He said nothing about agents and guards. My son died in the street with his head full of goodness. I can't pray to God to forgive him. I am sure there is no need for anyone to forgive him. And he hadn't anything against God either, to accuse Him or to forgive Him. The two of them had nothing against each other. I pray that he shall have peace and glory in the other world as he had in this world. Although he fought and they killed him, he always had peace, because he never thought one thing today and another tomorrow, and never said one thing and did another. And as for heaven, I think it is a place where everyone has enough to eat, all speak well of each other and see the best of each other and respect each other. It was that way my Germinal had peace and glory here, and I am going to pray that he gets them in the other world too.

But I don't finish. I sleep. I suddenly kick the floor and the corporal asks me:

"What's the matter, old lady?"

"Christ! I was sleeping."

"Don't get angry about that, mother. Go to bed."

And as I am not getting on well, I let myself doze off. A good thing to sleep—I dream a lot at night. Last night I dreamt that all the gentry and their women had left the streets and that we were the masters. There were no guards nor police and we were cooking on a stove in the Puerta del Sol and the Cibeles. Now and then a door opened, and some little lady pushed out her hand: "For the love of God, a pinch of salt!" We went and spat in it. A balcony window opened a bit and a marquis pushed out his snout:

"A match, for the love of God!"

And then my Germinal, who was alive although he was torn in pieces, got up and broke all the windows with a stone. Then we began to dance, and the widow Cleta lifted up her petticoats in the middle of a ring of people and waved her arms, saying that she was a soldier's widow.

That was the day before yesterday. Now—all right, we'll see! I am in bed and ask myself if I am asleep. Because sometimes I go to sleep sitting in a chair, and then when I go to bed I can't get to sleep again. It is all because of this old body which is like a broken clock. I hear new voices outside there. Lucrecia goes to the kitchen and makes a noise with cooking dishes. The voices are raised. Someone calls for silence and then I hear Samar speaking. Christ! This is not a time to stay in bed. I dress myself, and go to see what is happening. The door is open, and some men come in and creep along the wall like caterpillars without making any noise. They go to the corporal's bedroom, and when I look in there is no one. In a few minutes a lame old man comes out crossing himself. Samar asks him:

"What are you doing that for?"

The old man looks at him and says in a solemn voice:

"Oh, my boy!"

Then he points to the bedroom:

"It is like the Holy Mother for the poor. When you see, you'll cross yourself too!"

I go back to the bedroom. No one is there. I rub my eyes and go to the door of the house. Out there four or five ragged men are sleeping on the ground. A little way off two comrades are on guard. This is the poorest part of the suburb. There are only thieves and starving men. Lucrecia's house is like an archbishop's palace alongside such wretchedness. Madrid is in darkness. It seems as if they had cut with scissors all the wires that carry light to the houses. Well done! In this suburb among all these people, abandoned by God, light isn't much use. What can it do? Only show up lice and dirt! But there is Madrid over there. And my son?

"And you, what do you thing about Germinal?"

"Me?" replies a shapeless dark figure, breathing there alongside me, "what would you have me think? He is now at peace."

"But there isn't another like him, is there?"

"Well, there is a soul in every body."

We were silent for a minute and then I asked him:

"Why do you come here?"

He looked at me strangely:

"If you don't know, I am not going to tell you."

Damn their mysteries! The corporal, coming in, said with a mixture of alarm and pleasure:

"Everyone in the suburb knows about it, and the police haven't found out. But now we are going to shift it to a safe place."

At last, when two more passed into the bedroom, I followed them. At the side of the bed there is a trap door in the floor. They raise it and a steep staircase is seen. If it isn't for a woman they'll have to tell me. Down below there are about three dozen people. As the ceiling is very low, they have to bend their heads and some have to double up. Others, to be more comfortable, are kneeling. It is almost dark, except for two candles at the end of the room. All are still and silent, and as no one can hold his head up, it seems as if they are praying. Someone alongside me says:

"The day is drawing near."

"What day?" I ask.

"The day of true justice."

The man used to come to our house sometimes. Besides, I recognize almost all the faces in the room. I ask what it is, and they say a word I don't understand. Not to look like a fool, I don't ask anything more, but elbow and push my way to the front. People are talking in low tones. When I get to the front row, I see Graco snuffing a candle. In the front is a machine, tall and lean like a greyhound, with three legs. It doesn't surprise me, knowing what Lucrecia is, that it is clean and polished. I ask again what it is, and they say the same word as before, but now I remember it:

"A machine-gun."

I believe it can fire five hundred shots a minute. Never before had I seen one. The men gaze at it in silence, each of them thinking his own thoughts. I think that on the day of the burial this machine could have done in all the guards of Spain, and that with two of them my poor Germinal would be avenged. Alongside me a very lean man is breathing heavily, with his hat in his hand, like all the rest of them. The machine-gun is silent and strong, and at its side there is a heap of metal cases, and two boxes which must be for repairing it. They all look as if they are praying, and not to be different and because I don't know what to do on my knees unless I am praying, I make a prayer of my own:

"Dear God, praise and thanks because Thou hast allowed a machine like this to come to our aid; praise and thanks because Thou hast given us the wits to make it." I recite a paternoster, praying that those who use it do not come to any harm, and that their bullets find the hearts of those who killed my son.

Behind me I hear the anarchists moving up and down. Graco says that they are going to pack it up and everyone must go on as before, guarding the secret carefully in the name of Mother Anarchy. Two voices in the circle protest:

"Communists can keep a secret just as well."

Graco replies to them:

"Of course, I know that. But we mustn't have misunderstandings; you must not provoke people, for this isn't a moment for disputes."

I turn to look at them. If these men can do what they want, the machine will buzz, putting shots through the windows of the *bourgeois*. Tonight there won't be a *bourgeois* left in the world. Someone asks:

"Whose is the machine?"

Four or five reply:

"It belongs to the revolution."

Graco comes up to me:

"Look, at it, grandmother! How clean and swelling with

youth. It is one of the first that have come to our side. But there are others, whores, bitches, handled by the Civil Guard. Comrades," he went on, addressing them all, "here you have it! A machine-gun Hotchkiss, American model! It is the best weapon——"

An old man interrupts:

"Forgive me, comrade Graco. There is another weapon, still more effective—culture."

They all laugh. The machine is packed up. Graco says:

"Culture is a trick of the *bourgeois,* because there is nothing like *bourgeois* culture to enslave us."

"We don't want culture! To hell with culture! The machine-gun will help us to sink culture."

The communists cry out:

"Culture began with Marx."

The old man with the white whiskers said:

"And Greece? and Rome? Does not Demosthenes stand for something? And Plato?"

The youngest of them shout him down:

"Bloody nonsense! *bourgeois* dirt!"

As the old man is getting ready to make a speech, Graco puts out the candles, and goes off. I hold on to his jacket and go out first, lest they come to blows. From the staircase Graco calls out:

"Outside all of you, comrades!"

They come out lighting matches. The old man wishes to argue with the young ones, and they chaff him. Now I go to sleep peacefully.

I lie down and pray. I address the machine instead of St. Joseph. I don't know, but perhaps if we had turned to this Virgin before, they wouldn't have killed Germinal, and I wouldn't have colds or be the rough-tongued person they call me. Because there wouldn't have been these dogs of police in the world.

But we have them. Without muzzles, and with their tickets and badges. They will turn up their coat collars and clear out. It is for that, that all these young men, white or yellow, are in front of the machine, silent and purposeful. I say "yellow" because there was a socialist. But everyone prays to this Virgin. Talking stops there. Pray! pray! The men creep in like caterpillars, crouching down, but they come to the Virgin Hotchkiss, they raise their heads, speak their piece, and go back to struggle with hunger, but all the same, contented as one comes back from Mass. I can't tell what I'd give for Germinal to have had that machine. Now that something has come on Germinal's side, so strong, so sharp and cunning, so clean and so brave, it is easy to see that we can make a good job firing in the streets.

But I don't know what I am saying, because I am falling asleep. I see a sea of unshaven faces. Graco is standing up at one side and the old man with white whiskers at the other. Graco calls out:

"All machines enslave us except our Virgin Hotchkiss."

The crowd replies like an angry sea:

"The Virgin Hotchkiss is our Holy Mother."

The old man with the whiskers calls out:

"Our Mother will tell us that anarchy is the best."

No one takes any notice. Graco speaks again:

"With our own hands we have wrought the machine-gun."

"The Virgin Hotchkiss," they all reply, "is our daughter."

Graco stands up, holding out his revolver:

"Let us put our trust and our hope in the machine of the revolution."

"The Virgin Hotchkiss is our soul. Hurrah! Hurrah!"

Then Graco begins to pray as if he were reciting a litany:

"Ministers, Director-Generals, Archbishops, Duchess-bitches."

"You shall die at our hands!"

"Elegant highbrows! servile journalists! pimps of luxury!"

"You shall die at our hands!"

"Members of Parliament, Governors, Priests!"

"You shall till the land, harnessed to our plough!"

"Nuns!"

"For the first time you shall smile, pumping milk from your dry breasts!"

"Saints of the Church!"

"Splintered into chips they shall warm the soup of our cohorts."

"The Holy Vessels!"

"We shall use them to celebrate our great day of blasphemy."

"Certificates of Government stock, patents of nobility, wills and armorial bearings!"

"They shall blaze in the streets, and our children shall singe their shoes leaping over them!"

"The Holy Virgin!"

"She shall bring forth in sorrow!"

"Jesus, the Son of God!"

"We shall send him to a school for defectives!"

"God, One in Three and Three in One, the Almighty!"

"There is no God! We have done with God!"

"We shall use the holy napkins of His ritual as swaddling clothes for our new-born babes!"

"There is nothing but the revolution!"

"The revolution!"

"Nothing else?"

"Nothing else! And as its symbol we accept only one kind of machine: the Virgin Hotchkiss!"

FOURTH SUNDAY/HOPES AND FAILURE

Chapter 16

The Comrades Dispute: Star "Acts"

THE SECRETARY writes in his minutes:

"As a matter of urgency, comrade Samar asks for a hearing and says that the message to the national committee which has been redrafted must be agreed upon, so as to go before dawn on the aeroplane to Barcelona, and therefore his proposal must be considered before anything else."

Comrade Urbano opposes; several of those present know the proposal already and do not consider it urgent.

Comrade Graco also thinks that it is more urgent for the committee to consider the arrest of four of their members: Liberto García Ruiz, Elenio Margraf, José Crousell and Helios Pérez. The last-named has been treated with violence.

Several other comrades ask to be heard in support of Graco's protest, and it is agreed to report to the committee for prisoners.

Comrade Samar presses his request, and, as it is accepted, explains a plan of offensive based on the fact that the spontaneous uprising caused by the assassination of the comrades who fell on Saturday has reached its maximum intensity and has caused alarm among the *bourgeoisie*: noting that in the mineral zone of Arlanza, the workers have taken possession. That the communications have been interrupted to such an extent that the mail trains have to be staffed by the army: that the general strike has been adopted by the whole organization and that in places where we have not controlled the situation, the strike has been brought about by sabotage—notably that in Madrid the only newspaper is an official leaflet: considering also that in several places the army has remained neutral or has adhered morally to the revolutionaries, recognizing our successes: that in Madrid there is going to be a seditious movement in four barracks, with probable success in two of them.

Recognizing that there are many weapons in our hands and that we may gain more; that *bourgeois* activity is completely broken by panic: it therefore is necessary to begin to give coherence and a political purpose to the revolutionary energy, which has undermined the *bourgeois* organization and power——

Several comrades beg to be heard against Samar's phrase "political purpose". Samar withdraws the phrase and substitutes "efficient constructive purpose". They agree to that and Samar proceeds. He says that if we wait longer before going to extremes, there will be a *bourgeois* reaction and the struggle will encounter greater difficulties. He concludes by declaring that the committees of the suburb, with the soldiers who will revolt, the arms they already possess and those which they will secure, must go to extremes that very day, proclaiming their charter and the first decrees of the new revolutionary power, dissolving all the administrative and political machinery of the State, declaring the abolition of all class privilege, transferring to the workers the exclusive duty of carrying out the decisions of the syndicalist organizations, and ordering the soldiers to constitute their own committees, where possible reducing the officers to the ranks, taking all necessary steps. There would be four of these decrees, and each one of them would be based on, and, in theory, realize the four primary principles, which covered the fundamental aspects of the new power and were the springs of triumph.

Several comrades demanded a hearing, and as they kept interrupting, Samar sat down and asked that they should give their views, after which he would continue. Comrade Urbano strongly opposed seizing power and issuing decrees. He regarded authoritarianism as a dangerous vice, and was very surprised that comrade Samar had ventured to use such language.

Comrade Samar asks him if he believes that the workers who are risking their lives in the street agree with him. He demands that comrade Gisbert, who also had asked to speak, be heard, and Gisbert declares that he has nothing to add to what Urbano has said.

Samar insists that the meaning of the interposition be made more clear, and Gisbert declares that if the triumph of the revolution implies giving it a political basis, power and decrees, he did not want the revolution.

Comrade Samar says that he cannot understand the conduct of comrade Gisbert, who retorts that he would be against a revolutionary of Samar's type, because the struggle was for equality and liberty.

Comrade Samar reminds him that he has left out fraternity,

and that he is the more surprised because the comrade had been in France, where the gendarmes of the *bourgeoisie* had beaten his back in the name of Equality, Fraternity and Liberty. Comrade Gisbert explained where the French revolution had begun to go wrong, and ended by saying that if the world could be saved only by establishing an authority, however moral, to interfere with any individual, he would prefer that the world should perish.

Comrade Samar says that comrade Gisbert is terrible and that he only refrains from thinking him a monster because he knows him well.

Comrade Gisbert says that the *bourgeoisie* regard him as a monster, and that he thinks it an honour.

The President calls the meeting to order, and comrade Samar continues. The first decree is a reply to the "state of war" and proclaims that we are mobilized for civil war and gives rules for the organization of the soldiers' councils by those who accept themselves as proletarians and the soldiers of the revolution, as opposed to the capitalistic forces of the Civil Guard and the Shock Police.

The second proclaims the abolition of all contracts involving the labours of others, or economic privilege or exploitation. Thus, from that date, no one would pay rent, nor for public services, nor obey orders in factories or shops, except those given by the syndicates. It arranges that the miners in the revolutionary zone should, under the direction of their syndicates, prevent the mines from getting out of working order, and that in general two planes of the struggle should be recognized: civil disobedience, and armed offence.

Another decree reserved all revolutionary power to the committee until the central syndic should met in Congress with representatives of the autonomous syndics.

Comrades Segovia, Argüelles and Tarrasa interpose. The three urge that it is unnecessary to include the autonomous syndicates. Comrade Samar asks if they do not regard them as revolutionaries, but none of the three either accepts or denies that.

Comrade Urbano rises to order. He thinks that time is being wasted, and that a vote should be taken on Samar's view that the revolution should take an authoritarian and political form. If that should be passed, we could go on, but if it were rejected there was nothing more to be said.

Samar maintains that it is not a question of principle but of tactics, and that therefore it would be better not to vote until all the details were before them. Urbano and the three other comrades oppose. As they ask to speak again, the comrade president proposes that the vote should be taken, to save time, and Samar does not object.

By seven votes to five Samar loses, and the meeting passes to the first item of the agenda. Those who voted in favour ask that their vote should be recorded and——

Samar keeps looking at the rising dawn and thinks:

If instead of arresting the four comrades Liberto, Elenio, José Crousell and Helios, the police had arrested Urbano and Graco last night, nothing could have prevented my getting a majority. The four comrades who were arrested would have voted with me. Not because they are wiser or more intelligent, but simply because they are young, and understand that we mustn't sacrifice the revolution to a *bourgeois* prejudice in favour of liberty, which is what the old men have done. Our success probably depended on that accident.

A word sang in his ears: "Treachery". Unconscious treachery as always, without any idea of its consequences? What would the miners of Arlanza do when they found they had been left in the lurch? If they were to bring up against the great and powerful governmental forces a plan of attack that was concrete and resolute, the diffuse rebellion would become organized and a new impetus would be given to the indecision, the somnambulism of the revolution. A plan of campaign. A road. A light in the distance. But how were they to reach that, with men like the one who in a meeting burned his hand with a match to show what his will could accomplish, when he was only displaying a silly exhibitionist vanity? The plan of attack could be formed only by resolute intelligences, not by men who were always discussing and compromising. Samar recalled that when he was with the groups where these comrades were discussing, he went away giddy. And so did others. They disputed for the pleasure of disputation, they went on elaborating until they almost exchanged their points of view, and they had such a sense of competence and satisfaction in losing themselves in their petty intellectual labyrinths, that it seemed as if they really didn't wish for the revolution. Like priests, they always had a word to describe the "Miseries of this world", and the word once said, they were tranquil. That was an end. The workers who came to them in good faith for guidance, went off with their minds cloudy and unsettled, although, certainly, they were confident that the disputers had read all the articles in all the newspapers. And perhaps even some fat book costing a dollar. Samar shook his head and turned again to watch the dawning horizon.

Men who, although they are wholly opposed to a banker, are capable of admitting him to be right because of his fine tie when he utters some humanitarian opinion. Men who, although they are on the side of the proletariat, argue only to show that they have read the classic writers. Let them dispute with everyone, or be in agreement with everyone. What plan of battle, what manner of coherent faith, what logical order can bring them together?

Star stood in front of him with her aluminium pail on her arm. The cock followed her. Samar said to her:

"Go to the corporal's house and wait for me."

The girl went off, followed by the cock. Samar noticed that, since the tragedies, the girl was wearing a jersey of a different colour every day. Today it was white. He watched her going off and kept thinking:

"She is a revolutionary. Without the classics of anarchism or romanticism. She never thinks about the heroic. She has the revolution in her bones and in her careless smile. She lives and hopes in her faith, without thinking about it."

Star went off with the cock behind her. An Alsatian dog came along, and the cock hurriedly leapt to the other side of the girl, who stooped down and picked up a stone. When the danger had passed, she threw away the stone and the two moved off peacefully. The morning covered Madrid with its dome of blue and white. Samar went back towards the barracks, but before reaching them, slipped into a house on the left. When he came out, he was carrying a sheaf of manifestos. He felt rather pleasantly that if they were to stop him they would try him summarily and shoot him at once. As he liked to analyse his states of mind he began to think out the reasons why he was resigned to the idea of his own death.

The behaviour of some of the comrades, he said to himself, is against us. It is pushing us all down. Without meaning it, they are on the way to finish us all off, themselves and me.

Something deep down in him protested: "Not me; they can't do anything to me." Then he reflected:

Perhaps it is the inevitable result of the collapse of the *bourgeois* conscience. Its last kick in me.

Then he went on:

Or the reaction of humanity against itself now that it realizes the impossibility of raising itself by culture.

As he walked up and down alone with his reflections, he seemed to be in infinite space.

The revolution, he said to himself, is not in these, nor in the liberal radicals who gain from a dictatorship and then from a republic, and then, like the gamesters of a fair, play at revolutionary propaganda in which they offer a revolution at a discount of twenty per cent. And much less in the others who refuse salvation if at the cost of exalting another person, those who betray the revolution if they see their way to make themselves a personality outside. They are victims of an inferiority complex, and like the Argentine, are nihilists, because everything has been denied them. But the smallest praise from the *bourgeoisie* converts them. And now some are rejecting a proposal because it is Marxist, others because it is pure syndicalism, others because, although it seems sound, it is advocated by a more eloquent comrade, and they are upset that anyone should be more eloquent. They are all negative influences. Thin materially, dried up in their souls. And even in the morning light, all is negation. The trees waving in the air, the sun dreaming in the blue pools say, No, No.

Revolvers firing and hearts open and gushing through the mouth, all deny.

Samar meets Villacampa. He has slept in the open because the police visited his house last night and he has not dared to go back.

"Have you anything to do in the barracks?"

"Not me," replied Leoncio. "I thought that it was you who were undertaking that."

"Yes, but I have to wait until tonight. A few manifestos. Afterwards we shall have a meeting with two sergeants and the delegate revolutionary committee, and tomorrow we'll see if they will join in the attack or not."

"What do you think about things?"

"I am ready for anything. Now that they have rejected definite purpose or plans, we are without ideas and we go ahead in disorder. But all the same, we go unwearied and without stopping. Nothing will stop us."

They go on together. Samar says he is surprised to see that the streets of the suburb are not occupied by the army and that there are neither guards nor agents. Leoncio explains:

"They don't care what happens here. There aren't banks or

Cabinet Ministers or churches to defend. The forces are ready in the barracks, in the police stations, and in the country, all round about. The suburb is infested by them."

Villacampa discusses the recent arrests. They must have found many documents on Crousell. Samar shrugged his shoulders:

"The whole organization hasn't a single document which gives away anything. It is one advantage of the present way of doing things."

"As you think that," says Leoncio, "why are you 'acting'?"

"What do you mean? Why shouldn't I 'act'? In spite of everything the revolution is going on."

They reach the corporal's house. Star is waiting with her bucket on her knees. They put two thousand manifestos in it. Samar looks at Villacampa. His eyes are empty but resolute. There is nothing in them of *bourgeois* heroism, romanticism or aestheticism. For Star and him, the revolution must be followed absolutely but without emotion.

The manifesto is strong. No lyricism or highfalutin. The words are direct and have no need of purple intonations. Our revolution must be made without emotion, without the spiritual intoxication of the *bourgeois*. Numbers and deeds. Numbers are the backbone of deeds, and the two are inseparable. Numbers of Mauser cartridges and of sacks of flour. Numbers of rifles, of military coats, numbers of victims, of arrested men, and of the elementary ideas still in the brains of comrades which have to be thrust out because they are still poisoned by the *bourgeois* spirit. Numbers and deeds. The manifesto, short and precise, didn't please some of the priests of the old anarchist cult. But it has force in every line, in every letter and comma. It will be effective.

He gives Star the permit to enter the barracks, and the three go out together. The air is full of questions.

"And afterwards?"

"And afterwards?"

Villacampa shrugs his shoulders:

"It is no use bothering about 'afterwards'."

Samar says:

"My 'afterwards' isn't of the kind that seeks to direct the future. Enough to link deeds and numbers. To put a little compressed air inside each projectile, a little poison on each bayonet, to fix a telescopic sight to each machine-gun, and to place bullets and opinions where they may be most effective, and wound where we wish them to wound. To drive wedges into the existing social order, and to seek its disintegration by physical means."

Villacampa stood still and asked him:

"Do you know what I am going to say? That you talk a lot too much."

"Well! Well!"

"One kills or is killed. Anyhow there is this to the good: that if they kill us, a dozen new banners rise up from our bodies. That is what I think. And nothing more!"

Star disappeared on her way to the barracks. We lay hold of the cock which is trying to follow her at a run. Villacampa didn't say a single word to the girl. She read the manifesto, and after putting them all in her bucket, she made a casual nod of approval and went off to fulfil her mission without any fear.

The manifestos are going to the barracks like a rain of lead and bullets. They are white octavo sheets, badly printed but with shrewd and sharp words. Nothing much to look at. But they can stir up hundreds to revolt, even those not already eager to revolt. Samar believes in propaganda. Villacampa asks:

"What time was fixed for 'action' in the barracks?"

"Tonight," replied Samar. "There was a difference of opinion, as some were for waiting to see what success we should have with the infantry in other places. It was resolved by a single vote. I voted in favour. I can say that if the regiment rises it will be because of my vote."

Trumpets sound. In the sound there is a note of failure, of renunciation. She must be passing the night weeping. But nature would conquer. She would weep, bite her pillow—always she had to bite something when she was weeping—but slowly her body would relax, her breathing would become more rapid until she fell asleep. In the morning she would wake up, fresh and bright. But she would contract her forehead and set herself to write a letter which would be stained with tears. These thoughts made him suffer.

They went on. Somewhere near there was firing. Villacampa moved cautiously towards the shots, and Samar followed him. They met some groups laughing and putting away their revolvers. One of them explained: "We were very nearly killing each other. We were tracking down some blacklegs who were repairing the damage caused by the sabotage, and when we were close up against the guards who were protecting them, we met another group of workers who had their revolvers out. We thought that they also were there to protect the blacklegs, and we had almost begun to fire when I recognized that idiot Armengod and saw that his lot were there with the same intention as ours."

He laughed and ran off. They all ran. Samar stayed in the corporal's house until Star came back. He didn't find out what happened in the encounter, if there had been victims or who they were. His informant kept in a corner, ready to sell his life dearly. When Samar told him that if they caught him, they would shoot him, he replied: "Of course; they would be within their rights."

Samar found Casanova in the corporal's house. He was looking up at the ceiling and grumbling to Lucrecia about the sorrows of a man who couldn't get hold of a revolver. The corporal gazed at him, thinking:

"He has the face of a suicide. He is much better without a revolver."

Casanova wished to see the machine-gun which they had already taken off. The corporal refused, with cunning lies, to tell him where it was, and Casanova explained his excited state:

"I deserted the *bourgeoisie,* burning my boats. I could not and would not go back to them. But, damn it all, am I not a proletarian as much as the rest of you?"

Samar, also, saw that Casanova really wasn't one of them. He would put on a silk tie and go and be polite with nuns, if the chance came. He had been a butler in an aristocratic house, and had been discharged, leaving behind his image under the girdle of the oldest daughter. When she was told that, Lucrecia laughed until she almost cracked her jaws. But Casanova said that he was in love with the aristocrat, and the corporal and Samar joined in the laughter. Now that they were exchanging confidences, the corporal told them that a comrade in the transport syndicate was the chauffeur of a republican politician who was a regular visitor at certain "at homes". He gave himself out to be a philosopher, and the ladies called him the "journalists", because he owned a review and was associated with the Press. He thought himself a very elegant person, and the chauffeur never left the car at the door facing the main avenue, but took it off to an obscure street in the neighborhood, because he was ashamed to drive that lout.

Samar, who recognized the person in question, and knew him personally, laughed as if he were being tickled.

A shot sounded quite near. He turned to Casanova:

"Let us be off, for the police are certainly coming here."

At that moment Star arrived with her bucket. They opened it and Samar took out a paper from the bottom, kept it to use another time, and asked:

"Didn't they suspect anything?"

"I don't think so," replied Star.

Samar and Casanova went out. Casanova again begged for a revolver.

"Santiago is the man who could probably get one for you," suggested Samar.

"But has he got any?"

"Good Lord, as they haven't yet dealt with him in Geneva, the limitation of armaments is all humbug."

He went off to find Santiago, and although Samar knew that it was useless, he wished to leave Casanova with some hope. They thought over his love affairs.

"He is drunk with sentiment," they said, "and he might as well die, for he isn't fit for anything."

They thought about his committing suicide and they shrugged their shoulders. Samar knew that state of feeling well, and felt happy in thinking himself cured. "But perhaps," he thought, "this confidence of mine is no more than a return of the disease." He kept on his way to the country. After the day before with his sweetheart, and the rejection of his proposals by the committee, Samar felt the need of being in the open country.

He took a narrow path between a heap of rubbish and an unhealthy field of maize. Behind him lay the flat plain of La Mancha. The heavy sky threatened rain, and the dry soil seemed to expect it, to long for it, and even to rise towards it in little wreaths of mist. Suddenly he heard his name and stopped. Then he went on, thinking that no one here could possibly be calling him, and that in the absolute solitude only the stones and the dusty trees could be calling him. He kept walking on. "Were they foolish to reject my proposals?" he kept thinking, "—because our protest is not charged with political formulas, but is a question of the future against the past which traditionalists wish to prolong. They are men of tradition, we of hope. All that we are doing accelerates disintegration, demoralizes the traditionalists and their traditions, brings up to the surface the hidden force, the living reserve of humanity which we represent, we who alone in the western world remain faithful to nature and identify ourselves with it." He again thought he heard his name being called. That, and the fact that what he was thinking took him far away from Marx, disconcerted him.

He communed with the clouds, the trees and the wind, turning his back on the city. And these took away from him his confidence in his revolutionary position. The country is anarchical, he thought, the city communist. The country is elemental, straightforward and profound. Of course there are natural laws, and Marx appears again in them, but the country disdains agricultural science, the trees botany, and the river geography. The machine, on the other hand, is a lover of statistics. Physics and chemistry are its conscience, just as Marx is the conscience of rebellion. He identified the committees, the groups of action, the furious crowds, with the clouds, the rocks, the trees and the river, and he walked on. He heard a shot behind him, and a voice calling: "Put them up!"

He raised his arms and kept still, but turned round little by little. It was Emilia, the "virtuous Emilia" of the syndicate of various duties, who burst into laughter seeing him frightened. She came running up to him.

"I have been following you for quite a time. I called you and you disappeared. Pray excuse the shot, but I did so wish to hansel my revolver!"

"At what did you fire?"

She laughed.

"I fired at you."

Samar opened his eyes wide. He turned the revolver away, putting it in safety.

"You might have wounded me."

"You may have been hit. Don't you know that you don't feel anything at first?"

She spoke seriously. Samar felt his chest, bent and unbent his arms, took a deep breath. She helped him to search, feeling his back under the jacket, his belly and his thighs.

"I aimed straight at you," she kept saying.

"But," asked Samar, "what was your idea in coming out into the country this way? Did you come out to hunt syndicalists?"

"I came out to hunt a man."

Suddenly she seemed to be sorry. The air was heavy, and the clouds grew denser. There were great shadows. Samar felt that there was something unusual. They began to walk. And so without looking at each other they could talk more freely.

"A man?"

"Yes. Anyone. A strong man."

"But anyone?"

"How vain you are! I am glad it was you."

Samar saw that he had not understood her. He had put the question with his mind still confused by all sorts of vague ideas. Now he was sure that Emilia, apparently weak, was strong and lithe. But now that he knew what she meant, there was nothing for it but to approve. They stopped and he looked in her eyes. They were charged with electricity like the eyes of a cat. She said, with her eyes sparkling: "You will think me mad, but I want a son."

Samar stared at her, anxious to understand and absorb the mystery. She was a virgin. You had only to look at her eyes and her unformed childish nostrils. "This girl," he said to himself, "has made the revolution in her soul, she has accepted its victory almost with madness." As if confirming his thoughts she said to him hurriedly, nervously:

"I have left my family. They are worthless spongers. Now they'll have to break their heads working. I am independent and free and always will be so."

"But," he said, kissing her, "you'll have to confess tomorrow morning."

"Of course. But the priest will absolve me. He is more of an anarchist than you and me together. If I go on confessing to him he'll ask me to put a bomb in the archbishop's house."

The air grew heavier. It had begun to rain, and a kilometre off a rainbow stretched its coloured bow across the horizon. They sat down on a bank. A moist breeze came with the rain. Her breasts quivered under her bodice as if they wished to escape.

It rained on them. They melted together, under the warm rain of May, like the soil of the thirsty earth. Samar saw the rainbow in her eyes. And he also saw it in the pearly drops of rain on her black hair. She drank the drops from his wet cheeks. The soil sucked up the moisture and the bushes around them rustled. From the ground, from the turf, the dead leaves, and the roots plunging into the fertile earth, there arose a warm influence.

Samar satisfied her outspoken senses. He did not wish to satisfy the sentimental desire for a child, behind which the senses entrenched themselves. Emilia was sure that she had conceived, but Samar knew better. When the rain of May falls on the ground, it is not thinking of the satisfaction of raising bread for human beings. It sings its joy and gives its heat to the air and the clouds. Nothing more.

Chapter 17

Villacampa, Star and the Cock

THE SOCIAL brigade fell on the suburb in the middle of the morning. There were thirty agents and at least fifty guards. They thought it the best time to take us by surprise. In some places opposition was being made to them, not with the idea that they could be beaten, but to give the alarm to all the suburb, so that people might be on their guard, and anyone who had them might hide weapons, or documents. Star and I found ourselves at the corner of Mrs. Cleta's house, and seeing that the brigade was approaching, we went in and took refuge in the loft. The house has only one story, and the entrance to the loft is hidden by a kind of panel in the ceiling. We climbed a ladder, which we then pulled up behind us, and shut the trap-door. The sirens of the police motors and the whistles of the guards sounded in the streets, and a peculiar shot echoed, pleasant like a rocket. It is the signal that they are surrounding us. They try it in the morning because they know it is no use at night when everyone is taking precautions and is either not at home, or is waiting there for the guards, with revolvers ready. The explosions of the exhausts of the motor-cycles, sounding like machine-guns, almost drown the noise of the firing, and still shriller than these and the rumbling of the motors, rise whistles and sirens. The roof of the barn is covered with the red stems of maize. Seeds have been shaken from these and the cock pecks gaily amongst them making a rustling noise on the floor. Star is alarmed.

"The noise will betray us."

But there is no need to worry, for Mrs. Cleta doesn't know that we are here, and she'll make haste to boast to them that she is the widow of a soldier and that her husband belonged to the Corps of Public Safety, and most probably they won't want to search. We sat down on a roll of carpets. Suddenly I see Star's eyes growing round with wonder as she looks at something over my shoulder. With my hand on the revolver in my pocket I ask what is happening. Quickly I turn round:

"Hallo, sir. At first I thought you were Don Fidel. You are

very like him. Perhaps you are his reincarnated spirit in this loft, with his best black jacket, and his tall hat over his yellow, wooden face."

The unknown person sways his arms and his empty trousers in the morning breeze. The loft is at the corner and has two windows without shutters or glass, wide open to the breeze. I make a low bow. Down below, the hunters are seeking for the anarchosyndicalist machine-gun. All the suburb is in alarm. I bow again.

"I have the pleasure of presenting to you my young comrade, Star García, alone in the world, but an anarchist, which means that all of us are with her to ward over her. Here, comrade Star, I present to you Don Fidel, an honour and a distinction to the dead."

The wind raised the right sleeve of the scarecrow and Star took hold of it and grasped it with her hand. Suddenly she let it go, shivering, and said:

"How odd! It seems almost to be strong."

The cock went on pecking. The two of us sat down again on a heap of carpets. The scarecrow was really well-made, with something of the air of a judge, or a protestant parson, but rather degenerate and scrofulous. They had put it there to keep birds from coming in to eat the wheat which was in one corner and the fruit hung up to dry. We settled down to listen to the tumult in the streets. Because of the confused noise, the voices, and the shots, we couldn't get a notion of what was happening. Star wasn't afraid, but she took hold of my arm. We didn't talk, but when I looked at her, she smiled happily. She had her plated revolver in her grey cap, and it was lying doubled up on the carpets. I made her take it out, and I handled it. It was unloaded.

"Don't you carry cartridges?"

"No."

"Have you fired the one I gave you, the one on which you and Samar cut your initials?"

She became serious and shook her head.

"If we attack the barracks, then I'll shoot."

"But you'll need more."

"No; this one will be enough."

The cock leapt up, frightened, and came to us twittering. Apparently Don Fidel had kicked it. The wind must have twisted his trousers. Don Fidel hung from the roof, and although he was stiffened with sticks inside, sometimes he bent and danced in the draught from the two windows. His face kept quiet, but had a queer look when he twisted sideways towards the roof. We kept silent for a while. The cock looked suspiciously at Don Fidel, and I told the scarecrow that he ought to speak to us. His right sleeve lay against his stomach, and he bent slightly. It was his bow to Star. And Star wasn't grateful. We spoke about Samar. We agreed that he was demoralized and was losing faith in the movement. It was really his egoism and wish to tyrannize over us. Because it is quite certain that if his proposals had been accepted, his attitude would have been different. Star said that that was natural.

"There are many natural things that are not good."

"They are all good!"

I returned to my theory that the natural things mean violence. For instance—but I don't go on with the example, because it would be making a suggestion to her. She understands, and is quite willing. But this isn't the time for fooling. We have to keep an ear on the street and another on the floor below. The voices in the street surge up, coming nearer and nearer, mingled with shots. They pass on, and move towards the barracks. Star's house is near, and we hear the voice of her grandmother screaming at the agents. With the greatest care, and without leaning out too far, I see from where we are the grandmother in the street hurling insults at all the brigade. Then an agent comes to her and pushes her inside. He carries his revolver in his hand, and he must have pushed it into her ribs, because she stops and coughs. All the same before long she is seen at a window from which she continues to insult the troops, although not so steadily, and stopping now and again to cough. I take careful notice of the agent who drove her into the house. He has a face like a calf, and stoops, almost a hunchback. I won't forget him. The brigade moves off towards the barracks, and round about us things become quiet. We spread a carpet to deaden our footsteps and move across the loft. Sometimes the floor creaks, and we stop in alarm. Don Fidel, the honour and glory of the dead, begins to dance. It pleases me to chat with him:

"Is it really true that they shot your uncle, the Carlist general? Perhaps they did, but I don't think that he was a general. He might have been a sergeant, at the very most."

Don Fidel shakes from head to foot, in a fit of rage. He comes towards me, and the wind raises his sleeve. Star shrinks back instinctively, and the sleeve brushes my nostrils. Don Fidel looks very much as if they had just laid him out.

"What's the news from the other world, Don Fidel? Have you made your complaint to the Creator of all about that veneral disease you caught?"

Star bursts out laughing. She thinks she has seen Don Fidel assenting with a nod. I also saw it.

"Are you Don Fidel?"

He doesn't answer.

"Perhaps you are the defunct husband of Mrs. Cleta?"

He raises a sleeve in the air and moves it from right to left.

"Then you are Don Fidel, the man I flagged with a towel when he was dying."

The noise and shouts come near again. Apparently some comrades are following the brigade cautiously, seeking chances of firing at it. It is a matter of finding the right corners and getting at them first. Now the groups are close to us. Auntie Isabela signals with her hand from a window the direction in which the agents have gone, and talks in a low voice with someone I can't see from here. Star has kept back near the scarecrow, coaxing the cock with maize in her hand. Suddenly she cries out and comes running. The scarecrow has thrown his arms round her neck. She laughs, but all the same doesn't like it.

We sit down again, but this time on the floor. Star says:

"How lonely we are. In lofts it is as lonely as in churchyards."

I look round. Of course it is so. I ask Star:

"Could you kill anyone?"

"Yes. Sometimes I've thought over it. But certainly I could kill without hatred."

"I could, too."

We are silent again, until Star says:

"If I hated people as my father did, it would be different. But I don't hate the Civil Guards, and yet they tempt me to blow off their heads."

"To kill without hatred is the way we ought to kill, if we have to. But you ought not to worry about it. Reason behind the revolver. Not anger, as in murders in public-houses."

"And all the same, sometimes it seems as if we have come into the world to kill or to be killed."

That's how it is. War has been declared, and we have to be in one camp or the other, always on duty, ready and eager. The word "war" comforts the weaker comrades. War morality justifies everything. They seem to need a *bourgeois* code in order to act as revolutionaries. Star isn't like that. What happens to her is that quite simply she would like to feel hatred, but can't.

"All the same," she said, "perhaps I could. Here inside me hatred is being born."

She presses her left breast and looks sly in a pretty way. I recall how she asked me for a cartridge for her revolver. She wouldn't behave like this so deliberately, unless she did hate someone. But I am not going on talking about it, as it is giving too much importance to a poor girl who sells leaflets and badges, and hasn't succeeded in being made a delegate of her lamp factory. Just as a little while ago when we were talking of what is natural and therefore right, I nearly said rash things to her and looked at her as if I wanted her. She provokes me to it. And all because I wear a red tie. The cock comes up to us and tries to eat the flowers of the carpet. Star gets it some more shelled grains. At that moment shots sound down below. The brigade has withdrawn and our lot are following them up, it seems. Eight comrades have been arrested and they are trying to rescue them. A stray bullet hits the sheaves of maize above us. Down comes a rain of seeds which the cock quite composedly begins to pick up. All the working men of the quarter seem to have concentrated here. Down below Mrs. Cleta is screaming out in a fright, and the rapid shutting of doors and windows can be heard. The firing is heavier. A guard is working a machine-gun.

It seems as if the firing is receding a little and that the police are advancing. I lean out very carefully from the window, which is a little out of the line of the firing. In the corner at about four yards from my nose, with his back to me, an agent is shooting. I look at the other side. Nobody. The street is deserted. Windows and balconies are all closed. I draw my revolver, and, supporting my wrist on the sill, aim at his head. At the moment of firing I notice that he is the agent who ill-treated Auntie Isabela, and this discovery distracts me and I have to take aim again. I've got to get him in the head, so that if he doesn't die at once, at least he won't be able to speak and tell where the attack came from. I sight him about half an inch below his hat in the back of his neck. Sharp! Don't breathe! Up with the trigger. Aha! Paf! The agent drops his revolver and, tottering, clutches at the wall. Another still. Next shot; this time in the temple, because in his dance he turned sideways. There he lies with his toes turned up. No one has seen me. The exhaust of a motor in a side street has drowned the noise of the shots. I get back into the loft and stare at Star.

"Without hate, little girl, as in war."

I smell the revolver. It smells good after it has been fired. It is an excellent comrade. Star returns my satisfied look and repeats my words:

"Without hate, Villacampa.

But there is an inner pleasure more powerful than all the hates. Star looks in my eyes and repeats:

"Without hate."

Don Fidel seems to be saying the same:

"Kill without hate and love without grudging! We grudged our loving and fought with hate in our hearts. You do everything simply. Love and death! What would my uncle, the general, say?"

Star puts her arm round my waist:

"Without hate."

Her eyes have an odd gleam. Almost without noticing it, I find my lips on hers. But the touch sets up a current as when two wires join, and I jump off as if by an electric shock. I find myself two yards away from her. Star has shut her eyes and is laughing. I go to her and put my arm round her waist.

"What strange things one does in the presence of death."

She agrees and gazes at me with her head on my breast.

"It was the one who ill-treated my grandmother, wasn't it?"

"Yes."

"And you have killed him. You are splendid."

I stroke her head with my hand. Her hair is soft and her little ear is cold.

"I killed him without hate."

"Quite true, Villacampa, without hate."

I pointed out the place of the wounds on my own head.

"One here, and one there. Shots at right angles."

"If they knew it they would kill you."

I agreed. But they don't know it. The firing has gone farther off. It would be better to leave this place now. They won't search Star's house when they find the dead agent. It faces a different way. We could go off, leaving our revolvers here whilst we cross the street. Then in the evening I'll come back for them. Star agrees to everything. I tell her to wait a bit, and I set about putting the ladder in position. I want to see if we can get off without Señora Cleta knowing; she is sure to be shut up in the inner rooms. I place the ladder and go down quietly. I've hardly reached the lowest step when I hear frightened cries for help from Star up above. Shifting shadows fall on the wide landing where I am. The silence is whispering as if the shadows were rustling against the wall. I hurry up, not caring what noise I make. When I get up I see Star lying on the floor with her legs uncovered. The scarecrow is struggling on her. As I go in, the bundles of straw on the ceiling shake, and two jars are rattling against each other. The scarecrow has twisted his head and has seen me. His face is not wooden as I thought, but is a gourd. I see it as his tall hat falls off. A strong gust of wind blows his jacket and trousers out of the window. All that is left is his wooden skeleton. I smash the broom-handle which is his backbone, flatten in the gourd which is his head, and pick up Star who is pale and panting. The cock is strutting in the window frame, making a pretty pattern against the light. Full of corn, he proudly expands his wings. Star comes down with me. It must have been an accident that a gust of wind threw the scarecrow on my comrade, but most probably Don Fidel, who in life had his sexual desires unsatisfied, has made a lusty corpse. He can't get rid of the distinguished and elegant tendency so suitable to the nephew of a general who was shot. When we were in the street, before we went into Star's house, we saw the agent's body without looking at it. "Clearly Don Fidel is a distinguished corpse," and I added, with reference to the dead policeman, "a cut above your honour."

Chapter 18

Spain on a Relief Map

THE HIGHEST mountains lie in the Pyrenean zone stretching down to Catalonia. There are two or three other highlands, one in Castile, the other towards Vasconia, but the highest after the Pyrenees is the Sierra Nevada near Almería. How sterile and dry is this map of Spain without trees, without being coloured according to the contours, without railways, and signposts, without people, without even names indicating in letters of stone where each city is. How grey and stupid is Spain with mountain ranges of putty, plains of sand, and with rivers of green and stagnant water.

Galicia with its low hills has lost its green, and appears dead and leaden with its lakes without weeds, near the sea of rain-water. Samar thinks of comrade Monteleón on these mountains which define Galicia. In Miño there is a thread of fresh water. Monteleón writes his news and then will send it to the Centre fastened between the antennae of a pretty insect. The Galician Regional has the reputation of being moderate, but the hunger of the Galicians is a childish hunger, not avid of bread as in Castile, nor of oil as in Andalusía, nor of the early May fruits as in Aragón, but only of warm, sweet milk. Comrade Monteleón, garrulous as a woman, has told the Galician peasants the hard facts of the situation, and their hunger for milk has turned to a hunger for red blood. The Galician Regional has paralysed the activity of the four provinces. Smoke rises only from the chimneys of the villages and the manure in the stables. The factories are closed. The farm labourers are wearing their Sunday clothes. All Galicia is waiting with arms folded. From the civilian governors, by telegraph wires and the artificial highways of civilization, the nerves of the State vibrate with orders and counter-orders and with the rapid transit of the lorries of the Civil Guard, like a childish game of lead soldiers.

The State always begins with files in green jackets, and ends with the mouths of guns. A web of mutual interests! The money of the people devoted to support non-producers, and these in turn supporting the luxury of *bourgeois* politicians. Administrative difficulties, political upsets. Indifference of the green-jacketed files which are ignorant of the beauty of creative work, and the vanity of legislators astride of a tired and disillusioned land! Galicia waits with folded arms. With hands on their weapons, the Civil Guard waits. The four governors also wait with their ears to the telephone and their eyes on the white ribbon of the Morse. And comrade Monteleón replies from Galicia to the unspoken question of the good *bourgeoisie*:

"Certainly we wish politics; but not politics of rank and professions. Not a country-dance of vanities and feminine ambitions, but a combination of numbers, statistics and goodwill. We, educated by labour, know that it is possible."

On the tall hill of Cebrero there is a common ant. A black ant. It can't fly, it is nearly blind, but it carries a green leaf in its jaws and it knows where it is going.

"And the spirit?" asks a local poet.

"That is a sentiment for women."

A bee flies over Spain. It stops for a moment over a hill, and then, like a wide and shining aeroplane, alights at a streamlet. It slakes its thirst and rises again to alight on the heights of Llobregat. Catalonia is in two colours. Olive green, almost black, and a marine blue, almost the blue of the agave and cactus. The bee has alighted. It carries aromatic essences in its abdomen, and wishes to return to the hive with its burden of sweet honey. It feeds on flowers, makes honey, and yet its poisoned sting is thrust where it chooses. It is good to make honey, to feed on flowers, and to thrust the sting, but the bee has no definite goal. With its eyes and its wings, it flies, guided by the inspiration of the moment, by the wind, or the scent of a flower that allures it. Samar watches the bee over Catalonia, and the plain of Tortosa, near the River Ebro, which a tiny spider does not dare to cross, and begins to reconstruct the features of Abertain, of Ricart, of Magrañé. Catalonia has also folded its hands and carries a revolver under its left arm. Is there hunger? Hunger is not felt when we are drunk with ideals. The bee has taken flight and is hovering. In its humming, Samar seems to hear:

"Liberal ideas will carry us to victory. Let us sharpen our sting and fill our belly with flowers that the Day may come. We ought to inform the Centre, but the centralizing idea is anti-federal and we don't wish to inform it. Instead let us kill city guards and with luck amongst them an assault guard."

The bee flies away. Ricart and Magrañé write secret numbers, and write against them bombs and revolvers. They answer the good *bourgeois* Catalan:

"We are for independent communes."

The bee sees a Dutch rose on Mount Montjuich. It is the Dutch rose to which the industrialists of the country have given the name of a half-*bourgeois* Catalan, in tribute to his mild Catalonianism. Someone calls out:

"Hallo, young bee, the Dutch rose is a super-*bourgeois* flower!"

The bee alights on its heart and replies:

"What does that matter? Its scent is sweet."

To the clamouring *bourgeoisie,* Ricart and Magrañé reply:

"We must accept what comes from independent communes."

Samar's eye follows the coast line, but then, passing along the Pyrenees, returns to Cantabria. A winged ant with open eyes is crossing Asturias, Santander and Vasconia. It moves down to Aragón and there drops its wings, sprouts strong jaws and hefty limbs by which it can creep on the ground and not be blown by the wind.

In Cantabria the ant was carrying its bit of green blade. It drops it to rise into the air, scan the horizon and select its path. It came back to pick up the leaf. It walked some distance without difficulty. In the corner of Bidasoa, there is a black scorpion, a mighty worker in metals, with its pincers and restless and poisoning tail. The ant marvelled at the scorpion's precise and assured movements. The two got on well. Samar sees that the communist comrades there are troubled because the strike doesn't lose for a moment its revolutionary character. The strike there is for the *bourgeois*, but not for the striker, toiling and struggling day and night. Under the tree of Guernica the good *bourgeois* tunes his "chistu" which has carved on it the name of God, and prays and dances with one short and bandy leg, beside his carved blazonries. Sometimes he puts down his "chistu" and leans out from the window:

"And what do you want, then?"

A hundred voices answer:

"We want power."

The *bourgeois* draws back scratching his nose and muttering:

"These ones ask plenty, blast them! Power. That is nothing. There is the power. It is ready made and in the open air and perhaps not well defended. There it is for the taking. They know what they seek, damn it all!"

But he goes back to pray and dance round his blazonries of stone. The Revolutionary Committee has no authority over the scorpion of Bilbao, but when the struggle comes, they will work together without quarrel. Samar looks with melancholy at this corner, obedient to a proletarian party, and with the hope of seeing something different, descends towards Aragón, Rioja and Navarra. The Regional has its centre in Saragossa. The soil is calcareous and slippery. It acts with Barcelona and Madrid. And here the insect has fallen from a bough and passes its ringed body through the zone of sugar-beet and then reaches Monegros. The River Ebro is only a thread of steel. Samar remembers the noble river and says: "How unjust!"

The Saragossa comrades carry on the strike with tenacity and serenity. The insect is the caterpillar of a butterfly and crawls along politely and amiably, seeking the food with which to continue the development of its shining and coloured wings.

The good *bourgeois* also asks from his sunny balcony:

"May one know what you really want?"

"Of course. You may know!" The *bourgeois* continues:

"Tell us what you want, and if it is good, we'll all go with you."

The workers laugh. One of them asks him to stick out his snout a little farther. He has ready a huge old-fashioned pistol loaded to the muzzle. The good *bourgeois* is afraid:

"What is that for?"

"Not to waste a shot, what else?"

"But what is it you want?"

"To destroy everything except our syndicates."

The Regional syndicates are resourceful and enjoy unanimity and enthusiasm. The caterpillar is firm on his legs and one day will display his wings. Meantime Samar asks:

"Do you know what is being done?"

"We expect that they will return to work in Barcelona, and then hold a general assembly to see if they can agree."

Samar hastens to deny that:

"There must be no talk of resuming work."

The caterpillar raises itself on its hind legs and stretches into the air its head and first segment.

"What can we do? They have killed three comrades and arrested nearly all the leaders."

Next the two Castiles. On them there is a white salamander with its tail on Segovia and its snout on Zamora, slow and dreaming. Germinal, Espartaco and Progreso lie down below there, near the Guadarrama, under the creature's slimy belly. And what about Castile? Samar searches his heart for the answer. But he can find none, because Castile is Samar himself, and is not given to introspection, nor to prophesy about its own future, nor to play at understanding its own past. "It is me," it says, as a tree might say, or a stone or a cloud. And that is enough. But he imagines a Madrid of the future without officials, emptied by return to the fields, to the mines, to distant provinces. A lover of Madrid, he wishes for it the emptiness of a village. He recalls that at dawn, in the twilight, he has several times let his fancy play, and, thanks to it, has imagined it to be seven in the evening. The twilight of the evening, not of the dawn. An evening with the streets deserted, business at an end, the citizens shut up in their houses, driven there by panic; a Madrid deserted or a Madrid finally conquered by the revolution. The countryman has taken off in hostage the Director-General, the Archbishop, and the honourable bank manager. Without these, Madrid was delightful in its gentle civilization, cultured and clean. Some day, some day!—Samar wakens from his dream. He is in Madrid. This sun-steeped Madrid—for the clouds have gone, and the rainbow is distant—has something of the Madrid of the future. The revolution in Castile has an air of its own, dignified, sociable, well-mannered. It has a self-conscious elegance. For days the police pursued a comrade who was trying to escape after having shared in an attack on the blacklegs of an electric manufactory. Shots were exchanged. The comrade wounded one or two agents, and himself stopped a bullet. But he kept on fleeing and firing. When his cartridges were exhausted and he saw himself cornered, he threw away his revolver and restrained the police with a gesture, saying:

"All right; we've had enough of it. I forgive you."

Spain is again lying at his feet. Emilia looks at it from the other side. She thinks that she is carrying a child under her girdle and is happy.

"Look: there is my country!"

She points to mountains near the blue line of Málaga. A little higher up, a small and agile lizard is dozing. It covers the eastern part. Samar looks at it, asking:

"And you? And you?"

Puig and Ventoldra reply:

"We have gone back to work. We stopped only for twenty-four hours, in agreement with the demonstration of Madrid. But we are gathering our strength to go out for everything some day."

Samar nods his head and reflects: "Many oranges, many flowers, much of the East and much of the sea." He thinks that the East is restless when far from the sea, and that it is in the sterile wastes with their grey grasshoppers that justice is made and religion invented. But near the sea, nerves are soothed and men sleep in hope, as blue as the horizon which seems near enough to touch.

Turn to the fierce East, away from the sea. To inner Andalusía with its wide and green plains and white heights. The Sierra Nevada is not white but a grey blue. All the empty part of Spain without road or rail, volcanic Spain before the first tree and the first insect, is also grey or blue-grey. A black moth lies on the top of the Sierra Nevada. The caterpillar of Aragón has wings in Andalusía, but they are banded with black, wings that are sombre and dark. But the body of the insect is ringed with red and its antennae are red, except for their black tips.

"What have *you* done? What are *you* doing?"

"Forty reaping-machines and three farm-steadings have been wrecked, and the strike in Seville has shut up all the gentry in their oratories, or in their bedrooms."

"Whither are you going?"

"Where you are going."

"But whither?"

"To unfettered communism."

Andalusía is the country, and the country is anarchist. The comrades of the Seville Regional ask:

"And you? Whither for?"

"I am going to the revolution."

"We also."

Samar threw the stump of his cigar on Vasconia. The glowing end fell almost exactly on Loyola, perhaps close to the balcony on which elegant master Ignatius used to sit. If he had been there, thought Samar, laughing, he would have had to hop off, on his game leg, or be smoke-poisoned like a rat. Then he turned to the black moth.

"The same as you, no. I am for the grasping of power, for communistic tactics. But to destroy power next day, as is natural. But 'next day' in these times, may be one year or even two years."

"And then?"

"Then we shall all say what has to be. Socialism can meet every situation. Co-operative action and force are necessary from then."

All Andalusía burns in a clamour of proclamations and shots. Germinal, Progreso and Espartaco smile in the grave, happy because grubs creep from their lips today which tomorrow will be winged butterflies, flowers from the earth. In Extremadura there is a restless grasshopper, sometimes in a flash of coloured flight, sometimes placid on the ground, its elbows in the air, waiting until it be crushed.

Near Portugal there is an extraordinary insect. Samar takes some time in identifying it as a glow-worm.

"That little beast," he says to Emilia, "gives out a green light in the dark."

Then he notices exactly where it is.

"Do you know where it is?"

"In Castilblanco."

"That's right."

A light in Castilblanco, with Spain to the right, covered with shadows or under the light of the moon on the swamps. Samar and Emilia are resting on their elbows on the railing which encloses the relief map of Spain, at the end of Moncloa wood.

She points towards the Balearic Islands:

"Look. The Mediterranean."

"Yes," he said, "the sea of Christian civilization. The sea of Plato and Jesus Christ. An imbecile sea."

The sea was nearly dry. Samar sent off Emilia to walk up towards Rosales. Then he made water between Formentera and Valencia. The Mediterranean grew appreciably deeper.

Chapter 19

Comrades in Gaol

THE COURTYARD of the first gallery is a place of recuperation, like the playground of schools, and the comrades in gaol are much the same as school chums amongst the *bourgeoisie*. There are friendships to which people can abandon themselves peacefully. Moreover, civil prisoners enter in a sleepless condition, and if there are not too many legal complications, they can sleep in gaol and they do sleep with pleasure. They come to prison without sorrow, and this state of mind lasts a few days until the realities of the street are so far behind them that they have lost all contact with them, and only then the lack of freedom begins to be felt.

Liberto García, who is more than six feet in height, is grumbling about the prison beds which are too short for him. José Crousell, always taciturn and dry, walks up and down thinking about the Levantine Regional to which he belonged for many years, and cannot understand why it should have played a limited part in the rising. The other two, Helios Pérez and Margraf, are sitting on the floor, against the wall. Liberto has joined them and now there are three heads against the wall. As Crousell passes them they call to him, but he takes no notice and walks away. He knows that they are in a jesting mood, and want a butt. But at last he gives in, joins them and sits down. Silently they scan the courtyard. Now one of them asks:

"Who is that over there?"

They were looking at a tall fellow, well-dressed, with eyeglasses and a high-pitched voice. He fought on the proletarian side. He is a Spaniard, Americanized in Paris. That is enough to describe how far he has submerged his own personality by aping others. From his voice to his words—made up of cliché ideas and sentiments from newspapers—all was false and affected. Helios, not in admiration, but because he did not know his habits, and had exchanged one or two words with him, said:

"He is a vocalist."

He always had Marx on his lips. Sometimes Helios interrupted him, asking ironically:

"Do you say Marx or March?"

Then he swore that never had he been in relations with the Majorcan banker and that the question covered an offensive implication. He was pleased with his reply which he thought neat.

Now there came to Liberto's group three or four communist comrades, and an anarchist who was determined to acquaint all the journals of the organization with the injustice of his imprisonment. He had already written four sheets and begged paper from all his friends to continue the task. He was going to send them to twenty reviews.

"Will they all publish them?"

The anarchist was sure they would, relating that the last time when they arrested him in Algeciras, no fewer than seventeen journals printed his protest, but that this time he was going to add a little postscript: "All the anarchist and confederate press are requested to print this." The communists asked him:

"What do you hope for from all this?"

"What I am seeking? That the whole world shall know the injustice being done to me."

"But," said Liberto, "you think that they aren't already convinced about it?"

"Damn it all!" retorted the anarchist, "if they were convinced they wouldn't imprison me."

The communists burst into laughter. But no one took him seriously.

"Although you were to convince them, they wouldn't for that stop arresting you."

"Then," asked the anarchist, "you don't believe that men have a free conscience?"

"No."
"Why not?"
"Conscience is the slave of big battalions, of the needs and the moral code which the ruling class have created for themselves."
That didn't convince the anarchist, and he began to speak of the cruelties and irrational actions of the guards and the agents of public order. One of the communists became indignant.
"But that is childish! You have an organization of hundreds of thousands of workers, and you see no further than this: to write protests against the guards!"
Crousell in the depths of his mind was of the same opinion, but he defended the anarchist:
"There is some force in a protest. The story of it will circulate in some twenty periodicals and there are many simple countrymen and uneducated workers who will be excited by your protest."
Liberto added, perhaps with a trace of irony:
"We stir up the masses for the revolution, using such cries as justice and liberty. Take it that the most difficult part has been done. Now use your advantage and make the revolution! If you know how to do it, don't think that we'll put sand in the wheels."
Although he appeared simple enough in this conversation, Helios Pérez saw that although all was ready for the Spanish revolution, yet nothing came. The obstinate communist protested:
"You make the masses drunk with the idea of liberty, and thus you make them unfit to do anything!"
The anarchist asked with eyes rounded in wonder:
"Don't you believe in liberty?"
The communist shook his head in denial, and the anarchist was filled with dismay:
"And you say that in the courtyard of a prison?"
Helios and Liberto intervened against the communists, but without admitting that the anarchist was right.
"The Spanish revolution must be made in the name of liberty, and if the masses do not attain it, they will be against the revolution the day after."
The communists were dismayed:
"Then please tell us what liberty is. Isn't it the destruction of the reign of privileges? We'll secure that, as they have done in Russia!"

The anarchist denied it:

"That isn't so. In Russia there are plenty who feel oppressed."

"And there always will be people like that everywhere. Liberty as a sentiment, and not as a political fact, isn't our job, but a job for philosophy or medicine. According to your conception of liberty, there could be nothing better than to return to the *bourgeoisie* and make yourself a millionaire. A millionaire is a free man."

Now it was the anarchist who was in despair. He began to repeat himself in a way that was offensive to the communists, and they stopped the discussion by going off together. Such discussions between communists and anarchists often end badly. Liberto walked off with his red head in the air, very sure of his own opinions. He was a mason, and knew something of geometry and the physical sciences, and so his intelligence was solid.

As was evident from his name, Liberto was the son of an anarchist. His convictions came from a good stock. Although he was young, he never had thought seriously about any of the things that usually occupy men: love, economic security. In self-confidence he let himself drift, and be tossed about as time passed, without ever lacking necessaries. Although he had seemed to be involved in nearly all the deeds of blood carried out or attempted, and was well known to the police, he had never actually taken part in any of them. He excused them and even approved them, but he declared himself incapable of "acting" in cold blood.

"That," he would say, "is beyond me."

He called himself "syndicalist without revolver". On the other hand he always carried certificates of membership, news for such-and-such a committee, sealed letters to be given to a syndicate, slips with secret directions from the provinces, telephone messages. But he could not sit down at a table to write. He did everything by a nudge with the foot, a couple of words in a tramcar, a verbal message or merely his own presence here or there, now or afterwards. Liberto might have been a throwback, or an atavism of the Roman colonists, serene, determined and solemn, with clear-cut profile. He spoke little, but ideas glowed in his red head. He needed no formulas or heroic actions to give his natural disposition an outlet. For the same reason he did not require a revolver to give vent to his hatreds. He was not a communist, but he understood communism, nor was he an anarchist, although he was in harmony with the goodwill and the intellectual single-mindedness of orthodox anarchism. His faith was in the syndicates, and his enthusiasm in the revolution. He saw in that a new co-ordination of production, free from exploitation, rather than a blood-bathed violence. And so his activities in the revolutionary attempts had been restricted to co-ordination of the activities of others, to coming and going, carrying messages and documents. And also he was useful in times of peace. He interviewed harsh masters, and as they found in him neither class hatreds nor prejudices, they listened readily to his proposals. He was in no hurry. He took his time over negotiations, but as little was he guilty of idleness or of procrastination. It was not surprising that such a man would receive the most surprising news without being aghast, and would excuse all the activities of the revolution and would feel no impatience because there were unused machine-guns. He heard about the machine-gun in the corporal's house, just as he followed the ordinary proceedings of an official meeting. He had to be able to show certificates of all kinds, and for that purpose he had suggested to a companion that they should give him the title "Hotchkiss Machine-gun Corporal", obtained in the infantry regiment in which he had served. It was a diploma covered with seals and with the signatures of colonels and other officers, and was very useful to Liberto.

He would have been unnoticed in the prison but for his tall stature and his ruddy hair. The "Argentine" often sought him out. The latter, now that he was in gaol, regarded himself as a student well on the way to getting his doctor's degree. He had a supply of Egyptian cigarettes and was constantly talking of the exceptionally grave circumstances in which the law had placed him. Hearing him talk, it seemed to all the others as if it were a favour to them to have been put in gaol. At first, for two or three days, the Argentine walked up and down the courtyard without speaking to anyone. He strutted in theatrical attitudes. Some of the comrades tried to talk to him, but he held them at a distance with his hand. Then he put a finger to his lips, saying:

"Better not talk to me. I am a marked man."

He sought out Liberto when he decided that it was now safe to hold communications with the others, and put questions to him.

For instance:

"This movement may have an important international repercussion, don't you think?"

Liberto stared at him in astonishment, and the Argentine delivered one of his special phrases:

"The fear of international intervention will influence the whole country."

Then, as Liberto said nothing, he put his own interpretation on his silence:

"I understand that absolute secrecy is a duty of you leaders."

When he saw that they were paying no attention to him, he began to speak about the misery of solitary confinement, and of how there was no punishment like the loss of freedom.

"But when it is for a noble cause——" suggested Liberto.

Then the Argentine brightened and began to say that the thought of having done one's duty lightened even captivity.

"What have they against you?" asked Liberto.

The Argentine lowered his voice:

"Suspicion."

Liberto reflected: "No doubt he thinks it his duty to incur suspicion." He looked appealingly at the communists, who took notice and called the Argentine to them. They made him relate his revolutionary experiences and meanwhile smoked his cigarettes. Liberto stayed with the three other comrades thinking:

"He calls himself an anarchist and so we can't turn him away altogether."

Elenio Margraf took out a notebook and began to take notes, asking Liberto what documents he had on him when he was arrested. They made a long list. Elenio commented on the value to the police of such-and-such a paper, but concluded that after all there was nothing giving serious information. Then he related that during the morning visit his own woman had been badly upset by meeting in the conversation-room a young and pretty girl who had come to see him.

"And who was she?" asked Crousell knowingly.

"Well," said Elenio in a doubtful way, "it is a girl who has always shown a kind of affection for me. But I don't know who she is or what is her name."

That is Elenio's weakness, although in everything else he is serious. The comrades know that and press him:

"Then you only know her by sight?"

"I mean to say that I don't know who she is. We have spoken once or twice and the little girl certainly seems to like me."

Crousell asks:

"What does she say to you?"

"The truth, of course. It is a curious thing. I've been told that she found out who were in the gaol and had put down her name as a visitor to me."

Crousell and Helios keep laughing. They know the young woman and also that she is a wretch both vicious and sentimental who goes every day to visit "her prisoners". She asks the guard which prisoners have no visitors, and notes when the four or five prisoners who haven't come out to the conversation-room appear. She divides the visiting hour into three or four parts and goes from conversation-room to conversation-room to see "her prisoners". One of them, for one reason, and another for another reason, all of them please her, and she flatters the male vanity of all of them, pretending to be in love with them. She isn't really lying, because in fact the sentimental appeal of a prisoner stirs her much. In fact, their chief attraction for her is the idea that prisoners pass their time without touching a woman. She would make them, so to say, all violate her a little. Elenio insists:

"I can't complain of my luck with women!"

Crousell and Helios don't wish to disabuse him, and leave him with his illusion. Elenio smokes a cigarette of canvas which he puts up with instead of tobacco, because he may be a long time in gaol and his woman won't have his wages and will have to manage by charring. Elenio is a short man with a wide forehead with three horizontal furrows. His wrists are marked with scars made by cords with which the Civil Guards bound him, and he often relates that when he was led along the street, the guards removed his handcuffs and the corporal took out a waxed cord and bound him so tightly that in an hour or two blood poured out between his nails and flesh. The corporal called it an invention of his own. The cords left wounds which turned into permanent scars in the damp cold of the other prison.

"When I asked them to untie me so that I might relieve myself, the corporal preferred to open my trousers himself, instead of setting my hands free!"

The three made their comment in a single word and Elenio pushed up his sleeve, looked at the scars and renewed his hatred. He was a baker, and had the childish gloom of Gorki's bakers, and the tired air of those who work all night. Also, he had a tendency to metaphysics which came into play when he entered on any chain of thought. From the presence of the warder he passed to the authoritarian idea, from that to the crime of depriving him of liberty, and from that to his assured hope in a day to come without prisons or authorities. He elaborated these ideas with subtlety but became disconcerted at his inability to put his subtleties into words. That was natural, for he didn't think them, only felt them. After he had told what the guards had done to him, he became silent and self-absorbed.

Crousell, the printer, was much more taciturn. In conversation he revealed only a bit of his mind, and almost at once shut it up again hermetically. He himself spoke little. He thought that everything in the world had been said already, all questions discussed, and settled.

It was impossible to argue with him, because it was clear that he has passed beyond thinking, beyond human doubts, even far beyond certainties. Sometimes he gave the impression of being vacuous and at others of speaking like God. To value him, one had to know him very well.

Helios Pérez was also taciturn, as printers often are. As he came from the east, he always spoke in images. When he began to talk, it seemed as if he were taking a block of engravings out of his pocket and was exhibiting them. He was full of such blocks, and of things to say, but it was clear that most of the time, as his attention was fixed on current incidents, he forgot to speak. His sensibility was acute and responded to and registered the course of events just as a barometer registers storms. I believe that when things were going well, he increased in size, and when they began to settle down again, he grew smaller and shrunk into himself.

The four were silent, in a row against the wall. Liberto was thinking of nothing. His blue pupils contracted to pin-points in the strong light of the courtyard. The last rays of midday tinged his red head and were reflected from it, leaving him undisturbed. Elenio said:

"They won't try me. I am one of the leaders. They may give me a week or a year. But what is a year in the life of the universe? Or a century? Our notion of eternity is nothing but an instant in the reign of the physical laws which rule us."

Then he shrugged his shoulders. José Crousell was thinking that he had saved several pounds of type, and that the police would not find them. Another printer had them, so that if trouble should come, he would be able to set up the manifestos of the north district.

As for Helios, he was lamenting, in a rage:

"The Valencia comrades would already be drinking their coffee tranquilly with the radical-socialists whilst he was pacing the prison courtyard and feeding on rations."

There was a bald old man with a misshapen skull, and so thin and white that he looked as if he were a body which had been soaked in paraffin and hung on a wall to dry. He was a herbalist who had invented a specific for growing hair. He showed everyone a large document which he had addressed to the President of the Republic, the Spanish Academy and the Athenaeum. No one could possibly be more like a caricature, and as often as he told them his woes, they greeted him with jokes and laughter. His wife was young and gay, and cynically had taken a policeman as lover. Once the herbalist had made a scene, possibly to defend his rights in his own house, and the agent smacked his face, took him off to the Police Station and arrested him for "threats to the public authorities and the illicit possession of arms". They put him in gaol, and the agent and the wife were now undisturbed. The herbalist complained bitterly of the rudeness with which the judge treated him. The prisoners got much amusement out of him. The man was meanly abject, a mere spittoon, and seeing that, the comrades thought all the more of themselves, by comparison—except Elenio, who was saddened at the thought that they both belonged to the same species.

The warder summoned him and he ran like a blackbeetle. When he came back to the yard, Helios beckoned him:

"What was it? A visit?"

"No sir, a letter."

He pulled out several sheets from the envelope and said:

"It is my niece. I told her that while I was in gaol she was to write to me, and the poor girl writes down all she does and sends it to me. I took her with us to stay in Bilbao and now she is here with her family."

He took from his pocket some crumpled sheets and offered them to us, saying:

"They are the first ones she wrote to me when they put me in gaol a month ago. She doesn't know about my wife and me. Although she is twenty years old she is still a child."

As everyone was very bored, it seemed something to do if Liberto were to read them aloud:

"Saturday, April 9. When I woke up I wondered if I'd have as bad luck today as yesterday. I went down for the marketing and bought *The Liberal.* Two registries for nursemaids were advertised, one at the end of Serrano Street, to which I went. They opened the door for me and an old woman appeared and looked curiously at me and asked if I were in a hurry. I said I wasn't and she told me to sit down and wait. While I was alone I noticed that the house was very smart, furnished in the Spanish style, and quite new. I couldn't help wondering if they would take me. After a time the old woman came and asked me for references, and when I answered that this was the first time I was to be in service, she replied that they wanted a girl with experience in the care of children. I went to the other house, and, what with the time I had waited in the first and the time it had taken me to get to the second which is near the Botanic Garden, it was already half-past twelve. As I had done all I could, I went into the Retiro Park and sat down on a seat, and when I began to wonder why I was seeking a situation, I remembered being outside the School of Arts and Crafts in Bilbao, in doubt if I ought to join or not. If I had joined, I would not have come to Madrid and wouldn't now be seeking a situation. There they weren't my relations and didn't throw in my face what I was eating, and besides they were going to let me study, which they refuse here, and even my brothers keep telling me that they can support me, and besides that they don't wish me to study, but to take a job as they do. They are right. Money rules the world, and a person with money in his fist will be liked and respected, for there are very few who don't act that way, and have real charity in their breasts. In Bilbao the old people never laughed at me, and I could even tell them what I was thinking.

"Monday, April 11. Today nothing of importance happened. As strangers are going to come, I fancy all day that I shall like them because they are from Bilbao, and I am tired because we have had to make ready all the bedrooms.

Tuesday, April 12. I went to bed late, and with all the work I had done and with the fancies I had about the visitors, I didn't sleep, because between my dozing I heard that they were still arranging the house, and I heard someone saying that after all the trouble that had been taken, they wouldn't come, and then at last I heard the bell, and a number of people speaking, and got up and went to greet them, and found them having a meal. The father seemed to be a nice sort and the mother the same. The son seemed rather rough, but that doesn't matter. They then went to bed, and until two o'clock I was alone, and when they got up I served their dinner, and while I was serving, they spoke to me about Bilbao, which, although it is a dull little place, I like very much.

"Tuesday, April 12. The strangers asked me if I would like to go with them to Bilbao, and I guess that it wasn't necessary to ask. And so I'll be disappointed again if they don't take me.

"Wednesday, April 13. Today has been splendid for everyone, because it was a holiday, but much better for me. In the morning we saw the procession and at night we went to the Barcelona Cinema, but first we went to a café to watch the fireworks, and they spoke again about Bilbao, and I remembered every corner of it, and the more they spoke the more I remembered. The husband said to his wife that I knew all about Bilbao, and the talk got lively, and they asked why shouldn't I go, and that I would be a friend for their daughter, and that they would hunt up a sweetheart for me and marry me. And all night I haven't slept for thinking about it. And they also said that they would enter me at the School of Arts and Crafts.

"Friday, April 15. They are going off tomorrow, and I don't know if I am going to Bilbao. If they go off, I mustn't think about going, and it doesn't matter although I am suffering, because one gets accustomed to everything and tomorrow I'll go to look for a place."

Liberto didn't want to read any more, and handed back the sheets. The herbalist said:

"I am her Providence," but lamented, saying, "the poor girl is too clumsy."

How can that girl trust that man? And the man ought to understand her! He kept the sheets, and went off raising his feet so high that he kicked his own legs. Then two officers came and called for Liberto, Elenio, Crousell and Helios. The four stood up. The afternoon was still and silent. Across the walls of the prison, a youth playing football was heard calling:

"*Fau! Fau!* No score."

All these calls in the game had nothing to do with Fau, but they brought to mind the "Carnival Scarecrow".

They were put in separate cells. Next day they were taken in a lorry divided by partitions, and were returned to the dark dungeons of the Central Public Security Station. The Argentine walked up and down the prison-yard making slow gestures.

"They are setting the others free, and keeping me in gaol."

And added with unbridled delight:

"They know what they are doing."

He was delighted to be considered a dangerous man.

Chapter 20

Mass Intoxication

INTOXICATION HAS a point of climax, disease has moments of calmness, and war placid hours. The afternoon of the Fourth Sunday seemed drunken under a quiet and gentle sun, giving the sensation of a Madrid steeped in honey. The wide avenues were empty, but might suddenly become thronged, and the authorities had disposed agents and guards at strategical points, swift patrols with motor-cycles, whilst the chiefs themselves patrolled in cars. There was a silence of the country, a Virgilian peace under the trees of the avenues.

All the organizations, district, regional, local, the groups and the "cells" stretched their sensitive antennae, giving and taking information, tuning their activities to those of the others. In Madrid the masses wished only to arouse themselves from their intoxication enough to prevent blacklegging and make sabotage more destructive. If, for these purposes, it was necessary to wound or to kill, they would wound or kill. But without sentimentalism. And without avoidable misery. Hunger had not yet to be reckoned with. There were isolated cases of miserable people, just as there are always. But for the most part these were not the revolutionary workers, but broken-down men, without morale, in the last desolation. The strikers were living on food taken from the sacked stores which had been hidden in five different places, and had been carefully listed. It was certain that there was food enough for two or three days without pinching, and meantime plans could be made for more looting. Villacampa already had in mind a large warehouse with bales of dried cod, pickled pork and good flour. They would see about that. But they had also to try to secure supplies of arms and ammunition. For to eat and to lie in the sun was the kind of thing the *bourgeois* did, and there were more sacred duties in life. It had quickly become clear that they must not be too intoxicated by what success they had had. Even if all Spain had responded, it was plain that the State had quietly concentrated its black force of helmets and bayonets to conquer the situation. It appeared to have retreated, and to have left us the streets and the squares and the May sun. But we could not attack the Ministries, we could not get near the Central Postal System nor the Telephones. "If you like," they seemed to be saying to us, "you can burn a church and get away with it." The churches don't interest us. We go about the streets without a necktie, with a wide grin on our faces and breathe freely, rejoicing in an illusory triumph. All is ours. Everything belongs to everyone. Intoxication in a crowd is not vicious as it is in individuals. It is a more serious matter, which is called a "state of public feeling", and governors and political chiefs are prepared to negotiate with it. The intoxication of our multitudes is negative. It is not to be negotiated with. But many negatives may make an affirmative, as in arithmetic "many littles make a muckle". It is, above all, in negation of political authority, that crowd-consciousness hardly counts. If the crowd does wish to repudiate it, they can do it!

But in the intoxication of the masses there are three quite definite tendencies, corresponding to different sections of the city. In Vallecas, for instance, they are prepared to play the card of military sedition and let that take them as far as it will go. They have the view that in the revolutionary path, no effort is quite wasted. If one effort should fail, they must still go on, and if there are not other methods, they must still go on, even in despair. In Cuatro Caminos they believe in collecting all their resources and going straight to civil war. If that course should be rejected, they are ready to go back to work. Then there are the moderates of the lower parts of the city, who are influenced by socialist doctrines and wish to go back to work now that the protest at the death of Germinal, Progreso and Espartaco has been solemnly and impressively carried out. In the secret meetings which have been held—meetings of unauthorized delegates in the absence of delegates from the strong organizations—these three tendencies are apparent. Meanwhile, it is pleasant to drowse in the streets in the spring afternoon, and to let oneself become intoxicated by the strong wine of hope. Many splendid things appear to be near and certain. The committees are fairly resolute and there are few absentees. There are still in the streets many good comrades able to deepen and intensify the movement. To spread it more widely is not possible at present. Workers who don't know each other meet and stop to speak in the streets.

"Aren't you going back now?"

"Yes, but as soon as a couple of shots are heard in the street, we'll down tools and declare for action. Guards come in to protect us, if we are willing to go on working, but having guards at one's elbow doesn't encourage us to work."

"Are you a socialist?"

"Yes. But one is a worker first."

"Of course; I am, too. But in my trade we are not working."

"What trade?"

"Joiner."

They shake hands and move on. Men who don't know each other ask for cigars, sing duets in a low voice, and do all the unusual things which people do when they are happy. When a lorry or a private car passes, it is plain that their drivers are ashamed of themselves, and the revolutionary workers themselves, before firing on them, think sadly on the terrible and tragic divisions amongst workers. They would fire to destroy or puncture the motor tyres rather than to wound the drivers, from the surprising reason that they considered them already wounded in the class spirit by the terrible chance that they had been forced to be blacklegs. Of course such a reason was too subtle to stay the finger on the trigger. And the finger moved and the bullet was fired.

There had been a renewal of disturbances round about Atocha station and in the Paseo de las Delicias. It seemed that there had been an effort to restore the railway traffic. When they knew it, the comrades from Vallecas arrived early in the afternoon and their presence and the alarming rumour which they set going had been enough to stop the traffic. Some small groups had remained patrolling, and it was really pleasant to walk about together under the warm sun in the early afternoon, with so easy and simple a revolutionary task. The groups walked backwards and forwards. Soon after four o'clock, poor Casanova turned up, looking as if he were walking in his sleep. He had been five days without going to bed. He went up to a group of the syndicate of valets and wished to speak to them, but they took no notice. He pulled out his ticket and then one of them said:

"All right. What is it you want? Do you wish to join the gang?"

"I don't want to join. What I want is a revolver."

The three looked him in the face and said:

"You must be very unfortunate not to have managed to come by a revolver in times like these."

Another added:

"For it is easy enough."

Casanova's eye lighted up.

"Is that true? Are you really going to give me one?"

One of the group had two, but they all kept quiet about it. They excused themselves, and Casanova, convinced that it was no use to press them, left them, afraid to waste precious time. He walked off, unsteady on his legs, with the gait at once heavy and shaky of a man who hasn't slept; he went off, no one knew where, but in a hurry. He was afraid that tonight would end as the last two nights, without his getting hold of a pistol. No one would give him one, because they had not enough confidence in the way he spoke or looked at them.

And there was no reason to waste revolvers and cartridges on a suicide now, when they were so necessary, and when a suicide could accomplish his object without wasting proletarian powder. Casanova was an abject example of complete failure without any chance of recovery, the failure of failures. He wandered about in the afternoon, an afternoon clear and transparent, filling the air with rural joys, with bills of fairs, a novel full of wicked bishops and distracted duchesses, and a hidden child destined by the author to become an emperor in the last chapter. And Casanova poisoned it all.

As they saw that he was wandering aimlessly, they followed him for a minute. On turning a corner he sprang on a guard, contrived to knock him over and get hold of his revolver. He came out into the avenue with it and fired two shots in the air. The shots echoed along the evening avenues and faded into the uncaring void. It was like the shot in the air which starts a race on a sports ground. He fled, pursued by the guard he had disarmed and by two others who had come up at a walking pace. As he fired on them they surrounded him and brought him down like a puppet on the pavement. The workers saw the whole affair like a play arranged by strange mountebanks who spoke another language, and came from a foreign country and had set up their own stage. Casanova was dressed like a worker, and had an identification card. But that was not enough. He had debased himself too much. He had not subscribed even a miserable shilling towards vengeance, support or armed help. Whence had he come, they asked? They did not take him as a comrade. And a man dressed like a workman, and who begged a revolver and was not a comrade, could be anything. Even the most repugnant thing!

The affair broke the peace of the afternoon. Towards nightfall the secret backrooms and cellars began to be thronged. With the first darkness there came the first meetings. All with the same initial purpose: to keep up communications and contacts. Prodigious efforts of memory were made to recall addresses and telephone numbers. It was very dangerous to carry documents even when written in cypher. But it was not yet the night. It was six o'clock. As the sun sank the streets acquired a peculiar feeling. It did not seem surprising to hear the noise of crowds in the working parts of the city, or shots being fired, as some siren announced the closing of a factory staffed by blacklegs. At sunset, the sun steeped the tall sky in scarlet, and below, the city was in ashen shade. The mass intoxication reached its climax at the moment when the traitor sirens sounded, and then came the rising nerve-storm of the night.

At that crowning moment the crowds sang their song of peace. Whilst women hurled insults at the few female workers coming out from a manufactory of sweets, and some revolvers barked against the treachery from hidden corners, the crowds continued singing their song of peace. They were hidden, and no one knew whence came the sound, but Samar stood still for a moment, listening to the hidden voices. Villacampa also. But Star sang boldly, and in her voice was the spirit of the revolution. It was the high song of combat, of a combat now becoming more insistent. A new harmony, controlled by laws as yet unknown, laws unrelated to the old *bourgeois* law, laws unrelated to the old morality, the new joy created by violence. But a joy that was simple and pure, a joy in which Casanova could have no place.

The groups, and the "cells", as night fell, searched the horizon and awaited the work of the night. The committees arranged their papers and discussed the best way of getting to the places of meeting. Everyone, before starting on the path assigned, felt in his pocket to see that his weapon was ready. They joined in crowds singing the song without words that was dreaming in every heart, which without the use of words, without expressing feelings, thrilled the comrades until their pulses quickened. It is the hour when the worker, with the same song in his heart, says to his woman as he leaves her:

"If anything should happen . . ."

He departs for hours which might become centuries. Not figurative but actual. She listens to him and agrees to everything.

Chapter 21

Trapped. Samar and Amparo

THE MOON was hidden by a cloud shaped like a bear. It was surrounded by a pale halo. Was the cloud transparent at its edges, or was the fur of the bear filtering the light? But actually over the northern suburb the cloud stretched its short neck and hairy breast, and the bear grew larger, expanding without changing its shape. Graco, one of those who had shot at the "Carnival Scarecrow", lifted his head, saw the bear drifting in the sky, and said to Urbano:

"Look at what is happening. Look up there and see Fau!"

Urbano joined in Graco's merriment, and then from his place in the shadow, replied:

"Do you know that Fau business fell like a bomb on the Central Police? Have you read the papers tonight?"

Three sheets had been published, and in all three the account of the attack on Fau had been inflated by reports as to the motives for the deed. They attributed numberless virtues to the spy. He was a laborious workman, thoroughly steady, and of unimpeachable character. Graco laughed:

"They don't know about the South Bank or about the farm at Valladolid!"

"If they had know it would not have made any difference."

Fau had several crimes to his credit. Graco made a shrewd remark:

"Do you know what I am going to say?"

"What?"

"If you think it over, what I see in the comments of the reporters and even in what the editor of the *Vigia* himself says, is that we can take credit for Fau's good character, because it is only when you are dead that nothing but good is said of you."

Urbano shrugged his shoulders:

"No doubt you are upset about it."

Graco burst out laughing. The shade of Fau stretched over the workers' district. Graco finished:

"They may call themselves *bourgeois,* but they always degrade a man to the last depths, for treachery and spying are the lowest things a man can do."

It was clear that Graco was pleased by his own comment.

They walked on. There was no light in the district. Repairs had been stopped because each time the squad of blacklegs found it more dangerous. Fau in the sky was a heavy grotesque figure, dimly outlined, bright only at the edges. The people of the district were asleep round the free-water taps, and Graco and Urbano went cautiously towards the country.

They were to meet in a house outside the district, close to fields of barley. Behind it there was a stony waste ending in the fisherman's street called the Three Fishes. This waste was higher than the adjoining fields, and the area was surrounded by a steep slope of about ten feet on all sides, except on that of the house, where the declivity was gentle. It was almost level with the town, and from above nothing could be seen of the house but the chimney.

When they came out from the street of the Three Fishes, the cloud had begun to move towards the west. It kept its shape, and the moon was showing between Fau's legs. It was yellow. It was pallid and threatening. There were other clouds near it. Graco looked all round about him, in the cautious revolutionary habit. Then they set off to walk at a good pace. The night appeared to be suitable, and if nothing untoward happened at the meeting, at dawn they could renew the attack, and attempt subversion of the regiment, by agreement with the sergeants who were standing in with them. Of these there were two apparently ready for everything. They were blind visionaries. Two of the sort who perish at the first shock, or succeed. They hadn't the same faith in the third, who was stolid and steady. For the kind of business in hand, reflective men were of little use. Men mad with a contagious madness were wanted. Reflection has its place away from the firing line, pulling the strings. Graco said with decision:

"Action is our kind of reflection."

They had crossed three parts of the waste, when suddenly they heard revolver shots. They pulled out their own revolvers. Urbano said:

"They must be our lot," adding in a raised voice:

"Graco and Urbano, comrades."

Two shots sounded. Graco heard the swish of a bullet at his ear and Urbano saw the soil splash on his left. Bent until their chins almost touched their knees, they rushed forwards. The shots seemed to have come from the steep slope on the left, fifty yards off. Before they could take shelter on the slope, three or four more shots came. When they had almost reached the house, Urbano asked Graco if he had been wounded.

"Nothing," he replied.

They entered the house carefully. The silence made their steps ominous and intensified the loneliness. The house was empty. They struck a match and searched beyond their own shadows. On a deal table a note was left:

"The house is surrounded. Clear out by the right towards the little canal."

Under it there was a mark that seemed meaningless, but Graco studied it and said:

"They meant to tell us not to go that way. We must escape by the left towards the reservoir."

The night seemed to threaten them on all sides. Graco said:

"How can this have happened?"

"It was to be expected," replied Urbano. "We were too sure."

A window was open, and they thought they heard steps. Graco was going to fire, but Urbano restrained him:

"Keep that. Only with luck can we escape."

Graco obeyed him and withheld fire, cursing. They went out in the direction opposite to that suggested on the paper.

"The police," said Urbano, "must think that the house is defended and are planning how to catch us without risk."

Almost as soon as they went out, they found themselves surrounded by agents who pointed their weapons at them. They held up their hands. An agent searched them, took their revolvers and handcuffed them. No one had spoken. With a gesture they bade them march. Graco kept thinking of the "law of flight", and Urbano, carrying his head proudly in the air, didn't know what to think. When they saw soldiers with fixed bayonets they felt more easy. With them they would not be murdered in the open country under the legal pretext that they were trying to escape. Then they saw a dozen other comrades surrounded by machine-guns. They had all been caught. Fau was still looming in the sky.

As if they had been waiting for Graco and Urbano, they set off at once to the street of the Three Fishes. When they had reached it, they turned off towards the barracks. Samar was among the prisoners. He was third in the file, with his wrists crossed and bound to his chest. Graco thought it a pity that Samar had lost his nine-chambered plated revolver.

"Perhaps," he consoled himself with thinking, "he will get another weapon tonight."

Once in the barracks, the Colonel recognized Samar, and before the police made their depositions, he ordered them to take him to his office, and on his responsibility to remove his handcuffs. They had nothing to say. The Colonel knew Samar at once.

"What I didn't know," he said, "was that you were an active revolutionary."

Samar kept silence. The Colonel got still more human with the silence. Samar recognized in him the father of his betrothed, a formal man, weak in character, very little of a soldier, and with some of the straightforwardness and nobility of his daughter. He saw that of all the events, the only one that had deeply impressed him about Samar was to find him in the company of unshaven and badly dressed people. All the rest, ideas, revolutionary action, were respectable enough. He had on his desk a few copies of the subversive leaflets distributed that morning. He began to speak:

"I am not going to question you, and much less to scold you. Nor am I going to send you to the cells with the others."

Samar replied:

"You must do what seems best to you, but I must say at once that I am very sorry I can't be grateful to you about it. Your duty is to treat me like the others."

The Colonel seemed rather surprised. Then, playing with his pencil and not looking at him, he replied:

"I don't want your gratitude, and it doesn't matter to me what you may think just now. You are at my mercy and I'll do as my conscience bids me."

Samar looked at him coldly:

"Your conscience and the rules are against each other just now."

"That is all right," replied the Colonel; "when that has happened before in my life, I have decided against the rules. And for my acts, Samar, my friend, I am responsible."

Then he sighed, and with a sudden hardness due to the difficult and false position, and his dislike of bending his professional dignity to police duties, he said:

"I don't know what the army has to do with these affairs."

Samar didn't reply. They went out together from the office and the barracks to the wing in which the Colonel had his private quarters. They sat down to talk in the court of the entrance floor, and so out of the barracks' atmosphere. The Colonel said:

"I am glad that the whole affair has come to nothing; it is the best thing for you and for us."

Samar was still silent. The Colonel rang a bell and a servant came. "Bring coffee and brandy and tell the others to go to bed."

Then he spoke against the Republic. The Colonel was an aristocrat and monarchist. Samar let him talk. He was so assured, so well-poised and so confident that all these revolutionary attempts could come to nothing, that for a moment Samar felt his own convictions weakening. But it was not only what the Colonel said. His opinions were given a deeply emotional setting. It was his betrothed's house. In the arrangement of a curtain, the placing of a flower, even in the ashtrays on the table, he felt Amparo's influence. The Colonel made not the slightest allusion to these affairs of love in which he had never wished to interfere. Samar was his friend and he wished for his daughter's happiness. He cared little about anything else. Nor was there in the Colonel's manner anything that Samar could regard as protective patronage. When he had to go back to the barracks, to which he had been called by telephone, he said:

"They are calling me because there is a conference of chiefs at the ministry, and I must go. I have made myself responsible for you, and you can stay here until tomorrow. Until then you are a prisoner. Tomorrow we can see what is to be done. There you have coffee and brandy, and books; if you want anything else, ring the bell."

When he had gone, Samar reviewed his situation and put it into words:

"That man and I share hatred of the present Government and love for his daughter. These naturally unite us."

But as soon as he heard the outer door being closed, he felt free from the barracks, from the peril, from the feeling of defeat, from the menaces of which a few hours since, when he was arrested, had oppressed him. Amparo now dominated his thoughts.

"Things," he said to himself, "have happened too simply. Someone must have warned him."

This interpretation was confirmed as he thought over some of the details of what had passed. The Colonel had not been surprised enough at seeing Samar. Although he was a monarchist, and to a certain extent was pleased with difficulties made for the present Government, the revolutionaries had been primarily attacking the officers of the regiment. The attempt to make a regiment mutiny means rather more to a colonel than an intrigue or an escapade. The Colonel certainly had been warned. All the same Samar did not want to worry over the past. Always, when he was up against a defeat, he tried to wipe it out of his mind, and concentrate his energies on forgetting it and getting on with the next move. But for the moment he submitted a little to the comfort of these friendly walls. What about

Amparo? Was she sleeping? Was it possible that her father had sent her away from these perilous events? Complete silence reigned in the house. He rang the bell. Through the curtain which divided the Colonel's room from the hall, a charming auburn head appeared.

"What do you want? The maids aren't here."

She was smiling and seemed happier than ever. Samar frowned. She opened the curtains wide and appeared clothed in white from head to foot. She was wearing her wedding-dress and asked him with her eyes:

"Do you like it?"

Samar also wished to ask her a question, but he could not find the words for it, in the presence of that white radiance. All the same she had guessed it, and forbade it with her eyes. She would have replied, but she was not quite sure that if she were to answer, the question would raise a barrier between them. Samar looked at her, and she was submissive as always, but with a new joy. Her white arms seemed to shed light through the white sleeves. Her eyes, as always, were soft and steady, with an expression of restful and almost unconscious hope, a hope almost animal, and yet with a flavour of mystery and divinity. A little animal totem. Samar felt her at his side, confident and smiling. He asked her if she knew what had happened and she agreed almost without ceasing to smile. Her serenity disconcerted Samar.

"They have caught us all. I am angry with your father for bringing me here. What can I have to do with you people?"

She smiled. Samar went on:

"Now that everything has collapsed because someone warned your father and he warned the police, I wish to accept my responsibility, like the others."

Amparo came closer, passed her arm round his waist and leant on his breast.

"Don't think that, Samar."

"Don't think what?"

"That I betrayed you."

Samar kept silence. He felt her weight against him, on his left thigh. He looked into her eyes with a question. She gave them to him to read. Samar felt lost for a moment—to lose oneself for a single moment! To lose oneself for a single moment which is a life among the millions of lives which will succeed us! Amparo breathed through her lips half open, fresh and seductive. To abandon oneself to feeling, to the spirit, and to burn in it, and burn up in it! After all, who could say if his adhesion helped or harmed the revolution? And life is only an instant. After all, those who think that they suppress life only submit themselves, allowing themselves to be captured by its most childish side, the side of vanity. They play at being Titans, although aware that the rock they carry on their shoulders one day must crush them. Samar thought all that, and was weak enough to fly from it, taking a sudden futile refuge in a question:

"Why did you put on that dress?"

She repeated that she was trying it on, and thinking that he would like it. She had said the same words to him many times. Samar changed, quickly returning to his angry thoughts:

"If you didn't tell your father, how did he know about it?"

And then he added:

"Because it was he who warned the police."

She shook her head.

"Don't let us talk about that, Samar, my sun."

Samar felt her arms round his neck. Arms that were cool, rounded and firm. All the Spring was in them. They slipped through the hands like smooth apples. "Lucas, my sun." He kissed her, but without raising himself from the torment of his thoughts. He asked her:

"Do you know what happened yesterday when I left you?"

She withdrew from him in a sudden agony. Samar looked at her as an entomologist looks at an insect. She sobbed:

"When I heard the shots I thought that it was you who were the victim. Then I saw you escaping. A man died under my window. Did you kill him?"

Samar shrugged his shoulders.

"Pff. He was an informer. Someone who had given information."

She trembled:

"What kind of information?"

"He had told the police beforehand what we were going to do. He was a traitor and he had to die. Traitors must die."

Then he saw that Amparo was going to speak, but didn't know how to begin. She who never chose her words! But none the less she contrived to recover herself. Samar read in the depths of her eyes when he could scrutinize them, and read even better when, as now, she tried to keep them from him.

He was silent. He wished to know what she would say if she could bring herself to speak.

"My father's life was in danger, Lucas. I am glad that I was able to save him."

Lucas lighted a cigarette without looking at her.

"Your father! Your father!"

Amparo's anguish in her white dress made a picture of cinema anguish. But how harmonious!

"Yes, Lucas," she said. "My father—I know you understand."

But he retorted angrily:

"How can you think that in times like these your father means anything to us?"

Amparo was still serene and decided.

"As for me," she said, "we ourselves come first, then the others."

Samar made a gesture of disgust. He was about to speak, but she anticipated him.

"I know what you are going to say; you are quite right."

Outside this quiet house, in the street, in Samar's ambit, nothing was thought impossible. Everything was possible, everything was possible, everything could be surmounted. But her? But her? A voice that would cry out "Impossible" would be drowned in the waves of the multitude, drunken in their hope of the future. "More!" always "More!" But Amparo was impossible; Amparo meant an ecstasy; and ecstasy, quietude, is like death. In the course of the revolution to stand still is to go back. And the ecstasy of the happiness offered, Samar could not accept, as it was poisoned with failure.

She herself had said "Impossible".

In Samar's soul there were calling out the armed masses, the comrades, whom *bourgeois* morality oppressed and wounded and impoverished. "Everything is possible; we must advance." And the cry dear to his heart, "Always more". Amparo did not accept that secret impulse which impelled him against every obstacle. She was an end, her eyes a quiet harbour, and her arms open. She knew nothing of physical laws, of social morals, of the impulses of sex, of the mystifying music of the feelings, of the activity of the base and pimping spirit. She knew nothing of all these, and only felt her own mortal thirst which would lead her whither she neither knew nor cared. In Lucas's ears the imperative voice kept calling "Impossible". She kept saying "Impossible", and let herself be intoxicated by that delicate and frothy word, clinging to Samar's neck. He believed in the impossible as an abstract idea, but knew that it had no real existence, and kissed away from her lips that stupid and meaningless word. "Impossible." The depths of his conscience repeated it in the white and blue madness of May. "Impossible." But Samar was arrested by the red banners. "Always more." The two words moved apart. The first surpassed time and conquered it, the second, space. "Always more. Always more." And afterwards? There was no afterwards!

Samar held his head back to look at her. Her arms were a garland of wild flowers and her head swam in a new joy, a happiness that she had never before attained. She kept repeating, with a wild throb in her throat, "Impossible", and sought his lips and clung to his breast and body. She was not woman, not even one woman. Just as "always" conquered time and "more" conquered space, she in his arms was the infinite, but a negative infinite, denying the revolution and all his purpose. An infinite turned on itself, a less than infinite. The body took its revenge on its dreams, realizing them all in an instant, and Samar felt that something had exploded in his conscience, exploded in a sudden light which burnt up everything.

Suddenly she released herself from his arms.

"Papa is coming."

She fled out by the door through which she had come. Samar listened intently. He heard steps. He threw himself in an arm-chair, lighted a cigarette and put his elbows on the table with his hands in his hair to explain its untidiness. The curtain moved. Samar, his breathing quickened, his chest panting, deliberately swallowed a mouthful of smoke. When the Colonel came in he was coughing.

"What is the matter?"

He threw away the cigarette without answering. Then he picked it up and put it in an ash-tray. The Colonel remarked:

"Things are not going so badly as we could have feared."

Samar began to recover his presence of mind.

"I am not afraid of anything."

The Colonel remarked:

"Don't be such a child."

Samar began to explain:

"It would be stupid to pretend that I am not grateful for your kindness. But we know that we needn't talk of that. But as you have your conscience, I also have mine, and want you to understand."

The Colonel followed what Samar said so completely that it was unnecessary for him to go on speaking. He shrugged his shoulders and sat down again. It was clear from his attitude that the Colonel would make Samar compromise neither his loyalty as a friend nor even his gratitude. The Colonel kept repeating the words: "Behaviour of a gentleman and honour." Meanwhile Samar, who heard the sounds but not the words, was opening his imagination to wild dreams. The Colonel repeated, as he put on his gloves: "As I said. Things are going well, and I believe they will be better presently."

The chauffeur came in and stood at attention at the door. The Colonel bowed and the two went off. Presently the car was heard being started. Samar was alone, watching the curtain. For some minutes nothing happened. Then he drew the curtain, noticed some metallic reflections on the office table, and followed Amparo's steps on the carpet which ran up the staircase, and then he melted and was lost in the threefold whiteness of his sweetheart's garments, his sweetheart's body and the May night. But this time without turning to the light of his ambitions, the sacrifices to the light of things which exist and pass and die. Denying himself and denying everything.

Samar thought as he went into her room:

"In spite of everything, I may still save myself."

Now the poison was a delight. Thus they celebrated their festival of Spring, without astonishment, without tears, with a passive intoxication on her part, and with an undying hunger in his sensations. Samar did not recall anything comparable with that night. Not an actual night, or one of those dreams of a night, or the shadow of some sensual atavism from a remote ancestor, or the day of his own birth, or of the triumph of the revolution which they had not yet accomplished. He knew that in the last moments of his recollection of it there appeared a man murdered at the foot of a wall, and terrified female eyes which said:

"As they did not take him away until dawn, I was in terror all night."

It was the same eyes and the same fear which suddenly realized the impossible in their love. They saw the abyss and then closed as they fell through the air. Fau was at the bottom, groaning. But in fact, he remembered nothing but the last words when he was about to fly from the house, and to fly from himself, when she was raising herself to his lips:

"It was me. I betrayed you. I told it to Papa."

Samar said nothing. He wished to carry her away, a perfume in his lungs and a sweet savour on his lips. Amparo said, rescuing her breath from his mouth and throat:

"It is the last time we'll see each other. I could not let you go without telling you. Do you forgive me?"

Samar still devoured her lips. Then he tore himself away and fled. From the balcony she waved her hand in the air. In her white nightgown she was a flower-like image of May. She saw Samar close to the wall peering for signs of the enemy. She asked again:

"Do you forgive me?"

The motor-cycles of the police could be heard. Amparo asked her question again, as she sobbed good-bye, Samar came up to the wall: "Quick, find me a revolver, and throw it down." Amparo ran to the office of her father and came back with a revolver which she threw down from the balcony. She heard the soft shock of the revolver on the flower-bed.

"Lucas, for the last time in our lives: do you forgive me?"

Before disappearing in the shadows Samar replied in a clear and resolute voice:

"No."

FIFTH SUNDAY/COLLAPSE

Chapter 22

Assault on the Gaol

THE COMMITTEES are dissolved, the comrades are in gaol, our meeting-places and our newspapers are closed, and we are now given over to "free initiative". We aspire to "free initiative" as the state in which man reaches his sovereign dignity. Let us pay respect to "free initiative".

"Which? The free choice of being slaves? Are there any who wish that? Or perhaps to be bishops?"

It is comrade Samar who interrupts me. "What do you want?"

"I want definite proposals."

"But it is to that I am coming. 'Free initiative' lets men free themselves from the slavery of *bourgeois* conventionalisms. I don't know if I shall be understood when I say that although I deeply regret the imprisonment of our comrades and the closing of our centres, against which I protest with all my power, our organizations are not indispensable for accomplishing the revolution as that cannot be complete and true until the free initiative of each individual leads us to unite in common revolutionary action. The period of syndicalism has gone, and, after its collapse under the superior force of the *bourgeoisie,* our turn comes, with our 'free initiative', and we ask, 'What motive impels us in these days of revolution?' It is single, unique and holy, 'Liberty'. We seek liberty for ourselves and for our brothers. If we can attain it only by making an end of the armed mercenaries in our way, we must move forwards without counting the cost. We shall tear down the prison gates, the hateful shame of humanity. . . ."

I see that comrade Samar is impatient and I beg him to be calm. My concrete proposal is this:

"Let us bear the light of liberty, or at least of the hope of liberty, to our comrades who are in gaol."

Comrade Samar agrees and directs:

"Let everyone who has a weapon go off to Moncloa Square separately by different routes, and not in groups."

The comrades needed no persuasion. That is what I have

been saying. In every breast lies the love of liberty. "Comrades, we go to carry the light of . . ." Samar interrupts, saying that all talk now is only rhetoric. We separate. The comrades go in different directions to make the plan known to others. And so in the darkness, along different routes, the streets leading to Moncloa Square with its frowning prison become thronged with single individuals who gradually assemble all round the Gardens. A scruple comes into my mind and I say to Samar:

"But what if we accomplish nothing?"

"Always something is accomplished," he replies. "Anyhow, our comrades will dream in their cells."

Although I am often at variance with Samar, who is poisoned with Marxism and is always falling out with me, I see sometimes that he is right. What he has just said shows the loftiness of his mind. "At least our comrades will dream." Those words could have been spoken only by a man with a fine sense of liberty.

"What I wish," I say to him, "is to carry the light of liberty and, if possible, liberty itself to these poor souls."

"So talk parsons."

It was impertinent, but that is Samar's way. The best way of converting others is to be tolerant oneself. . . . "I never take offence and if other people would only . . ."

"So talk the Jesuits."

Samar and his group have always treated me badly. Let them do it. When he sees that I don't retort, that I say nothing, Samar will think all the more of me. I am sure of that. When we were near the Square, a comrade comes running up and warns us. We must go cautiously because the guards have been reinforced. Samar jests:

"Perhaps they are not going to let us enter!"

I look at the brick wall and can't help protesting:

"Prisons are a ridiculous affront!"

Samar laughs and digs me in the ribs.

"No theories, old man."

And so if I had replied to his impertinences we would now be disputing or would have quarrelled. But you can see that I can enjoy chaff. My way is best. We go on in complete good temper. The darkness is deeper in the middle of the Square. To the right are booths of a fair with their fragile doors and shutters closed. What is all that?

"The May fair."

Some of the comrades have posted themselves between the cock-shies and the lucky-wheels. There is also a windmill with its sails arranged in a star with little curtained boats at their ends. One of these windmills is higher than the trees and even higher than the prison itself. As these preparations for the fair occupy the whole quarter up to Moncloa, they will give us excellent cover in case of need.

Samar and I stayed a minute at the corner. Several comrades passed us. Roberto, a hospital orderly, told us:

"There are at least thirty of our people in the Gardens. Look out for their firing!"

It is now after midnight. It is not true that time passes quickly when one is "acting". Samar wishes us to go through the district, and the region round the barracks, to see where our comrades are, and what they are about. Although it is dangerous, and I don't see what good it can do, we go there. Noises come from among the booths.

"Comrades!" I whisper softly.

In the darkness I hear: "Right-o! Right-o!" There must be a pair of sentinels hidden there, like bugs in a bedstead. From outside you can see nothing. In a booth with the title "This way for the Sea Monster", one can hear gulping sounds like those made by a Metro train when it is starting. In the booth alongside there is a shadow close up against the curtain.

"Comrade!"

"Blast you!"

Samar, surprised, stops.

"Who are you?"

It is a bad-tempered old man.

"You might bloody well keep out of here and not bother me. You are frightening the monkey."

"What monkey?"

"The monkey which is my bread-winner. If I lose it, the soldiers won't come to my booth."

"We have nothing against your monkey, old boy."

The old man protests:

"You are all coming with revolvers. The fair is ruined. As the electric light is shut off, we have to spend our money on petrol flares, and now you come and frighten my monkey."

"Is the monkey delicate?"

"Of course it is; as delicate as a young lady."

From the way Samar is looking at the old man, I can see that he is thinking that the old man has no right to live. When he sees that I know what he is thinking, he explains:

"Life is for men who earn it. Not for those who grovel behind a monkey. This old man is less than a monkey."

I don't say anything. Samar has a feeling for human dignity which pleases me. He continues:

"This man is able to live as he does, because without doubt he believes in God. It is not him we ought to kill, but God. With belief in God, these people can live upon a self-abusing ape and still go on thinking themselves of divine origin and divine purpose!"

Then, as if he had settled the matter, he raised his revolver and fired in the air. It looked as if he were firing at God, but it was only the signal for the attack to begin. The old man crossed himself, and there jumped out of his lap a hairy little creature, fastened to his master by a chain round the waist. The old man cursed us: "You bloody swine!"

He walked back, the monkey following him in leaps, as if it were being dragged along. Sometimes he turned this way, and that way, as if he were dancing to the monkey's orders. Samar and I ran off towards the Gardens. He asked me:

"Has a plan been arranged?"

I replied that revolutions are not revolutions unless they are carried on by free initiative.

"But do you think they'll attack the prison?"

I said, "Yes. We are going to carry light to the spirits of our imprisoned comrades." I don't know what Samar replied, because the prison guard fired a volley, and I didn't listen to him and his words were not audible. Villacampa came to us:

"I am going off," he said.

"Where to?"

"I want to sleep. I haven't undressed for three days. I am going to the country."

He took out his revolver and emptied its magazine, firing nine shots against the darkness round the prison gates. Then like a man who has done his duty, he put his revolver away and disappeared. Samar thought that Villacampa believed everything to be lost and wished to save his skin. For what? Possibly Star was the motive. He cried that out whilst he took refuge and flattened himself against the awning of a booth. The hoofs of horses could be heard, and I hid myself in the same way. Inside I found the sea-monster shut in a box lined with zinc and filled with water. It was a kind of seal or walrus, oily and shining, without room to turn in its shallow and dirty water. A peevish attendant in linen drawers came out. Samar and I kept quiet. When the attendant, striking a match, saw us with pistols in our hands, he pointed to the box, saying:

"Don't hurt Philip!"

I heard the beautiful creature snort as if he were drowning. That box is not fit for him. His home is in the Baltic sea. We must also free this animal from its prison. Samar said to me:

"And that other animal? Isn't he the gaoler?" pointing with his pistol to the attendant.

The peevish attendant, trying to push aside the pistol, said:

"Call me what you like, but point another way!"

Then he assured himself that the animal was safe, and to show it off, took a stale fish from a bucket and went up to it.

"Philip, dance the Charleston!"

The animal struggled spasmodically trying to get the fish. Then he swallowed it. Samar saw the black and glistening back of the animal and commented:

"It is like a priest."

Shots resounded outside, as if the Square were full of horse-breakers cracking their whips. Samar thought about Villa-campa again, and then said:

"Let us move on; if they hit us, so much the better."

Then he pointed to the sea-lion's box with his pistol.

"In our lives we are just like this animal in its box. To get our fish, we have to dance and to fill the pockets of the patron."

And so we go out. From the prison windows come shouts of enthusiasm and encouragement. Above the rapid note of the pistols, there is heard the heavy discharge of the guards' muskets. No one can be seen. Neither guards nor comrades. No one comes out of hiding. The darkness is thick, and one could believe that it was going to last for a whole lifetime; or which is much the same, that one's life was going to last only two or three minutes. Every now and again the monkey is visible, jumping and pulling along the old man, who crosses himself and groans at the bullets. The fire gets heavier. There must be many casualties. A booth alongside is stripped of its awning and a man cries out, pointing to two others:

"Here they are; here they are. I don't want trouble."

He thinks that it is all due to two revolver-shooters having hidden themselves in his booth. The booth is called "The Rout of the Moors". Inside there is a group of life-sized puppets, representing bearded Moors. Presently he sets the mechanism going, and the Moors begin to glide along a pathway, jumping over each other, all very solemnly. Samar says that the owner is a Visigoth, and that the show is an atavism. Meantime it is plain that the attack is failing. No one can go out of his shelter, because the defences have been reinforced, all the gates shut, and bullets come from every window-slit. They must be surrounding the Square. We'll have to get out somehow, if we are not to be killed like rats. Individual initiative is leading people towards the Iron Gate, and we descend with caution towards it. The owner of the Moors has been shot down and volleys from the Civil Guards are raking the Moors.

We get behind the prison-wall pierced with windows, and descend with great care, because outposts have been placed to prevent escape in that direction. We have to lie concealed in brushwood for more than an hour. The firing goes on above us. The guards must now be shooting at one another. The monkey, the old man and Philip all must have perished. The crockery booths and the pottery stores must have been thrown down. One can hear the horse galloping. We meet more fugitives, and when at dawn we have reached the other side of Moncloa, we see that we are at least fifteen. Samar is thoroughly upset, as the light rises. He walks along in a temper saying:

"Don't you wish to carry the light to our comrades in prison? There it is."

It is true. We have come up against the dawn. But what is the matter with Samar? He seems always to be discontented and to show it with reason or without it. The truth is that we also know quite well that it is difficult to succeed, now that daylight has come. In the darkness everything seemed easy, but now in daylight the trees, the houses, the air itself, seem not to be on our side. They are neutral, and to conquer the neutrality of the green of the trees and the blue of the sky needs more strength than we possess.

I don't know how it happened; someone called out, jumped and ran off. Almost all of us followed him. When I realized what was happening, there were three rifles pointing at us. Then came questions and searching.

One of them said in reply that he was an active anarchist. Did they give food in the gaol? Very good. Active anarchist!

Another replied, not looking at his questioner:

"A working man; do you know what that is? A man who lives by earning his wages."

An officer struck him with the flat of his sword. They bound us and took us to the highway to a prison van divided into cells. We had to go in, each of us stumbling into a separate division. At the Central Station they took us down to the basement with grated cells along one side. There were Crousell, Liberto, Margraf and Helios, each in his cage. All four visible. Two agents questioned us and a third wrote on a typewriter.

It seems that they are going to take us to prison today. We cannot deny having taken part in the attack, but we do deny it, because in our contest with the police the worst thing is to confess.

They don't put us in the cells, and that seems a good sign.

We are kept standing in a row in the cellar for hours and hours. Liberto asks us some questions from the bars of his cage:

"Have they caught Samar? Has the central committee met?"

A guard throws a full cartridge box weighing a couple of pounds at the grating.

"You, there, get back."

They go to the back of the cells. Why do they think it necessary to be so harsh with these men? A guard explains:

"We have been on continual duty for six days and that has ruined our health!"

The basement is rectangular and the guards keep walking up and down. They won't let us talk or even sit on the ground. The old ones among us have done military service ourselves and know how it limits one's movements and deprives one of free initiative, and understand the behaviour of the guards, keeping us from speaking and making the prisoners go to the back of their cells. When I was twenty years old I was just like them; devoted to authority and discipline. But the blows of life have shown me that a man is nothing without free initiative. An agent arrives.

"What was your idea in attacking the gaol? You got what you were asking for, when you tried to attack it without a plan."

We saw the four comrades through the bars of their cages sitting in the shadow about a yard behind the doors. The agent began to talk with an officer of the Security, and said to him:

"The information given us by the secretary of the Local Federation of Syndicates is not quite accurate."

"Who is the secretary just now?"

"Miguel Palacios."

They are talking so that we can hear, to make us think that comrade Palacios, one of the best of our organization, is an informer. To make the trick go better, the officer warns the agent:

"Be quiet; they are listening to you."

But they were wrong. In the first place, because all of us knew that kind of fake, and next, because Miguel Palacios has been in gaol for several days. Apparently they forgot that.

Liberto is sitting cross-legged. Helios with the soles of his feet on the ground and resting on his hands behind his back. Crousell with his chin on his knees and his legs folded, and Elenio quite stupefied. Although it is nearly full morning, they haven't slept, because they have been made to get up perpetually; to appear before the judge; to appear before the Chief of

Police, to be confronted with others recently arrested. Even during the day, they didn't give them a moment's peace. It seems that their case is to be taken seriously; sentences of at least ten years. You have only to look at their beards of six days' growth and their eyes beginning to wander, to realize that they are in a bad way. As for us, they are putting us back in the prison van, to take us to gaol.

Later in the morning, an officer of Security goes up to the gratings.

"Stand up."

The four obey.

"Which of you is Elenio Margraf?"

"Me," replies Elenio.

"They have picked up your wife in Infantas Street with her baby at her breast and have taken her to the hospital half dead."

"What from?"

"From hunger."

Elenio knows that it is possible. The police had turned her out of her house in agreement with the owner. They were hopelessly in arrears with their rent. The officer awaited Elenio's reply, but he muttered a few words that could not be heard. Then the officer added:

"You people would leave your wives to starve!"

Elenio said nothing, and the other kept taunting him. Elenio finally burst out with insults. The officer threatened:

"Just let me open the door." . . .

Elenio bade him open it, ready to rush at him and quench his fury with teeth and claws. Another officer and an agent come up and tell their comrade not to waste his breath on useless words. But why? They say it in such a queer way that the four are very curious. They retreat whispering and shrugging their shoulders. One of the agents laughs and repeats:

"But why?"

Then he turns towards the guards:

"Don't dispute with them. Say 'Yes' to everything they ask. And if they want anything, get it for them from the street."

The conversation is over. They don't talk again or get into a discussion. They no longer consider these four men as enemies, or even as criminals, or even human beings. A guard comes up to them: "Do you want anything?"

Liberto, who has a receipt for a few shillings in his pocket, gives it to the guard.

"The prison has the money. Take the receipt and get coffee for the four of us."

The guard grumbles.

"That isn't fair. Here outside are we three who have been on duty all night, and our morning coffee is two hours overdue."

Liberto sits down again, passes his hand over his red scalp and says in a tired voice:

"All right. Get coffee for yourselves, too."

Chapter 23

Amparo Decides to Die

AMPARO GOT up as usual at eight o'clock, and went to her bath. She filled it so that it didn't feel warm, although she had never been able to bear a cold bath. She had drawn the blind of the wide window which opened on the country, and the steel-grey morning light came in. The reflection from the sky turned the water a pale blue against the enamel of the bath. She got into the water and stared at the polished taps in which her neck and shoulders were reflected. Then she looked through the window up at the sky. She felt isolated from all the world. Since the night, she had a secret, and that secret surrounded her with high walls from which she could look, as she was doing now, only at the sky and the clouds.

She thought of Samar and of how surprised he had been when she told him that she never had dreams. She no longer felt for Samar the impulse that had driven her towards his revolution, towards his hatreds, towards his arms. She had lost all that for ever and knew that she would never return to it. She had been torn away by a hurricane which would drive her away further every day. Everything was impossible. She thought over it placidly, with the tepid water splashing over her shoulders and breasts. Two years of intoxication and illusion, and the wedding-dress of last night, a dress irrevocably stained. Then an astonishing thought came into her mind. The lovely thought that a baby girl might be born from her intoxication.

She finished her bath, and, coming out of the water, surveyed herself in the mirror. She was proud of her whiteness and freshness after the night. Would she continue to be in love? She didn't know and didn't wish to stop to think about it. It was all impossible. Samar could not find happiness with her, but far from her in regions to which she could not follow even in imagination. He was bound to reject her for having betrayed them by informing her father. The murder of the man under her balcony opened up abysms and distances which could not be crossed. It was a different world where there were laws under which a man or a thousand men could be murdered, and yet the murderers remain good. She understood it, but didn't wish to explain it to herself. She began to think again, against her will, of the monster riddled by bullets, collapsing on the blue morning-glory and the green creepers. Until then she had never heard revolver shots, and she thought of them as diabolical little games of extraordinary beings who could play with death. Wrapped in a white dressing-gown, she leaned at the window. Down below there were still visible spots of blood torn by the wall from Fau's wounded and bleeding body. These men, the friends of Lucas, were killers. Lucas himself would kill, if it should seem necessary. Death did not require prayers and tears and black clothes, but only a wall and some strange men. There was Samar engaged in that circle of laws of iron which needed no judges with their caps and lace sleeves, nor guards nor printed codes. She could never go there. Even if she wished to follow, she was separated from Samar for ever by the words she had spoken to her father: "They are trying to make the regiment mutiny, Papa." They called these words a treachery. A treachery. That was the crime of the monster murdered under her balcony. A treachery!

It was that which made her feel unworthy of Lucas, of her own family, of her childish dreams, of her wedding-dress already stained, of the sweets of a home. She was an impure woman, not because of her night of love, but because of her treachery. And the idea of treachery kept piercing into her life, reached its roots, the memory of her dead mother, and began to blemish and corrupt them. Then she felt giddy, lost in the labyrinth of her thoughts. Never had she thought over so many things in so short a time. She left the bathroom. The corridors had the bareness and coldness of the early morning. The dining-room had no homeliness. It seemed a room in a hotel. The maids were now remote creatures, and when one of them spoke to her, her voice sounded as if she had never heard it before. She didn't like to look her in the face. The maid said that a young girl was asking to see her. She was in the kitchen and had come up by the service stair. Amparo found a young person seated on the edge of a rush chair, very trim and with her hair dressed. She was wearing a blue jersey and had a red cock under her arm.

"Lucas, still Lucas," she thought with distaste, but all the same invited her to follow her.

They went into her room and sat down face to face. Star had a terrifying serenity, and her eyes were wide open and steady. Amparo hoped that she would speak, but as she said nothing, she asked: "Are you Lucas's comrade?"

The girl nodded assent and Amparo reflected that "comrade" was much more than betrothed. Amparo had never been his comrade. She took up her cap to put it on the toilet table, when a little plated revolver which had been inside it fell on the floor. Then Star smiled and stooped to pick it up. As to keep it in her hand seemed rather theatrical, she placed it on the cap. Amparo reflected that as the girl was Samar's comrade, she naturally had a revolver and would use it when necessary. That girl had come from the strange and alien land of Samar's friends. At last Star spoke:

"As I know that you are betrothed to him, I have come to see if you can tell me what happened to Samar and the others who were arrested at the barracks."

Amparo would have been glad to give her full information, but knew nothing except about Lucas.

"Is he in the cells at the barracks?" asked Star.

Amparo hastened to answer, although she was letting her life ebb away with her words:

"Oh, no, he is at liberty."

Star did not understand how they could have let him go, and Amparo explained:

"He escaped."

As Star's look still was questioning, Amparo told her in a rush of words what had happened. She did not understand how she came to say these words:

"Papa brought him to the house here on his own responsibility, but he escaped."

It appeared as if she were making an accusation in these words. And so she added hurriedly:

"Of course I helped him."

They were silent for a little. Star gazed at her, and Amparo returned her stare and made a questioning gesture. The grey light suddenly became clear, faded out, and flashed again. Then distant thunder rolled dully and continuously. It was a storm unexpected and almost theatrical. The cock under Star's arm heard the thunder and seemed to growl. As they didn't know what to say, Star began to talk about the weather, and said that she would go before it began to rain, but Amparo kept her back.

"You think that he is in danger?"
"Who?"
"Lucas."
Star hesitated in answering.
"At present, certainly. They will pursue him and arrest him at any cost, at least while all this is gcing on. Don't you see that they caught him in action?"
She received this information with a gesture and an exclamation: "Ah!"
Star looked at Amparo with curiosity, wishing to see what a *bourgeoise* in love was like. Until now she had only seen in her a concealed restlessness, which however was plain enough, and threads of silver and gold on her hair when the darkness was lit up by flashes of lightning. Star asked her:
"Are you really his betrothed?"
"Yes. Why do you ask?"
Star shrugged her shoulders and then held down the cock which was trying to escape.
"Just asking."
Amparo frowned rather gracefully. She remembered that at school direct questions of that kind were thought in bad taste. She ought to explain why she had asked, so as to prevent the questions being impertinent. She seemed to see the ghost of a smile at the corners of Star's mouth, and then, as if one of the flashes of lightning had freed her from sentiment and had filled her with a new energy, she looked at the silvered revolver, and felt that she wished to kill that girl. But she confined herself to asking the question:
"I think that you wish to tell me something and can't make up your mind to it. Speak quite frankly."
She had hit the mark. Star said to her:
"Your affair can lead to nothing. Samar doesn't love you."
"What reasons have you for saying that?"
The conversation sharpened. Amparo's eyes sparkled, but Star's kept steady and tranquil, as if they had been glass eyes bought in a bazaar. Star went on:
"I have my reasons."
"But what are they? I suppose . . ." She was going to speak with suspicion.
Star interrupted her:
"You needn't suppose anything. The reason could not be simpler. Samar hates you."
Amparo dug the nails of one hand into the back of the other. She stammered, affecting indifference:
"Did he tell you that?"

Star said nothing, and Amparo looked one way and the other, wishing to speak and not knowing what to say. The worst of what Star had said was that Amparo had also said it to herself before then. Now by Star's silence she found her former sweet uncertainties finally and definitely resolved. Star went on:

"His hatred of you, you can't understand, because the only harm you have ever done to him is to love him. Even I, who have received from you nothing but linen and food for my comrades, hate all of you."

Amparo was hardly listening and Star went on:

"All the same, you could make him quite happy."

Amparo didn't venture to ask how, as she feared the answer. Without being asked, Star replied with a look. Their eyes met. Star declared:

"I tell you in the name of the cause, in the name of the revolution."

Amparo thought that Samar had no need of such interference. He had settled it all by himself. She replied with an indifferent air:

"I told you that we were engaged, but it isn't quite true. It hasn't been true for three days. If that is what you wished to know, put your mind at rest. All is finished."

Her nerves were all to pieces, but she kept up an air of quiet resolution.

"For always?"

There was an insolent doubt in her words. In all the words of that girl to whom she gave the soiled linen and worn-out shoes, there was a balanced firmness independent of her surroundings. Instead of replying, Amparo looked out across the balcony. She saw the barracks, their walls of a reddish-grey turned to scarlet purple under a lightning flash. Amparo had nothing more to say or to hear, but all the same she would have liked to keep Star beside her always. As for Star, she stayed where she was because she had suddenly forgotten the phrases which ought to be used in taking leave. Amparo looked at her, and it was enough to look at her eyes to assure her of the gulf between Lucas and herself. They were sealed eyes into which light could not penetrate. It was kept out by another interior light still stronger which gave an amazing brilliance to the pupils and cornea, like the blue of linen put out to dry.

"Perhaps you love Lucas."

It seemed natural that she should love him. Star nodded assent and added:

"All we comrades love each other."

That was the kind of affection Lucas sought from Amparo.

It was a first necessity to be comrades, to think and to live in unison. But that they could never do. In her ears echoed the last words of her last conversation:

"Do you forgive me?"

"No."

Just before he disappeared in the darkness. She repented of having saved her father. But only now, when repentance was of no avail. It was impossible that they should be comrades now. Star looked at her, thinking: "She is ill. She has the *bourgeoise* disease of love." Amparo, for her part, returned the look, thinking: "She is serene and unfeeling like a star; she is visible but infinitely remote. She is candid and simple and yet she is surrounded by mystery." She asked her:

"You are going to see him, see Lucas?"

Star said that she would see him within the next half-hour.

"You live near here, don't you?"

"Yes."

"With your parents?"

"With my grandmother. They killed my father in the street last Sunday." Amparo started, but as she saw that Star was quiet and serene, she forgot it almost at once. She rose and then asked:

"Would you like some old clothes, as before, for the poor?"

"They are not poor," corrected Star without offence. "They are workers without work."

Then Amparo said that her father, the Colonel, had caused the rations to be estimated in such a way that there was a good daily surplus for the out-of-work. She wished to prove that her father was a good man, but Star saw in that an offensive flavour of patronage. Amparo disappeared a minute and came back with an open envelope in which she had put a sheet on which she had written five words: "Will you be happier now?" Then she gave Star two jackets, a pair of trousers and three shirts. Star thanked her and promised that she would deliver the note within half an hour. As she said good-bye she felt Amparo's hands and especially her voice trembling as she said:

"If you love Samar, make him happy."

As she was speaking, she saw the silver-plated revolver and would have like to seize it and empty it into the blue jersey. Passion still governed her. But when she closed the door of the service stair behind Star, whose image remained before her eyes as if she had been one of the heavenly messengers of the Bible, carrying the envelope in her raised hand, she felt happier. She returned to the dining-room and then to her bedroom. The morning had become darker. Amparo opened the balcony widely at the moment when a flash reddened the skies. She remained almost in a trance gazing at the heavy air and putting a question to herself:

"What of this afternoon?"

In her thoughts of the immediate future, there were no persons. Only volumes of light and of sound. Neither her father nor the maids.

"What of this afternoon?"

Thus she asked herself again. Then she saw clouds passing, white wind drift that covered a high window. She smoothed her cheeks with her hands and flattened her pretty hair. Smiling, but in a trembling voice, she said:

"All these illusions of my life!"

But suddenly she drew back and left the room, trying not to see Star's revolver which had been left forgotten on the dressing-table. It would be an hour until her father got up. She took underclothing from a chest of drawers, went to see if there were enough fire to heat the water in a thermos flask, and asked them to get ready the electric iron. She went out, came back from the lobby with some newspaper cuttings. There was an article in French on Paul Valery, and two articles by Samar, two of these high-toned articles in the *bourgeois* style, which Samar wrote for her to keep. The article on Valery didn't interest Lucas, but she wished the collection which she was making to include the gentle aspirations of the old spirit. And she had had pleasure in searching them out as flowers which one day would suit the peace of their home, the serene silences and windows open to the sky. A day which Lucas, on the other hand, knew would never come!

Amparo damped a piece of linen. The cuttings were crushed, as Samar had carried them in his pocket. She smoothed them out with her hand, put them on the wet sheet and ironed them carefully. Then she went to her father's office, gummed them on large sheets, numbered them in the corner and docketed them. All that pleased her. The cook put her head in to ask something, and she did nothing except agree to everything. Then she reflected that she had ordered lunch without thinking about it.

Once she had put the sheets in her collection she went back to her bedroom. She stopped in the passage a minute. A distant peal of thunder made an insecure glass rattle in the sideboard of the dining-room. She thought:

"Who will give Papa dinner tonight?"

She walked up and down steadily. She saw that everything was ready for her father when he got up. She filled the bath flask with eau-de-Cologne from a large bottle, using a little glass funnel, which she noticed was dirty. She wished to scold the maid for her carelessness, but forgot about it. She went back to her room. She didn't understand why everything seemed to have no relation to her. Everything wished to blot itself out. In the distance the high wind of the storm swung the trees. From the direction of Moncloa came the sound of shots, and each seemed to echo, "Never, Never, Never." But some without an echo were harsh and flat negations. Even the sky was a negation. The morning darkness of the house seemed the darkness of falling night.

She began to dust the marble slab of the dressing-table. To do that, she had to pick up the revolver and put it on the night-table. And she didn't finish dusting the table because she stood alongside the bed with the weapon in her hand. She stared at the walls, the mirror, the country beginning to be soaked by the storm. "Afterwards," thought Amparo, "what will happen to my room and who will look in my mirror? Will there be storms and lightning? Will the sun come out this afternoon?" She looked at the trees, nodding under the wind, and thought: "In September their leaves will fall and I shall not see them." She wished to laugh or to cry. Her cheeks trembled between the two wishes. She noticed a picture hung on the wall by a blue cord. The lightning flashes gave fiery reflections from the glass and the water in her basin. It was raining furiously outside. The streaming rain lulled her a little. "Illusions of my life." Amidst the roar of the storm she fired. She felt nothing but that the revolver gave a jump and fell from her hand. Then a feeling of burning in her left breast. She was on her bed. She stared at the ceiling and without knowing what she was doing moved her head from side to side.

The maids came running and fled to tell her father. But he wasn't there. He had been in the barracks, and possibly had not gone to bed all night. When they raised the revolver, they found that it was empty. It had carried only one cartridge, and when it was fired the case had been pushed out. Amparo did not speak. When she died, the blood from her heart blotted out another stain that had been on the sheet since the night. A small stain, of a *bourgeoise* marriage. The last words she spoke were commonplace.

"My darling mother!"

In good faith she believed that she had found the right path. That she was no longer the pretty little wandering animal. That her mother was awaiting her. That perhaps she would rise to heaven in the fashion sung by a popular poet, "on the luminous staircase of a ray". The electric iron, forgotten on the sheet, had raised a little column of black smoke like the silhouette of a cannon.

Chapter 24

Samar Becomes an Automaton

HE HAD just read it in a newspaper, for the evening papers were coming out as usual. The announcement was in the news columns, but the editor gave it prominence by placing it at the head of a column. The lettering was very black and beside the initial "D" there was a blot where the stereoplate had not fitted exactly. The title occupied three lines, and ran as follows: "Daughter of Colonel García del Río Victim of a Fatal Accident in her Home." As soon as he read these lines, he folded the paper, put it in his pocket, and set off walking as if he were in a great hurry, but in fact hesitating at every corner. He kept the paper in his pocket, as an inexperienced thief might keep a pocket-book he had just stolen. He thought that everyone was staring at him, and for his part he stared at people, without seeing them, with the self-conscious pride of a murderer. Thus he walked from eight until ten of the evening. He felt that he must be alone, but could not succeed in that, as there were people everywhere. He walked straight ahead listlessly. He walked quickly, not knowing where he was going. Soon he came to the Chamberi water-reservoir, tall and rounded like a Byzantine dome. His feet felt warm. His forehead ran with sweat. He stopped. A star shone behind the dome. The air was cold and clear. He thought of prison with pleasure. There, in a cell, alone, isolated from the world, he could think over things quietly. Now he could not co-ordinate his thoughts or reflect on his state of mind. He began to walk again like an automaton. At midnight he realized that he was tired out, and sat down in a dark doorway, very far from the centre of the city, in a street of Tetuan de las Victorias, at the end of the city most remote from his betrothed's house. Without thinking, he had been fleeing from her. He lighted a match and began to read the paragraph.

"This morning the Police Station of the Bridge of Vallecas received information as to an accident which had caused the death of the only daughter of Señor García del Río, the colonel commanding the 74th Light Artillery, a lovely girl, eighteen years old, whose name was Amparo. The casualty occurred while she was examining a revolver in her own house. Without doubt because of the said young lady's inexperience of weapons, or from some defect in the weapon, it discharged and penetrated the fourth left intercostal space, causing a wound which the official surgeon stated to be inevitably fatal. The court impounded the weapon in accordance with the usual procedure. Many officers of high rank called at the house of Señor García del Río to express their condolences."

Samar had at once suspected that it must have been suicide, and in every way the paragraph confirmed that. It was the only reflection he made. Then he crouched down in the shadow and leant his chin on his hand. He needed a shave. He must be looking like a tramp. Tramps were people who wandered through the streets under the stars believing in nothing, neither in their own bodies nor even in their absence of belief. To walk under the stars singing when one felt like singing, a stupid childish song or a pretty country song. To drink, thinking that the water in the pond has slaked the thirst of gentle asses and simple sheep, to lie down in the ditches alongside the high roads, to strip oneself in storms under torrents of rain, and to fly from fields in which there are torn shreds of newspapers with paragraphs. To wander thus, speaking with no one, seeing no one, to endure the storms of summer, to climb the desolate hills, to undress in the darkness and to await the dawn.

He tore the newspaper into pieces. He drew out his revolver, the weapon of Colonel García del Río, and threw it into the mouth of a drain at the edge of the pavement. He stood staring at the wall in front, where there was a closed window lighted up. Through the curtain, a gas-mantle with its white globe could be seen. In Spain, he reflected, there had not been the age of gas, the democratic and humanitarian epoch of gas-illumination through which other countries had passed. In Spain they had passed directly into electricity. He thought that that might make a good subject for an article, but what article could he write? How could he write when he was without the vital energy necessary to translate an idea into written words? He sat down again in the doorway. He had no hat, and the door-post was hard against his head. He stretched out his legs wearily. He felt as if he were going to pieces in the darkness. When he was a child he was full of enthusiasm. He got excited about everything which was going to give him pleasure on the day or the next day. Later on his enthusiasms were more limited, but still strong. Then love brought him delirious intoxication. Amparo's love called on and strengthened all the reserved forces of his spirit, which had been wandering and uncertain. He made his final effort. And she had dissolved that miracle, because for Samar her love was miraculous, breaking his heart with one shot. With her death, everything that she had put into him died. He set himself to analyse what she had taken from him.

"She has taken," he said in a firm voice, "what was left of my faith."

And a voice hidden within him repeated old words he had spoken:

"The spirit is *bourgeois*. Señor Lenin, Señor Roosevelt, is the spirit of any use?"

With her, his own spirit had died. And Samar was left completely empty. Without a spirit to consecrate one's faith, to transform emotional faith into moral principles, and to raise these to something more than human, life was impossible. He stared at the wall in front of him.

"The spirit by its sole action," he said, "made it possible for those bricks and tiles to become a house. But as it is impossible to disintegrate the spirit of *bourgeois* morality, and as pure spirit does not exist, but is always *bourgeois* spirit, the heap of stones and bricks does not remain merely a house, but becomes a property and a sacred home."

The spirit must be killed, even at a sacrifice, demolishing the house if necessary. But these reflections rose up outside the dying present which was still alive, as if they were spun by a flame of Jewish fire burning above his head. The ideas did not come out of his head, but arrived already framed from outside him, and surged against his closed brain to be reflected and so seeming to issue from it. He knocked his head lightly against the door. Then more strongly. Then he hurt himself and rubbed it. He withdrew his hand, spotted with blood. He had cut himself slightly and rose up in alarm.

He sat down again. He felt a little trickle of blood on his neck. What did it matter? "I'll probably be infected with tetanus," he thought, "and die in a few hours." That did not disturb him, and he leaned his head against the door again and stretched out his legs. She didn't exist. She had gone, as she was bound to go, without his forgiving her. But certainly he could not write his article on gas-lighting, nor return to "action" with faith, nor weep, nor laugh heartily. He could let himself exist. Let himself exist! Abandon himself and be like a chair or a table. That was what he wished now, but for a "now" as long as possible.

He had his hands at his sides, his legs stretched out loosely, his forehead spotted with blood. He felt blood trickling down inside his collar. He was drunk with negation. "Never more," rang in his ears. The "ever more" which was his own refrain, the refrain of the dusty road, of the crowds thirsty for the future, of the implements of labour, and of the rebel weapons, the "ever more" which made him forget everything, now did not reach his heart. The heart said "never, never, never", and the "always more" faded away. He remained half an hour, desolate, motionless, without thinking or feeling. He heard uneven steps and the voice of an old woman who was mumbling to herself, saying something soothing, probably to a child in her arms. The woman came up to the door at which he was sitting, and squatted in the other corner with a "good evening" —the sign and password of a beggar. Samar didn't reply. His eyes were wide open and he was staring into vacancy. His heart was beating "never, never, never", and he felt in the back of his hand the chill of the pavement. But he couldn't speak. Nor look. Nor think. The woman began to mutter, and her lamentations were a mixture of violence and blasphemy.

Three days without sleeping under a roof. And you, little wretch, sleeping and sucking happily. Your mother will die if she has to, and you'll go on sucking her breast, won't you? You are killing me, little darling!

Odd endearments! She was carrying a child at her breast. She was old and thin, but the child had fat legs.

"You see, my friend," said the woman, addressing Samar, "I am condemned to die in the street, and life goes on just as usual."

By "life" she meant her baby. Samar heard quite well, but he didn't move or answer. The old woman stared at him and then jumped to her feet:

"He is dead, Mother of God!"

All the same, it isn't bad to be thinking one is dead. While he was thinking that, life still went on. The baby was laughing in her arms and the mother fled, shaking her skirts.

"God Almighty, a dead body!"

Samar heard it all. The old woman was speaking the truth. Samar agreed with her. He was dead. Dead, although he was waking up and would have to resume daily life. He had died, and his only wish was to concentrate his mind on concealing it, until he could see if he could contrive to take up life again. Although his eyes were already open, he had made an effort to open them and to pull himself together. Blood had ceased to flow from the wound in his head. The poor woman was running far off. He got up and felt a new peace. He thought coldly of Amparo's suicide. He was only surprised at thinking that, as she was dead, he had not to send back letters and photographs, because death was different from a simple breaking off. He forgot the thoughts of desolation and of hopeless ruin which had assailed him at first. When he saw the spots of blood he had left on the doorstep, and those that had stained his shoulders, he explained his changed condition: "the loss of blood has cleared my head." A few drops of blood had cleared away the infinite desolations which had been overwhelming him!

But the moral vacuum continued within him. He went down an avenue with resolute steps. His senses were alert, and clear ideas rose from them, ideas in close touch with facts and not transcending them, and so leaving peace. These ideas directed him to his house which he had left five days before, in case the police might seek him there. Without doubt it would be watched, and it seemed clear that as soon as he reached it, they would fall on him, handcuff him and take him to the Central Station. "If that is what happens, tomorrow I'll be in gaol." After what he had gone through, he would go to gaol as people in despair go to a convent. Samar, who had always laughed at that sort of thing, felt inclined to go into the lay convent, Moncloa gaol. It seemed the obvious thing to do. He went to his house so that they might arrest him.

All the way, it was downhill. It was half-past one o'clock, and before he came to the lights of the suburb near the city, he tidied himself as well as he could, smoothed his hair, and generally straightened himself. The night-porter looked at him with curiosity. Samar saw from his face that he had been questioned by the police on the previous nights. He didn't bother about the police and the revolution, gaol and the cemetery. He went upstairs, and as he reached his rooms, he had the feeling that nothing had happened. The black piano, the green curtain over the opaque glass of his door! Not a single cigarette-end near the ash-trays! He went in and passed his eye over his three shelves, filled with books, his writing-table and his narrow bed. He sat down on the corner of the table, lighted a cigarette and looked at her photograph on the wall. "She is dead, she is dead," he said to himself. And he tried to see if it had more effect on him if he said it aloud. He went up and kissed the glass for the first time in the two years of their intimacy. Always when she used to ask him if he kissed it, he said yes, lying naturally. Then he opened a drawer and saw three large packets of letters. He glanced at one and threw it on the table.

"They are all the same," he said.

In all of them the same phrases were repeated. Day after day, year after year. He began to undress and opened wide the balcony windows to hear better Schubert's military march which was one of his earliest memories of the time when he became engaged. An old man was playing it on an accordion. The chords tore the shadows of the night and filled the world with loops of blue and rhythmical movements. Blue mazes and an intoxication of illusions and wide dreams. The spirit has the mission of surrounding us with infinity. But Samar no longer felt or dreamed of the impossible. All that was of the past, of the time when he himself was a dream, an unsubstantial thing, of shifting and wayward outlines. Now——

He had undressed and put on his pyjamas. Before going to bed he had put on his slippers. The right one was burst and through the hole his toe stuck out. He went into the passage and went through the house to reach the terrace where there was a douche. First he leaned over the street, and saw a group of night watchmen. "And so life goes on," he said. But the phrase had no deep meaning for him; it was casual. He took his shower-bath. He returned to his room completely refreshed. He felt warm, although his shoulders and arms were cold.

He went to bed and slept. Next morning the housekeeper came into his room rather upset. She began to tell him about the visits of the police, and to say that although she knew him to be a respectable person, the visits of the police annoyed both her and the other lodgers. Samar stretched himself and interrupted her:

"All right! All right! Send up my breakfast."

When the maid came in with the tray, he told her to look in the pocket of his jacket and bring him cigarettes. The girl took out some papers, and among them was a long envelope. When he saw it, he told the girl to bring it to him. He wished to see it again. Star had brought it to him at noon the day before. He opened it, and read, "Will you be happier now? Amparo." He took his coffee and opened the balcony wide. He heard the telephone bell, thought it might be for him, and made sure. It was Star speaking, saying that she had to speak to him about something terrible and urgent.

"Yes! Yes!" he said, not knowing what tone to take, "I know it already. Horrible. Poor Amparo."

Star corrected him with "No, of course not that," which sounded angrily. She meant that she had more important things to speak about than a fiancée. Samar was pleased, because he was coming to the same view. They fixed where to meet, and he went back to his room. Then he looked at Amparo's letter again. "Will you be happier now?" And he answered aloud:

"Yes."

He looked at himself in the glass and found himself changed. Before he took off his pyjama jacket, he studied his own eyes. They were not his. That empty and vague look was not his. He could not understand it, as he had forgotten that he was dead.

The light and the sounds of the street came in through the balcony as usual. He went out, and leaned his elbows on the railing. He concluded that the police had stopped watching his house as they thought he wasn't there. But he withdrew, fearing lest there might be an agent in the street who would see him. He dressed. Things had returned to normality. The police had been destroying communications with their arrests and their searching, and the crowds would require a new battle-cry before they could respond to it and multiply it. And every day it would be more difficult for the new voice to sound.

Samar shrugged his shoulders:

"What can it matter?"

It was inexplicable that all that could matter to him. The dying forces of the revolution every hour were more scattered; up went his shoulders:

"Why not?"

Although most probably the decay was only in Samar, and he was colouring everything with the bilious tint of his own collapse, he leaned over the balcony and watched the sky like peasants when they see a shooting star.

"Everything is going down," he repeated.

Perhaps he was thinking of the movement, or perhaps of himself.

THE MOON (*shining through the azure morning sky*). "Three new planets: Espartaco, Progreso and Germinal."

Chapter 25

The Devil's Automobile

AT NINE o'clock the four arrested men were still in the cells. The guards and the agents kept to the letter the instruction given them in the morning. "Do not talk to the prisoners."

They said "Yes" to everything. Liberto looked at everyone who came in, in the hope of an explanation. Crousell asked questions, but got no answers. The chief shrugged his shoulders the three times he was questioned. One of the guards with whom they had shared their coffee in the morning risked an opinion:

"I suppose you won't get out of this until they take you to the court."

Crousell could not understand why they should have to go to court again, as without doubt it would simply send them back to prison. It was a weaving and unweaving which gave to the early hours of the night the uncertainty of not knowing what the next hour was going to bring, in a storm where anything might happen.

Margraf thought of the family of his parents, far off, which he had not visited for years. As for his own family and son, that was settled. When they shut him up he had been confident that no one would harry his wife. Although the notice to quit had already been given. It was a more bitter cruelty than a question of money could have caused. The few shillings they owed to the landlord were no reason to throw a woman into the street, especially considering that Elenio had paid his rent so often. The landlord knew that he would settle and ought to wait. But the police paid the money and forced him to throw the woman out in the most cruel way. She had few resources. There was great misery in the quarter, and sympathy could be little more than moral. Moreover, just as among Bedouins and other tribes, when there was a prospect of war, the men disappeared, going off to fight, the homes were abandoned to chance, and women sharpened their own selfishness under the responsibility of having to maintain the household, and so were hard with one another. It did not surprise Elenio Margraf that misery had overtaken his wife. The smallest push from the powerful hands of a lawyer, a judge or the police, was enough to destroy her.

Liberto didn't wish to think out what was happening. He preferred to let the hours slip by, knowing that time would bring the answer. He had no fear. He expected to find himself in the prison cell next day, and prison did not frighten him, for it was the desert retreat of mystics. Men who have been in prison know that the forty days in the wilderness of Jesus Christ are necessary for those who are going to die for the people.

Helios was much concerned about the fate of a pair of new boots which he was wearing and which he knew he would have to sell either in the gaol or in the penal settlement. He felt that he would be forced to wear boots he didn't like. In his opinion boots were the essential part of a man's wardrobe, and always, when after a long spell of work, he had succeeded in getting himself a new pair, of horse hide, troubles came to him as now from the fifth gallery where there were traffickers of all kinds, makers of weapons, sausages, lamps, receivers, second-hand dealers . . . who valued them at the first glance, and proposed all sorts of fantastic bargains. Although Crousell used to defend them, always he had ended by selling them for tobacco and money for newspapers. Of course in part exchange they used to give him a pair of old string-soled shoes. Now he looked at them with pity thinking that he would have to wait seven or eight months, after he was set at liberty, before he could buy another pair.

At eleven o'clock an order came which caused activity amongst the guards near the cells. They took them one by one to the guard-room. To each of them the same question was put:

"Who killed the agent?"

They knew nothing. All the same the chief persisted in his interrogation, which did not surprise them, as they knew from his questions that he had sufficient evidence about them. Liberto began to hesitate. Doubt is always a bad thing, but much worse at times when one's thoughts are not under control.

Instead of returning them to the cells, they kept them in the lobby, which was a kind of reception-room for those coming out of the gaol or going into the street. Next their detention changed to a journey of a thousand gates. A journey through a labyrinth, which in the end led to the point from which they had started. There were those who never found the end in all their lives, and others, who without knowing why, after the opening and shutting of many doors, found themselves in the street. The lobby had several exits from which flight was impossible: the door, the window, the telephone box. It would be very pleasant to call from here on the telephone to the hut of a forest guard on the Sierra. Then three agents came with open handcuffs asking for their hands. They went out in a file. There was in the street an open automobile with six guards carrying rifles. The automobile was huge and shabby. It reminded Helios of a story of his childhood called *The Devil's Automobile* in which there was a car like this one, its gears out of order, without a carriage, and with no privacy. Two agents and the six guards mounted with them. The car swayed like a big straw-laden country wagon. The speed varied, and suddenly when they came into a wide, straight street, the car jolted heavily so that hats had to be held on. Neither the agents nor the guards spoke. The eyes of the four syndicalists roved over the streets festive in the Spring night, for the strike was now fluttering out. No doubt but that they were being taken to the gaol. Up Princesa Street, well they knew the way! But Liberto was not so sure; suspicion lay deep within him.

In Moncloa Square the fair was in full swing, the lights all blazing, but there were not many people. Helios feasted his eyes on the lights, the roundabouts and swings, so that afterwards, in his cell, he might be able to place each barrel-organ and booth in its proper place. When they were expecting the car to stop, an agent spoke to the driver, and the car went on towards the Puerta de Hierro, slowing down; the prisoners were baffled, and Helios looked back at the massive prison as if it were his own house to which they were denying his right. Liberto tried in vain to interpret the looks of the agents and guards whose faces were stony. Margraf was grinning hysterically. They were all thinking the same thing, but shrank from putting it into words, although they searched for it in each other's eyes. Presently the brakes jarred and the auto stopped. The driver tried to start it up from his seat, but the switch didn't work. Margraf, who understood cars, said under his breath:

"Humbug; that is all humbug!"

And Helios thought of his horseskin boots with some alarm. An agent got up and opened the door.

"We have to walk now, as the car has broken down."

His voice and gesture were so natural that no one was surprised. There were no houses near. Two miles or less lower down, there was a smart suburb with a factory and some better class villas. Perhaps they were taking them with unusual haste to some place where there were other prisoners and a judge. Helios declared ingenuously:

"In a working-class Republic surely we ought to be told where we are being taken?"

Helios had repeated these words, and Liberto heard him and remembered how at school when he was a small boy a companion had shown him his hands all red with chilblains and had said to him:

"Must I really go to the geometry class with hands like these?"

Then he began to try to find some relation between these two phrases, so different and spoken in places and circumstances so different. It pleased him to distract himself with such trifles because in that way he could keep out of his mind a terrible suspicion: the "Law of Flight". And yet Helios was asking his question. Didn't he see that the answer was the Law of Flight? The relation between the question of Helios and his childish memory lay in their hands bruised by the handcuffs, in their present defencelessness and in the dread of the unknown facing them.

"Must I really go into the geometry class with hands like these?"

The boy's ears stuck out widely from the side of his head, and when he wanted money to buy cigarettes, he went in the interval between classes to the Bishop's palace opposite, wrapped up his head in his scarf, and stood with the beggars. Sometimes he cut the geometry class and went with two or three others to the fields near by. There were usually small flocks feeding. They would get hold of a lamb, tie a scarf round its neck and lead it to the police station:

"We have come," they would say, "with this lamb which we found wandering without an owner."

The police praised the little boys and gave them six-pence, thinking that the owner would repay it when he came to recover his lamb. Liberto remembered all that. But the Law of Flight. . . . The State has laws for everything. Anarchists or communists, if they kill, are murderers, if they steal are thieves. The State has laws for everything. When it wishes to kill anyone, it puts him on the highroad, plants a couple of shots in him in the name of the Security of the State, and then goes before the judge and says:

"He was trying to escape, and we could do nothing but shoot him."

The judges might say many things. For example, that a prisoner is bound to try to escape. That the guard is bound to try to prevent him from escaping without using arms against a man who is unarmed and manacled. The judges might say many more things, especially those that are not yet old and have preserved some of the generous instincts of youth. But the State anticipates any reflections on the part of the judges by laying down a law for them; the object of the law is to remove the power of reflection from the judges. There is no need to maunder about justice, when there is at hand Article 487, nor to go into fine considerations about responsibility, when there is a final section defining deeds and punishments. There is no need for individual skill in reflection and interpretation. The code, like a blue print, is placed over the record of facts, until they coincide. They get a mechanical correspondence and read off the sentence:

"Six years and a day."

Or

"Imprisonment in chains for life."

Up to, where it is printed, the death sentence. The "Law of Flight" is a standard applied not by judges but by the police in cases where they think it is required by professional dignity, public security or their own *esprit de corps*. Then the judges make no comment. They know that there is a law of flight which keeps up the appearances, and people with authority to apply it.

Here now was the Law of Flight. The shadows all round proclaimed it. The four, handcuffed, were walking in file. Alongside them, also in file, were the six guards with their short street carbines. One agent marched in front, the other at the rear. Here was the Law of Flight! Liberto showed what was about to happen, and Helios, who was behind too, by dragging their feet and stumbling at every pace without cause. Liberto was in front. He did not know how the others were taking it, but he would have liked to look at their faces. As the road twisted he was able to look up and he saw on his left the massive block of the prison. He said:

"Up there the comrades in the fifth ward are sleeping; also those of the first. For them everything is going on. And for us everything is ending.

"What a pleasant home, the prison. How human-like and cheerful with its sunlit yards." He looked at it as if it were an enchanted castle, a salvation which they were refusing him, and which they were losing although it was within arm's length and they had a right to it. Now there was nothing for it but to abandon hope. The police who were using the Law of Flight made their victims leave the highroad so that they might establish, from the place where the bodies would be found, the intention to escape. And they were still on the highway.

Helios was humming under his breath and marking time with his feet. He didn't understand what he was doing at first, but soon found that he was singing "The International". Liberto felt that the new certainty, the knowledge that Helios also was expecting death, confirmed all his suspicions, and the certainty was too much for him. He felt his resolution slipping away, and his feet trod the ground carelessly as if he were barefooted and had been so all his life. Margraf and Crousell joined in Helios' song. Their voice was the voice of men who were drunk or who had not been to bed for days. They sang in a low voice. Liberto saw the darkness round him and recalled his childish fears, and wished to die in the full sun. To die in the darkness was a fate for beasts of prey, for highwaymen, for tramp criminals with garments infested by lice caught in houses of Peace and Charity. He would have wished sun, air, the wide horizon.

When the agent led the file off the highway, the three ceased their singing. Liberto was seized with the urgent wish to shout, to warn citizens still awake behind their distant lighted windows, to hurl his voice out into the night, to hear it himself, let it resound in his ears. Crousell directed short phrases to the others as if they were parts of a speech.

"Courage, brothers; the revolution goes marching on."

The footsteps of the four were much firmer than those of the agents and guards. It gives strength to know that one is dying without guilt. It has an unnatural beauty. To kill an innocent man is to exalt innocence, to heights inaccessible to the human mind. On the other hand the killer has lost peace, lost moral equilibrium. He in his turn will die in the darkness, and self-disgust will in the end close his eyes.

When Liberto saw that the agent and the guards were slackening their pace and falling behind, he thought simply:

"Now."

If he could have bitten his own heart, he would have done so. Helios also realized it, and called out with delirious strength:

"Long live anarchy!"

Liberto replied like a man who shuts his eyes and throws himself over a precipice. Now they would begin to fire. There was no escape. The four walked on obstinately, indifferently and aimlessly. The guards had become an escort, at two paces behind Crousell. The sharp voice of an agent was heard reproving someone for being unready, and the sound, partly concealed, of a bolt being snapped as the magazine of a rifle was charged.

The vibration of Helios' cry was still in the air and it was a gallant challenge which the guns did not accept. Liberto then called out:

"Cowards; why are you not firing?"

Although the guards had said nothing, the four stopped, and strained at their manacled hands. No one of them trembled. The first to fall was Helios. When they heard two shots from a revolver, they tried to fly, but could only separate into a longer file as long as the cord binding them allowed. Helios had two shots in the back. Liberto could be seen to fall by the flashes from a volley. He must have died instantaneously, as his body gave only one convulsive movement. When they were all on the ground, the guards came up, removed their handcuffs and the cord that bound them together. Three of them were still alive. All except Liberto were breathing. They blew out the roof of Helios' head whilst he was still thinking about his horsehide boots. They put the muzzles of their rifles against the hearts of the others and fired several times.

From the first shot neither a sound nor a word came from any of the four prisoners. Only a rattle in the throat and the sound of unwilling bodies falling. Then the agents hurried back to the automobile on foot. As it was uphill, the oldest cursed and grumbled:

"That he-goat of a driver might have come down a bit to us."

Under the brushwood in the bend of an irrigation ditch, there was a pool of water. A star was reflected in it, through a break in the foliage. From a stone hollowed into a groove, there fell a trickle of water, and the water, the darkness and the star, spoke together in the deep silence that followed the shots.

"Why do men die?"

"Because they have invented death. For birth and death are poems with which they think they can adorn life. Things do not die nor are born; they are and they continue, like you, lovely Star, you, mother Darkness, and you, lady Water."

Chapter 26

The Mortuary Again

SAMAR WAS on the platform of the tramcar. The life of the city, after the crisis which the Movement had suffered in the last two days, was on the way to recover its tranquil activity of production and toil. He was thinking over the primary impulse which throbbed in the depths of their souls and led them to break out into collective passion. Why do we fight and risk our lives? There must be an impulse, a reason in the vital and elemental logic of our youth. We are sane, strong and generous. Agree that a man may be deceived. But not a crowd, not a million men! What is it that moves us? The craving for liberty? Liberty as a feeling, not as an idea. And no one can give us this nor can it be found. Only he can reach liberty as a feeling who has conquered his own spirit and has resolved the infinite unknown which every man carries within him. The slave whose will is not his own, whose dreams are not of time, but of immortality in an eternal life, has no responsibility to his own conscience because he is governed by a will that is not his own. On the other hand he is free from the anguish of creating out of ideas a living material, because he has given to his life an ideal range wide and extensive as his imagined eternity, and a dream of nothing less than absolute perfection. "I have to do only what they order me. I can have no dreams except about the eternal and absolute." Such a man, for whom day by day his daily bread is a secure gift, is the only person who can feel himself truly free. Jesus Christ said that he brought freedom to men, and he was right as he knew the deceptions of illusion and hope. "Do not seek for perfection in yourselves or in your fellows, for you will not find it. Do not expect justice on the face of the earth, for you will not find it." Absolute perfection was divine in the beginning and the end, without end and without beginning. The same infinite which breathes within the man without religious faith, and which the believer thinks he has found in the doctrines of the Catholic Church. Samar was inadvertently paying homage to the church. "How admirable," he thought, "is the attitude of archbishops, cardinals and Popes who are the upholders of faith and who, of course, don't believe in God."

The Christian fact, the death of Christ on Golgotha, is not unique. On the sacrifice of any one of the comrades who fight and die there could be founded a doctrine and a propaganda of the same kind. There is no interest in that. The ecclesiastical organization has lost its meaning for all intelligent people. The Catholic Church which has dazzled so many simpletons! The House of Singer is better organized. It is more catholic, more universal. What surprises me is the capacity to make human beings happy and free.

Freedom as an emotional value can be attained only by a man without a sense of social responsibility, without a spiritual ambition in the political sphere, without faith in justice or in the beauty of humanity. There will be justice some time and it will be administered by some being similar to man, a superficial concession to weak imaginations—which will be the Supreme Perfection. And the old church which does not believe in God gives happiness in the name of God to millions of free individuals, really free. To call such men slaves is a political judgment, limited in its nature, and leaves out of count the intimate possibilities of mankind. The sense of liberty can be satisfied only that way.

Samar stopped in his reflections and breathed deeply. He felt that his profound reflection had cooled his blood. "I can think like this," he said, "only because she is dead." If these ideas had come to him a few days earlier he would have repelled them with alarm.

They might be a way of life. But he cared no longer. He realized that, with a deep satisfaction which pained and frightened him. He clenched his fingers on the metal bar which separated him from the conductor. He bit his lip until it hurt. He had a momentary impulse to lean out of the car and let his head crash against one of the standards. Then, resuming his train of thought, he reflected, "If I had religious faith, these impulses, which may be the symptom of a serious disorientation, perhaps the threshold of madness, would not come to me. Religion would make me tell myself that nothing is perfect in a human being, that I might rejoice that she has died, or even have killed her myself without thinking that I was going out of my mind or loathing myself, without the torturing dread of insanity. For I could confess my sorrow to another human being and save myself, save my soul. God, absolute perfection and absolute mercy, would judge me not with sternness but with wisdom, giving freedom and bliss eternal to my soul. And those who tell me this and would convince me of it, do not believe in God." Samar was still wondering at the Catholic Church when the tramcar passed a wide avenue and began to twist through narrow streets. He could not think of liberty as a feeling, except within religious faith. "It is impossible," he said to himself, "and yet we wish to make it possible. We try to satisfy, by our very limited political formulas, this longing to live which oppresses us and always will oppress us." Then he put to himself a more definite problem. "With us the political aspect is slight. Politics are opportunism and doctrine. It is the human factor that influences us. And the most human of human factors is feeling. And so political doctrines never solve anything for us. And so in swift and unconscious intuition our masses declare themselves apolitical. And so, from the strictly human point of view to which we are tied, if we face our conscience, we must put to ourselves a question in complete sincerity. Is it not our object to make man more happy by satisfying his sentimental thirst for liberty? If that is so, shall we not accomplish it better by the system of absolute faith, by religious faith, than by explosions of violence which at the best can only achieve a play of formulas which are limited, relative, and always subject to doubt and imperfection? On that system shall we not always have beside us the cosmic longing, the thirst for justice and the Good? Does not the Church of Rome accomplish a humaner task than all the international atheisms?" When he reached that conclusion, Samar smiled, not taking himself seriously. He closed his eyes and tried not to pursue his thoughts. He plunged his own brain into shadows, but thought happily, "This effort to stop thinking is at base religious. It represents a faith in something absolute. If some time this faith should fail me . . ."

He descended from the tram, without looking or hearing. A motor-car jammed on its brakes and stopped within half a yard of him. He just missed being killed. He walked on placidly, crossed the street and entered the hospital. As he thought that this time they would not let him enter the mortuary in order to verify the reported death of four comrades, he went to one of the rooms in search of a doctor he knew. He got permission, and went down acompanied by a hospital orderly. When they reached the courtyard with the solitary acacia, the orderly left him. As he went in he recalled the visit they had made a few days ago to see the victims of the "Royal Paranymph". The lonely dismal cellar was in a golden dusk which reminded him of the light of chapels at matins. Gentle memories of his childhood. He stared round. Deep in his consciousness, independent of his will, a voice called to him:

"But now I believe that death is real; now I believe it."

He said it, recanting what he had told Star. "I sought," he said, "to give her faith. In the presence of death, we have to believe either in God or in absolute negation." Samar had wished to replace Star's feelings by a faith in moral negation, faith in our life which is the life of the air and the rocks and has never been in us, but only in the air and the rocks. Consciousness of a wider harmony in which our birth and our death have less meaning than the accidental kindling and quenching of a ray of the sun on the eaves of a house. He wished to give her that faith. But Star was an anarchist and feelings conquered. And now they were conquering Samar.

"Now I believe in death."

Five slabs were occupied. The bodies were covered by sheets. Samar was cowed by the loneliness which the five mounds made solemn. But he went up to the nearest. Outside, in the passage which led to the janitor's quarters, a woman was disputing with someone, and from what she said, he inferred that she had the job of washing the mortuary sheets.

"A sad job," he thought.

Everything was cowing him, but he felt quite different from the day before; serene aloofness, presence of mind, peace. He felt as he had quenched his soul. He smiled and thought:

"I gave my soul to her and she has taken it away with her."

The reflection pleased him; it was sweet and concrete like an apple. He had stepped back, but drew near again, and with his finger-tips raised the edge of the sheet. The distant voice of the washerwoman gave him confidence, and as he raised his arm, the sheet uncovered the head and chest of the body. Still holding the sheet, he drew back reeling. He stumbled against the sharp edge of the next slab and a pain shot through his loins. He let go the sheet, which fell down, and he tried to rub his back, but could not. His arm remained bent over the slab and his shocked body almost collapsed. His head fell on his breast, his mouth open, his eyes staring in an agony of terror.

"It is you! It is you!" he stammered.

On the slab there lay a woman's body, with black stains under the left breast. Samar spoke, but his thoughts and his words were at variance. He was unaware of what he had said or what he thought. The light seemed to take pleasure in revealing the mortal whiteness of Amparo. He said dully:

"There are five instead of four. The victims of the 'law of flight' and her."

And at the same time he remembered that that body was in his arms two days ago. His habit of speaking aloud gave his words an apparent indifference. His thoughts were far away and his words were empty.

"The four of them and you, Amparo. They were murdered, but you? I thought you had gone. And now you come to me again. What do you want?"

He kept interrupting himself, his voice almost breaking into sobs. And the white body was dumb.

"Speak! Speak! You have sought me and you have found me!"

He sighed deeply, and repeated:

"What do you want?"

Anyone who heard his moans would have thought that he was weeping, but his eyes were dry. The distant voice of the washerwoman still came to his ears. The dead eyes were becoming purple and falling in. Samar called out:

"It's not my fault. I was mad about you. One of us had to die."

He thought that she had been with him truly, only then, only when she died. And he added:

"You were death. Your love was death."

He wept without tears. His soul wept. He leaned his forehead against the slab on his folded arms. His anguish was answered by the frozen silence of her dead nakedness. In the end she had been at his side. She also had embraced the revolution, sacrificing more than the four comrades of the law of flight. They gave only their lives. She gave her life and her faith. A suicide dies abandoning faith, abandoning the Church, and she did not hesitate to fly from life and from the Church, to lose the smile of God. Samar moaned, but still the answer to his moans was the frozen silence of her dead nakedness. He leaned over and kissed her on the lips.

"Speak! Speak to me!" he implored.

The black darkness behind her teeth spoke. The hand lying on her marble body spoke. The shining little nails of her rounded toes spoke. But most of all that flagrant whiteness in the golden light. But when Samar begged her to speak, he really wished her to be silent. And the more he beseeched, the more surely was his voice quenched in her clamorous silence. At last he stopped and let himself fall down. He remained crouched on the floor beside the pillar which supported the end of the slab. Minutes passed in silence. She was speaking. From where was she speaking? At last that voice which days ago had moaned with trembling lips "illusions of my life!" had had to travel far to a region of naked truth. Truth is thus; naked, white, dumb. It is lovely and its eyes are closed. But where? Where are you?

Samar stood up and hurled his questions at her head. The breath of his words made a lock of her hair tremble.

"Where are you?"

The echo from the corners of the cellar wrung his heart with its message of unconquerable loneliness. Truth was in it. Truth is empty and lonely and it echoes despair.

"Where are you? Who has taken you there? I must share your truth to be with you in your silence. From where are you speaking to me?"

He wished to know what in his own personality had caused Amparo's death and her eloquent silence. And he, too, was far away, and away from life. "I have killed you. But where am I and what am I?" He sought to find himself, with the fury of a wild beast hunting its shadow. What was the being within him which had brought all these things to pass? He wished to encounter it, annihilate it and then go with her whither she had gone, that he might understand the tongue in which her white silence spoke. He kept looking at her and broke into silent tears. His tears swept him away from what was around him. He wept, conscious only of his own despair, and his tears fell in floods. And so for long. All his sobs and all his sorrow needed few words. He loved her still with the love he had given her when alive. She was asleep and away. And he loved her, jealous of the shadow in her mouth, of the light which shone on her. She was away, or asleep. And never again could she awaken, never again come back. Asleep for ever! Away for ever! Amidst his tears his grief took coherent shape in words:

"Liberty, Justice and the Good were in your eyes, your body, your words. I have lost you, I have lost everything. Do you hear me? Where are you? Listen to me as so often you used to keep silent, listening. You were Liberty, Justice and the Good. I was a blind force of nature with the sun poisoned in my soul. I took you all into my arms and I killed you, and scorned everything. Have pity on me if you hear me! You live and always live in beauty and harmony. I am dead and will drift on, desolate and wandering. Wherever you may be, listen to me!"

He bent to her ear and murmured against her cold cheek:

"I love you in death as I loved you in your garden and in your bed. Take with you these words of mine!"

His head reeled. He seemed to hear Amparo's last question:

"Do you forgive me?"

He passed his hand over his forehead and looked round wildly. Again he wept. His sobs in his handkerchief sounded like the idle sobs of visits of condolence. He was alone, but the room was pervaded by her. He was almost demented. He thought that her left hand had moved and her eyelids had fluttered. He had a shock as from phantasms that were terrible and friendly. Again he seemed to see a flutter. He wept. The light was stronger and her pale skin and shining teeth seemed to be its source.

He was sincere. Justice and the Good were for him simply aesthetic conceptions. As for Freedom, the intimate freedom which makes us masters of ourselves and of the universe, he had never realized it more completely than when he took Amparo into his arms. He was sincere. The sincerity of hallucination is always excessive and theatrical, and Samar raised his arms, tore his hair and plunged his nails into his neck. All his anxieties, all his longings could be solved on these lips, now for ever dumb. And now, now that he had lost her, life would be a desert through which he would have to wander, barefooted, struggling against himself, telling the sand and the stones his dream that was now impossible. He turned towards the four walls, and clenching his fists, muttered, "Scoundrels! scoundrels!"

Once more he thought he heard her last words. They were graven on his mind as on a sheet of ebony. He rushed across the cellar with his clenched fists. When he came to the door he saw framed in it, against the light, the figure of a man. He was wearing a blue blouse. Samar rushed at him:

"What do you want?"

The unknown man retorted:

"Who are you to talk to me like that? What are you doing here?"

Samar didn't reply. He kept looking at him. The man in the blouse pointed to the slab on which Amparo's body was lying, and excitedly said:

"The sheet has been lifted and it is disgraceful, for a woman is always a woman," and added again: "Who are you and what are you doing here?"

As Samar didn't answer but kept staring at him, the man turned to go out and spoke to three others, one of whom was carrying a costly white coffin on his shoulder. He looked into the mortuary again and entered, followed by the others. The one with the coffin placed it on the ground and the man with the blue blouse went up to the slab. As Samar put himself in the way, he said, plainly in a fright:

"We have come to put her in her coffin."

Samar pointed to the door:

"Get out of this!"

"We have come only to carry out our duty," said the man, excusing himself, he didn't know why.

Samar took him by the arm and dragged him towards the door. Then the others came to the aid of their companion. Samar saw that the four were terrified, thinking that they had to do with a raving lunatic. Samar let go his man to attack the others. The man, in an effort to resist, let go and slipped to the floor. Then Samar stepped back and yelled:

"Don't you touch her!"

Then the three tried to soothe him. After helping their companion to rise, they came to him and said:

"We understand that you must be her husband, but now there is nothing for it but to cover her up in the earth. Let us do our duty." They came up resolutely. One put his hand under Amparo's head. Samar struck him on the chest and then pulled him back. The others were about to throw themselves on Samar when he drew back and pointed his revolver at them.

"I'll blow the brains out of the first of you who stirs."

Then he smiled grimly and muttered:

"Put her under the earth, you fools? Is that all you have to say?"

The four retreated slowly and then fled. Samar kept his revolver in his hand and looked about with staring eyes. Then he remembered about the four comrades on the other slabs and uncovered them one by one. There they were. Out of respect for Amparo's body, he pulled the sheet up to the waist of Helios Pérez. The sheet had slipped back to his knees. He stared and his sight became confused. The windows seemed much smaller. Flies were buzzing over the bodies and the noise was as loud as the drone of an aeroplane. His eyes were dry and he could not think consecutively or remember where he was and why. He tried to count the bodies and the slabs, but made them out to be fifteen, twenty, a hundred. Then he sud denly ran to her side. He looked at her forehead, but it was forehead of stone. He thought he heard the voice of Helios:

"Love! love! love!" it said.

He stood attentive. He gazed at the four comrades, and they seemed to smile. Helios went on speaking:

"Our comrade in love! Just look at him! Can't we tear him out of this place? And the manifesto protesting against our death! Who is going to prepare it?"

The four cried out together:

"The manifesto! Clear out! They'll come to arrest you and the manifesto won't be written."

But Helios Pérez continued with his refrain:

"Love, comrades. Let him stay. For it is love." The four smiled again. Samar could not resist that smile. Suddenly he found that things round him were rearranging themselves in their normal order. The laughter of the four comrades had risen to a guffaw.

"Love! love! love!"

He bent over her and kissed her lips again. A noise of footsteps in the passage came nearer. He drew his revolver, covered Amparo's body with the sheet, went to the bodies of the comrades and lowered his voice which was not yet under control. He heard it as if it were not his own.

"Comrades!"

He pointed to Amparo.

"She is a new comrade. She stays with you. Bear her company, as a comrade, in the desert to which you are going. Go with her, and all of you remember me."

Again he felt hallucinated. The last words of Amparo echoed in his brain. The words she spoke from the balcony:

"Do you forgive me?"

From the door he turned back to the comrades:

"Forgive her, all of you, in the desert, under the stars. Forgiveness is possible there, because everything begins and ends in forgiveness. There is nothing but darkness and light."

The footsteps were coming up behind him. He went out, climbed a grating and reached the top of the wall from where he saw two agents aiming at him. He fired at them and slipped down the other side. He was able to escape.

Chapter 27

Night in the Pacífico[1]

AFTER THE strain of the fight, nerves became relaxed, and man, things, and the air went to sleep. Towards the Pacífico, Madrid began to wake up and to accept the old servitude. Compulsory work, without knowing why or for whom. That was the business of others. Hundreds of workers, indifferent to the use of their labour to Society, brutalized once more by the degrading rule of the daily wage, without the joy of creating . . . creating what? and for whom? . . . in a simple, unthinking animal greed. They toiled that they might eat. Efforts forced by the entrails to continue the same forced labour and fill the same stomach. Always just that.

Many comrades in flight had left Madrid, and they were all making for Andalusía. It is strange, whilst we are still in hiding, an invisible hand beckons us to the south. An inference can be drawn. When a main-spring has broken within us, we direct our life towards the south, just as birds after the love season has come to an end . . . for love always comes to an end . . . in October go towards the equator. Samar went southwards. He had met Star, Villacampa and the cock on a seat in the Retiro Park near the Observatory. The three looked in each other's eyes, asking mutely if the death of the four comrades were not the end of everything. That was what Star wished to say to him. Compared with that Amparo's suicide, of which the other two were still ignorant, paled and lost significance. Life was becoming normal in Madrid. Everything back to its normal channel. Villacampa looked at Samar with the same silent question. Samar himself replied without opening his lips:

"Facts can control us. We can do no more with our revolution than a meteorologist can do with the weather."

Villacampa corrected him:

"All right! But what has happened?"

Motor lorries rushed up the avenue, shaking the pavements; tramways passed sounding their bells; people came and went on their affairs. "All right! but what has happened?"

[1] A street in the south-east of Madrid.

Samar replied:

"Everything has happened as it had to happen. The revolution rules us and the day will come when it rules everything."

Meanwhile here and there it has crushed a comrade. Star broke the silent exchange of question and answer, telling them that since the day before, the cock and the cat had been quarrelling all the time.

The syndicates were still closed. As nearly all the leaders were in prison, it was useless to try to hold meetings. But before long there would be meetings in the gaol itself. Regular meetings with definite resolutions and minutes. Star and Villacampa looked at each other, and Villacampa was pleased to see his reflection in her eyes.

"Tomorrow," she said, "I'll have to go back to the factory to work."

Villacampa could not understand why everything was finished.

"Why not?" asked Samar.

"Damn it all! In my calendar there are seven red Sundays, and yet today is only the sixth day of the general strike, and yet all that is going on."

With a gesture he pointed to the traffic and animation of the streets. Samar said to him:

"If you are keen on symbols and superstitions, remember that seven is a Jewish number. The bearded God of the Hebrews made the world in six days, and our creation is in progress, and our triumph will be after the sixth day."

"What do you mean?" said Villacampa, amused by these subtleties.

"Nothing much. That we are living in the sixth day of our creation. It is a day that may last for years, although I don't believe myself that there will be many years. Then will come the seventh day, the day of rest."

"Then my calendar was right."

"Certainly. What we must do is not to turn over these sixth and seventh days until we have won."

The three kept silent. They didn't speak about affairs of the revolution or of the syndicates. "We are safe——" they said in silence, with a dim pleasure. Villacampa kept looking at Star with a pleased expression. Samar thought: "He has seen death all around him. He has seen good comrades fall, and he has lost force and resilience. And now he is turning to Star, although she doesn't wear stockings." Samar also looked at her with his eyes vacant, as they had been since yesterday. Star got up, took Samar's arm, and the three went downwards. The evening was quiet and the angels and emblems on the Ministry of Reconstruction were foreshortened in purple shadows. Behind Atocha station the sunset glow shone, and the Basilica, with its white turret, was soft as butter. That Basilica recalled memories of *bourgeois* weddings, the Retiro Park and its pleasure establishments. When they reached the station, they turned towards the Pacífico and kept on beside its parapet. Then, after passing the offices of the Madrid-Zaragoza-Alicante railway, they turned to the right and descended a narrow street leading towards the railway lines outside the station and the complexity of the shunting lines. Star kept asking:

"Where are we going? Are you going to upset the points?"

Samar had not told them about his visit to the mortuary, concealing it as a shameful secret of madness.

The sun's rays fell on the slope of houses and work-shops of minor trades dependent on the railway, and reflected changing lights, thin and delicate. From the slated and glazed roofs of the station there came a smell of coal-dust and metal, of steam and waste iron, constricting their throats. Star was walking with the cock:

"Where can I put you down?"

Villacampa growled:

"I am fed up with that cock of yours!"

They followed the direction of the railway track. The track was a wide expanse sown with trucks going towards the South, seemingly endless. Above this strange highway there was a steel forest of signal-posts, small cranes, water-tanks and the tall, glass-fronted signal-boxes. Sometimes the railroad bent in a semi-circle and eight or nine engines could be seen in a row, like horses in a cavalry camp. The signal-posts and their disks were an iron net, woven by the night. In the joints of these arms and legs, of these huge gallows, which suddenly stretched out an arm at an obtuse angle, there were points of light, blue, green, red, yellow, flaring out or disappearing in obedience to some unknown will in the loneliness and silence. Star looked about her:

"It is more beautiful than the cinema or the theatre."

Villacampa was strongly impressed, but kept silent lest Samar should score over him. Star kept hold of the journalist's arm. As the cock was heavy, Samar told her to put it down as it would follow, which it did, at not too great a distance. Star looked up at the sky, now without the glow of sunset, a sky of porcelain, and let her eyes rest on the line of signals which made a lovely bridge of lights above their heads. As she kept looking at it, one of the lights would flash out or disappear, or an arm stretch out as if in threat, or drop down, and she laughed aloud. Samar smiled contentedly and said: "Just see how all these are alive! Because they are natural, they are imaginative and artistic. Isn't it all better than the Prado Museum?"

The Prado Museum was poor and pretentious in campari-son. "Art" was imitative and monotonous. Here they saw pure line and colour, based on mechanical activity, labour, and mystery.

They walked on towards the country, following the road of steel. Along one of the lines a huge and snorting engine came up slowly. It was tall, and the low smoke-box with its open escape-valve emitted short explosive clouds of expanding steam. It advanced steadily and gently with its boiling belly, a harmony of black and grey. Samar kept looking at the fading horizon. The engine passed close to them. The piston and connecting-rods shone as they moved in and out. The cranks transferred the power to the wheels, and the huge mass advanced, stopped, went backwards, with smooth certainty.

Behind in the cab was the engine-driver, elderly, bold, his face black with coal and dripping with moisture from the steam. In front of him Samar had a momentary glimpse of the manometer with its needle, the regulator, the injector, the speedometer, all of shining brass, the levers and the level-indicator, an arsenal of instruments as delicate and as necessary as the heart, the brain, and the kidneys of animals. Samar looked at them with delight. Villacampa, who had gone on with Star and the cock, turned round to call him, and Star replied:

"He is in love with locomotives."

"If you are trying to find an excuse for your love of tramways I can tell you that it is no good. There is no sense in it." Villacampa sat down on a little mound near the signal-wires which ran along about a foot above the ground. The others joined him. They had gone on a good way, and the railroad narrowed down on a high embankment which shut them off from the rest of the country. Samar pointed to a set of metal standards rising on the other side into a forest of steel. The railway branched, and there were the signal-posts, the signals, the eyes of green, red and yellow and the arms of steel raised, or stretched out like a cross. The night had drawn down, and across the horizon, disappearing in purple, there was left a wisp of the day, a rosy band from north to south. Samar was silent. He kept Amparo out of his thoughts.

Here he felt strong and new. The engine came back and passed in state before them. The wheels were at the level of their heads. Samar dreamed of a new, a higher, strength and harmony, a liberating force such as the engine showed. Star said:

"The engine is not an anarchist."

Villacampa retorted:

"What nonsense you talk!"

Star pointed to the engine which had shunted back again:

"There you have your sweetheart."

Samar replied:

"And not a *bourgeoise,* you mean?"

But as he listened to his own words, he knew them to be thoughtless. Amparo had been buried that morning. He was ashamed of himself and didn't listen to Star's reply. He looked down on the ground between his feet, staring at the sand. His cruel words, of a cruelty that was stupid, piercing and devastating, echoed in his heart and almost stunned him. He sighed deeply. Star kept on talking, but he didn't hear what she said. Then he closed his eyes and recovered himself just as the engine passed again. He spoke again, but now accepting his own cruelty:

"The engine is not a sentimental sweetheart—don't you agree?"

Villacampa protested:

"Why do you sneer at sentiment? Sentiment raises us."

Samar burst out laughing:

"You have got that idea from some silly speech!"

Star came to the rescue:

"I understand a man's being in love with an engine."

Villacampa couldn't understand what it was all about, but Samar dropped the subject, because he saw that although Villacampa could never understand, he was himself a living example of that kind of being. Star couldn't understand either, but she accepted in complete faith everything that Samar said.

"I foresee," he said, looking at the engine, "a future in which men will be as perfect as machines. That must be our goal. Then the world will have reached a new and true beauty of which we have been robbed for centuries by religion and spiritualistic philosophies."

All three were silent. Such serious thoughts were out of place. In the darkness, the under-surface of the engine showed scarlet reflections from the glowing furnace. They could not see each other's faces, and the darkness made confidences easy and inevitable. Star asked:

"And your other sweetheart? Your *bourgeoise* sweetheart? I left her my revolver."

With a great effort, at last he replied in a careless tone:
"She killed herself."
Star shuddered, staring at him anxiously:
"It can't be true!"
Samar nodded. "Yes."
Star asked:
"With my revolver?" And she continued, feeling that she wasn't being quite honest, "And so I have lost it! It was a lovely revolver, all silver-plated."
Then it was Samar's turn to stare. Villacampa commented:
"The oddest things happen to our Samar!"
It was plain that he wished to laugh. Samar understood his indifference. He also was trying to adjust his mind to a mysticism of steel and cog-wheels, not of human affections, but Star and Villacampa would always be ahead of him. They had no need of a mysticism either of cog-wheels or of human affections, or of scarlet dreams, or of a remote metaphysic. Samar admired them. He recalled Amparo and tried to picture her illusions, her surrender of herself, the delicate delights of her voice and her lips, but he was surprised by his own placid indifference. He recalled it all as if it were a story in a book, something that had happened to someone else. It was her instincts that had been in play as always. She had asked him:
"Will you be happier now?"
And without thinking, he had told her that he would be happier. For besides passion, feeling and reason, there was also a watchful instinct. And so he had answered "Yes". Even she had an intuition of the truth. Love awakens in us unknown powers of discernment. He said "Yes", unreflectingly, and now he had to face the incontrovertible fact that he had recovered, had rescued himself. It was true. At heart he was happy. The indifference of Star and Villacampa didn't disturb him. It must be as it was.
They had risen and were walking southwards. The cock was almost invisible, as its red feathers were black in the darkness. When they reached an iron bridge, they heard a train approaching. At the side of the bridge, wooden planks made a narrow footpath. They went in file and waited, leaning against the railing. There was a road forty feet below them. As they felt the approach of the train they turned to face the railway. It came on the upper way. When it drew near, the engine whistled in two notes, repeated nervously. It was an express, and was being braked down. The machine thrust its way through the air, panting, but smoothly, in a cloud of black and grey. The noise was deafening and the planks shook under them. A

vacuum was made in the air, sucking them in and then thrusting them out. The blinding passage of that torrent of iron, making them gasp, was a moment of magnificence. Then they stood deafened, their senses numbed. Star laughed:

"It was a shower-bath of steel!"

She looked for the cock and found only one of its feet and a handful of feathers. Villacampa grunted contentedly:

"At last; now we won't be bothered with that bird."

But she clenched her fist and ground her teeth, threatening the train which was vanishing into the distance. The signal-lights made smiling grimaces, as if laughing at her. Samar's mind was still filled with the image of the locomotive in motion, and he said nothing. The mental image, precise, strong and powerful, kept him away from a reality which in itself was fantastic. Villacampa stopped and suggested:

"We must now go down towards Vallecas."

It was late and they had to return. The embankment was twenty-five yards high, and there was a little path by which they could go down to an esplanade. Children were playing football there, almost in the dark. It was surrounded by one-storied houses and there was a water-stand in the corner. They took a narrow street. The suburb had a peaceable countrified air. They came out on Pacífico, high up near the bridge. They were tired and wished to sit down, and went into a café. Star mourned the cock's tragic end, but Villacampa took it coolly.

In the café they asked for raw tomatoes, bread and wine. These were brought and they had a pleasant meal. Villacampa looked about him and then went out to read the number of the house.

"Helios and Crousell and Fau lived here."

Star bit into a tomato and thought: my father is dead; the comrades are dead; the *bourgeoise* sweetheart is dead. What is going to happen next? She has a bullet in her heart with my initials. The anarchist newspaper will now come to me, with my name on the wrapper. The syndicates will reopen, and everything will begin again. Villacampa repeated:

"Here the two printer comrades lived, and Fau."

"A bad lot, that Fau!"

It seemed that even when dead he was a danger to the cause. He could still whisper into the ears of the police evil-working messages.

The three were silent. A woman, at once vicious-looking and timid, with a timidity which her neighbours had forced on her, came in and began to speak to the landlady who was getting ready a pan to fry fish. Samar heard what she was saying. "I have come," she said, "to pawn some clothes to put an advertisement in the papers for paying guests. Three of my boarders have been killed in this revolution." And she added apologetically:

"They owed me a month."

The landlady asked carelessly:

"Didn't they leave any clothes?"

The woman replied in a contemptuous way which showed the misery of her life:

"Amongst the lot they hadn't enough to make a candle-wick."

When they left the café, Star and Villacampa went off together, and Samar returned secretly to the railway. He sat down in the same place and waited until an engine passed. Before long an engine came and halted a long time opposite to him. Samar recovered his lost soul and carried it to the smoke-box, satiated with white clouds of steam, with the clouds of May which it sighed out. He foresaw a future, articulated with wheels, pistons and spirit-levels. "Perfect as you," he muttered, "a perfect future clear as the clouds you digest and strong and agile as your steel." He remembered his own sentimental past with grief, and lay down to sleep, so as to see the engines at dawn before taking up life again, a life which, he thought, would now be simple, active and unemotional.

Chapter 28

Burial of the Cock

SAMAR LOOKED at the shuttered and blind windows of the *bourgeoisie* on the distant amphitheatre of Las Delicias to the left, and of the Pacífico to his right:

"Sleep peacefully, good citizens, whilst your gentle souls lurk in your special coffee machine, your newspaper, in your curtains, and in the lazy indolence of your women which very presumptuously you take for faithfulness. Faithfulness! Your women deceive you every day!"

A pair of knickers hung out to dry on a cord at a distance inquired:

"With whom do they deceive them?"

"With the Sacred Heart of Jesus."

Samar continued:

"Here am I, at dawn, far off, and near you in spite of the police whom you pay to pursue me and who will not succeed from lack of imagination. Many things separate us, good citizens. We think and feel in ignorance of ancestral thoughts and feelings, and are yet inflamed with the anger of all the slaves of former days. We have come out of the void and we keep free from the sense of time which is a low political sense. We create and invent everything. From our first look and our first step, we create the world around us, stamping it with the impression of our will. We are creation, progress, the sharp edge of the future. You are reflection, complacence. Degeneration and death. We have nothing to do with you. We have taken nothing from your ancestors."

The knickers hung out to dry inquired:

"And the spirit? Whence came the spirit? Did it also arise spontaneously? Please give me your answer to that."

"Bah! It cames from different factors, differently combined from those of the intelligence. These factors must be *bourgeois,* for you have poisoned the world with your fancy conscience. But in most of us the spirit sleeps."

"Does not culture awaken it?"

"Yes."

"Culture is wholly ours, wholly *bourgeois."*

"Certainly."

"And love; does not love awaken your spirit?"

"Certainly; it also."

"And love is *bourgeois."*

"Of course. But when your culture and your love infect us, and awaken our spirit, we are aware of the danger and avoid it."

"What danger?"

"You don't know it; for your spirit is a feeble thing, and when it troubles you, you can incarnate it in a good fat coin or in the Virgin Mary. And then you remain in peace for ever. But if our spirit is awakened, it can never go to sleep again. It labours to make living flesh of the infinite, strives in longing and anxiety to reduce to simple formulas the vast, the invisible, Nature and her laws, the universe and its secret entrails. When our spirit is awakened, the first consequence is that we bind the gods with ropes and tear their sawdust out of them as a child does with its doll. And that is only a first step in our longing to know and to rule. Then comes despair at our inability to penetrate all secrets, and then there comes sometimes the need to worship a negative truth-mystery. And our will seeks to stretch out to infinity and to beyond infinity and to all the past, to the beginning and to beyond the beginning."

"You are a curious set of people! On that path you'll come to a bad end."

"We shall end as you end—in death."

"Is there another way of coming to an end?"

"Yes; before dying we can kill the spirit, which is to kill death. Death broods in the mind of men, like many other follies, only because man has invented the spirit."

"How do you kill the spirit?"

"Everyone has his own method. If no other can be found, then bullets."

"By suicide?"

"It is the least satisfactory way."

"But then you can't say that you have conquered death."

"But we can. The suicide subjects it to his will. To kill oneself is to conquer death. All the same, it is a trick of the spirit which says: I allow you to conquer death if you submit yourself to me completely. The suicide falls from a hypertrophy of his spirit. He is not a conqueror, but a victim of the spirit."

"Then what can you do to kill the spirit?"

Samar said very gravely:

"I told you before that everyone has his own method."

The knickers continued to swing, and after a pause, asked again:

"What happens to you when you have killed the spirit?"

"What happened to the world when the nebulae cooled and the solid earth with its woods and rivers appeared."

"And what was that? I haven't studied geography much."

"The dreams of the nebulae became solid earth and made the faith of the inorganic, the faith of marble, of the mountain, of sharp and harsh quartz. And in the depths of that faith remained the dreams which became physical law and which we can oppose to your stupidity. Against your frivolous laws, your fripperies and your tendencious leading articles, we oppose the secret truth by which the world moves. If sometimes we wish to be frivolous and light, our lightest words are meaningless to you and unpronounceable. We have the serene ultimate truth. Our frivolity is to you as unnatural and as terrible as the cosmic frivolity of volcanoes and cyclones."

Sirens began to be heard. Two gardeners passed along the foot of the embankment with their donkeys, on the way to their morning work. An old woman appeared at the window with the knickers, pulled the cord and the knickers disappeared. Now that he was alone, and without anyone to speak to, Samar sat down and lighted a cigarette. He had hardly lighted it when he felt hungry and was relieved to find a shilling in his pocket. He would go to breakfast in some little inn in the quarter. He looked at the sky. Dawn was coming slowly. There was some mist low down at the foot of Carabanchel. The sun could not be seen yet, but a distant little cloud was beginning to glow. On the lower branch of the railway, two engines were shunting. The smoke was purple against the dark land down below, but as it rose above the horizon it was grey against the clear sky. A siren continued to sound from the distant station. The workshops were still closed, but it must have been the time to relieve some nocturnal squad. Samar gazed all round him, absorbing the dawn, without fixing his eyes on definite objects. Dim tints, vague sensations; the rigidity of the signal-posts against the acacia in flower, and the distant shining cloud. The dawn was bathing them in a damp and coloured haze, rising into a grey cloud above, and purple against the earth. The clear crystal of the sky seemed to have light above it. But there were still shadows below hanging over the damp ground.

The station siren was arousing other sirens far off and close at hand. Under the shrilling sounds the horizons seemed wider, and simpler his terrible position. The loneliness was soothing and sweet, and after the disappearance of the knickers into the window, he seemed to have the world alone to himself, as in a complicated game of his childhood.

He hadn't finished his cigarette, when he was startled to see in the sky a single star, not blue, but white. He was engrossed by making observations on the light, remembering things he had read long ago in Goethe's *Theory of Colours*. When least he expected it he heard Star's voice behind him:

"What are you doing?"

"You can see; a lovely and stupid thing; watching a star."

"Did you sleep here?"

Samar looked at her clear and moist eyes, and nodded, and then added:

"I am sure that if I go into Madrid the police will catch me."

Star commented:

"But you can't be here always."

"Of course not. Now I must think what to do."

Star was wearing a blue jersey and a yellow skirt, and under her arms she carried an empty cardboard shoe-box. She was going to find the rest of the remains of the cock and bury them.

"Thinking about it, I couldn't sleep."

She was looking at him in a manner that made Samar know she was thinking about him, and not about the cock. And at dawn she had hastened there, anxious lest he should have committed suicide. He smiled. The idea of suicide had not passed through his mind except in his dialogue with the knickers, and then only as a term in an argument. Possibly Star had seen him, the night before, going towards the railway and the embankment. The two were silent. The factory sirens were stopping. Star said:

"Everyone is going back to work."

"And you?"

"I shall go back to the factory, presently."

She opened the box and showed him the little heap of feathers stained with blood. Just then a dog passed, with something in his mouth. Star handed the box to Samar, picked up some stones and ran towards the dog, which dropped its booty and ran off. She came back with the cock's leg in her hand and put it in the box.

"Now we've got the whole of it," she said with satisfaction, and added:

"Will you help me?"

They went down to the foot of the embankment and opened a hole. They were still at work on it when the dog appeared at the top of the embankment and sat down quietly to wait. Before putting the box in the hole, Samar opened it and turned over the remains with a dry twig.

"We ought to offer a prayer," he said.

But Star closed the box and became livid. Samar stared at her in surprise and she tried to speak, but couldn't. Samar, curious, opened the box again. Under the remains of the cock there was an envelope in his own handwriting addressed to Amparo García del Río. He opened it. There was the last letter he had written which Star ought to have delivered last Monday morning. The letter she had read on the first night she was an orphan, and which had seemed so beautiful to her.

"You didn't take it?"

Star could not reply. All her life was in her staring eyes, round with dismay. She had not delivered it. Shrugging his shoulders, Samar put it back in the bottom of the box and they buried it in silence with the remains of the cock. The dog kept watching them from above. Samar made the hole shallow deliberately, to give the dog a better chance, but Star noticed that and put a heavy stone on the top. The dog licked his chops and ran off.

Pushing the soil in with his hands, Samar asked if she had been very fond of the cock, and Star, compressing her lips, replied without looking at him:

"Very."

Samar laughed.

"Perhaps you sometimes called it 'My life!' or 'Light of my eyes'? Didn't you, now? These are the things one says when one is very much in love."

Star conquered her confusion enough to retort:

"That is the kind of thing the *bourgeois* say."

"And you, what do you say?"

Star ventured to look at him.

"I don't know, but never that sort of thing."

"But you must say something."

Star looked vaguely into the air:

"Is it necessary to put it into words? Isn't it plain without speaking?"

Neither spoke for some minutes. Then Samar said:

"What a lovely morning to walk, walk, walk on without stopping. What a splendid thing to walk on and always reach new country and see new horizons! To go beyond the dawn, beyond the sun and live always in this hour!"

"Let us do it."

"It can't be done. Don't you know that the earth is round? We would come back to where we started from."

Star laughed.

"Quite true! That is a difficulty."

Samar asked suddenly:

"Why are you laughing?"

She started.

"I don't know," and became grave again.

A train passed above them exhaling an odour of soot and oil. Samar climbed up and Star followed him. Once at the top, they sat down. The white star was still shining in the distance. On the top of the embankment Star had recovered her serenity, and even had a brave and audacious expression. Samar said:

"Why didn't you deliver the letter? Why did you lie about it?"

She was no longer confused.

"I'll tell you," she said, "if you'll tell me first something which has been bothering me for days, and one thing about which I've been curious since I came here."

"Very well."

"The last one first. What were you thinking about when I came and found you looking at that star?"

"I wasn't thinking. I was feeling and I don't know how to tell you what."

"When you are staring, and not seeing or speaking, and are quiet, what are you thinking?"

Samar laughed.

"I don't understand you."

"Sometimes you are staring into the air and are seeing something that can't be seen by anyone but you."

Samar laughed again.

"And what do you think it is?"

"I think that you know everything and can do everything, and that if you wished the world not to be round so that there would always be unknown country to cross, you have only to wish it and it would happen."

Samar was silent, and then said:

"The holy women think that about God."

She said hurriedly:

"They know what they are about. It is lovely to have a God."

Samar smiled and tenderly pulled a lock of her hair as he said:

"What wise wisdom!"

But he said to himself:

"The Spirit has been born in her, a new thing. As much as two Springs it has rounded her breasts."

He laughed and dismissed the question he had asked her. They rose and began to walk back. The morning sang for them as when they had bathed in the Manzanares.

In the air with the scent of the river,
In the wind with the scent of May,
Through the air it came laughing,
Through the air it departed singing,
What shall we call sweet love?

And Star, taking no notice of Samar, repeated under her breath phrases from the letter: "I would like to give you a life you don't know and to fill it with light and with peace." She didn't understand it before. Then she remembered another sentence, "There are persons like us in whose hearts something of the sun remains." The noise of the city was louder as they drew near. Employees thronged round the workshops and factories seeking their toil. Life was rising to the fundamental and fecund plane of production. Star said before they separated:

"Is it true that the sun sometimes turns to poison in the heart?"

"You understand?" asked Samar.

He stared so fixedly at her that she laughed foolishly, and the familiar dimples appeared in her cheeks.

Chapter 29

The Movement Never Dies

I HAVE come back to the shop and send off peas or fulfil the orders of *bourgeois* households. I've got hold of our newspapers, those that have been able to appear in the provinces. I see that the pulse of the organization has slowed down, but before long it will beat more strongly than ever. But before I forget. Star has now promised herself to me and before long we are going to live together. We have spoken to Auntie Isabela and soon I shall be living with them. Star has put on stockings today and they are going to make her delegate of her factory. That is another matter. I thought that she belonged to Samar, but she told me that they had killed him in this uprising, although he still seems to be on his legs and to come and go. Star made me see that, last night when we left him. This morning we went to the country and we sat down under the Manzanares wood. There, where there were no people about, Star became as pretty and as serious as a grown-up woman. Quite clearly she was very pleased that I, who am going to be her mate, am likely to be a member of the Committee of Groups. She will be even more surprised when they come to reopen the syndicates and she finds my name proposed for the Local or perhaps even for the Regional. Moreover, my boss has told me that he intends to raise me if I do well for him in the branch which he is thinking of opening in Vallecas, in the quarter where Star lives. I think the rise will be to put me in charge of the branch. Of course with a bigger screw. Naturally all that makes our plans easier. When we were in the country, all these things had a pretty good effect. Star told me that she would have to speak to Auntie Isabela again. We have spoken to her. I went to see her, and from the first she received me very well.

"It seems all right to me, if you remember that I don't want children here."

What advice to give a man like me, who believes only in deliberate parentage and in not producing more slaves for the *bourgeoisie*! Afterwards Star told me that Auntie Isabela didn't want great-grandchildren, for then she would be a great-grandmother and she was tired enough of being a grandmother! But I still believe that Samar is after Star, although she says "No". In the wood she had annoyed me with her song about Samar being dead. I've had enough of that, although I don't understand it yet. She says that Samar will never be able to have a real feeling for any woman and he can no longer feel passion or joy or grief. That, to put it in a nutshell, he is just like a machine. Perhaps women will want him, but he won't want any woman.

Then I said to Star:

"And what do you know about it?"

Now she seems to be much more knowing, with her stockings and with being a delegate of her factory. She was quite confident:

"Isn't it enough if I tell you?"

She became quite serious, with her eyes secret and with an air of being alone, as if I had no business to be with her. I wasn't going to stand that superior way of behaving.

"You think you know a lot!"

She sighed and fixed her eyes on a little pool of water beside a tree. A beetle was about to drown between floating leaves. She ran down and rescued it. She put it on its legs and clapped her hands to frighten it into walking. As it was still making swimming movements, she pushed it, and when it began to walk she came back and sat down beside me again. I kept looking at her. As she is going to live with me, I must try to understand her.

"How did it happen that Samar's *bourgeoise* sweetheart shot herself with your revolver?"

She flushed for the first time. Then she began to laugh in a hard sort of way:

"What do you think?" she said.

"Me?—nothing. I want to know what really happened."

Then Star turned away a minute.

"This is the truth," she said. "I forgot to take away my revolver and she shot herself with it."

"But don't you know what happened between her and Samar?"

"Yes."

"Then why did you go?"

She shrugged her shoulders and flushed again.

"When I knew what had happened, I wished to go and look at her face."

"You always kept the revolver unloaded and you hadn't cartridges."

"I had one. The one you gave me the day we had our lunch with you."

"Why did you load the revolver that day?"

She started, then said quickly, with her eyes wide open:

"Just a chance!"

To the devil with such chances. I kept staring at her and she said:

"Do you think that I killed her?"

"Why should you have killed her?"

"Of course; why should I have killed her?"

She sighed. Suddenly, like a scene-shifter when he changes a scene and wipes out all that was on the stage, she gave me a smack and ran away laughing. I followed, caught her behind a tree and ate her up with kisses. Then it seemed as if we had been living a dozen years in the same room. I said nothing, but she saw well enough how much I liked her when I caught hold of her. Now we are in a hurry to set up together. I think it will really be tomorrow. After one of these uprisings, one has a thirst to live. There are gaps in the committees and syndicates, and although we seem to forget them, they have an effect. Certainly it wouldn't have come into my mind to live with Star, or to seek another mate. It must be the same with her. I'd like to see Samar. He is a good comrade and he will be pleased to see that Star has now got someone to look after her. I see that I was wrong in thinking that Star and Samar were fond of each other. She has denied it, and there is no more to be said.

Actually tomorrow comrades will be chosen to fill the places of those that have fallen. They will arrange about replacing their own victims in Catalonia. Our people will go to Andalusía and Extremadura and make themselves felt there. The Government has beaten us for the present, but within a few months the blood of our martyrs will redouble the strength of the Central, and many regions still moderate will be influenced. The best of our organization is that it can never be conquered. The more of our blood is shed, the stronger we are. It is their part to persecute us, ours to raise new legions. There is our strength, because although a government cannot recover from collapse, with us every collapse brings to us new masses of workmen, who feel compelled to protest and can protest only by joining us. The Local will resume its meetings in prison. Our secret committees have been saved and in a fortnight the Government will be compelled to reopen the syndicates and to free our prisoners, so as to prevent another rising. In my opinion we ought to go tonight to interview the Home Secretary. He is a weak man equally afraid of the Government and of us. All the same, going to see them immediately after a rising is dangerous. I became sure of that, less than a year ago, when we went to see the Director of Public Safety. He would not let us speak and spat in our faces, but I thumped on the table with my fist until the inkpots rattled, and I told him:

"We have come here to speak, not to listen to you!"

Then he got up and said that he would give us an hour to clear out while the going was good. After that he would have us arrested. He said that he was a gentleman and did not wish to take advantage of the chance of capturing us that we had given him. We went off and each of us took his own way. He had given us an hour, and ten minutes would have been plenty! Of course they didn't catch a single one of us. All the same, we must protest against their oppressive measures and present our petitions. It is shameful that the centres should be closed still, our newspapers suppressed and our comrades imprisoned. In what civilized country are workers treated that way simply because they wish a juster state of society? And the Law of Flight? But it would be useless to talk to him about that. We shall talk to the comrades. The Home Secretary won't take much notice of what we say. Although they say that he is a good man at his job, the poor devil is tied to the service of the *bourgeoisie*. Perhaps he is an anarchist at heart and has passed through bad times, because he looks very underfed, and he may have sold himself to the State for his salary.

I've begun to pack in my house. My calendar is on the table. I am going to take it to Star's house, although I don't like the picture with the white wigs. When I had nearly finished getting my clothes together, Samar came in, saluted me with a nod, sat down on the bed and began to turn over a bundle of manifestos which I had collected to put in my trunk. He saw me hesitating about the calendar which I had in my hand, and I told him what I thought about the picture. He said at once:

"They aren't two women; they are a man and a woman."

"The one with the pig-tail is the man?"

"Yes."

I burst out laughing so that I had to hold my stomach in my hands. "And when did they dress like that?"

"Two hundred years ago."

Dirty fops! But to tell the truth, I am relieved about it. When I was just going to put it in the trunk, he asked me what

Sunday it was. I had already told him, but he must have forgotten.

"It is the sixth."

He sighed and threw himself down on the bed. For half an hour he didn't speak. His eyes were shut. Then he muttered something and I asked what he was saying.

"Nothing."

"Damn it, you were saying something."

"Nothing. I'd like to wait here like this for the seventh Sunday, the Sunday of rest."

"The triumph of the revolution?"

"Yes."

We fell silent. I had closed the trunk. Samar said that there must be a national manifesto as soon as possible.

"We must make the most out of this failure," he said, "and move upwards from it as if it were a springboard."

We heard a bell outside. Samar started up and asked if it were the door-bell. When I said it was he got up:

"Hide the trunk!"

Hurriedly we pushed it under the bed. Meantime he told me that he hadn't dared to sleep at home the night before, and that when he came to my house he thought that he was being followed. Sure enough the door of my room was opened without knocking and two agents appeared. They cast a quick glance round the room and I saw that they realized that someone was about to leave. They asked:

"Lucas Samar?"

My comrade stepped forward. They seized him. They took papers from his pockets and handcuffed him. He looked at me, shrugging his shoulders: "All right," he said, "I'll wait for it in gaol."

He meant the seventh Sunday. One of the agents stopped to look at me.

"Are you leaving Madrid?"

"No."

"Where are you going?"

I gave Star's address. My friend Samar turned to look at me in great surprise, but recovered himself at once.

"Good luck to you, comrade! May you both be happy!"

But what about me? Why didn't they arrest me, too? I feel a little neglected. But no matter. All the better for Star. I've already said that we are setting up together today. I am pleased for her sake. When they leave me, I look out of the window. It is an evening as if there had been a bullfight, or at least as if the fire-brigades had been parading in the streets. I am going to the shop. When I leave it at seven, as the syndicates are closed, I don't know where to go. I shall have to stay with Star. That is what I'll do.

By the by. Why is it that although the rising has collapsed, I've had the odd feeling in the depths of my heart that we have triumphed? During the day there have been moments when the revolution seemed to have been made.

Chapter 30

Epilogue. Death the Only Freedom

SAMAR HAD a strange dream in prison. When he rose in the morning he wished to write it down in case it might serve as a poem or the scenario of an ultra-realistic film. There was a city humming like a beehive. All factories and workshops. The air had a crystalline purity as if after a storm. Red flags blazed from the upper windows of the houses, but he didn't know if they were political emblems or simply the cloths with which builders cover wet plaster. Of course the completion of a house has political force and value—Samar couldn't think of anything of higher political value—a kind of impersonal accomplishment inspired by collective enthusiasm. But the enthusiasm came neither from passion nor from the spirit, but simply from the joy of living activity. The fact was that there were the red flags, some faded by the sun, others torn by the wind. A full moon was shining in the daylight, and, like Villacampa's calendar, it bore red numbers. Through the middle of the city an endless wide avenue ran, paved with glass, and the Metropolitan trains could be seen running across it, filled with elegant moles and otters. On one side of the street there was an endless procession of naked women, white, brown, pink or dusky. On the other side naked men of all shades and ages. Although they were naked, certain characters showed that they were *bourgeois*—their trim hands and well-dressed hair. The street seemed endless and in the far distance the two columns merged. The men were singing of love, the women of liberty, whilst the city toiled in its factories and workshops.

Ricart went up to them calling out:

"Anarchist comrades!"

But they went on singing. He took a Gillette blade out of its case and sharpened it on the palm of his hand. Then he went to the nearest woman on his right and with the blade cut off one of her rosy nipples. The woman raised her hand and cried out:

"Unhappy me!"

Then Ricart crossed to the nearest man and kicked his behind. The man sang out:

"What bad manners! I am a martyr."

The same happened with the second, third and fourth woman and man. Ricart was at length lost to sight in the distance where the two columns met. A he-goat ran from side to side along the street, stopping to groan in front of each man and to bellow in front of each woman. Ricart came back, and, looking at them, said:

"These are the constitutional reformers."

Then the men and women declared that they were the protagonists of love and of liberty and claimed a decoration and a pension. The beehive humming still resounded from the workshops. The he-goat changed into the Christian God and went along indignantly displaying a written charter and swearing by his Father that he would not pay land-taxes.

So far the dream, but Samar went on writing as he didn't know what to do until the reveille sounded. On his sheets of paper he wrote on for the mere pleasure of writing, without thought or coherence, mingling sayings of his comrades in gaol with vague sentimentalities. But before long the writing turned into a kind of dialogue.

Feeling is a luxury for which men pay dearly. And also societies.

It depends on the societies. The protection of animals and plants is a different affair.

I speak of free societies organized by civilization. Rights and duties. Mechanical progress. Prevention of disease and eugenics. Liberalism and motor-cars. Rotary clubs and democratic bishops.

There is in the world one country of luxury.

Which?

Spain.

What is its luxury?

"Liberalism."

Then came a fragment of an argument he had had with a communist in the courtyard:

"Spain has not given up sentiment. There is sentiment behind the nihilistic idea. I don't say that it is good or bad, but only that it is there."

"Sentiment ruins man in society."

"Very good, and what of it?"

"And also civilized societies. The nihilists, without wishing it, as their sentiment had no part in it, brought about the dictatorship. The nihilists brought down the dictatorship and the monarchy. The luxury of getting free from everything not only made the Republic, but now wishes to destroy the Republic and is destroying it. The Republic thinks sentimental luxury is too great a luxury for a country in which tradition is powerful and careless."

"And what of that?"

"This. Do you want to hear more? Sentiment decomposes individuals, and an organization of the masses based on sentiment, decomposes the masses. A bloody monarchy cannot destroy you because every day it throws fuel on your sentimental hearth. A serene and tranquil republic will destroy you because all the time it is exposing your lazy and luxurious sentimentality."

"But even allowing all that, the revolution is not the loser. The masses will find their way in the end."

"Certainly."

The communist and Samar had shaken hands and separated. Then Samar went on writing. Rather incoherently, but probably a faithful image of what was going on within him and around him.

Neither Star nor Villacampa have come to see me. Villacampa, without knowing it, is living in the triumph of a sentimental revolution. Star is simple and clear as crystal, but sometimes under light a crystal flames out, and sometimes refracts the light, focuses it and causes fires. I don't want to probe deeper into Amparo's death, because I know that behind all my suspicions I shall find Star's simple face. Work is now resumed everywhere. Work brings joy. I would like to go out, to plunge myself into the sleep of work. Dreams for prison. The spirit for the mortuary. Life is in the streets and life is mechanical and materialistic. If we could reach a mechanical and physical religion everything would be solved, because, as things are, the spirit is unwilling to die. For the present all we can do is to convince it and subdue it. We might be able to give it that mechanical and physical religion to occupy it, and then we might take advantage of its force, as the wind is used by windmills.

Coming back to dreams—the prison is the house of dreams—I remember that the army of naked *bourgeois* had a general staff: Liberto, Elenio, Helios and Crousell. In the sky the heads of Progreso, Germinal and Espartaco were not planets, but comets with long, red and glowing tails. Fau's shadow threw sudden storm-clouds. Sometimes it came down and wandered through the wide street between the files of naked people, crying out:

"When is the Carnival?"

It wished once more to destroy everything. That men should

look like women, wear masks, forget the routine of the days in their masquerade. Fau reasoned with Ricart:

"I have a broom and can't use it until the Carnival."

Samar saw himself seated on the ground with his feet dangling over the outlet of a gutter and thinking:

"I hate men, and yet I think that I could make them happy."

His thoughts appeared written along the length of the street and all the naked people called out:

"Scoundrel! You have a devil's ambition."

Samar saw himself standing up and calling to the naked crowds:

"I hate you all! The unhappy and the happy! I hate you and I despise you! For the imbecility of your outlook, for the feebleness of your passions, for your doubts and for your beliefs. But I could make you all happy, you fools, as no one else could. Don't get startled, don't curse me. Remember that Jesus Christ thought much like me. But he didn't dare to tell."

"Why did He not dare?"

"It is quite simple. His supra-renal glands weren't active. Someone knows that even better than me, a particularly learned bishop. For example, Father Zacarías Martínez."

The example pleased the naked people. The city went on working and the noise of two hundred sirens deafened the approving comments which the men and women exchanged across the street. When the sirens ceased to sound, they were talking about something else. The word "syndicates" was heard hear and there. The syndicalists were coming out from their work. They would return to their work.

"What are they making in such a hurry?"

"Sun, for our baths."

"And you, are you not working?"

"We are singing of love and of liberty."

At the sight of the naked people, the workers returned to their factories, in disgust. Their nakedness was silly and disgusting. Some of the workers vomited. The noise of their labour increased, grew much louder than before and drowned everything else. The naked people continued to speak, but although they made ear-trumpets of their hands they could not be heard because of the noise. The noise of labour obscured the light, shapes and words. There was nothing but a vague cloud in the air within which there were millions of working hives. Everything became silent and disappeared. There was left nothing but the abstract idea of labour. And an abstract that was serene when everything else had dissolved in a storm. The syndicates exist and the syndicates existed.

The door of the cell was opened and was left partly open on the chain. Through the opening a hand appeared with a bundle. Samar laid down his pen and asked what they wanted. The hand made an impatient movement, bidding him come to take the package. He obeyed.

"Who sent it?"

No one replied. The arm disappeared and footsteps faded away in the passage. Samar thought for a moment. It wasn't a warder's coat-sleeve. It must have been one of the prisoners. He opened the parcel. Inside was a revolver and a written sheet which, instead of a signature, had a badly drawn star with five points. "It is Star," he said, and laid down the letter and the revolver for a time. Star's letter said, "There are three charges against you, carrying a total sentence of fifteen years and three days. And so the best you can do is to try to escape. For that here is a good help." In the magazine there was a single cartridge. There was another, separate, wrapped in paper. He unwrapped it and found two initials on the bullet, S. G., Star García. He took out the one in the magazine and found that it was marked in the same way. He rose up, smiling. He stretched himself, and said, smiling:

"You aren't a fool, little girl. You thought that you would make me happy with Amparo's death. Certainly you did so."

Then he laughed aloud.

"Then you found out what happened in the mortuary, you looked into my eyes, you heard me speaking, and you wish me to kill myself to make you happy. Perhaps if I kill myself you will make a scene about me too in the mortuary, won't you? Then you'll be reborn and would live free from the spirit which I kindled in you and you have put in me. But live with it, dear, and if it infects and inflames you, die with it."

In the damp greyness of the cell, these words of Star, written in pencil, full of mistakes in spelling, came with the clear fragrance of the river bank or of the dawn beside the southern railway. Memories. They came charged with obscure motives. The shadow of these motives was in Star, but, unlike the shadows of other people, it was a white shadow. But there is mystery even in whiteness. Passion does not reside only in red jewels nor fatality in blackness. Star's mysteries were simple and shone clearly. More clear than those of a woman with complex reactions were the unfathomable mysteries of the will and intelligence of a child under extreme strain. Samar tried to search out the motives of her final determination, with its strange glances, snatches of sun, of the dawn and all kinds of mingled suggestions in which the cock kept appearing. Star, from contact with Samar, had felt the spirit growing within her and with it the power of imagination, of fancy, and the longing to reach the infinite. Samar thought: "I have poisoned the sun in your heart. You think that the earth could cease to be round and become an endless plain which I could traverse and always have new countries unrolling before me. You believe more. You believe that my will would suffice for that miracle. And that can be expected only from a God. It is very useful to have a God, is it not? To allow the feelings to spin their dreamland, airy web out of sights and sounds, love and desire. And to place a God in the web, and people it with dreams, realizing all the impossible. Do you wish a God? Look elsewhere. I can be now only a cog-wheel or a connecting-rod in some great machine. I don't wish to be more. Is that not ambition enough?"

He had filled Star's soul with visions of divinity. She could not live without them, and much less hope to find them encouraged by one who had rejected the spirit, who was empty of it for ever. Her reactions must have been very like those of himself with Amparo. Star's mysteries had been transparent like the pictures seen by a crystal gazer in oblique light. Samar laughed aloud, looking at the bullet with the two initials scratched on it, "S. G." The cock should have been there too, he thought. A ray of light struck silver flashes from the polished barrel, like lightning in May. "You would like your spirit to die with me, little Star! And then you would be born again. Sad to wish for re-birth at eighten years old! Live, little comrade, with your spirit infected and sick, and with your new wisdom!"

He began to laugh again. He went to the window, pushed the revolver through the bars to the sill outside where they would not look for it if there were a search. He heard in his brain the two hundred sirens of his dream-city, and laughed, feeling himself free. Free in prison! But an actual noise came from the galleries, rising to a hoarse and roaring clamour. The prison vibrated. Not the workshops of his dream-city, but the ninety closed doors in the galleries. A mutiny! A mutiny!

Samar smiled joyfully. Life had begun again. He turned to seize the revolver, and throwing himself against the door, yelled:

"And now, let us fight for freedom!"

In his brain the metallic thunder of the blows on the doors was mingled with the two hundred sirens of his dream-city and the grey cloud enveloping the creative labour of the syndicates of industry directed to dreams, directed to the future. The day became thronged with red and blue shadows under the anarchosyndicalist storm in the prison.

"Freedom or death!"

The prison-guard clattered the bolts of the mausers drawn up where the five galleries met.

"Freedom, or death!"

His heart was nearly bursting in his breast under the clamorous shouts.

"Freedom or death!"

And death, metaphysically and actually, is the only possible freedom.

Ramón J. Sender (1902–1982) received Spain's most prestigious literary award, the Planeta Prize, in 1969. He had supported the republican cause during the Spanish civil war and was forced to leave Spain in 1937. He eventually settled in the United States where he became a professor of Spanish literature. He refused to return to Franco's Spain and died in San Diego in 1982.